ANGELS WILL CRY

DIVINE GRACE
BOOK 1

RAJA LYN

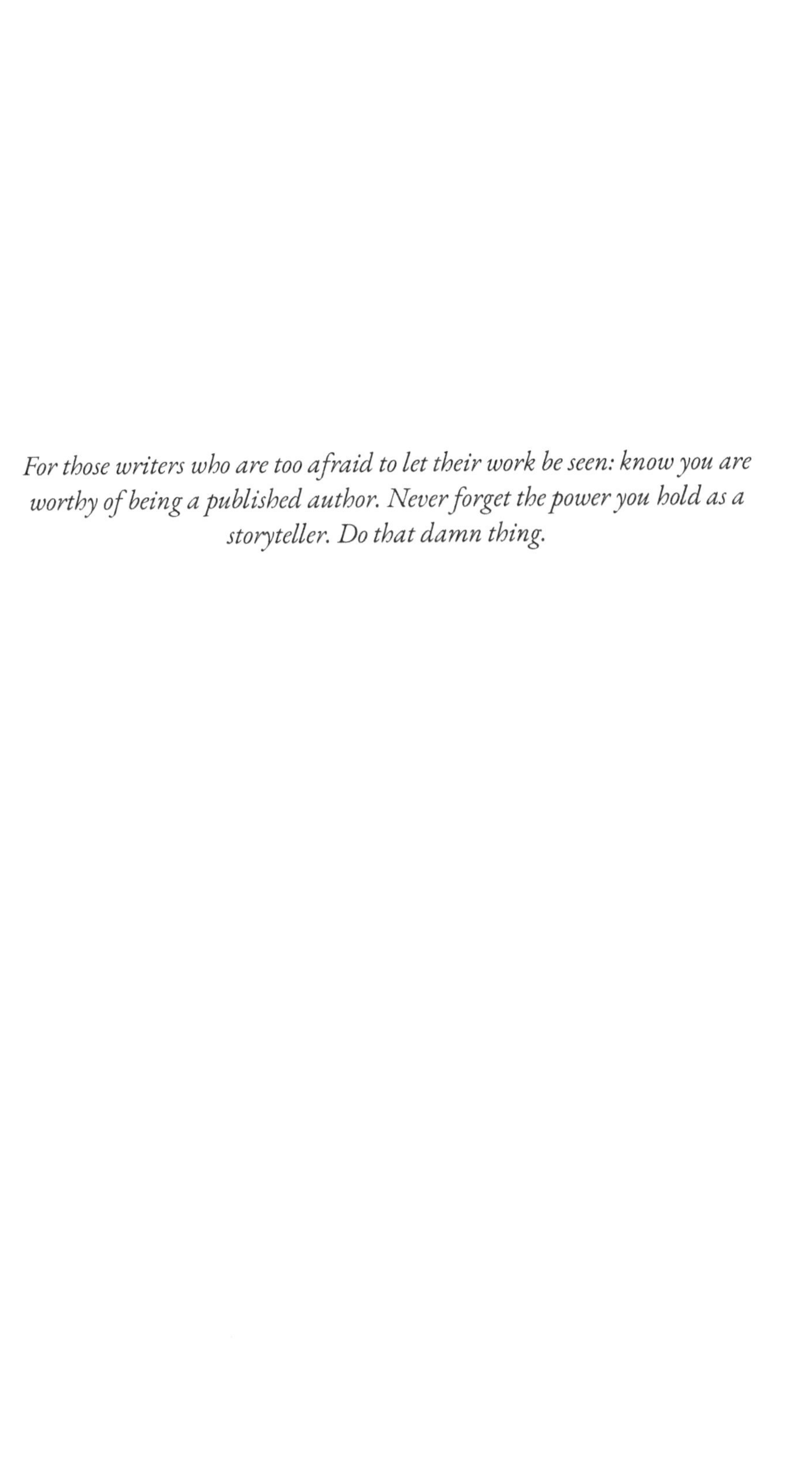

For those writers who are too afraid to let their work be seen: know you are worthy of being a published author. Never forget the power you hold as a storyteller. Do that damn thing.

CONTENT WARNING

This book contains adult themes. Please see the possible trigger warnings below. Though I tried to list them all, there may be some people that can be affected by certain tropes and triggers more than others.

Additionally, if you are a person of strong Christian faith, it is recommended you also proceed with caution. This book draws on religious stories told in some teachings and morphs them into something that may not align with your studies.

This is a fantasy/romance novel. This story is intended to demonstrate how one can open the door to many others.

I'm just here to write a banging story, y'all.

Read at your own discretion. Your mental health is important.
War
Violence
Gore
Torture
Death

Abandonment
Sexual activities
Graphic language
Forced relationship
Religious themes

CHAPTER 1

THE SCREAMS STOPPED. Only hours after the questioning and the executions, just as the moon had reached its peak, did they finally stop. The blood-stained cobblestone glistened in the moonlight.

Blessed silence.

I crouched closer to the stone wall. These weren't optimal conditions for an assassination, but I had a contract to fulfill, and tonight was my last opportunity.

At the highest point of the prison, I was tucked away under the brass bell that had rung only minutes before. It was a perfect vantage point to map out the guards' steps.

The prison was smaller than most. It held common thieves, murderers, rapists— the usual. Not my biggest hit, but the money was good. One hundred pieces of silver for the warden's heart in a sack. In all honesty, I would've done it for twenty. More than ten was a blessing.

The family who wanted him dead must have been desperate. Any coin was precious to a commoner. But I didn't ask for more information, because I genuinely didn't care. They wanted someone dead and had coin— that was good enough for me.

Two guards strolled along the eastern wall, murmuring to each other as they had done all night. If there was a siege, they would surely fall in minutes, if not seconds. The men who held the swords and spears, so-called guards, were nothing more than criminals themselves. Those who looked better than the rest and who the warden had deemed sane enough to arm, since the Emperor didn't find it worth his time to send real soldiers. They had the chance to be guards rather than take a trip to the executioner's block.

Death would have been easier—maybe even more enjoyable—than marching in the mud. It had rained hours before, and the pathways of the compound were still drowning in it.

Luckily, it wasn't summer. Hot air would do this place no favors. If the ground was wet, like it was this night, then I'd imagine the warm breeze would sweep up the smell of vomit, blood, and any other fluids a body can produce. And, by the gods, the sun would only add to the pot of waste this prison had swirling around, like a soup over a roaring fire just waiting to boil over.

Thankfully, all I could smell was dirt and wet stone.

As the guards drew closer, their words drifted over to me.

"Think we'll get those supplies from Darn?" one asked.

That was the next town over, about a full day's ride.

The other guard snorted. "You think they give a shit about us here?"

The first shrugged. "We might be criminals, but we're paying our dues. Maybe the Emperor will show mercy."

"You won't last long here if you put your hopes in that doll." The guard's tone was scathing. "He doesn't even know we exist, and the Clergy would rather see us dead than put us back into society. Just do as you're told, and you might live. And pray to the Divine the warden sets you free."

There was a moment of silence before the hopeful guard spoke again. "I heard the pup was coming in early this morning."

My ears pricked up as they passed right below me.

"Can you believe he's more than fifteen years younger than us and he's got all that power?" He scoffed, kicking the loose gravel under his boot. "I was hard at work feeding a family before he could even spit out the words *da* and *ma*."

And now you're manning a prison no one gives a second thought.

More guards came to do their rounds, all of them human. The prisoners, though, could be of any race. Most of them were human, but a few witches were in the mix, their necks bound in collars that kept them from using magic. Never any lycan or fae, though. May their Divine help them if they were ever found in a place like this.

The second patrol of guards came and once they did, I scaled down the wall and landed without a sound.

These men were untrained and unqualified to guard anything. They constantly left blind spots in their defenses, so slipping through to the barracks was simple.

It hadn't been hard to find plans for the prison, either. A few pieces of bread to the poor, a few more blades to throats, and it was done. I knew they'd never see me coming. Not just because of my skill and planning, but because I practically blended into the night.

My outfit was practical. It was early winter in Arabrosa, so most of my clothes were thick, dark leather lined with wool. Gloves shielded my hands from the chill, and a hooded cowl covered most of my face, leaving only my eyes exposed.

Two daggers were fastened to the outside of my thighs, pressed down tightly to ensure their security. Usually, the bow was my favored weapon—it required less work and got the job done—but I'd always been particularly skilled with a blade. Any type really, though my instincts had always been drawn to daggers, which was why I'd selected these for tonight.

Scurrying down into the barracks, I couldn't help but note how beautiful the night was. The air was crisp, and there wasn't a cloud in the sky, allowing the moonlight to shine brightly. It was the first time in days the snow had ceased.

Behind the prison walls, the picture was ruined. The blanket of snow was muddled by the footsteps of the guards and prisoners, the crisp white turning black or red, depending on where I looked.

Slipping behind some crates in the corner of the barracks, I waited for the guards to create another opening. Predictably, it happened rather quickly, and I continued bobbing and weaving through the prison until I reached the warden's quarters.

I was standing outside behind a pillar when I heard voices coming from the room, but I couldn't make out what they were saying.

Some more time passed before the wooden door finally opened. A person came out and walked the opposite way. I didn't see their face, and I didn't care. They weren't my target.

With my back still on the wall, I inched towards the door, dagger in hand, and lightly knocked.

"The Divine above, what else is there?" a voice boomed.

I knocked again.

"Come!"

I waited a moment, then knocked again. There was a huff and footsteps came closer to the door until it was thrown open. I acted quickly, pushing my dagger against the warden's throat and maneuvering us so he was placed against the now closed door and the bolt was settled. It wasn't until I had him where I wanted him that I realized this wasn't the warden.

This man was much younger than the bastard I'd been sent to kill.

I scanned his grey, almost silver, eyes for an answer but found none.

The man held his hands out and away from me, keeping them in my view. One held a cup and the other was free.

"And who, might I ask," he said, voice dripping with fluidity and caress, "are you?"

I didn't speak, examining him closely.

He was tall, towering actually, but that wasn't what fazed me. It was his eyes. They were framed by thick, structured brows and dark, fluttering lashes. Below his high cheekbones was an impressively strong jaw. He had the build of a warrior, not too muscular but not too lean. A perfect soldier. So, what was he doing in a place like this?

"No name?" He spoke, distracting me from my assessment. "Then, how about why you're here to kill me? Or am I not the one you're looking for?"

I narrowed my eyes ever so slightly.

"Ah," he sang, bringing the cup to his lips.

I pushed the steel deeper against his throat.

He stopped, raising a brow, then slowly continued to take a sip. "You're here to kill the warden."

Did I get the mapping of his quarters wrong?

"Don't fret, you're in the right place," he continued. "However, I'm staying here for the night while I ride through to my destination."

Possibilities raced through my mind.

I didn't kill anyone who wasn't a contract unless they attacked me first. This man seemed at ease, even with a blade to his throat, so he was either an idiot or didn't see me as a threat.

"Where is the warden?" I forced out.

"She speaks! And with such a lovely voice."

I gritted my teeth. *"The warden."*

"He's staying in the guest quarters down the hall. Though you needn't go there."

I stilled.

"I'm dangerously low on wine, and he was kind enough to get more. He should be back any minute."

"Good, then I have no more use for you."

"Indeed," he said simply.

"You want to die?"

"Sure. Kill me."

No survival skills, I see.

I tried to remain as impassive as possible. "What?"

"Kill. Me."

Huffing, I stepped back, releasing him from my hold. "You must be someone of importance, otherwise the warden wouldn't have given you his room. He's a proud man, so he doesn't *give* anything." I looked him up and down. "I'm guessing you're very high up, to the point where he was practically ordered to give it to you. Now, why would someone of such importance want to die so badly?"

He shrugged. "A mild curiosity of the afterlife."

"Or, maybe you're buying yourself time so when he comes through the door, I have two people to worry about and you'll be able to alert the guards."

He shrugged again, but a smirk stretched across his face. Taking slow, swaggered steps back to the warden's desk, he sat in the chair and placed his chalice on the table. He leaned back, getting comfortable as if it was *his* desk, *his* prison, *his* place to command me.

"So, what do you want to do?" His tone was casual. "Kill me and wait for the warden to get back, or keep talking and let him come in and kill you?"

I didn't kill those who I hadn't been paid to kill, and he hadn't attacked me. The only thing he was doing at the moment was placing his elbows on the armrests of his chair and fiddling with a gold signet ring on his right index finger.

The thumb and index finger of his other hand twisted the yellow metal around, slowly stroking the face of the ring. He flexed his hands ever so slightly, and my eyes darted to the veins covering them and his smooth, muscled forearm.

My head cocked slightly to the side, taking stock of him. In another life, I could see this going very differently.

His right hand balled into a fist, making the muscles under his tan skin flex and relax as he uncurled his fingers. The tips of his fingers traced the veins on the backside of his arm.

It wasn't until a cheeky smirk was setting into his face, his eyes gleaming in triumph, that I realized what he was doing.

My nostrils flared and my cheeks heated, but I pushed the feeling down as quickly as it came.

"Any chance you'll keep quiet and let me kill him?" I tested.

He shrugged again, grabbing the cup from the table.

I waved my dagger at his face with irritation. "You're a bore to jest with."

"Ha, you call this jesting? Maybe you haven't given me enough to work with."

Cocking my brow, I rounded the table to stand in front of him, between his widened legs. He looked up at me with amusement, took another sip of his wine, and waited.

"You want entertainment?"

"I prefer it to whatever this is."

Irritation brewed within me as I placed a foot between his legs on the chair and kicked, making him slide back against the barred window. He landed with a thud, the wine spilling from his cup.

He shook his now-wet sleeve in annoyance. "He hasn't even come back with more and you went and spilled all I had left."

"You wanted entertainment. You're getting it."

He scoffed. "Spilling my drink. I'd prefer something else."

"Like?"

"Seduce me."

My chest tightened. How did it come to this? I came to kill a horrible man, and now I was trading witty remarks with a pretty lord who was too upset about his wine to worry about his life.

I held out my dagger. "You seem to forget who has the weapon. Do you have any regard for your life?"

"Well, I did say 'kill me.'"

I sheathed my dagger and swiped a pair of iron shackles from the desk.

"I don't have time for this."

He stood, but I immediately pushed him back into the chair, placing my knee on his chest.

He quirked a brow. "Into bondage, I see."

Rolling my eyes, I quickly shackled him to the bars that were welded into the window. He used his free hand to grab mine and pulled me so close I could feel his breath on my lips.

"You still haven't told me your name," he whispered, gazing into my eyes.

"Luna."

"Liar."

I raised my eyebrows. "Oh, so now I lack a sense of humor *and* I'm a liar?"

"Also a tease," he added.

"In that order?"

"The latter could use some work, but I think you're off to a great start."

He was toying with me. Somehow without knowing anything but my skill with a blade and the color of my eyes, this man knew how to make my blood boil.

"Don't test me, there's still a warm body in my hands that can turn into a corpse."

"We've been through this—"

"Kill me," we said in unison.

I went to pull away from him, but his grip turned impressively strong. Enough to make me pause.

"My name is Vork."

"I don't care."

"Tell me your name," he commanded.

"Luna."

"Lies again."

I was wasting time playing his game, and yet I couldn't stop. "How do you know I'm lying?"

"Your eyes."

"My eyes?"

He gazed harder. "Yes, they're beautiful."

"They're dark and brown and the only skin you can see on me. How could they show you I'm lying?"

"The eyes can tell a lot."

"Are they telling you how annoyed I am right now?"

The tip of his mouth curled up slightly. "A bit."

Using all my strength, I pushed away from him. "Good night, Lord Vork."

Finally, my attention could move back to the task at hand. Killing the warden.

"Commander."

I kept walking.

"Commander... Vork Lacelle."

I was mere inches from the door, to freedom, but I stopped at his words.

"What did you just say?" I asked quietly, my back still to him.

"I'm no lord." He spoke with such softness. "If you want to address me, then you should do it right. Commander Vork Lacelle of the Arabrosa pack."

"Damn," I breathed.

The iron shackles clinked, and I closed my eyes, taking a breath before turning to him.

Vork stood, rubbing his now freed wrist.

Lycans, the perfect warriors for Masos, were truly feared in battle. Especially ones who came from the Arabrosa pack. And *especially* the son of their High Chief. Subsequently, word of the prince of the most powerful pack and his... vigor had travelled well.

Lycans were plentiful in Masos, and many of them were part of the

Arabrosa pack, though there were smaller ones in Saar and Ekros. They had the ability to shift into wolves, but not normal wolves. These beasts could walk upright on two feet and could stand over ten feet tall.

The only weakness a lycan had was the same disadvantage of any other race; they could be killed with a stab to the heart or a beheading.

Strong, fast, and agile, they were the ideal weapon for anyone's army. Lucky for the packs in Masos, they were able to stay within their own and were not forced into the Emperor's army, unless they willingly joined. Though an agreement had been signed stating if the Emperor ever were pulled into a civil war and the safety of Masos was in jeopardy, then the strongest of the lycan warriors could be drafted.

Vork was a well-known warrior. There was said to have been a war between his pack and the pack of Ekros a few ages past, where it was told he was on the field for a solid week with maybe four hours of sleep in total. The story goes he would not leave a fellow pack member to fight his battles while he was safe asleep. It was due to his inability to rest off the field that he was captured and kept as a prisoner for weeks. The horrors he went through could not be spoken of, but they said he went into the battle as a soldier and came out as a man, as their commander.

So now, here I was, trying to kill a contract and just happened to stumble upon the prince of the Arabrosa pack, who I had heard would arrive in the morning. Daft guards.

I widened my stance, keeping my hands very close to my daggers. "You could have subdued me at any point."

He was taking slow, calculated steps towards me. "True."

Now that I knew the truth, his aura had changed. The smugness of the lord was still there, but his body held a power that would make anyone second-guess their next move. Though I couldn't let him know that. I was cautious. He had received expert training that I hadn't.

I stepped back as he circled me, a predator ready to take down its prey. "So why didn't you?"

"I wanted to see how this would play out."

"Didn't your mother ever tell you not to play with your food?"

"Are you offering? I could use a midnight snack."

A huge wave of adrenaline surged through my stomach and moved down to my core.

You have a job to do. Stay focused. The warden. You're here for the warden.

I shook it off, my blood boiling. "Only if it means you'll choke."

His eyes gleamed at my promise.

"So," I said, backing up to the door as he got closer. "What's your end goal here?"

"You won't tell me your name, so a look at your face will suffice."

He couldn't. I wouldn't let him.

My back bumped against the door, and he placed both hands on either side of my head, caging me in.

His breath was hot on my face. "Is this something you do often?"

"Do what?"

"Kill the innocent."

"The warden is hardly innocent," I argued.

"I know of the warden's history."

"Then don't speak as if he hasn't done wrong." My eyes threw daggers his way, my anger about to reach a boiling point I was growing accustomed to in his presence.

"We've all done wrong."

"I haven't taken a man from his bed, held an unfair trial, skinned him as punishment, and then fed his body to dogs in front of his family."

Vork let out a small huff. "What the warden does is of no concern to me. I am simply here to rest."

"Then go rest while I kill a murderer of the falsely accused."

"Perhaps," he said in a low voice, his hand reaching for my mask. "After I see your face."

"No."

His hand stilled, and he raised a brow. "No?"

"I'm sure, being the little prince you are, you aren't used to being told that. So, let me try again. *No.*"

"I hear it plenty. It's just so pretty coming from your lips."

Piss off, I wanted to curse at him.

What were my options here? I was cornered by *the* lycan commander, with no way to subdue him. Although I had strengths, I also knew my limitations. He wasn't an opponent to take head-on. I had to play it smart.

His hand rose to my face once again, and my heart was pounding loud enough that his lycan ears must have heard it because a faint smirk played across his lips.

The warm skin of his fingers brushed against my cheek as he released the mask and let it fall to one side, exposing my face.

He was silent, examining me. I couldn't read him.

"Well," I said. "Am I as attractive as you had hoped?"

"You've got a bit of a plain face, but it'll do."

A scoff escaped my lips. I knew I wasn't unattractive with my long dark hair, perfect golden skin, decent cheekbones, dark brows, and lashes that added a dainty feature to my appearance. A pretty face with lethal skills. I wasn't the most stunning girl by any means, but I was comfortable in my own skin and knew I was beautiful in my own right.

My chin rose a notch. "I'm attractive and you know it."

Vork's smirk widened. "Is that so?"

While he was mildly distracted, I armed myself and pressed the dagger back to his throat.

His stormy eyes darkened, and he bent into the blade, almost making it cut the skin. The same hand he'd used to uncover my face lightly hovered over my cheek, his thumb briefly touching my lips.

"You're perfect."

That surge of adrenaline came back, covering my head like a veil of fog. For a split second, I couldn't think straight, and so I didn't see his next move coming.

It was simple, unfortunately, which made it all the more embarrassing.

His other hand wrapped around my wrist and squeezed so hard I feared his lycan strength would shatter the bones. My grip on the blade faltered, and now *he* had it pressed against *my* throat.

He studied my face as if I was a specimen on the table of a witch's altar.

My confused gaze searched his face. What was his end goal? Where did we go from here?

I was brought out of yet another trance from this lycan by an alarm. Multiple bells followed by someone banging on the door behind me.

"Commander," a man yelled. "There's a riot taking place in the pit. We advise you to stay in my quarters till it's safe."

The warden. *Focus*.

While Vork was distracted, it wasn't hard to disarm him and this time I took my second dagger and used the hilt to land a blow on his head.

He staggered back far enough for me to rip the door open and waste no time in sinking my blade into the warden's heart. It happened so quickly the only reaction my target could give was a strangled gasp as his heart began to fail him.

With Vork at my back and the riot at my front, I didn't have time to retrieve his heart as proof, so I settled for his silver necklace, which held a small sapphire jewel. A known luxury he carried.

I didn't give the lycan prince a second thought as I leaped over the warden's body and scurried through the halls, fixing my mask back into place. This time I wasn't as careful navigating the prison as before.

Guards ran past me shouting orders and curses at one another, but I paid them no mind. My destination was a few hours' ride from here, and I had to get back before dawn.

The stables were at the entrance, just as I remembered. Taking the nearest saddled horse, I rode into the night.

I was free. Finally, I began to breathe easily, listening to the hooves hitting the snow-covered road. But that easy breath turned ragged very quickly when a familiar wail sounded in the distance.

Sazari.

CHAPTER 2

It was always peaceful in the mornings before anyone was out in the halls. The sun had just risen over the horizon, and the freshly fallen snow hadn't been disturbed yet by the hundreds of feet that would soon pace the grounds.

Silence. Beautiful and pure. Just like that night at the prison a few weeks ago.

Clamore Academy sat at the base of Arabrosa's three-hundred-mile mountain range. It had been founded by the Clergy ages ago to ensure the young minds of Masos were properly educated in the ways of the Divine.

I had to admit, the sight of it could make anyone stop in their tracks and gaze upon the ethereal place.

Every hundred feet, lamp posts illuminated the walkways on both sides and showed the trees lining Clamore's courtyard. Snow weighed down their branches, so much so they looked close to breaking.

Electricity was only in places where it was most needed on Masos. The Emperor and his Clergy granted this privilege to the main cities, temples, schools, and those of high stature. Small towns far away from any central city were stuck living as the people on Masos had before, by candle and moonlight.

Clamore was special enough to have this light, though, and as grateful as I was for it, the fact we'd been granted it showed I held privilege I had done nothing to deserve. Luck of the draw, I suppose. My life wasn't full of lucky circumstances by any means, but I wouldn't question the good fortune that fell to me unless it seemed too good to be true.

There were many less fortunate than I. Not just the ones who had been slapped in manacles and sentenced to death from the prison the other night. These particular people were those who felt the wrath of the Clergy when certain expectations were not met or a knee was not bent to the Divine—but everyone knew it was the Clergy themselves we were meant to pay fealty to.

The punishments varied, depending on what class the offender was in. It could range from a hefty donation to the Clergy's purse, imprisonment, crucifixion, or what people call *the journey.*

When I was young and naive, I fantasized that the Clergy were good men who respected and honored their Emperor by allowing the Divine to work through them. I learned quickly they were the rot so deeply embedded in Masos, and the land was doomed so long as they stood near the Emperor. Seeing *the journey* for the first time spurred the revelation. Even all these ages later, the memory still haunted me. Even now as I was safe within Clamore's walls.

A pair of horses pulled a simple cart where two soldiers sat comfortably. Behind them, a man and a woman walked, tugged along by ropes extending from two hooks in the back of the cart. Their hands had been bound in vinegar-soaked rope, rubbing their skin raw, the acid burning as it exposed their flesh. In the cart, one soldier held the reins of the horses, and the other held an infant, whose face was red with stress and wet with tears, constantly crying for its mama who was just out of reach.

The mother and father had been badly beaten. The mother's eyes were almost swollen shut, her lips bruised, and a bald spot bled from the top of her head where her hair had been ripped out. The neckline of her shift dress was ripped open, and a tear ran along the side all the way up to her waist. She walked in a shuffle, hardly widening her legs enough to take full steps, every small movement making her wince.

Blood pooled at the man's feet as he walked with jagged rocks in his sandals, puncturing the pads with every step he took. His back was painted with red slashes from the whipping he had been given, the blood draining down into his trousers and ultimately mixing with the bloody footsteps he left in his wake. His face was badly bruised and beaten as well, but at least he could open his eyes.

What had truly made me cry that day was the sight of the child being dragged in front of them, lifeless and blue. He couldn't have been more than fifteen ages old. A noose was woven around his neck, creating creases as the material pulled his skin together. Other than his skin being the color of the sea to the south of the continent, no other bodily harm was evident.

The parents watched his body as they made the journey to the Holy City and back as a reminder that their defiance of the Divine's plan had cost their son his life. For four whole days, they looked upon his corpse and heard the screams of their youngest, so they would never forget how a proper citizen should act.

I knew the Divine wasn't real after that. If they were, how could they allow such evil to do works in their name? What is it that kept them from saving Masos' people from the tyranny of the Clergy?

There was no Divine. I would be my own savior— my own protection and religion. Nothing mattered besides staying alive and out of their way so I could go on living how I pleased.

That way of thinking had ultimately led me to the school I was currently sulking in. It was early, and I didn't sleep well the night prior. Though at least I had a bed to sleep in. So, I'd continue to count my blessings.

Only a few more moments until the courtyard would flood with bodies. The colossal bronze gate came into view at the front of the grounds. It was the first marvelous thing a visitor would see. The entrance was guarded by two marble angels holding swords. Once they entered, they were welcomed by an oak tree which stood about two hundred feet in height and another one hundred in diameter, but it was what was in front of the oak tree that truly awed visitors.

A marble statue of the angel Michael stood tall and proud; beautiful wings speckled with an iridescent material to add to his spirituous stance. In his left hand, he held a sword, and in his right, a shield, both said to have been given to Michael by the Divine. His hair lay over his shoulders, and his eyes pierced anyone who walked through the gates.

On either side of the courtyard were brick hallways and buildings that led to classrooms. The school was so old I was sure the brick could crumble under a simple touch, but it had stood for over five hundred ages.

I tightened my arms around my torso, trying to keep the cold at bay. The bell rang, and people began scurrying to their first classes.

As an assassin, I favored the crowd—easier to blend in—but as a normal person, I hated the hot breath and shoulder touching that came with it.

The students ranged from twelve to twenty-five ages old. Gifted children traveled from all across Masos, from Arabrosa, Ekros and Saar, to attend Clamore and learn in the arts– for a fee, of course. Not just any child was allowed through the gates of this school. Only those who had the coin, which meant the sons and daughters of diplomats, politicians, and wealthy merchants.

"You stare any harder and I'm sure fire will sprout from your eyes and onto their backs."

Leena. She was one of the two people in the world who I gave a damn about and knew about my past life. It was hard to keep anything from her. She told me once best friends don't keep secrets, and though I hadn't known what that was at the time, I trusted her anyway.

I stood still, continuing to look at the sea of people.

"Wouldn't that be a sight?"

"I have a few options you could start with."

Leena had to be one of the most simply beautiful people I had ever met. Her face was hardly ever painted since her beauty was natural, and her straight red hair aided in that.

Leena was one of the Emperor's, or rather the Clergy's, golden children— a nephilim. Nephilim were half angel half human and were the closest to the Divine the people of Masos could get. So, they were revered as the most important beings to walk the continent, besides the Clergy and royal family, of course.

The poor girl had been pulled into all that madness thanks to her *ascension*. It translated to a revelation of their true selves, when their lineage and powers were made known. There wasn't a set age for when this happened, and sometimes it was at very inconvenient times.

Leena was an empath and her *ascension* happened when she was eight ages. She can interpret people's emotions, moods, and temperaments without them even knowing. Though, she swore to me she had never once used her powers on me. I believed her.

She explained she had just known how people felt at first, then it slowly developed into more. As her training progressed, so did the strength of her power. Now, she could manipulate other's emotions. In a sense, it seemed like a hell of a power. It was essentially mind control.

Sure, a witch may be able to use magic to do the same, but that was a simple cover over one's mind that could easily break with another spell or the person's willpower. With Leena's power, she could tap into an emotion the person already had and amplify it to where they couldn't help but react how she wanted.

Everyone has fear, anxiety, and rage deep down in them. She's a puppet master.

Curious how such a dainty creature could hold such a manipulating power.

It was believed nephilim's angelic blood could not be tainted with human blood any more than it already was. To remedy this, the Clergy insisted the Emperor enact a law where arranged unions were made for nephilims with races they deemed worthy.

Leena was only twenty-one ages old and had yet to be given a suitor. Most nephilims are promised as soon as they discover what they are, but for Leena they had not yet found another for some reason.

It was likely she'd be paired with a fae, that was usually who the Clergy chose. The Fae were at the top of the social ladder. They were everything every human wanted to be—graceful, but strong. Their appearance nothing short of immaculate, naturally tall beings with long hair and pointed ears. Two characteristics which gave them away. The natural wit and cunning most of their kind possessed was why they held a majority of the office positions in each territory.

Meanwhile, I was human. And humans should feel especially lucky to be friends with a nephilim.

"Amara." Leena pulled me out of my daze, bumping my shoulder. "We'd better get to class."

It seemed so unimportant, seeing as how I was plunging my dagger into the chest of a warden not too long ago. I was here learning about history, finance, and how to be an upper-class citizen on Masos, when I was a killer for hire during the night.

Technically, I wasn't a student, but I also wasn't a teacher. I liked to think of myself as an add-on. Diana Vocova, the headmistress, was kind enough to let me live on the academy grounds for the ages I'd been here and engage in the classes I liked. However, she had some say in what I did while on the grounds, which had led me to the class Leena and I were headed to now.

Diana had taken me in when she found me on the streets, pickpocketing at a young age.

It had baffled me, seeing how Diana was fae, but who was I to deny a free home?

I later realized that maybe training to be a warrior was in the cards for me. Of course, I didn't plan to fight for the Emperor, but I could use my available resources. It would help me achieve my end goal of getting the hell off this continent, and my nightly jobs enabled me to save for passage through Arabrosa and the west.

Every day my feet touched the soil of this land, I was reminded of what I couldn't do that night. Who I couldn't save.

Some days I swore I could taste the smoke in the back of my throat and feel the heat of the flames rising across my face.

When we made it to the classroom, there were two seats left in the front, which was less than ideal. Having people at my back made me uncomfortable. I needed to see the whole room.

On the board in white chalk read *The Cleansing*.

Leena groaned, sinking into her seat. "I've heard this story way too many times."

Professor Crane turned from the board and clapped his hands together. "Today, we will be discussing the Cleansing. Does anyone know of it?"

Who didn't?

He chose a girl in the back of the room. "It was a war that happened over fifteen ages ago. All of the races of Masos came together to fight on the coast of Mahlar Isle against the demons and the Defiants."

"Correct. And why exactly did they go to war?" He asked the class.

Another girl spoke. "Demons were turning nephilim."

At that moment, all eyes were drawn towards Leena. The air around us was stale, and Leena slumped in her seat ever so slightly.

"That is correct," Crane spoke, returning the class's attention to him. Leena took a breath. "Demons are the product of Lucifer's hateful and demonic power to change those who would defy the Divine, the Clergy, and the Emperor. Unfortunately, he later realized he could not only corrupt humans, fae, witches and lycan, but also nephilim. This was the ultimate crime of disobedience to the continent, tainting the blood of that which is so pure and good. The Clergy gathered the Emperor's forces, which was composed of the best warriors and witches, and waged war against the demons and their resistance. Can someone tell me what the Defiants are?"

A boy next to me coughed, shifting everyone's attention to him. "The Defiants were formed shortly after the Clergy built our society. They consist of members of all races who fled the main continent and wished to join the demons. They assisted in Lucifer's plan to dominate Masos and bring all the nephilim to his army."

Crane nodded and walked around his desk, leaning against the front. "This is why you are all here. You are the future of Masos. Some of you will go on to take public office or enforce the security of our borders, some will become warriors in the Holy Army and others..." he paused, trying to find his words. "Will go on to assist those in power. Nevertheless, you all are poised to be great assets to Masos. Study hard."

I internally rolled my eyes. It didn't help that none of the teachers in the academy were human. Humans at the school were not treated poorly necessarily, but any other race tended to keep their distance, except for Leena. Most humans were grouped together in classes for this reason, but today's class had some witches as well.

Witches were easily the most powerful of the races, but they fell second in social standing due to their lack of intelligence compared to the fae. Witches, men and women alike, looked exactly like humans, but they had powers and could do anything. They could cast spells as shields, curse an enemy, manipulate the people around them, and raise the dead. The list went on.

One could distinguish a witch from a human in two ways, by the lavender color of their eyes when they wielded magic and by the silver markings that formed on their arms and hands when they came into maturity.

Those tattoos, as people like to call them, are said to be a remnant of the power of the first witch of Masos, Hazem. When he came into the full might of his power, they burned into his skin as a reminder of the gravity of his potential. These marks were passed down to all those who came into their witch powers after him.

And then there were humans. Humans were almost nothing in Masos. They were neither dirt nor slaves, but they were not favored in any household. Those who held a position only did so because the Emperor decreed it, and his word was law. Most humans at the academy were there because their parents were wealthy enough to send them, not because they were gifted. Humans who did not hold office or any seat of power were typically maidens to the fae, worked in the fields for the witches, or were so desperate they traveled to the Mahlar Isle to escape servitude, and rumor has it, to join the Defiants.

The Mahlar Isle was a large island of sand and blood on the east side of the continent. The west side of the land was rumored to be covered in bones and stained with the blood of the Clergy's enemies.

Some of those who were a part of the rebellion fled to the Morge Isles at the Southernmost tip of Masos instead of retreating to Mahlar. These humans were miners of Morgean iron, an essential mineral needed throughout Masos to produce quality weapons for the Clergy and Emperor's warriors.

I had found, very quickly, living on this rock, that the Clergy was the ultimate power and was not to be crossed.

IT WAS after dinner when Leena and I made it back to my room. A loud rumbling sounded beneath us. I was lying on my bed, nearly about to fall asleep, and— gods I had been so close. Sighing loudly, I sat up. Leena sat across the room at my desk.

A crack rattled against our ears, and the floor shook so severely the ceiling crumbled a bit. The rumbling didn't stop as we approached each other and held on until the movement finally stopped.

When it did, there were shouts outside the door.

"An earthquake?" I asked.

Leena shook her head. "We've never had any on this side of the continent before. At least not that big."

Another crash hit the ground so hard it caused us to fall to our knees. The screams outside continued.

Leena ran to the door and flung it open, revealing a hallway full of crying students. "We have to find out what's going on."

And risk our lives for what? The sake of curiosity?

"Are you mad? Whatever it is could kill us as soon as we step foot outside."

"You want to just stay in here hoping it stops?" She yelled back, her face scrunching.

"Yes," I said simply.

Leena shook her head and ran off.

"Leena!"

She was already down the hallway and headed towards the courtyard.

I chased after her without a thought, and when I reached the courtyard, I was genuinely at a loss for words.

Everything was on fire: the bushes lining the walkways, the grass, even the ancient oak tree behind the statue of Michael.

I had seen countless sunrises cast their rays over the school, but I'd never seen it glow like this. While the heat felt good against my skin in the winter air, the light it emitted was daunting and filled my gut with worry.

"Get inside! Everyone, get inside right now!" Across the courtyard, professors guided students back into their dorms.

Through the flames and smoke, I finally found Leena, who was also helping get the younger students to safety. Before I could take a step towards her, a professor stepped in my way and grasped my shoulders, violently shaking them.

"You have to get to safety now! Do you hear me? You have to go! You have to—"

Blood spilled from his mouth, and he coughed, splattering it over my face and neck. He fell forward, and I couldn't do anything but grab hold as he crumbled to his knees.

Protruding from his back was an arrow running straight through his heart.

The screams continued, and the low rumble of the fires began to spread.

I was too exposed.

Move. Now. Pushing the professor off, I quickly climbed to my feet, squinting in hopes of seeing past the smoke, but too soon it began to fill my lungs. My throat closed up, and my eyes began to water as I gagged and coughed.

Two bodies walked out from the flames a few feet in front of me. They weren't rushing as if to help but stalking like I was what they were looking for. Understanding the danger I was in, I turned to run in the opposite direction but was stopped by a brute with a menacing gaze that burned into me.

The whole sclera was pitch black; the darkness bleeding out of the lower waterline in cracks like a lightning strike. The iris was a glowing crimson, contrasting against the rest of the eye, the pupil just as black as the rest.

"This was easier than I thought it was going to be," he laughed. A disgusting smile split his face as he took hold of my shoulders.

"Stop fucking about," someone shouted from the side. I didn't take my eyes off the brute, though. It was a death wish to take your eye off a predator ready to pounce. "Take her and let's be done!"

Don't think, just survive.

I brought my knee up swiftly to his groin and shoved him aside, making a run for the hallway again.

I didn't make it far.

Hot, piercing pain gripped my right leg, and I fell immediately. An arrow shot clean through my thigh. The brute hoisted me up by my hair. I went to land a blow to his face, but he caught my wrist and took a deep bite of my forearm. His sharp teeth ripping through my flesh with ease.

I howled in pain, letting tears fall. He tightened his hold on my hair and pushed me forward, closer to the fire.

"You do that again and I'll peel your lips off your face."

Nausea flooded my whole body as I struggled against him, but his grip was iron. Blood was pumping so rapidly through my ears I couldn't make out what he was saying to whoever was out of my line of sight. The heat was unbearable.

Any closer to this fire and all the hair on my face would burn off.

Get a hold of yourself. They're demons— bodies. They bleed just like everyone else. They can be hurt. They can be killed.

A thin man stood to my left, a vicious smile playing on his lips. I had to make a run for it or this would be it.

Taking three short breaths, I brought my elbow back to collide with the brute's nose. He dropped me, and I held my breath as I dodged through the small spaces untouched by the fire.

The hallway was in sight, a smile crept across my face, but the sliver of relief was short-lived when I was knocked to the ground.

The thin man flipped me over and held a dark blade to my throat.

"Finally, a little bit of fight!" He hoisted me up by my shirt, pushing the blade deeper against my skin. "Please, fight some more. It will make all this worth it."

"If you insist." I kneed him, slapped the knife out of his hand, and darted for the hallway again.

He made a quick recovery and grabbed my ankle. The rough cobblestone of the courtyard bit into my palms as I landed on the ground once again.

Picking up a fallen branch smoldering with flames, he secured his grip on the unburnt end and swung it at my face. My eyes widened, and I did the only thing I could think of.

I grabbed the branch.

My hands felt warm, but not the burning, searing pain fire should bring. My heart skipped a beat as the flames danced around my skin and extended onto my arms. The man was surprised, a hint of fear glimmering in his eyes as he looked at me through the fire.

"Get. Off!" I screamed, and the fire grew around my grip before exploding in the man's face, shooting him backwards, and hurling him into another pit of endless flames.

Still holding onto the burning branch, I looked into the flames, astounded. It was just me and the fire. Like the flames somehow knew me and found solace in my grip. I melted into its blanket of warmth.

Abruptly, everything slowed. I dropped the branch as a wave of nausea washed over me, making me fall to my knees, then my back. I'd lost feeling my leg, and my eyes were beginning to shut.

I fought the urge to close them, curling my hands into fists and digging my nails into my palms.

With fuzzy vision, I saw a figure standing above me. They swept me up.

My eyes had already shut, and I couldn't open them to look at the face of the person who held me. I took one last, heavy breath and let the warmth of the fires carry me away.

CHAPTER 3

A STALE SMELL greeted me as I awoke, a mix of soap and linens. The infirmary? I balled my fists under the sheets, feeling them crinkle with stiff resistance. Definitely an infirmary bed.

It wasn't until the headache pulsed that I realized it was too quiet. There was an attack on the academy, and I know for a fact not everyone made it out alive.

I knew what I had heard. Screams. There's a difference between screams of fear and screams of pain. I should know. I've given both.

A hand coasted across my thigh, moving the bandage down while someone fumbled with something on the bedside table.

"If she catches you touching her there, she might just throw a punch your way."

Leena. She was safe.

"Good thing I'm into that," a mysterious voice said.

Leena scoffed in response.

"But if I don't do this, she might lose the leg."

The voice was feminine. I hadn't heard it before.

"Well, the warning still applies."

I smirked, my eyes still closed. "Don't worry, I only bite when needed."

Leena's hand was on my forehead, wiping the sweat that had

collected at my hairline. I couldn't see her, but I knew her touch—I always knew.

"Hey," she whispered.

I finally opened my eyes and batted away the fog.

"Hey, you alright?" I reached out from under the covers and tried to wipe the soot covering her face away. Dried blood was crusted on her knuckles and cheeks as well.

"I'm fine," she said, glancing at the dark-haired girl stitching up my wound. "The arrow they shot you with was poisoned."

I took note of my mender.

She looked at me with dangerous, graceful, slightly narrow eyes. My gaze landed on a small cut gracing her upper lip, but that didn't hinder her image. She was slender but not overly so. Although she might have appeared breakable to some, I highly doubted it. She looked like she would be trouble, and every time she glanced at me, I could see it. She moved a piece of black hair that had stuck to her face, and I noticed a short cut with two braids at the top of her head.

"I'm Dasyra."

I swallowed some saliva to lubricate my throat. "Amara."

"Pretty name for a pretty girl."

"Stop flirting, D, and fix her damn leg."

Dasyra huffed a laugh and continued her stitching.

I looked back at Leena. "D? Do you have other best friends besides me? I'm hurt."

"Hush," she said, sitting on the side of my bed. "Dasyra is... like me. A nephilim."

Ah. That's why the scar on Dasyra's lip looked more like a birthmark. The mark of her angelic parent. It was said that when the nephilim came into their powers, they formed a mark on their bodies in the exact spot where their angelic parent had been injured in battle. It was one hell of an inheritance, I'll admit.

"What's a nephilim doing helping me? Was the nurse not available?"

"You're not in the academy's infirmary. You're in ours."

Bracing my arms on the bed, I pushed myself up to a sitting position, ignoring Dasyra's breaths of irritation and the pain in my leg.

"Ours?"

"Against our words of wisdom," Dasyra said as she pushed the needle through the last piece of skin. "Though your friend here is very persuasive when she wants to be. We have our own separate wing of the academy, which most people don't know about. The academy's infirmary is overflowing with those injured from the attack, so you were brought here."

My gaze went back to Leena. "Thanks."

"You have no need to thank me. I'd save you every time, but I have to admit if it weren't for the lycan, I wouldn't have been able to get you out of there."

"A lycan helped you to save a human?"

"Yeah, though I've never seen him before. He had you in his arms when he ran over to me, demanding that I get you to safety. Which I would have done without demand, of course, but something about his intense... grey eyes had me moving double time. Like if I didn't do it that second, he would throw me into the fire purely because of the delay."

"Grey eyes..." A memory pricked at the back of my mind. "Can you describe him more?"

"Really tall, built like a damn weapon, long brown hair but it was pulled back in a low bun. I don't know. I feel like I'm describing any ordinary-looking guy."

I was overreacting. There's no way he was here. The prison was the last place I saw him, miles to the east. He'd have no reason to come to the academy.

Footsteps sounded against the hard stone floor, possibly another nephilim coming our way.

"Heard we had a human in the infirmary."

The man standing at the end of my bed gave me a goofy grin and began to unwrap the bindings around his knuckles and palms. He was drenched in sweat and breathing as if he had just run laps around the grounds.

He had a short but stocky build and soft brown eyes, so friendly I couldn't help but grin.

I gave his body another swoop and noticed the mark of his parent on his forearm. It was faint, but there. The three bands that looped around his forearms were a few shades darker than his caramel skin tone.

"Luca Turner. Second son of the angel Gabriel." He gave me a slight bow and continued unwrapping his hands, throwing the used cloth on the table beside him.

"Amara. Daughter of who knows."

He chuckled. "Nice to meet you. What got you in our infirmary?"

"A poisoned arrow, it would seem. Does anyone know who was responsible for the attack?"

Luca glanced over at Leena and Dasyra. "The headmistress plans to address all those on the grounds."

Or I'll just ask her myself. Why's he so quiet about it? Was it sazari? I didn't see any when I was fighting, but then again, I was busy.

So, I asked. "Was it sazari?"

"Demons," Dasyra blurted out after tightening my bandage and wiping her hands clean.

Luca threw the last of his wrapping at her face.

"D, we don't involve humans if we don't have to. What happened to following the rules?"

She shrugged and balled up the cloth, throwing it back at him. "I only follow them if they benefit me, shorty. Look, she's alive, and Leena said she was fighting two by herself. Or at least that's what the mystery man had to say. Telling her the truth won't hurt."

"I won't tell anyone," I said, interrupting before Luca could reply. "How the headmistress wants to handle this is on her."

Dasyra got up from her seat and walked to Luca's side, patting him on the shoulder. "See? Nothing to worry about." She casted a glance back at me before taking her leave. "Try not to see me again anytime soon, yeah?"

"Nice to meet you." Luca smiled and walked after Dasyra.

"You're going to go to the headmistress, aren't you?" Leena sighed.

Yes, yes, I was. I needed to know why those demons had taken an interest in me, and if anyone could help me figure out why, it was Diana.

"Get some rest. I'll return in a few hours to check on you."

Leena rested her hand on mine before walking out of the infirmary.

It wasn't until it was quiet in the room that I realized how banged up I was. Everything hurt. Bruises were beginning to form under my clothes, and my muscles tensed every time I moved. Some of my ribs had to be cracked, because taking even the smallest of breaths made me cringe. I hadn't been hurt like this since before I started this life.

I lay my head in my hands, willing the pulsing headache to go away, and that's when I heard footsteps entering the room and stopping at the foot of my bed.

"I'm fine, Leena."

"You're a terrible liar." It was a sinful purr that racked against my skull, sending chills over my arms, forcing me to grip the sheet and cover myself.

I lifted my head and gritted my teeth. "Vork."

He stood with his arms crossed.

I had almost forgotten how tall he was. He towered over me, his eyes never leaving mine. He was dressed in a mundane-looking shirt with a leather coat that pulled slightly at his crossed arms. My gaze finally moved to his face. For a lycan commander skilled in combat, his nose was in perfect shape and his face had no imperfections whatsoever. How strange.

"You took a hell of a beating."

"What are you doing here?"

"Checking in on you."

"No," I snapped. "Why are you here at the academy? Surely you have better places to be."

"What?" He said with a bit of hurt. "You don't want to chat with an old friend?"

Friend? Ha.

My eyes narrowed. "Are you here to rat me out?"

He moved to the side of the bed and sat at the end, his feet planted on the floor.

"No, I'm not. I'm here on pack business. The attack happened shortly after my arrival. You're welcome for the save, by the way." I went to respond, but he kept talking. "No need to thank me. It's all in the day's work of helping pretty thieves and murderers in the event of a demon attack."

"Did you come here for another reason other than to have a conversation?" I asked again.

"As I said, just here to check in on you."

"Why?"

"Curious."

"Curious little thing, aren't you?" I spat.

His smirk grew into a grin as he stood. "I guess I am. You seem well, so I'll leave you to your healing."

I lightly rubbed my bandage-wrapped forearm. It didn't hurt, but it was itchy.

"I'm fine," I muttered, more to myself than him.

"So you are. Before I go, do you mind if I look at your bite?"

I was so injured, I had forgotten the bite from the demon, right where it was itching.

"Why?"

"Demon bites can be a bitch."

"I have a nurse looking after me. She said I'll be fine."

"You've healed, haven't you?"

"What makes you think that?" I shot back. I was bitten hours ago. There's no way it's healed, but his abrasiveness made me want to deny him either way.

He turned to me and crossed his arms over his chest. "Show me your arm."

I scoffed, "No."

"You have something to hide?"

"No, but there's no need for you to see any of me besides my face."

"Show me your arm."

"No."

He took a step forward, his eyes darkening. "Amara, show me. Your. Arm."

I let out a short snort. "Is that look how you normally get people to follow your orders? No means no. We've been over this before."

"I'll tell Vocova what you've been up to."

"I'll kill you," I said simply.

"You think that would solve any of your problems? Killing a lycan commander?"

"You've seen what I can do. I'll make sure your untimely death isn't linked to me in any way."

"Yes, I've seen what you can do, and isn't that a problem for you? I've *seen* you, angel."

My eyes darted towards his, and taking on a darkness of their own. "Don't call me that."

"Ohhh," he sang. "Hit a nerve, have I?"

"I have some healing to do. You can leave now."

"I think you're done healing."

Vork took a step towards me, taking my wrist in his hand and ripping off the bandages.

"Enough!"

Just like he assumed, there was nothing there but bruising.

"What tricks do you have up your sleeve, angel?"

That fucking name again.

"I don't have any tricks."

"You're not a lycan, a fae, or a witch. How are you healing so fast?"

I didn't answer as I looked forward, keeping my eyes away from his.

"What are you?"

That made me look at him with a dumbfounded expression. "I'm a human."

"Humans don't heal that fast."

This man wouldn't leave, would he? He had plenty of time to find me after our night at the prison, but he never came searching, and now he's asking too many questions.

I sighed.

"I have a witch friend who is crafty with healing potions. He gave me some."

"Who's the friend?"

"I'm not telling you my supplier."

"You mean to tell me a trained assassin has a friend? No, the lot of you are taught that connections are weaknesses, so I don't believe you." He rested his hand on the back rail of the bed, leaning in so he was inches away from my face. "The truth this time, if you please."

I lifted my chin and met his gaze dead on. He wasn't going to intimidate me. Most couldn't.

"What I told you was the truth. I have a witch friend—fine, an acquaintance—who I have a deal with. I show them combat skills, and they supply me with healing potions for when I get banged up in my classes. What we're doing is against academy rules, so I won't tell you who it is, but that's the story. If you don't like it, feel free to concoct a different version that will make you happy."

His stare could burn a hole through my head with how hard he was pressing.

A minute passed, and he closed his eyes and took a short but deep breath. "You smell like berries."

"And you smell like a wet dog."

That put a smile on his irritatingly perfect face. He pulled away and fumbled with the ring on his pointer finger, still gazing at me.

"I recommend jusha tea if you're taking healing potions. It'll help with the sour stomach you'll feel later on."

With one last soft smirk thrown my way, he strutted away back down the infirmary hall, his boots clanking beneath him.

Letting out a long breath, I slumped down in bed. Great. Exactly what I needed, a lycan prince asking questions.

But the questions he was asking...I wanted to know the answers, too.

CHAPTER 4

THE NEXT DAY at Clamore went on as if nothing had happened. A thin blanket of snow covered the burned grass and bushes of the courtyard. The official story was a group of raiders thought they could come and steal anything of value. I wasn't sure how that obvious fabrication was accepted without further questioning, but the headmistress was a persuasive woman.

Luckily, the oak tree still stood, but the statue of Michael was scorched. No one seemed bothered by the black patch of land that was once a vibrant green oasis.

I stood in my usual spot towards the back of the courtyard and watched everyone pass by. Were they really just going on like everything was normal? They had to be terrified of what happened. Someone, maybe the headmistress, must have silenced the worry somehow.

Though no one knew the truth, it was the first time demons had entered the academy. The school and the grounds were supposed to be protected by some of the best witch magic, so how were they able to get inside?

These followers of the Emperor and the Divine had no idea the danger they were in, or maybe they did, but they didn't care because the best of the best was protecting their walls. But it wasn't the best, because the demons still got in.

How was the Emperor going to handle the attack? The better question was, how was Diana going to handle it? The Clergy made the majority of the decisions regarding the school, but Diana was a strong leader on her own.

I pushed off the cold stone and headed to her office.

Knocking at the large wooden door, I let myself in, but stopped when I noticed she had a visitor. Diana stood behind her desk, her hands gracefully placed on the top.

A thick line was between her brows, and her eyes looked down at her desk. Her hollow cheeks, thin lips, and short blonde hair were tucked behind her ears. If her intimidating appearance didn't deter people, then her expression certainly would.

A man leaned against her desk with his body turned towards her, seeming to be in deep conversation.

Their heads snapped to me.

"I thought you had a free period, headmistress," I said with an apologetic nod. I started to close the door, but Diana beckoned me in.

She glanced at the man and slowly walked around the desk with her hands in front of her.

I kept my eyes on the visitor as he nonchalantly moved from his position and aimed for the door. He had hints of Luca, but was taller and leaner. His hair was also a stark contrast to Luca's brown curls. My suspicions were solidified when I saw a mark on his arm identical to Luca's.

"Son of Gabriel?"

His eyes locked with mine as he came to a halt and raised a brow. "And you would be?"

"Amara. I met your brother Luca."

He held out a hand. "Corym."

I took it and gave him a firm shake.

"What can I help you with, Amara?" Diana pulled my gaze to her.

Corym released my hand and glided out the door, closing it behind him.

"Last night," I began, "I know it was a demon attack."

"How did you—?" She huffed and cursed. "Luca."

"Don't blame him for wanting to tell the truth, but now I need the whole truth. Do you know why they were here?"

Diana sat back in her chair and placed her forearms on the table. "No."

"Do you know how they got inside the academy walls?"

"No," she sighed.

"Are you saying 'no' because it's the truth or 'no' because you don't want to tell me? I don't intend to tell anyone, Diana. I just need to know."

"Why are you so adamant about this?"

Crossing my arms, I went to the front of her desk and stopped to look her dead in the eye.

"Two of them tried to take me."

The emotions on her face came and went so quickly I couldn't decipher her reaction. Anger, concern, curiosity, annoyance.

"What did they look like?"

"I don't know, Diana, one was huge and the other was a sickly looking man. Why does it matter? The point is, I think the whole reason they raided the school was to take me and everyone else was just collateral damage. If that's the case, then I need to leave."

"No," she said quickly. "You're safest here. If they truly are after you, we will do what is needed to protect you."

Diana Vocova wasn't my mother, but she was as close as I would ever get to one. At fifteen, she took me in and did everything a mother should have done. I was a full-time student when I first came, but when I hit twenty ages, I started taking fewer classes and assisting with a some I enjoyed. It was my way of "paying her back," as she would say.

I didn't mind as much as I initially thought I would. I assisted mainly in the combat classes, because I was good at it. This part of my life was all I really wanted to remember. The past was full of painful memories, and I pushed them down deeper with each passing day and every coin I lined my pocket with.

What she was doing was typical of someone who cared; however, I wasn't a child, and she knew very well I didn't need to be coddled.

"No," I said just as quickly as she had.

"No?"

While there might be witches and warriors guarding the academy, staying would give the demons and whoever commands them full knowledge of my whereabouts. There was a target on my back, but if I left, I could make my way west and leave like I had always wanted to. I could really disappear.

"I'm leaving, Diana. Don't think I'm not grateful for what you've done for me. You took me in when I needed it most. I've learned so much from you, but you must know I didn't plan on staying here very long. This is the push to get me on my way."

Her eyes narrowed, and she rolled her shoulders. I could tell I wouldn't get the answer or acknowledgement I wanted.

"You will be guarded by a witch every day. One will be posted at your door when you sleep and accompany you to your classes. You are not to set foot outside of the academy walls."

"So, your solution is to treat me as a prisoner?"

Her fists balled, and her tone went rigid. "If that is how you want to view it. Though I would prefer you see it as a mother looking out for her child."

"Don't back me into a corner, Diana."

"You're not an animal."

"Then don't treat me like one. Give me enough motivation, and you'll see a whole other side of me you didn't even know existed."

Her eyes softened as she approached me and placed her hands on my shoulders. "Amara, I have kept you safe the entire eleven ages you've been in this school. You were so close to being taken last night. I almost lost you. I will not make the same mistake again. Please. Stay."

"Lose the bodyguards."

"Done."

I nodded. "Fine, you win."

The air was now calm as she visibly relaxed and rubbed my cheek with her knuckles. "Thank you. This will allow me time to discover who wants you and why."

I gave her a closed-mouth smile and stepped away, making my exit. Before the door shut behind me, I could have sworn I heard her curse.

CHAPTER 5

I DIDN'T MAKE it a habit to lie. Stretch the truth, sure, but lying was a hard business. If one wasn't careful then the web of deceit could become so tangled that something would slip. I only did it when necessary, and, unfortunately my talk with Diana fell under that category.

The following night, a few hours after the sun had finally set and covered our part of the world in darkness—where I truly thrived—I changed my clothes, wrapped my cowl over my face, and secured a bag of coins to my hip. Two long daggers were strapped to each thigh and a small knife was hidden in my boot.

I believed Diana wanted to keep me safe, but if demons got into the academy once, they'd do it again, and I'm not waiting.

It was quiet since it was just past midnight. I quickly scurried down the hall and outside.

Tall brick walls circled the outer perimeter of the academy and iron gates were located throughout them. The gate on the southeast side finally came into view when a hand caught my arm and twisted, making me drop to a knee.

"And where the *hell* do you think you're going?"

"Leena." I glanced around, looking for anyone else. "What are you doing up?"

"Are you my mother?" she chastised, then pushed on my arm again.

"Easy!" I yelped.

"Do I need to ask again?"

I pulled off my face covering. "I have to leave, Leena. I'm not safe here."

"This is—"

"Do not say the safest place for me," I interrupted. "It's not. There's a target on my back."

"Why? Who is after you?"

Clenching my fist, I tried to rise to my feet, but she brought my arm further behind my back and forced me down. I was on my knees, my face inches away from the stone walkway.

"Come on, don't make me fight you." I couldn't tell if it was a challenge or a plea.

I had never fought her.

I could take her.

Placing my free hand on the ground, I pushed back and brought my right leg up to kick her away and finally gain some space to free my arm.

To no surprise, she recovered quickly and pounced before I could make it to my feet.

I dodged her first punch, air blowing across my face from the path she carved through it with her fist. Another flew all too soon, and I ducked, taking the opening and landing a blow to her left kidney.

My next punch was caught and used to whirl me around. For a moment, I lost my bearings as the world spun around me. She took the opportunity to execute a powerful back kick and by the gods was it powerful.

Okay, maybe I can't take her.

My ass landed on the stone beneath us. I winced as my spine rolled back and my head met the ground. With the breath taken out of me, flashes of light sparked in my vision. I wheezed, fighting to find my bearings. Leaning on my left elbow, I rolled to my side.

"Had enough?" she chastised.

"I— I have," I gasped, dragging in air, "to go."

"You're being childish. You won't even talk to me." Hurt crossed her face, and her voice softened. "You always talk to me."

It hurt me too, but talking wasn't going to solve this problem. My absence would. She could see my mind was made up, so she advanced on me again.

I obviously wasn't going to be able to beat her in offense. So, I needed to switch up my strategy. I was used to being the stronger opponent, but there was no way I could take on a nephilim.

The air was hardly fully restored to my lungs, but if she landed one more blow I was going to wake up in my bed— probably restrained.

I grabbed her arm right as it came hurdling towards me and stepped up in a crouch, flipping her on her back. The next part was important because if I didn't do this, all the energy I just used would be for nothing.

I maneuvered behind her as quickly as I could and placed her in a hold, locking my arms around her neck and squeezing.

Leena clawed at my grip first, trying to pry them apart. When she saw that wasn't working, she went for my face. I scrunched my eyes shut and turned my head.

"Bitch," she choked out.

I couldn't help the quick smile that formed.

Her struggling finally began to ease as she slipped further into unconsciousness. When she stopped, I let out a breath and lay back with her on top of me.

"I can't put you in harm's way," I said between heavy breaths. "I hope you'll forgive me."

After I finally caught some of my breath back, I carefully placed her against the wall and adjusted my coat before making my way towards the gate.

It was huge and spikes were at the top, making it hard to climb. Hard, but not impossible.

As I grabbed the iron bar the gate opened at my touch and loudly creaked. I flinched but then relaxed when I heard laughter and shouting coming from ahead.

Students were congregated around a huge bonfire, cups in hand. I had forgotten; it was a late celebration for the harvest moon. This night had just turned out to be the best cover I could have hoped for. The warriors and witches who guarded the school were probably too worried about the safety of the entire student body to be concerned with one human making a run for it.

Those around the fire were clearly intoxicated, a good number of them hardly standing upright. Others were trying to catch up or were excessively kissing.

They're lucky there are additional protections around the school grounds and this field and forest was within them. If it wasn't for the wards, then this would be much more dangerous for them.

I ducked through the gate and scurried across the field to the forest's edge, finally close to making my escape.

Though the fire was the main source of light in the field, the full moon illuminated the path once I was under the cover of the forest.

Thick roots covered the ground, making it difficult to keep my eyes ahead. I had to constantly look at my feet to stay upright. That was my first mistake: not scoping out my escape route, because if I had then I could have avoided them.

Two men—boys, rather—stood in front of me. One with a cocky grin and the other with a face full of curiosity.

"I thought I smelled a human," the cocky one said.

Must be a lycan.

"Something I can help you boys with?"

"Yeah," the other said, taking a large gulp from the jug in his hand. "We're wondering what you're doing out here."

I stood straight, my hand itching for the blade connected to my thigh. "Is that all?"

The cocky one stepped forward. "We're warriors in training, and we just want to ensure you're safe. It's dangerous for a human to be this far from the academy and so deep into the woods."

He kept taking steps towards me until he was a foot away. A move to intimidate.

"You don't need to worry about me. It seems like you should be looking after your friend instead." I gestured over to him. "Looks like he'll be ready to keel over any minute."

"No doubt. But it's you I'm worried about."

I didn't have time for this. "No need. Enjoy your night."

I went to move past him, but he caught my arm.

The drunk one got closer then and sighed in my face, the smell of wine hitting me hard. "Don't leave so soon."

"You both have seconds to move away from me before I break whatever bones are closest."

"Oh, come on," he hiccupped, moving his face closer to mine. "One taste."

I brought my head back and connected with his nose, an audible crunch sounding as it broke.

The drunken lycan howled in pain, dropping the jug and cradling his injury. "You bitch. You fucking bitch! My nose, Wren, she broke my nose."

Before Wren could tighten his hold, I twisted out of it and pushed him away before taking some calculated steps back.

"I'd like to be on my way."

"Not a chance," he spat.

Not as nice as he was before. How predictable. I motioned him forward.

"Come on then. I don't have all night."

He did a cute battle cry and lunged.

I dodged out of his way, rolling on the ground and back to my feet.

"Slippery little human, aren't you?"

"Wow, Wren." I nodded toward his fingers, where his nails had elongated. "You need to shift just to beat a human? Must be depressing knowing you can't get it up without your wolf."

He lunged again, and this time he didn't miss. His hand wrapped around my neck, and he squeezed, lifting me off the ground. He was strong and on the verge of shifting. Those claws started to dig their way into my flesh, stinging as they began to break skin. His eyes took on a red hue and his canines sharpened.

There was no way I could beat him in a full shift.

While struggling for the last bit of air I could get, I reached down to grip my dagger and brought it up, slicing his arm and forcing him to drop me.

There was hardly any time to catch my breath as I took off sprinting deeper into the forest. A yell echoed behind me, but I paid no mind and picked up the pace. Lycans were extremely fast. I had to be smarter if I was going to lose him.

Numerous plans raced through my mind, but those ideas were quite literally knocked out of me. Blinding white light assaulted my vision, and a thick ring of searing pain wrapped around my throat as one of them caught up and landed a blow.

I coughed until I was retching up saliva and dry heaving.

"That wasn't very nice," the drunk lycan said, sneering down at me.

I placed my knuckles on the forest floor and pushed myself up, more coughing and ragged breaths tore their way out of me as I did.

"I'm going to have one hell of a field day with you." Wren laughed to my right and launched a kick to the side of my head that had me spitting up more than just saliva.

I lay on the earth, a pool of blood coming from my mouth, dirt and leaves stuck to my face.

The lycan I had yet to learn the name of kicked me in the abdomen, then again in the face. "Red is definitely your color, human. Let's add some more, yeah?"

Blood kept spilling from my mouth and nose before I spat again.

"If you touch me again," I said with the breath I had left, "I'm going to rip out your eyes."

Testing my resolve, he went to kick me again, but I had moved enough to where I could sweep his legs out from under him, giving me the perfect opening to sink my dagger in his left eye.

His scream pierced my ears, and I ripped out my weapon, glaring at Wren as I stood.

"You next?"

He bared his teeth and went to lunge.

"I wouldn't, if I were you," a smooth voice came from the shadows.

Wren stopped in his tracks, searching for the intruder.

"Who the hell are you?"

Vork emerged from the shadows, covered in darkness as if they were hugging him in protection, but he needed none. Wren knew it. He swallowed in trepidation.

Dressed in all black with his hair hanging wildly around his face, he leaned against a tree, his arms and legs crossed.

"That's not what's important. I think your companion there," he pointed with his eyes, "needs medical attention. You should take him to the infirmary."

"Stay out of it," Wren snapped. "This doesn't concern you."

"Oh, but it does. You seem to have my friend here in a tizzy."

I scoffed. "Friend?"

Wren looked back at me. "What? Is he like your boyfriend or something?"

"He *is not* my boyfriend."

Vork had a devilish smirk on his face. I would kick it off if he were close enough.

"I don't need your help, Vork."

"You're getting very close to the border," he tsked.

"I know," I gritted out. "I don't need your guidance."

"So then you know what lies beyond it?"

"I'm kind of in the middle of something." I gestured towards the boys, one still screaming on the ground, clutching his injured eye.

"Oh, of course," he said, matter-of-factly. "As you were."

I turned my attention back to Wren, and before he could look back to me, I sent a series of blows to his kidneys and kneed him in the face so hard it rendered him unconscious.

"Could you take care of the howling one?" Vork asked, annoyed. "He's got a hell of a scream."

Rolling my eyes, I gave the lycan the same kick he had so kindly graced me with moments ago, and he too fell silent. Now the only sound in the forest was the students getting drunk.

I seated my dagger in its place and used the back of my hand to wipe the dried blood off my nose and chin.

Vork's eyes tracked the movement, his lips tightening. "You alright?"

"I'm fine." Not giving him another glance, I walked towards my intended destination.

He followed.

Of course he did.

"Is there something I can help you with?" I snapped.

"Why are you trying to leave?"

I pushed the branches out of my path, but didn't hold them for him. "I'm not safe here."

"Not safe from what?"

"You," I sneered.

"For an assassin, you sure have a sense of humor."

I was wondering when he was going to bring that up. He had my secret looming over my head. But I was leaving, so it didn't matter if he told Diana. What mattered was if he told the regulators of Arabrosa, because then I would have a price on my head. I've never been caught before, but this lycan held the status of my future in his hands.

"Mind telling me the purpose of your presence?"

"Sure." He stopped walking. "You're very interesting to me."

I turned to him.

"You have very low standards, then. I've been trained to be as boring and forgettable as possible."

He chuckled and took a step forward, looming over me. My whole body suddenly flushed. His eyes held mine with such intensity, it was almost impossible to look away.

"I hate to tell you this, angel, but you've failed miserably."

"In all my ages of life, I haven't had this problem. This might be a malfunction on your part, not mine. It's okay to be obsessed with me, Vork. It's flattering."

"Firstly—" another step forward. "—You came into my room that night and thought I was someone else. That's poor planning as an assassin, not knowing your target's whereabouts. Second, every damn time I see you, I can't help but lock eyes with you. They're mesmerizing. Like the leaves of autumn just after they've fallen."

He lifted his hand to brush my cheekbone. His touch was cool but burning at the same time.

"Lastly, I find you here at the academy almost being taken by demons, and now you're fleeing your home into a sazari-infested forest just to get away." His eyes narrowed. "I want to know why they want you."

I tried to back out of his grasp, but he matched my steps until I felt bark piercing my back.

"I don't know why they want me," I admitted. "And I don't want to find out. I just want to leave."

"Running from a fight?"

"I'm *surviving*."

"No," he said softly, never moving his gaze from mine. "You're fleeing."

"Yes, are you going to let me?"

His eyes searched mine, looking for another response. With confidence, he pulled down my hood and placed his hand under my chin, so I was forced to look at him. It almost made me lose sight of what my purpose was.

Leena would wake up at some point and either come after me or tell Diana.

I placed my hand firmly on his and ducked under his arm, twisting around his back and pushing his chest against the tree.

"Goodbye, Vork."

He let out a low, short growl and turned, breaking free of my hold.

I took a few hesitant steps back. The moon's light was now blocked by the cloud cover, so I couldn't see when he wasn't right in front of me.

A presence stirred to the right and warm breath brushed across my ear. "How much can you actually see?"

I turned and reached out for Vork, who was no longer there.

He chuckled again in the distance. I couldn't see him, but I could feel him staring.

A fae would have easily been able to see him, and a witch could have simply cast a spell, but a human, oh, a human had no chance.

Vork was enjoying this. I wasn't accustomed to being on the other end of a hunt; I was always the one doing the hunting.

My chest rose and fell as I tried to still my rapidly beating heart. Small beads of sweat collected at my hairline.

The heat of his stare burned into me, and nervousness crept into my belly, I shed my coat, dropping it to the ground and stepping over it.

"Make a move," I said, my arms out in invitation. "Let's finish this so I can be on my way."

Vork happily accepted.

I didn't have enough time to react as he charged, picked me up by the shoulders, and threw me to the ground.

I groaned at the pain shooting up my back.

He lay on top of me, his hands on either side of my head.

"That's your idea? Tackle me and get between my legs?"

"I'm pretty comfortable right now."

Wrapping my legs tightly around his waist, I shifted my body to one side and gripped his head putting it in a tight hold. He was face down now, puffing up clouds of earth as his breathing turned heavy.

"Amara." He tried to speak, but his voice was strained from lack of air.

I didn't let up. I needed him out of the way. My mind got too muddy when he was close. My gaze turned up towards the trees as I squeezed harder, but he didn't fall as quickly or as easily as Leena.

His hands came over mine, and gripped them so tightly I thought he might rip them off. He pulled and growled as he pinned them above my head.

"It was a good attempt," he rasped.

"So," I said curtly between breaths, my legs still wrapped around his waist. "You have me pinned on the cold forest floor. What are you going to do now, *lycan*?"

He licked his bottom lip, which my eyes locked on.

"There is a very, very fine line between what I'm going to do and what I want to do, angel."

"Call me that again and you'll regret it."

"What could you possibly do to me in this position?"

My eyes narrowed. "I have a wicked bite."

"Don't tempt me with such promises," he said in a low, gruff voice that had me sinking into the earth beneath me.

I needed to move. *Now.*

Planting my heels in the dirt and bucking my hips up, I was able to take the sliver of a second to change positions. Now, I was straddling him.

"Good idea," he boasted. "I like this better."

A familiar wail sounded in the distance, sending fear slithering through my entire body and saving Vork from a punch to the face. A sazari was close, or rather, we were close to the border, as Vork had said.

I wet my dry lips. "I thought the witches put protections around us. The ward should be strong."

"They did. But strong doesn't mean foolproof."

"Goodbye." I pushed off him and stood. I could head east and hopefully circumnavigate the sazari.

Snow crunched under my feet, and small streaks dropped onto my face from the tree's low-hanging branches.

There was another screech from a sazari, but I kept moving. The hairs on the back of my neck stood up, and my heart stopped.

Closing my eyes and taking a deep breath, I slowly turned, careful not to make any sudden movements.

Exasperation coursed through me when a figure emerged. "Damnit, Vork."

"You know there are sazari out there, and you know you're getting close to the witches' ward. You won't be protected much longer. I thought you had better survival skills."

I jumped when another screech came from the distance, but this one was closer, much closer. And it was different from the others. Almost painful.

I didn't wait for him as I stalked toward the sound. My hands held onto branches and trunks of trees as I maneuvered through the roots and bushes.

Growling filled our ears, and Vork grabbed me around the waist to stop me from going further.

He was nervous—that worried me. I let his hand be as I reached out to the limb covering our view and pulled it down.

The moon's light slowly started to peek through the clouds, giving me sight and what a horrid one it was.

A sazari was just outside the ward, its hind leg caught in a trap. That was the source of all the noise. It had been captured.

And it was hideous.

It looked like it used to be a female fae, with hints of green skin visible against the grey, cracked hide. Its ears were slightly pointed, a lobe missing from one.

Moments passed and the sazari didn't make a sound, only taking short, loud breaths and thrashing in an attempt to gain its freedom. Blood dripped from its mouth and hands, which was strange considering it had no prey.

The sazari reared back around to its legs, and the source of the blood becoming clear. It was biting through its own flesh.

I tried to take a step forward, but Vork tightened his grip. "Where there is one, others will follow."

He was right. The sazari traveled in packs. The smallest group they ran in was threes, but their packs could get as large as two hundred.

"But we're behind the ward. Even if more came, we'll be fine."

He sighed, easing his grip on me. "Your faith in the witches is touching, but every magic has weaknesses."

I didn't respond. I was too focused on the beast still biting at its leg, halfway through now and hitting the bone.

How could anything have the will to gnaw off its own leg? The pain must have been excruciating. Then again, when someone was turned into a sazari, they slowly lost their wits and became a rabid animal. And animals would do anything to get out of a trap.

Snow crunched under footsteps coming from the right.

A group of witches came stumbling into view with smiles plastered on their faces, excitement in their eyes, and their silver marking shining in the moonlight. Some had cups in their hands, which barely made it to their lips as they fumbled to consume the drinks. Others simply hung on one another, cackling endlessly.

"Well," one of the young men slurred as he came to the edge of the ward protecting the academy grounds. "Look at what we have here. Our first catch, ha!"

The witch clapped his hands and stared at the sazari while the others snickered.

It lunged for him, but was flung back when it hit the ward and cried out in pain. Its snarling never ceasing as its gaze locked onto the witch.

"Any idea why witches are catching them?" I whispered.

Vork stepped closer, his chest mere centimeters away from my back. His hand dropped from my waist, leaving me feeling surprisingly cold.

"To practice magic. Practicing magic on other living creatures is forbidden, so it looks like they've opted to use something no one cares about."

The witch then did something I didn't expect. He stepped outside the ward.

"Sayer, get back inside the ward!" One of the others pressed.

"Pipe down. I'll be fine." He brushed her off as he kneeled down to the sazari's level.

A low growl vibrated past its lips.

They stared at each other for a moment, then something changed in the sazari. It was no longer fighting. It was calm.

Sayer picked up a small bushel of weeds growing at its feet and crumbled them in his hands before opening them and blowing the dust into the sazari's face. It started to convulse in pain, but this was different from the pain of the trap. This time, it was from within.

It twisted and turned, trying to escape the spell the witch had cast on it.

He gleamed.

"Well, would you look at that. It worked! By the Divine it—"

"Sayer!"

Sayer was pushed to the ground as another sazari pounced on him. Before the witch could utter another spell, it lifted its fist and smashed it into his head, twitching each time it brought it down.

It roared, looking around at its surroundings, knowing the other witches were there but unable to see due to the ward.

Within seconds, two dozen more sazari followed behind and charged at the ward, their claws sharp and their teeth ready to feast.

The stench of their flesh burning reached us as they attempted to push through the ward. It must have been painful, but they didn't care.

"We need to leave," Vork said, urgent. "They're going to get through."

I knew he was right, but I couldn't look away. I'd never seen this before. Despite all the pain they must be feeling and the easier kills waiting in the forest, the sazari were pushing to get through.

My eyes scanned behind the horde, and I took a step back.

A sazari the size of five of them combined stalked forward and let out a roar so powerful I had to cover my ears for fear they would bleed.

The enormous beast ran full speed towards the ward. It landed with a loud thud, not quite breaking through, but it was close.

The witches still present gasped and began their retreat. Vork pulled on me once again, with more force this time.

"Run, now!"

For once, I listened and followed behind him. There was another loud thud, and screams filled the air.

It had gotten through.

CHAPTER 6

Vork was already hundreds of meters ahead of me, and if I didn't think of something, I would get caught.

Stupid, stupid, stupid.

Survive. Do not get curious. Those were the rules I had lived by. Any human should live by them if they wanted to survive.

This was where curiosity had led me. With a sazari hot on my heels, and panic setting in.

I wasn't going to outrun them, so I did the only thing I could think of.

Climb.

I hoisted myself up the first tree I could and began my ascent. The bark jabbed into my palms, but adrenaline was coursing through my veins, so I paid no mind to the pain.

I pushed higher and higher, not looking back at the ground as I went, but I could hear the beasts as they darted past me. I sneaked a peek at where they were headed, and it was straight for the group of students who were still celebrating. My panic truly set in then.

Leena.

After the bonfire, the sazari would go to the school.

I cursed and started to descend. Snarls erupted below, and a sazari jumped up, reaching for me.

I attempted to climb even higher, but the next branch wasn't within reach. There was no way out.

The sazari growled as it made its way up, and I waited patiently until the monster hoisted itself up to my branch. It balanced as best it could while slipping its tongue over its teeth.

I whistled it forward, and it attacked.

I quickly stepped off the branch and dropped to the thick one below. However, my abrupt weight was too much for it, and it snapped.

The first blow, a branch, landed only on my stomach. The wind was knocked out of me, but before I could fully register it, I fell backwards and another thick branch hit my back. I flung forward, landing on my face with a thud.

I was getting flashbacks from when Leena sent that kick to my abdomen. This wasn't nearly as painful, but it brought back the same feeling. Soreness radiated from every part of my body.

Luckily, I had put my hands under my face before it connected with the ground, so there wasn't any bleeding, but if I walked away with nothing more than a concussion it would be a miracle.

With a groan, I pushed against the snow. There would be bruises everywhere, but for now, I needed to push on.

I mustered up all my strength and began to rise to my feet to run. When I took my first step, the sazari had already returned to the ground and grabbed hold of my right leg.

I reacted on instinct. With my hand on the ground and my leg in the sarazi's claws, I whipped my left leg around to collide with its face. It released me, and I scrambled to my feet to run again, but it wouldn't be so easy with these beasts.

It let out a shriek that sounded like a call, a beacon.

Gods, stop. Stop!

I pulled the knife from my boot and flung it, the blade sinking just between its eyes.

In depths of the woods, return calls from the rest of them sounded. Fear plucked through my body like a harp string.

I took off again towards the school, adrenaline pumping through me. The beating of my own heart filled my ears as it thumped against my chest, almost jumping out of my skin to find some reprieve from the anxiety it was under.

Ease up. You've gotten away. You're fine.

I finally made it to the fire, and it was carnage. More sazari must have flocked to the opening in the ward, because there were too many to count. Blood shined brightly against the snow, and with the fire still lit, I could see everything.

Dozens of students lay dead, sazari still feasting on their corpses, while others tried to fight their way out.

I scanned the field, but there was no sign of Leena.

Students were still running, trying to escape, and I joined them.

I ran back towards the academy with the group when we were met by the enormous sazari I had seen penetrate the ward minutes earlier.

"Run!" Someone hollered, and the students dispersed.

Screams erupted behind me. I pushed my legs harder and harder until something slammed into me.

Dasyra.

She grabbed hold of my arm. Her face was covered in blood, and her shirt was ripped in the front from claw marks, but she was still breathing.

"Where is Leena?"

"Safe," she assured me. "Come on, we have to get out of here."

I couldn't agree more.

We moved to make our way to safety, but our path was blocked by three sazari. Their mouths were filled with drool, and blood leaked from between their sharp teeth.

I took out the two daggers held at my waist and readied myself.

"I hope you know how to use those," Dasyra said, unsheathing her katana.

The sazari lunged for us.

I rolled out of the way and regained my footing, but one managed to tackle me to the ground.

The teeth. The teeth. The teeth.

I held my forearm under its neck. If it bit me, all hope would be lost.

Gripping the dagger, I stabbed it twice in the neck, but it still wouldn't stop the assault. I pierced its neck five more times before it finally gave up and fell limp right on top of me.

I tried to push it off, but its weight was too much. I pushed again, and it instantly became heavier.

Above the dead sazari crept another, peering down at me with black, soulless eyes. Its claws curling around the corpse and inching towards my face. I tried to move the hand that held the knife, but it was pinned. I closed my eyes, waiting for its attack, but it never came.

Looking back, the sazari was no longer there, and the dead one was lifted off me.

"Need some help?"

Corym gripped my arm and pulled me upright. He was armed with a long steel blade reflecting the fire behind him. Thick, brown leather armor stretched across his chest, and silver bracers covered his forearms. A small line of blood trickled down the side of his cheek, but other than that, he didn't look harmed.

"What are you doing here?" I asked in disbelief. "You're a nephilim. Aren't you too valuable to get caught up in this?"

Despite the death surrounding us, he found a way to flash a smile. "You know little about us."

I furrowed my brows, and then my attention was brought to a sazari running straight for us.

Corym swiped his sword through the air, easily decapitating it. The body dropped, but with the momentum of its run, it slid across the ground and stopped at my feet.

"Show off," I scoffed.

He grabbed my arm, pulling me forward toward the academy. "We need to get you to safety."

"Where's Leena?"

"She's fine. She can take care of herself."

I twisted out of his grasp. "Where is she?"

He pointed his sword to my left where Leena and Luca were fighting the sazari like it was what they were born to do.

Leena moved with a swiftness I would have never expected—her movements stunning and lethal.

The spear in her hand sliced through the air and her enemies with ease. The shaft was made of dark wood and capped by a long metal point, nearly the size of my forearm. Just below the tip, where metal met wood, a short horizontal blade jutted out, almost making a cross. Another gleam of metal flashed at the butt of the spear, which she used when being attacked from behind.

Leena bobbed and weaved through the clutches of the sazari as Luca wielded an axe that slashed through their hide effortlessly.

I was about to dash to her side, but a thunderous howl came from behind, bringing me to a halt. It came from the school and was followed by numerous others.

"Ah," Corym sighed, placing his sword on his shoulder. "Looks like the cavalry is here."

A pack of lycans ran through the clearing, snarling as they lunged for the sazari still coming from the other side of the ward.

I had never seen a lycan in their full form, and I was in awe.

They were enormous. Just standing on all fours, they stood way above my head. On their hind legs, I could imagine them being at least ten feet tall. Their snouts were the length of my hand, and their teeth were menacing. They were killing machines and wasted no time ripping each sazari they came into contact with to shreds.

As more of them flooded the field before me, I saw Dasyra join the fight. I itched to use the knife in my palm.

"You feel it, don't you? The urge to fight?" Corym asked.

I peered up at Corym, attempting indifference.

"I need to get Leena out of here."

"Come now," he jested. "I know a killer when I see one. You want to cut down every beast here."

"No, I want to get my friend and me to safety."

"Well," he said, clearly not convinced. "Let's head over there and kill a little on the way."

Together, we ran deeper into the field. I didn't look for sazari to kill, but I attacked whenever one got close enough. A few scratches grazed my skin as I went on fighting, and my body was starting to feel the pain. I didn't know how much longer I could keep my strength up.

The nephilim and lycans, on the other hand, were doing just fine. They didn't even seem to be breaking a sweat.

I was the only human on the field. Witches had joined the fight as the sazari kept filing in, but no other humans were here. They knew better. No human would be reckless enough to get caught in this fight. Even I usually wouldn't have.

Another one came towards me, but a lycan sideswiped it, hurling it into the fire. I stared into familiar eyes.

They were storm clouds.

"Vork?"

All the lycan did was huff in response.

My gaze moved behind Vork's shoulder to Luca, who was fighting two sazari with his axe. He was winning, and it was impressive. A smile began to grow on my face, but it quickly faded when a third sazari came from behind him, about to pounce.

"Luca!" Leena ran toward him, slicing through the two sazari that stood in her way. She gripped the small amount of hair still remaining on the third's head, and Luca sliced its throat.

More kept coming, and Leena was losing sight of her surroundings. Another was slowly stalking her, and amid her last kill, she had lost her weapon.

Without thinking, I left Corym and Vork and rushed towards them. Twisting the knife in my hand, I flung it forward, luckily connecting with the head of one of the beasts. More were still coming, and I was out of weapons, so I used the only one I could think of.

Myself.

I tackled a gigantic sazari to the ground and rolled until we separated. It broke through the barrier, and my stomach turned in nausea. I had no weapons, and this creature was five times my size.

It eyed me and slowly stalked forward, growling.

Beads of sweat fell from my face, which had little to with the fire at my side. Panic gripped me.

As it advanced towards me, I tried to maintain the distance between us until I tripped on a corpse and was forced to scurry back. A flash of black whipped past me and tackled the sazari to the ground.

Vork.

He was a great warrior, but he was losing this fight. I didn't know if it was because he was exhausted or because the sazari was a bigger opponent, but I couldn't watch him die because of me. I rose to my feet and tried to step forward, but immediately fell, grasping my twisted ankle as a cry tore through me at the unexpected pain.

For fuck's sake. It must have happened when we collided.

Pain shot up my leg, but I tried to push it aside to get to Vork. The lycan was putting up a hell of a fight, but I was nervous. He was there because of me. If I hadn't left Corym's side, then he wouldn't have been about to die to save me.

All at once, the past I had tried so hard to bury within myself reared up, the emotions coming over me in waves. The armor I had fortified myself in began to crack and chip away, allowing them to drown me. I blinked away tears as the sazari wrapped its arms around Vork's chest and squeezed, piercing him with its razors. His howl of pain snapped me out of my thoughts, and guilt festered inside of me. The sazari let him go, and he fell at my feet.

I crawled over to him and took hold of his front paw. "Come on, you hardheaded dog," I pleaded, my voice cracking as I looked at his unmoving form. "Get up."

He didn't respond.

The sazari had probably cracked his ribs and pierced his lungs. It would take him time to heal. But we didn't have time.

"Vork, don't you dare die on me. *Not for me.*"

The sazari stalked back over, the same as before. Slowly and painfully. It might have been a crazed monster, but it knew when its prey was helpless.

"Stop," I whispered as rage-fueled tears began to fill my eyes.

The sazari barked, making it known my time was almost at an end.

I shook my head and gripped Vork's paw harder.

"Stop it."

I didn't know who I was speaking to. To Vork, for him to stop bleeding and to heal. To myself, to wipe the tears away and fight like I knew I could. To the sazari coming to end us, or to the entire battle. I didn't know. What I did know is I wanted the killing to stop.

I was tired from the fight. And I was furious that I had an inconsolable feeling that the lycan in my lap was going to die.

Trembling, I blinked away my tears and turned my gaze to the sazari. "Enough!"

My voice carried over the fighting and the screams filling the air until it was only mine everyone heard, and with it came a fierce heat.

The heat from the fire still raging at my side seemed to fuel my anger. I was a succubus, taking heat and power from the flame. It grew to new heights as I breathed heavily, my sight never leaving the beast.

It staggered back momentarily as it acknowledged the flames but quickly remembered its original goal and lunged.

"I said *enough!*"

The bonfire's flames swirled around us and shot at the sazari. They engulfed the creature, the power never letting up. Its splitting screams ripped through the air, but I refused to let go of the anger. The flames kept growing, and so did my fury. I couldn't let it go; it began to consume me.

It felt good. It felt like power. I wanted it. I craved it. The flames circled around Vork and me, not harming, but protecting us. I was becoming so drunk in the heat that I hadn't even noticed the sazari had died and was nothing but a charred corpse.

I didn't care.

"Amara."

Amid everything, Vork had shifted into his human form. He was naked, covered in blood with gashes all over his body. He strained, attempting to roll over to his back, but his injuries were still trying to heal.

He looked up, blanching at the fire surrounding us, worry in his eyes.

He squeezed my hand. "Amara, look at me."

I tore my gaze from the fire with heavy breaths. My shoulders sagged when our eyes met, and the flames subsided, returning to their source.

"You okay?" I asked, my voice raspy.

There was an eerie silence around us. The fighting had stopped.

Vork smacked his dry lips together. "I think I have a few cracked ribs, but I'm going to be okay. Are you alright? What was that?"

Worry settled in my gut as I looked around the field. There were no sazari left. They had all fled when the fire broke out.

"I have no idea."

CHAPTER 7

THE SUN HAD JUST LIFTED over the horizon when I was summoned to Diana's office the next day. Despite my strange ability to heal minor cuts and scrapes, the bruises from last night ran deep. My whole body was stiff, though my ankle had already healed.

If last night's events weren't odd enough, a new scar had appeared on my right hand. A deep brown mark swirled from the top, wrapping around my wrist and climbing up my forearm before stopping on the inside of my bicep. There was no pain when I touched it.

By the gods, I was pissed. I was a nephilim.

Panic and confusion had gripped me when I realized what the mark meant. I had passed out from exhaustion after the fight, so I didn't have a chance to give anything a second thought in the moment. But when I awoke at the witching hour, I began to deduce who I could be. What I could be.

Now wasn't the time to lose my wits. I needed to be calm and see if I could learn anything from the other nephilims without them learning any more about me. With everything that had happened last night, I needed to hide what I could. If I didn't have a target on me now, there definitely would be when people discovered my immunity to fire and the apparent ability I had to control it. Not to mention my newfound parentage.

I sat opposite Diana, hands in my lap, trying to hide the mark. Behind her, Vork stood with his arms crossed over his chest. His face was free from bruises and scratches, and he stood straight as if no ribs had ever been broken, breathing easily like his lungs had never been pierced. Not a single sign to indicate he'd even been in a fight.

After the battle had ended, we were carried to the infirmary together, but this was the first time I had seen him since.

Part of me was relieved he was alive, but something burning inside kept me from fully enjoying his company.

My head was spinning when I woke up. It wasn't the random powers I had developed, the drunk lycan's assault on me, or even the sazari. No, it was the way the man standing in front of me could make me feel with nothing more than his whisper brushing over my skin.

The other nephilim were standing behind me, scattered across the room. The only one I could see without turning my head was Corym.

He rested one leg on a table with the other planted firmly on the ground, glaring at the lycan commander across the room.

Vork ignored him.

"How do you feel, Amara?" Diana asked.

I shifted in my seat. "Better than I did when I fell asleep, but I'm still very sore."

"And your ankle?"

"Still hurts," I lied.

Diana pursed her lips. "I will get right to the point. While I realize the danger those witches put everyone in, that is not why you are here. You lied to me. You attempted to flee the academy grounds even when you said you would stay—"

"I never made any such promise, Diana, and you know that. Don't twist my words."

"Nevertheless, you knew where we stood on your safety, and you put yourself in danger by trying to leave."

"Am I a prisoner?"

"By the Divine, no. This is your home."

"Then I should be able to come and go as I please. I am a woman, Diana, not a pet."

Her lips tightened. "Is there anything you would like to tell us?"

Silence filled the room.

"Amara," she pressed, but this time with a soft voice that caused me to look away. Her moment of emotion wasn't something I was used to. "I am only trying to help you. At least try to see that."

"I honestly don't know what happened to me."

"The night when demons infiltrated the academy," Vork began, "Amara defended herself with fire."

I shot him a glare.

He had made no promises to keep my new found powers a secret, but I didn't know he had been in the courtyard when I fought that demon, so he's known longer than I have.

Diana laced her fingers together and looked at him. "Fire?"

"It covered her entire body without hurting her. Last night was different, though. She took control of it."

Shut the fuck up.

"There is no way out of this," Diana pressed, turning her gaze back to me. "Tell us."

With gritted teeth, I began that recollection of that night, "I was trying to find Leena. The demons came out of the fire and attacked." I held up my hands in defense when I was met with unsatisfied faces from those gathered. "I swear I don't have anything else to tell you. I'm immune to fire, and now—apparently—I can also control it. The demons tried to take me, but you already knew about that."

Diana and Vork's eyes landed on my marked hand and I quickly put it back in my lap.

Damnit.

Diana stood slowly. "Were you injured?"

"It's just a nasty scratch. It'll heal."

"Liar," Vork muttered from his dark corner.

My eyes narrowed. "If you don't stop talking, I'm going to punch your teeth in."

Wrinkles creased his forehead as his brows shot up and a smile on his lips.

Diana walked around the desk with her hand out. I looked up at her, but didn't move. "Your hand, Amara."

Reluctantly, I placed it in Diana's and flinched as she pushed up my sleeve. She traced the mark with her fingers, and I sucked in a small breath at her touch.

"No way." Dasyra walked up from behind her and leaned over.

"This," Diana began, "is a very, very old mark."

"Okay," I drawled. "Whose is it?"

"Your father."

"And that would be..."

She released my arm and leaned against her desk. "It would appear your father is Michael. The angel Michael gave you this."

All I could do was let out a small, quick laugh. The angel Michael himself. Well, wasn't I lucky?

"We all have marks," Dasyra said as she circled around and sat in the empty chair next to mine. "I'm sure you're familiar with the fall of Lucifer?"

I nodded. She thought I didn't know this, but I played the part.

"Well, during that battle, our parents received some gnarly wounds. Mine, or my mother's, Tirel, is on my lip. Michael has the same mark on his hand and arm."

"That must be where your powers come from," Vork added. "His ability to command fire is legendary."

"I'm sorry," Corym interrupted, making us all turn to him. "Why is this lycan here? This doesn't concern him."

"I see you still haven't learned to respect those in command," Vork calmly said.

"That's enough," Diana demanded. "Leena, please show Amara to her new room. Dasyra, Luca, you can return to training."

Leena took my hand and pulled me up from my seat, not allowing me another look at them before we left.

A long hallway framed with dark wood and a gothic ceiling that seemed to go on forever greeted us as we left Diana's office. On the walls were paintings of biblical events, weapons, and armor. At the end of the hall was a door that looked like any ordinary door, but when Leena placed her hand on it, there was a huge thud on the other side. Multiple mechanical dings followed, like a lock turning, which was exactly what it was.

The door gave way, swinging open for us. Leena smirked as she went into another never-ending hallway. She took a quick turn, and we were in a room filled with so many modernized weapons and armor I was convinced we couldn't possibly go through it all.

Leena saw my expression and laughed. "Don't get too overwhelmed. Your armor has already been picked out for you."

"I don't have a say in what I wear?"

"Not when you're the offspring of an angel."

I winced. I didn't want any of this—not the group of nephilim, not the shiny armor, not the title, and especially not the baggage or restriction that came with it.

We made our way down the rows of what seemed to be endless weapons until we came to a white wall that housed a wooden mannequin.

Leena reach for the armor that was a thin, black matte chain mail fashioned to look like reptile scales. The material was smooth to the touch. It extended up the neck, flowed down into long sleeves, and laid flat along the midsection.

Leena unclipped the armor and laid it on the floor before undoing the black leather under the chain mail.

"This," she said, handing me the leather breastplate, "is your base armor. You wear this underneath the pure luxium."

"Luxium?" I shrugged it on. "So, this thin piece of leather is supposed to protect me?"

Leena began to tie the strings so they fit snugly. "The leather is more for training than anything, but it provides extra protection when you wear it with the luxium. This is all from your father. He had the armor crafted for you as soon as you were born, hoping you would never need it, but if you did, it was always here. It's made of luxium, the same material the angels' armor is made of. It's nearly impenetrable."

Nearly.

"We never knew it was you specifically," she went on. "But we did know the heir was a daughter. How lucky I am that it just happened to be my best friend."

Her smile warmed me.

I reached out, the metal scales cool against my fingertips. "This material— luxium. I've never heard of it before."

"And that's how the Clergy would like to keep it. Luxium is found only in the ground of the Garden. That's why angels have exclusive access to it."

"You mean *the* Garden? The Garden of Eden?"

"The very same." Leena put the armor over my head, slipping it over the leathers. "It's extremely rare and very valuable. Luxium isn't public knowledge, so don't go around flaunting it. If demons got a hold of this, we would have a serious problem."

If my father had commissioned this armor for me, then that meant he knew of my existence. Visions of him flooded my mind. Though I had never met Michael in the flesh, I had walked past his statue in the courtyard countless times.

"There's a war raging right now between angels and demons," Leena continued. "Your father is the general of the Divine's army. He left you in good hands. Vocova has been with the angels since the beginning. You couldn't have asked for a better caretaker."

I didn't care much that my father had taken no interest in me. I had survived this long without him and would continue to do so, but what Leena said about Diana made me pause. What didn't I know about my so-called mother figure?

"How old is Diana?"

Leena shrugged. "Truthfully, I don't know. But I do know she's someone we can trust."

Despite the secrets, I never doubted that fact.

Leena finished strapping on the armor then dipped to the feet of the mannequin, bringing the arm bracer back with her.

These were also black leather, but they were trimmed in silver. She collapsed them around my forearms, and they conformed to me naturally, starting at the middle of my forearm and extending over the tops of my hands, with two large gaps for the fingers ang thumb.

With my hands in the bracers, I squeezed them into fists, stretching the leather out. "Do you know who your angel parent is?"

"I don't know much about her."

"So Otto is..."

"My real father." Leena made a circle around me, adjusting the armor. "His wife is my stepmother. A wonderful woman, but it's clear she doesn't love me as much as she loves her own, which is understandable."

Leena grabbed two short steel swords adorned with a fiery red ruby on each handle. The blade had a slight curve to it and a very sharp end.

"Your father never... realized he slept with an angel?"

Leena chuckled. "No, of course he knew. Human parents are sworn to keep their children's lineage to themselves until their powers come naturally. An odd rule, I admit." She held out the swords for me to take. "Go ahead."

I took them from her and turned to look at myself in the mirror. I wasn't surprised. I was empowered. The dark luxium armor that lay across my chest was a perfect fit. The bracers made me feel strong as I clutched the swords.

This was a power I hadn't known I craved. There was a glow to my swords that was so intoxicating I couldn't look away. I stood taller, something I wasn't used to doing. A life in the shadows kept you from drawing attention to yourself, but I almost wanted all eyes on me after putting on the armor.

The two short swords weren't weapons I was used to handling, but they were blades nonetheless, so I had no doubt I could adapt.

"Your training will start tomorrow," Leena said. "You should get some rest."

I furrowed my brows, finally coming to. "Training? No, I need to leave."

"I understand you were taught to flee in your past life, but doing that won't help you now. You have a dangerous power, Amara. You need to learn to control it or you'll hurt others."

She could no doubt sense all the emotions flooding into me because she placed a hand on my face and smiled.

"Hey, don't be like that. You might not know the others, but you know me. Just do me the favor of at least staying for your training. After that, if you still want to leave, then we'll talk about it. But learning to control your powers will help keep you alive."

Leena was right. If I ran away now with powers I didn't know anything about, it could kill me, and at that point, what was the purpose of running anyway?

I nodded. "What should I do for the rest of the day?"

"Rest. You're a new nephilim, but you took a beating. I'm serious. You're a capable fighter from the past training you had with the guild, but what Vocova is about to put you through... It'll be much different. You'll need all the energy you can save."

"Can you at least show me around?" I had found out the secrets Leena was keeping. Who knew what I could find out now that I was one of them?

One of them.

The last time I was part of any group, it ended in fire and death. If I didn't leave at some point, it could end the same for them and for her.

"Sure. Let's get this off you, and I'll give you the grand tour."

The Hold, as they called it, was enormous.

There was a library that housed every battle and legislation ever proposed by the Clergy and past emperors. A long white marble table stood at the base of the room's winding staircase, with one chair at the head and more on each side.

The training room took my breath away.

The Hold sat on the side of the closest mountain above the academy imbedded into the rock. The training room was filled with natural light due to the floor-to-ceiling windows on the west side. The windows were cut into long panels that swung open and led to a balcony overlooking the school grounds and the surrounding woods.

I couldn't believe I never noticed this place before. My only thought was that it was so well camouflaged into the mountain that I nor any other students gave it a second thought.

While Leena tended to some business I had no interest in, I took my time on the balcony. The cold breeze graced my face, and it felt like I was breathing in clear air for the first time. I leaned against the stone railing and looked out onto the land of Arabrosa.

The sun was at its peak and gleamed off the snow falling on everything in sight. Pine trees surrounded the Hold, filling the air with their delicate scent. I enjoyed this part of my life. The beauty of Arabrosa. Since most of my time was filled with classes and contracts, I hadn't had a chance to experience the rest of Masos.

There were rumors of lush land and warm air in Saar. Rolling hills and vibrant green covered the entire land until the Southernmost tip at Sacro Port. The area surrounding the Port had been overrun by merchants and those less fortunate than others on Masos. It was an important location for the whole continent, but as the ages went on, more areas of the Port became slums, making it a dangerous place to go in Saar.

The Port was a few miles from the Morge Isles, where mainly humans resided. There, the majority of the steel mined was used to create the weapons needed for the warriors of Masos.

The innermost part of Ekros was covered by the woods and mountains that ran through Arabrosa, but in the east, it became just like Sacro Port. Deserts covered the area due to its closeness to the land off its coast, Mahlar Isle. Ekros' coast was so close to the land where the war raged that it was scorched, though not many people traveled far enough into Ekros to see it.

A clanging from below pushed me out of my daze.

I peered over the edge to get a better look.

Corym and Vork were sparring.

They both had tall, thick sticks in their hands, sweat glistening along their brows as they let out heavy breaths.

"Come on," Vork teased. "You're going easy on me."

Corym let out a hearty laugh, then charged.

They both moved with such precision, their muscles flexing with every blow.

"Like what you see, Amara?" Corym shouted, a smirk on his face.

I snorted. "I've seen better."

Vork took the opening and hit him in the stomach, then in the back, pushing him to the ground. "I suggest you leave before he gets so distracted that I push him off the mountain."

Leena joined me a few minutes later, looking down at them. "How long have they been at it?"

"Not too long." My gaze lingered on Vork. "What's he doing here?"

"Well." Leena turned her back to the stone railing and leaned her elbows on it. "I'd say he's taken a liking to our newest recruit."

I rolled my eyes. "You're telling me the commander of the Arabrosa pack has stayed at an academy in the mountains because of a newly found nephilim?"

Leena cocked her head. "Did you sleep with him?"

"No." I grimaced. "I didn't sleep with him."

"Well, why not? Look at him. He's attractive."

"And cocky as shit."

"Hmm," she hummed with a growing smirk. "Wonder who that sounds like."

"Shut up."

Her smirk turned into a chuckle, and she turned to lean on the railing next to me.

"Fucking someone doesn't tie you down unless you allow it to," Leena said. "You've enjoyed yourself before with men and women alike. All of which never looked or acted like that lycan down there. I think you might have met your match."

I looked down again, and though Corym was impressive, it wasn't him I was looking at. Leena was right. Vork wasn't like anyone I've been with. I was honestly intrigued by him.

The thought of us together, as sweaty as he was, in bed, sent a jolt of energy through my body that almost knocked me over. His hand on my chin like he had the other night, the deep hunger in his eyes boring into mine, his iron grip painted on my backside to draw me closer.

How would he like it if the roles were reversed? He's a man of power, but the thought of seeing him submit sent a new jolt straight to my core.

"I see he doesn't even have to say anything to get you going," Leena observed dryly.

My eyes darted to her. "I'll have to keep my emotions in check around you.

"Oh, I don't need my powers to see what's right in front of me."

CHAPTER 8

"Looks like it's you and me, sweet cake." Dasyra flashed a wicked smile as she circled around me.

When the sun went down, I'd reported to the Hold's training room as instructed. Dasyra had been assigned as my partner for the evening.

"First lesson," she said. "Be aware of your surroundings."

I already knew all of this. So much for the nephilims' *elite* training. Rolling my eyes, I glanced at Corym and Luca, who were paired to the side. When I turned back, a fist was hurtling towards my face. I caught it just in time.

"Leena!" I threw her arm down. She'd come out of nowhere.

"Sorry, babe, you won't get any slack from me in this room," she said, grinning.

I sighed and looked back at Dasyra. "Nice try, trying to use Leena as a distraction. Anything else you want to throw at me?"

"Now that you mention it." She began throwing punches left and right, and I dodged each one. I pushed Dasyra's right fist away from my face, only for her to swing her left fist around and collide with the side of my head.

The world came crashing down as my face met the floor.

"Get up," she said curtly. All traces of her earlier flirtatiousness gone.

I stumbled to my feet, putting up my fists. Dasyra came at me again, but this time she had a knife in her right hand.

She swiped up, down, side to side, and jabbed, actually slicing me a few times. The slight but burning sting lingered for a moment, then healed moments later. Though, I wasn't able to feel much reprieve from the feeling because at one point she was nicking me every other slash.

I threw my leg under her, and she fell on her back but quickly recovered with a backward roll. She came at me again, and I sent a hook kick with my left leg towards her abdomen. It must have been more powerful than I intended because a loud crack sounded as she crashed into the wall.

I winced at the sound as Leena quickly ran to her side.

"Shit, I'm sorry."

I was. I had no idea where that power had come from.

Dasyra shrugged. "You just broke my arm. I'll be fine. We heal quickly, remember? Leena, train with her until I get back?"

"Yeah, you got it."

Leena turned to me, ready to begin another lesson, but before she could, Corym stepped in.

"Leena, go with Luca, I'll train Amara," he said, finishing wrapping his hands with tape.

"But D—"

"An order."

Reluctantly, Leena pursed her lips and joined Luca on the other side.

"So, you give orders?" I asked with an arched brow.

Not answering, he walked to the rack of weapons and picked up two sets of short, thick sticks wrapped in leather. He threw one set my way and twirled his own in his hand before bringing one down on my left shoulder.

A hiss escaped my lips, and I had to take a knee to recover from the impact.

Corym was unimpressed by my reaction. "Stand. Now."

"I thought this was training," I grunted, forcing myself to stand and grip my weapon. "You're acting like I'm a real enemy."

"If I take it easy on you here, you'll die as soon as you see a real fight."

There was barely any time to process his response before he struck again.

With each hit, the clanging of our sticks rang through the room, and it was all I could focus on. He jabbed forward, and I took the opportunity to hit his hand instead of the stick, which made him drop the weapon. I lunged, but he took hold of my left arm, twisting it so I had to drop the stick in that hand. Huffing in irritation, I moved away and twirled the other stick, waiting for him to attack.

Hours passed and by the end, I was lying on the floor with my eyes closed, legs sore and hands raw. Everyone else had turned in for the night, but I had yet to make myself move.

"You did well today."

I opened my eyes to find Diana towering over me—her hands were on her hips, her black dress spotless. Not a hair out of place.

"I got my ass kicked. Me," I said in disbelief. "I'm a good fighter."

"It's your first day of training, and you still have much to learn. Your combat classes helped, but fighting with your fellow nephilim is a much different experience than what you've learned in the past. Give yourself some credit."

"Combat is combat."

She sat beside me, leaning back on her palms and looking at the empty room.

"You've only been taught self-defense and evasion. You're quite adept in those, the best I've seen to be honest, and in someone so young..." She smiled down at me.

I covered my eyes with my forearm, my cheeks heating.

"But what you're learning here is more than that. You've been shown different strategies and ways of moving that you haven't had to do in your twenty-six ages of life. I don't expect you to master it in one day."

"What about two?"

Diana gave me a rare laugh, which made me smile.

"Not even two, child, but you'll catch on fairly quickly. You have a natural talent for these things, and your level of discipline is hard to come by."

I unveiled my eyes. "Thank you, Diana."

She gave my head a quick kiss before standing up—gracefully, of course.

"And who knows," she said, brushing off the dirt from her dress. "You may even surpass Dasyra."

I snorted as she walked back to the academy.

Despite Diana's kind words, I was still angry I couldn't beat Corym. So, I stayed in the training room a bit longer. Practice makes perfect, right?

It was almost midnight. I had been working on my form with my new swords, bobbing and weaving through an imaginary opponent. I wasn't used to short swords. They were heavier than a dagger or a bow. More clunky.

Vork walked into the room, his arms crossed. "Isn't it past your bedtime?"

I pushed my loose hair from my face. "Why are you still here?"

"I'm a bit of a night owl."

I raised a brow.

"I figured I could help with your training, but it's getting late. You should get some rest."

I holstered the weapons at my waist, resting my hands on them for support. "No, what are you still doing *here*?" I gestured to indicate the academy as a whole. "Your pack must need you back at home. Our meeting here was by chance."

"Wanting to be in your presence isn't enough?"

"It's a good start."

He smiled, but it quickly fell. "There's been an influx of demon and sazari attacks near my pack's borders. Vocova is an old friend of my father, so he sent me as an emissary to ask for assistance. Though it's put on hold, thanks to Michael's newfound daughter lurking around the halls."

"Apologies for disrupting your affairs."

"No apologies required. It's a welcome distraction."

I tried to hide the twitch of my lips, but he noticed. "Well, you're right. I ought to retire—"

"Have you ever fought sazari before last night?"

"No," I confessed. "My targets are normally more... coherent."

All the warmth in the room went out then. It was all charged toward him, walking up to me.

"Let me teach you one thing?"

In truth, I wasn't tired, but flirting was not my forte. Fighting, though...I reached for my swords, but he placed his hands on mine.

"You won't need those."

I untied them from my waist and set them aside, feeling naked. Not because I didn't have my weapons, but because his gaze made me feel positively vulnerable. He wasn't undressing me with his eyes; in fact, his gaze never left mine, but I felt helpless in that moment. Raw.

"What do you plan to teach me?

He began to circle me just as Dasyra had. "When the sazari first change, they still resemble their original form. A few days after the transformation, their body starts to shift." Though he was feet behind me, the hairs pricked on my neck. "If you can't get the momentum to decapitate them and need a more efficient kill, you'll want to aim for the heart. Their ribs encase their heart like every other creature, but the space between them has grown small. Their bones are also harder than ours, so it's a small window."

"The perfect killer."

"Correct." He wrapped an arm around me to show what was in his hand: a dagger.

Vork put it in my hand before coming around front. He took my free hand and laid it over his ribcage.

"See how far apart our ribs are? Cut that in half, move down three, and you'll have your opening."

I nodded.

"Try it."

He removed his hand and motioned for me to explore his torso. My light touch began at his collar bone and traveled down his tight chest. There was no logic as to why I started so high. Maybe my hands wanted to explore and they have a mind of their own. I wouldn't blame them.

This was the first time I'd had the chance to really feel his body without worrying about evading him or a sazari trying to kill us.

My touch skidded across his nipple and he shivered. I quickly tried to force my concentration back to the task, but my hand faltered and twitched as my fingertips pressed into his chest and continued their journey. I did as he said and counted by three, but cut the ribs in half. When I got to the sweet spot, I smirked up at him.

"Nice job."

Turning the blade to face me, I pushed the hilt against the area and caused him to move back a step. "Anything else you want to teach me?"

"You have no idea," he smirked.

"Well," I said, straightening my back and flipping the knife. "Show me what you got."

CHAPTER 9

OVER THE NEXT WEEK, my body was beaten down more than I'd ever experienced. Bruises formed along my skin, and I was certain Dasyra had dislocated one of my shoulders, not once but three times.

Due to the fast healing I'd inherited, the pain didn't typically last longer than a night. Plenty of time for my body to prepare for another training session.

I was so exhausted from tonight's training that I rushed back to my room for rest but once sleep had almost taken me, a loud noise from outside my room jolted me awake.

I groaned, rubbing my face, and slowly made my way out of bed. My eyes widened when I saw someone standing before me, leaning against the door.

"You must be Amara," the stranger said, his voice deep.

I reached for the dagger Vork had given me on the bedside table. The figure appeared beside me, grabbing my wrist.

"Calm down, I'm not here to hurt you."

He stood over me, peering from under his hood. The only feature I could make out was his pale hair which fell just below his collarbone.

I elbowed him in the nose and pushed against his chest to create distance. He held his face and ripped off his hood, causing his honey blonde hair to fall uncontrollably.

"Dammit. I said I'm not here to hurt you."

"Then what are you doing lurking in the shadows?"

He stepped into the light of the moon coming from the window. "I admit this probably wasn't the best time to approach you, but I had to ensure no one else was present."

He had a scar that ran from the bottom of his right ear across his neck and into his chest.

Minus that imperfection, everything else about him was perfect. Pale, jade green eyes locked onto mine. His jaw was as sharp as the weapon in my hand coming to a point to form his chin. A dashing grin showed his straight, white teeth with canines a bit more pointed than an average person's. Perfectly shaped blonde brows sat within perfect distance of each other, complementing the slender nose he'd been blessed with.

My grip on the dagger tightened. "Now that makes me think you're here to do more harm than good."

He stood a bit taller, his lean form taking new heights, and causing me to crane my neck further. "I understand why."

"Are you going to tell me who you are and what you want?"

"Call me Abe. I've heard a lot about Michael's heir. It's an honor." He put his hand over his chest, and bowed slightly.

My eyes tracked every movement. His shining eyes. The formality of his bow. Something was behind it. I raised a brow. "How have you heard of me?"

"Oh, word travels fast up there." He pointed and glanced up while twirling his finger around. "I'm especially interested in what powers you have." I didn't lower my weapon as he paced around the room. "So, do you?"

"Do I what?"

He stopped walking and faced me with his hands behind his back. "Have any powers?"

"If angels know about me, then why don't they know about my powers?"

"I try to stay out of gossip for the most part, but I couldn't help but overhear about you."

"I don't have any powers."

Abe raised an eyebrow. "No powers?"

"No."

He nodded and continued to walk around the room. "And your friends, do they have any fancy powers?"

"Who are you exactly? Do you work for my father?

"Oh no, I do not work for your father. We, uh, how do I put this—?" He drummed his fingers over his mouth. "We have our disagreements, Michael and I."

"Then who are you with?"

"I work for myself."

My irritation spread. "What. Do. You. Want?"

"To take you home." Before I had time to react, two massive bone white bat-like wings that almost took up the entire wall length developed from behind him. A dark aura radiated from him engulfed the room, inching towards me.

I backed up and gripped the dagger tightly. "What the hell are you?"

A black shadow materialized and slammed me against the brick wall, pinning me down. The shadow hit my right hand, forcing me to drop the knife.

Abe stalked forward and motioned for the shadow to move. It did, but its grip was still tight.

"Wouldn't you like to know," he teased, inches from my face. "I have so many fun things in store for you, Amara."

"Piss off," I spat.

"Well, you sure do have your mother's mouth."

I stilled.

"What do you know of my mother?"

He chuckled at my struggle. My nostrils flared, and I head-butted him in retaliation. He lost his grip, stumbling back.

"Alright, little pest." Once he got his footing, he grabbed my jaw and stared into my eyes.

I gasped as the whole room around me disappeared. The shadow's grip released, and I was in a dark abyss. The only thing I could make out was the sound of my deep breaths. I began running, and that's when I heard another person's breath. There was light then, though where it was coming from I couldn't be sure. Squinting my eyes, I saw Luca.

He was clutching his stomach. "Amara, help!"

I reached for him. There was so much blood I wasn't able to locate the wound.

"Please don't let me die. I don't want to die," he pleaded with tears swelling in his eyes.

"You're not going to die. It's going to be okay." I franticly continued to look for the source.

"Don't lie to him," a voice whispered. My head whipped around, but no one was there. "You can't save him. You're Michael's mighty daughter but can't even save your friend. And to think, this is all your fault. He's dying because of you."

I held onto Luca, helpless, as he slowly started to wither away into dust.

No, no, no.

Not for me.

Not for me.

"Where are you?" A shout sounded in the distance.

"Leena?"

"You—" My best friend sneered as she drew her spear. "You did this!"

I put my hands up in surrender. "What are you talking about?"

She swung her weapon at me, and I dodged it— barely. She turned again and landed a bow on my cheekbone. "Leena, stop!"

"Or what? Are you going to kill me, too?"

I gave her a puzzled look and pulled her close. "Of course not. Why would I do something like that?"

"You already did."

I pulled away and saw there was a dagger in my best friend's heart. My own hand gripping the hilt. My breaths became fumbled.

"Leena, no. I'm sorry, I'm so sorry. I didn't— how did— what can I do?" My words became uncontrollable as I started to cry, holding the dying girl in my arms.

She spat up blood. "You have to end it, Amara. It's the only way."

"What?"

"If you don't, I will," another voice said.

I looked up to see Corym walking towards us, but then it was just me as Leena disappeared like Luca had.

Corym reached down and pulled me to my feet. "You bring nothing but death everywhere you go. You are a leech. Worthless. You killed my entire team, my brother—" He choked on the words. "You are incapable of any good."

He grabbed either side of my head and squeezed.

My body was burning, as intense cold seized me and I struggled to breathe. Everything around me was starting to fade. Corym's eyes were filled with pure hatred. I gripped his wrists, trying to break his hold, but everything became frigid. The end was coming.

My body couldn't take the heat anymore, and I screamed.

Corym's grip left me as I was flung through the air, slamming against the wall before falling to the floor.

Unable to get up, I simply rolled over. When I opened my eyes, the dark abyss was gone—I was back in my room. A bright light shone, leaving me temporarily blind.

"You can't protect her forever," Abe growled.

I grabbed onto the side of the table, struggling to stand.

The walls and floor began to rumble, the light growing brighter. I shrank into a ball and covered my head as a massive gust of wind blew forward, followed by broken glass.

When the wind subsided, I peeked through my lashes to see the bright light and Abe were all gone. The windows were completely shattered, letting in the rain that had just begun to pour.

My heart was pounding so fast I could hear it over the ringing in my ears.

I slid down the wall I had been thrown into.

What the hell is happening to me?

CHAPTER 10

So far, being a nephilim had given me nothing but bruises, dislocated joints, bloody noses, long nights, and an episode in my room where I wasn't sure whether I'd simply had a nightmare or if my life had really turned this chaotic.

What had Abe meant by he was there to take me home?

As an orphan, I didn't even know where my home was. I had moved around a lot after the guild, so the closest thing I had was this academy.

It seemed he knew more about me than I did about myself.

I was reluctant to tell Diana of my visitor, but if I was going to stay here, she needed to know. It also compromised the safety of the entire academy that another person, angel, being whatever he was—could get through the defenses.

She was already having a tough time consoling the parents of the children who were killed in the sazari attack and the demon breach before that. I hated to add more stress to her docket, but whatever she was doing to keep the academy safe wasn't enough.

There were days and nights I would go into her office to check in on her, and it didn't look good. The always poised headmistress I was used to wasn't there when I first walked into the room. When she noticed my presence, that changed, and she was back to her usual elegant self.

Though I knew she was tired, hearing the Clergy was getting involved was not good news either.

She never specified anything, and I didn't want to make it worse, so I let it be.

Another month of training quickly went by. It seemed as if I had only become a nephilim a few days prior. I had two reasons for deciding to stay. The main one was Leena. She was one of the only people in my life I gave a damn about, and I knew she would try to leave with me if I tried again.

I could live with the regret of my killings and the souls that haunt me day and night, but I don't think I could live with myself if something happened to her because she followed.

It also wasn't smart of me to leave without gaining actual training like a nephilim should. Going out into the world untrained and on the run was a recipe for disaster.

I would take this day by day, at least until I finally had enough coin from my contracts to get safe passage off Masos. Part of me had hoped Leena would come because she really wanted to, but I found she had a strange attachment to the other nephilim that I couldn't understand.

One step at a time.

As I trained, I became more advanced until I was fighting two of the nephilim at once and was able to fend them off successfully. It didn't take long to realize I was becoming stronger. Underneath my loathing of this place from feeling like a prisoner, I reveled in my new strength. The others could tell I was getting faster, better, stronger, and they didn't hold back during training.

Luca and Leena had a knack for using their powers in the middle of combat whenever I had the upper hand. Leena would control my emotions mid-attack and force me to take back control before I could continue the fight. Countless times, Luca used his, making me two steps behind him, until he turned the tables in his favor.

Luca could manipulate time, though his powers were still developing at their most basic level. Time was a very sensitive and dangerous instrument to control, so it didn't surprise anyone his power was limited for now. He could only control one person or thing at a time and slow time down, not completely stop it.

With practice, I was able to adapt to Luca's counterattacks. I could judge my opponent's next move regardless of time manipulation.

It was later found out that Dasyra was gifted with clairvoyance and was the best tracker in the group because of it. She could gain visual information without any physical contact. It wasn't an active defensive or offensive power, but Dasyra was the most aggressive fighter.

Corym's power was the exact opposite of mine. His control was over ice. He was able to form and manipulate it. Though from his experience in combat, he said he'd rather only use it when near his opponent, and he did so often in practice with me. And I didn't know any better, I'd say he'd try to clink my arm off right after giving me frostbite.

There were times when my vision from Abe came flooding back with Corym using his power against me. Did Abe know everyone's power but mine?

I shook off the thought before it took hold.

Today was brutal with Dasyra as my sparring partner. She always had the strongest punches, and I seemed to be the only one to suffer from them.

Just after training ended, I was called into Diana's office. She sat in her usual spot behind her desk, and Vork was sitting in one of the leather chairs in front of her.

The air was completely charged with tension when my eyes met theirs.

"Did something happen?" I asked, attempting to cut the silence.

"Please sit," she instructed. "I trust you understand that you are very valuable. Your blood comes from the Divine."

I internally rolled my eyes as I took the chair next to Vork. Blessed with the blood of an angel but caged like an exotic bird. This wouldn't end well if we were starting with that.

"There are now only five nephilim left in existence. We must keep you safe, and that includes your future. Unfortunately, you all do not have the freedom others have, but that comes with your lineage. As such, your partners are chosen for you. They are chosen to strengthen your bloodline as generations move on and to strengthen the bonds of the races in Masos. This—"

My nostrils flared. How could she even dare try to speak the next words? It was as if she didn't know me at all.

"There's no way I'm accepting this."

"Amara—"

"No," I said curtly. "You've known me far too long to think I will take this quietly. Are you out of your mind?"

"You know I have no say in this." She sighed and pulled her brows together. "It came straight from the Clergy."

So those letters weren't just about her inadequacy in protecting the academy. They were about me—*about my life.*

"Fuck the Clergy."

"Amara—"

"You went ahead and told them who I was?" If my eyes could bore any deeper into hers, then she'd be blinded by the absolute rage that was itching to claw its way out.

She knew I didn't want this, and she did it anyway.

"If they had found out any other way, then—"

"Who have I been promised to, Diana?"

She sighed and flexed her fingers that rested on the armchair. "When the time comes, you will be bonded with the Chief of the Arabrosa pack."

A deep frown formed on my face.

"The Chief of the Arabrosa pack," I deadpanned. "He's almost three times my age. Isn't he already married?"

Diana laced her fingers together on the desk as she leaned forward. "I said *when the time comes.* Meaning the future Chief. The next in line for the title."

My body stiffened. "No." The sudden chill of the air ran down the back of my neck. "You *did not* allow this to happen."

"As I said, it was not up to me."

"Then I will speak to them."

"You will do no such thing."

"Why not?" I almost shrieked from anger.

"I feel as if you've both forgotten I'm here." Vork's voice was smooth and calm like he already knew ahead of time this was happening. The initial shock had worn off. Or maybe this is what he wanted all along.

"I didn't forget," I spat. "I just don't care."

"It is the word of the Clergy and is not to be changed," Diana said. "Amara, this is bigger than both of us. You have a duty."

"And that's to be promised to someone I hardly know?" I stood, gesturing to Vork. "Absolutely not. I am not ready to marry anyone, nor do I want to. Even if I was on board with being promised to another, why him? There has to be other fae or witches out there who need a nephilim to marry."

"Ouch," Vork said in a low tone. "That hurt, angel."

I whipped around to meet his gaze, pointing a finger in his face. "If you call me that again, I'm going to shove my dual swords so far up your ass you're going to be spitting up luxium."

"Amara," Diana said firmly. "It pains me to see you put in a situation you did not ask for, but please try to understand. In all the years Masos has existed, there has never been a descendant of Michael. You are his first and possibly his last. There has never been a nephilim who was joined with a lycan pack. It is the will of the Clergy, on behalf of the Emperor, that you be the first nephilim to bring together the Arabrosa pack with—"

"The Clergy," I finished. "This has nothing to do with combining the packs or the races, but all to do with the Clergy's power. They think they can control me since I am a nephilim. I am not a bargaining chip, and I am not a weapon."

"No, you're not," she agreed.

"I'll leave. The Clergy thinks they can have me. Well, they can't."

Diana sighed. "Live a life on the run?"

"It's what I was doing before I came here. I'll survive."

Diana rounded her desk and stood before me, leaning against the oak.

"I have been alive a long time. In my opinion, far too long, but if there's one thing I know, the Clergy always finds a way." Her head tiled to the side, and her brows pulled together. "Please do not make the mistake of trying to flee from this."

My lip curled in a silent snarl. "Is that a threat?"

"It's a warning from someone who cares deeply for you."

She stood and straightened her skirt before her eyes flashed to Vork, then back to me. "I'll give you both time to discuss."

Diana left, shutting the door behind her.

I was frozen solid, my fists curled into tight balls.

"I don't know if you know this," Vork said, rubbing his thumb across his bottom lip. "But when you get angry—and I mean foaming at the mouth angry, like you are right now—a tiny dimple forms at the side of your mouth when you frown. It's quite adorable."

That frown deepened.

"You knew," I seethed. "You knew this whole time."

He shrugged. "Whether I knew or not wouldn't have changed the situation."

"So, you thought starting a relationship out on lies would be a good idea? How long have you known?"

"About a month, and withholding information is not lying."

"It is," I gritted.

"No," he said matter-of-factly. "I didn't tell you because you never asked. It would be different if you asked and I said I knew nothing. That, angel, is a lie."

"Do not call me that."

He tsked as he walked to Diana's desk and sat in the chair. "Temper, temper, Amara. That will most definitely be passed down to our children."

I stood and slapped my hands down on the desk. "I won't be giving you children. I won't give you a damn thing!"

"Your past actions say otherwise."

There was nothing but red. "You asshole, you know that isn't true!"

Something snapped in me, and I jumped over the desk to wrap my hands around his neck, pushing him out of the chair. He chuckled at my attack, *chuckled*, which only fueled my anger. Vork easily pushed me off him, making me land hard on my backside.

"I wouldn't have children with you if you were the last male on Masos. I would rather live a life of celibacy."

"Ohhhh," he sang with a beautiful vibrato. "So, you're a virgin."

My face twisted as I picked up the first thing my hands could clutch, a book. I threw it at his head, but he dodged easily.

"Not that it's your business, but that's not the case. My point is, I don't want anything to do with you."

He circled the desk till he was standing in front of me. "Why all this hostility? You seemed to like me not too long ago."

I threw another book, and he shoved it out of the way.

"That was before I knew your reason for being here." I moved around him and began shuffling through the endless papers and note-books scattered on Diana's desk. Neither the countless opened letters from the Arabrosa pack's chief nor those from the Clergy—their seals still unbroken, but addressed to no one—escaped my notice. "You knew they were going to pair you with me. This whole time, I was wondering why you might be staying here. It didn't make sense for someone of your standing to squat at an academy, especially with nephilims, but I see now. As soon as you found out I was a nephilim, you just had to stake your claim."

"Look—" he began, but the sharp letter opener I pointed at him cut him off.

"Well, let me tell you this, Lycan Commander, I belong to no one. You do not claim me. I am my own."

"I didn't claim you."

"Bullshit."

"If you keep up with your hostility, we'll get nowhere, and one of us will end up hurt."

"It's going to be you."

He held his hands up and let out a small laugh. "Amara, be honest with me for a second. What is so bad about being mine?"

The audacity of this man. For fuck's sake, he couldn't even see what the real problem was here. It wasn't being with him that was the prob-lem, it was the terms.

"How about the fact that I don't have a choice? You can't force love, Vork. If you force it, then it'll fail. That's not what I want for my life. I don't think anyone wants that kind of life."

He sighed, his hands on his hips, looking down for a moment before thinking of his next words. "Why don't you give it a chance before you say no?"

"This is exactly like when I thought I was a human. Now I'm seeing no race has a choice. Everyone's always wanted to control what I do, and it's worse now being a nephilim. I'm considered a favorite of the Emperor, but I still have to play by the rules of others and be what they tell me to be."

I was breathless by the end. Specks of red dancing in my vision.

"Are you done?"

My nostrils flared, and I adjusted the metal so it was clutched with the blade facing my body.

"Keep talking, and I'm going to rip your precious canine teeth from your mouth."

Vork stood at the edge of the desk with his hands on the top and leaned in. "I think you're all talk and no play."

Like lightning, I raised the blade to rest against his neck and pushed slightly. "Want to see just how playful I can be?"

"I'm begging."

I raised a brow. "You begging for something. Now that's new."

"Tell me." He leaned in further, the blade creating a small slit on his neck. Red collected and drained down onto his white shirt. "Why is it you truly loathe me at this very moment? Is it me, or is it the situation you're in?"

Up until now, I had fantasized about this man, though I would never let him know it. I was an idiot if I didn't admit to myself how physically attractive he was, and, over this past month, his ability to have actual conversations made him even more so. Am I upset about being tied to this man? No. But being forced to marry is ridiculous and a leap too far.

Marriage... No. Absolutely not.

"I don't like my freedom of choice being taken away."

He looked me dead in the eye, and with a soft voice said, "Neither do I."

I blinked. "What do you mean?"

"I didn't lie when I said I was here because of sazari on our borders, but once your identity was revealed, my father and the

Clergy saw the opportunity of our union. My choice was taken away, too."

I eased up on the knife but still kept it hovering near his throat. "Why don't you fight?"

"For my pack. If I refuse the marriage, then everything could break. Masos is more fragile than you think. The Emperor and Clergy don't have power over our lands, but our independence is always threatened. Other packs across Masos have always been envious of us. We've been here the longest and hold the most power. Our alliance would strengthen the pack and keep my people from harm. A union with a nephilim—the daughter of Michael, no less—would ensure we survive."

My grip loosened, and I stepped back. He was unwilling, just like me.

"Vork, I can't do this."

He said nothing.

"You have reasons for going along with this, but I don't. As soon as I can, I'm leaving Masos for good."

Still, he remained silent.

"People like me don't marry. I don't get a happy ending." My voice broke, then softened. "But if I were ever lucky enough to marry, it would be to someone who deserves my affection. This forced union... we wouldn't be together for the right reasons. It won't work."

"What you're looking for is a fairytale, angel."

It was, and I knew I was never going to have a life like that, but he didn't. "It's basic. It's what everyone should have."

"This life is not kind to us all."

"So I'm noticing," I mumbled.

"You've been given a lot to digest." He said, moving to the door slowly. "I'll allow you some time alone."

The fact he thought my mind would change irritated me. What part of *no* does he not understand?

"It's not happening, Vork. You aren't enough. I don't want you."

Something snapped in his eyes, and for the first time since I'd met him, since I fought him and stood beside him, I was startled. His flirtatious, womanizing demeanor was gone, replaced with determination and vexation.

"This is about more than you and I." He said, stalking towards me till my back hit the desk. I had to bend back to look up at him as he continued. "You are very ignorant if you think you have me figured out from watching me fight a few hours a day. Despite what you think you might know of me, I am a man of honor and duty, and I'm starting to see that it is something you know nothing about. You have no pack, coven, or place here in Masos, and as soon as you are offered that, you tuck your tail between your legs and run. It's pathetic, really." He pushed away and looked me up and down with disgust and disappointment. "I expected more from Michael's heir. Oh well." He paused as he was walking out the door. "I guess we both were let down."

I suddenly felt small.

I didn't know much about Vork, but I had learned enough about his type of person through observations. It didn't matter what he had been through or was currently going through.

I wanted to give him the benefit of the doubt, but my head was screaming not to.

My heart, no, my body, was telling me something entirely different. Every time I thought back to that night in the woods when it was just the two of us.

"Childish," I cursed at myself.

Remember your training.

Self-preservation. Survive. Do not get curious, do not get careless, and do not love.

My body might try to pull itself to him, but I knew better. My head and heart know better; I would have to rely on them to keep me from ruin.

CHAPTER 11

Over the next few days, I tried to keep my distance from Vork. But despite our argument and my refusal of the engagement, he still tried to get into my good graces.

He could go to hell.

I wouldn't be pushed into a marriage I didn't want. Not to mention the attention I would get as the wife to the Chief of the Arabrosa pack. I wanted to be left alone. Now, later, all the time—I just wanted the silence.

I was in the lounge, sharpening my daggers, when the others came in. I ignored them until Leena shoved my shoulder and I gave her a small smile before going back to my work.

The lounge was a decent-sized room with two leather couches, one of which I sat on, and two other leather chairs surrounding a table in the middle. To the side of the room was a small bar that held basic wine and cups, and on the other side was space for sparring.

The lights were dimly lit but enough to see clearly if one didn't help themselves to too much of the readily available drink.

Everyone moved on to their own conversations, and everything became background noise until Corym's voice rang clear a few minutes later.

"It's time to discuss our next mission."

I didn't stop sailing the stone across the blade as he spoke.

"The next den is not far from here. It shouldn't take us but a few hours to complete it."

"You plan to raid a demon den?" I questioned, looking at them all.

Dasyra poured herself another drink before leaning on the bar. "Come on, Amara. They're training us like we're going to be in a war, but the Clergy wouldn't dare put us in the middle of it. We're too precious for that, so we do what we can. What we are doing is strictly forbidden, but that's why Vocova doesn't know about it, so keep your lips sewn shut."

"You're insane."

"You think we practice with our swords for fun?" Dasyra scoffed. "We are born fighters. The Clergy wants to keep us in protective glass cases and have us breed with those they choose. But we're not made for love. We're made for war."

"Jeez, D, lighten up," Luca teased as he sat beside me. "What she means is we're resources the Clergy should be using in this war, but instead they want to protect us. They make it seem like they use us to make people feel safe, but we've quickly found they would never do that. So, to do our duty and uphold our lineage, we do what we can to help. That includes raiding demon dens, helping towns that are attacked by them, and sometimes killing a few sazari along the way."

The stone glided down my blade with a sharp hiss. "And you do all this without Diana knowing. How have you managed to keep it a secret?"

Leena lay on the couch directly in front of us. "It's not easy. Sometimes our raids will go on just before sunrise. Corym has a good way of covering our asses."

I shifted my gaze over to him. He stood behind the couch where Leena was lying, his hands lightly grasping the leather.

He dismissed the praise.

"I've long known Vocova, and she trusts me."

"Let me get this straight," I said, halting my sharpening. "You nephilim go around Arabrosa raiding demon dens, liberating towns, and saving women and children, all for what? So you can rid them of the demons for a few days, maybe even weeks? They will never stop coming."

"Why not?" Dasyra countered. "You want us to sit here like pretty ornaments?"

"I don't care what you do, but you won't pull me or Leena into it. We aren't risking our lives for a lost cause. You have no plan. You go, conquer, move on, and then new demons come. If anything, you put a bigger target on your backs by doing this."

"Amara—" Leena began.

"How long have you been doing this?"

She sighed and tried again, "Amara—"

"We survive, remember?"

"We do this because we want to, because it's our purpose. Neither you nor the Clergy will dictate what I can do with my life. And besides, you risk your life multiple times every week..."

My heart skipped a beat.

She rolled her eyes. "Don't act so shocked. I know what you do in the shadows, and I don't judge you for it."

My mouth closed in defeat. I couldn't stop her from doing this. If I did, I would be no better than the Clergy forcing Vork and me together. But how did she know about my contracts? I always covered my tracks. I was good, no—great, at what I did. How the hell did she know?

"You're not as good as you think you are," she jabbed.

I winced a little.

Corym stepped in.

"So, we have a new mission to complete, you in?"

Gods.

"Fine."

The corner of Corym's mouth curved slightly as he came around the couch and produced a piece of parchment. He rolled it out onto the table between us.

"Here." He pointed to a spot to the east of the Hold. "There is a large farm where demons have taken over. Normally, we'd save simple nests like this for last, but they have something they shouldn't."

I gave him a quizzical look as he paused for effect. "And that is?"

"A luxium blade."

"Any idea how they got that?"

"Not a clue," Dasyra chimed in as she plopped on the chair at the end of the table. "There should be no way to get it. Only angels can get into the Garden, so the only way we can think they got hold of this one was by taking it from an angel."

"Or it was given," Leena speculated.

"Given by Lucifer to the demons," Luca finished, shaking his head.

I sat back in the seat. "Why would Lucifer give his only luxium weapon to demons?"

"We think," Corym sighed, "they're trying to make more weapons like his to arm demons all over Masos."

"But you just said getting the luxium is impossible because it's in the Garden. How are they making more?"

"That's what we want to try and find out. If anything comes out of this mission, we must get Lucifer's sword and bring it back here. Once we find evidence of our theories, we've decided to go to Vocova with the information. Hopefully after that, the Clergy will see our potential and allow us to aid in the war."

"So, what exactly is the plan?" I asked.

Corym sat with his elbows resting on his knees. "To the east of the farm, there is an old watch tower with a guard that switches out every four hours. Dasyra will position herself up there as our eyes. Once we have an idea of the layout, we'll split up accordingly and begin our search."

I scoffed. "That sounds too easy. There's a lot of room for error."

"There always is when doing these. We do the best we can with what we have."

A good leader wouldn't just throw their team into a situation and pray everything goes alright.

"Have you done any recon?"

His brows knit together.

"Of course we have, but the number of demons keeps swelling with every passing day. We can estimate how many are at each post, but the exact number would be impossible." He paused, and his tone became harsh. "If you don't feel confident doing this with us, then you can stay here."

I didn't want to do this in the first place.

"It's not that I lack confidence in myself," I argued. "I'm trying to make sure we're prepared before we go into a situation that could get us killed."

"Amara." Luca threw his arm over my shoulders. "We've done this dozens of times before you joined us. We even did a few while you were training weeks ago. Trust me, we got this."

I turned my attention to Dasyra. "I'm guessing you have some Morgean iron for your arrows?"

She huffed in shock. "Of course I do. I'm always prepared. Morgean iron doesn't fully kill demons, though."

"What do you mean? They seemed pretty dead when I saw them struck with it during the attack on the academy."

"It's effective to get rid of them, but all it does is send them back to Hell. It takes some time for them to crawl back out, but they'll return sooner or later. The only thing truly lethal to a demon or an angel is a weapon made of luxium."

My head cocked. "Does the Clergy know we possess luxium?"

"Yeah, but they won't take it. These weapons are our birthright."

Which means the Clergy would fight this war forever, because they don't have enough luxium weapons to actually defeat the demons. They would just keep coming back to continue what they started. A never-ending cycle of death and war.

I sighed. "When do we leave?"

Corym shooed Dasyra's feet off the table and rolled up the parchment. "We'll meet in the training room at midnight, so be ready. We have to be back before sunup."

That shouldn't be a problem. Everyone would be asleep by then, so I wouldn't run into—

My stomach dropped. "Vork. I haven't been able to shake him for days now. He follows me back to my room each night. He'll know I'm up to something."

"What a crush he's got on you," Leena snickered.

"I will gladly take your place," Dasyra purred, rolling her eyes. "I'm jealous. That is a hell of a man... Or lycan. Whatever."

"Just stay in the training room longer than usual," Luca suggested.

"He'll get bored sooner or later and leave. When he does, go change in the armory, and we'll meet you back there."

"Don't underestimate his patience. He'll stand there all night and watch me train if he wants to." I shook my head. "I'll think of something."

Everyone said their goodbyes and went their separate ways for the rest of the evening.

Corym caught up with me on my way back to my room.

"Hey. I wanted to talk to you for a second about tonight." We stopped walking, and he lowered his voice. "I take care of my team. They're my family, but I won't lie to you, tonight will be dangerous. You've been excelling at your training and are resilient, but being out there in the real world during this war will be different from the training room. I want you to be careful. Don't do anything just to show off. The objective is to stay alive."

"Look, don't take this personally, but my only family is Leena," I said. "I will do anything to protect her. My main goal is to stay alive, and I'll do anything I can to make sure she comes out of it, too. You worry about your team, and I'll worry about mine."

"That kind of mentality will get you and us killed."

"That's how I've stayed alive so far." I turned on my heel and walked back to my room.

Once there, guilt from my words washed over me.

Corym and the other nephilims have been nothing but kind to me since I joined. They were good people. The problem was I've never had anyone care for me like they do, and my only reaction was to close myself off.

Not to mention Vork. Gods he was a pain in the ass—and I was *betrothed* to him.

I knew how to enjoy the little things, and maybe I could do that with him, but marriage?

I had a single objective. I was going to get off this forsaken continent and sail to a new world.

None of my plans included the lycan.

CHAPTER 12

It was an hour before midnight, and Vork was nowhere to be seen.

Odd. Usually, he was everywhere I looked. Though I was grateful to have one less thing to worry about, I *was* still worried. I blamed it on my inexperience fighting demons, but what I was truly concerned about was the lack of detail we had. Poor planning often led to death.

Had they done this every time they went on a raid? How they had stayed alive each time was beyond me, but we did train hard.

The moon was full and so bright it illuminated the entire training room. There wasn't a single torch lit, but I could see perfectly. It was calming, which was curious because I had a feeling there would be chaos tonight.

The moon's position showed it was almost midnight.

I put away the practice swords and met the others in the armory, where we all suited up. From there, we made our way to the Hold's stables.

Corym opened the doors, and everyone walked to their horses—all but me, who remained at the entrance.

"Surely you know how to ride?" Luca called.

Corym motioned me to a beautiful Palomino horse. Her coat was shimmering gold, with a tail and mane as white as the snow on the ground.

I held out my hand to the horse's muzzle. To my delight, she leaned into me and huffed.

"This is Eos. She's Diana's," Corym said. "Do you know how to saddle a horse?"

I nodded and began to unlock the gate to Eos when a sound in the distance caused every muscle in my body to freeze.

It was a howl, a deafening howl so strong and loud that the horses began to bang against their stalls and whine.

I tilted my head back with a sigh, closing my eyes. "Shit."

"Sazari?" Luca asked, trying to get hold of his horse.

"No, something much more aggravating."

Another menacing growl came from the stable entrance, and everyone except for me prepared to draw their weapons.

I waited to see if my prediction was correct. A muzzle puffing smoke-like air rounded the corner of the door and attached to it was an enormous black lycan.

Even with all the disdain coursing through my body, I couldn't deny the sheer beauty of Vork's wolf. I had vaguely been able to remember what he looked like during the sazari attack, but this was the first time I was able to get a solid look at him.

As he strode slowly into the stalls, he locked eyes with me.

When he got closer, I noticed a very small, but visible, white patch of fur on the right side of his muzzle.

Moving directly in front of Vork's line of sight, I locked eyes with him. "Are you going to shift so we can speak?"

He glanced over at the rest of the team and then back to me before he shifted to his human form. I wouldn't dare look anywhere else besides his eyes.

Though his bare chest was testing me to lower my gaze. I couldn't. I wouldn't.

A playful smirk pulled at his lips. "Hello, angel. Going for a midnight ride with your new friends?"

Don't look down.

"What are you doing here, Vork?"

"I didn't see you return from your training earlier tonight."

I placed my hands on my hips. "You know that's considered stalking."

"I am only looking after my betrothed. And anyway, I was helping with the routine patrols when I caught your scent out here."

My brow scrunched. "Caught my scent?"

"Betrothed?" Leena said from behind.

I grimaced. I hadn't gotten up the courage to tell her yet. Truth be told, I was a bit ashamed how I went from being single to being engaged so quickly. It was embarrassing to admit to anyone that this was out of my control.

"Don't call me that," I gritted out.

"Why? It's what you are." Vork mused.

"We are going for a ride." I ground my teeth and turned back to Eos. "You have nothing to worry about. You can go back to your quarters."

"I'll accompany you."

"No," I spat, turning around on my heel. "Can you not take a hint? Leave me be."

"I would if I believed you were simply going for a ride. But I see your friends are armed, which leads me to deduce you are up to no good, and I can't have my betrothed running into danger, especially a nephilim."

"I am not your betrothed."

Vork shrugged. "Fine, excuse me while I notify Vocova of your ride so you can be properly accompanied."

He turned and began to walk out the door.

"Wait!"

Dasyra whistled in approval, her eyes roaming from his face all the way to his toes and back up, cocking her head to the side.

"Will you cut it out?" I groaned, pleading with her.

Vork smiled and turned back to the group. "Well, it's nice to see a nephilim notice all I have to offer."

"Oh, don't worry," Dasyra flirted. "I've definitely noticed."

I turned, pointing a finger at her. "Shut it!"

"So, here is what's going to happen," Vork said. "Either you take me with you for whatever it is you're doing, or I go to Vocova about your little 'ride' and see what she says about it."

"There aren't any more horses," Corym interjected.

"No matter. I'll ride with Amara."

"Not a chance in hell," I barked.

Vork sighed. "Off to Vocova I go then..."

"All right," I breathed, defeated. "But at least wear some damn clothes. You're going to give Dasyra a heart attack."

"Not necessary," she sang.

Pinching the bridge of my nose, I groaned again before finishing putting the saddle on Eos. As I led her out of the stall, Vork approached, fully clothed.

He wore deep brown leather trousers which fit perfectly and hung just off his hips. A black shirt stretched across his chest and a fur-lined leather coat covered his shoulders. On his hip rested a great sword, no doubt made of Morgean iron. His hair was pulled back in a low bun, small pieces falling effortlessly and hanging against the frame of his face.

Vork stretched his hand out and offered me a cloak of deep red velvet

"I thought you'd be cold," he explained. "Luxium armor can only keep you so warm."

"Thanks." I hesitated before I took the cloak from his hands and put it on. The fine material cascaded down to the top of ankles. At the neck's opening was a grey fur softer than anything I'd ever felt.

As I guided Eos to join the others, I turned back to him. "Why the niceties?"

"Was I ever not?"

The others were already mounted on their horses, so I hurried to do the same. I was about to hoist myself up when a pair of hands wrapped around my waist.

"What are you doing?" I demanded, frozen in place.

"I'm helping you on your horse."

"I got it."

Vork put his hands up in defeat and stepped back.

I mounted Eos, and Vork quickly followed, settling in behind.

"We need to ride fast," Corym announced, shooting Vork a stern look. "Keep up." He jerked his horse's reins and took off into the night, the others following.

Vork shifted behind me. "He's a charming fellow."

I tightened my grip on the reins.

Eos took off quicker than I expected. So quick that if Vork hadn't wrapped his arms around me, he would have been left in the snow.

Too bad.

It took me a moment to steady myself on top of her, but soon, the memories of riding returned and we found a rhythm. I had forgotten how much I enjoyed it. Most of the time riding was simply a means of transportation, but before I took on the odyssey of gathering coin to leave, I would ride outside of the academy grounds weekly for pleasure. It was freeing, knowing I could take off anywhere the moment I let the horse run at full speed.

Though now I was trapped by a lycan's grip around my waist, holding on for dear life.

I twisted my head and shouted, "You alright back there, Lacelle?"

"Why wouldn't I be?"

"You seem a little tense, is all."

"You would be too if you were about to fall off a running horse!"

"Never rode before?" I teased.

"I have!" he shouted back. "I'm just usually the one with the reins in hand."

I smirked at the idea of taking a power he was so used to having. It brought me a pinprick of happiness.

We rode through the forest behind the academy and luckily managed to avoid any sazari. The path we were on began to narrow, and the group fell into a slow trot as we approached the farm.

It was far bigger than I had imagined. Our horses stood just under the cover of the tree line, their huffs of air creating faint clouds around their snouts.

Assessing the farm, there were at least ten bodies standing at the perimeter. I would say nothing looked out of the ordinary except for the weapons in the guards' hands and those tell-tale signs of glowing red irises.

Memories of the academy attack flooded me, and I shivered. It was the first time I had ever seen a demon up close like that.

I pulled my horse up beside Corym's.

"What are we doing here?" Vork asked.

Corym kept his gaze forward. "The mission."

"Elaborate."

Corym's jaw ticked.

I butted in. "We suspect they have luxium in their camp. More specifically, Lucifer's weapon."

"That's a bold accusation," Vork said.

"Do you want to take that chance?" I snapped.

One of his hands was still wrapped around my waist, and his other rested on my thigh. I tried to ignore the weight of it.

"You think Lucifer gave them his sword. Why?"

"So they can mimic the luxium metal and reproduce it."

"Dasyra, go to the watchtower," Corym ordered, apparently deciding I'd given a sufficient explanation. "Position yourself, and from there we'll split."

She nodded and retreated into the forest. The others began to do the same, but Corym remained next to me.

I nodded, and reluctantly, he followed the others.

"I think he likes you," Vork said. "One might say I share the same emotions."

I despised the chill that went through my body at his words. "Fantastic. I was so worried you didn't."

He chuckled in response.

"It would be a huge help if you stayed here while we did what we needed to do."

"Not going to happen."

I didn't think so. "Then don't get in our way."

"My only concern here is your safety. I will not be in anyone's way."

"I don't need your help. And there will be demons in there trying to rip my throat out every second. You can't protect me from them all."

"Watch me."

I nudged Eos' reins, motioned her back to the others, and tied her to a nearby tree once we dismounted. I adjusted the armor under my cloak.

"That looks uncomfortable," Vork observed.

"It's not." I cut off any further attempt at small talk and leave to join the others.

In the distance, Dasyra had already made her way to the watchtower and disposed of the demons. She gave Corym a series of hand signals which I couldn't translate.

He signaled back to her, then turned his attention to us. "There are two buildings we need to clear out. The house, which is a few yards away from the barn, and the barn itself. Luca, you're going to take out the demons in the house. According to Dasyra, there are a total of four."

"Not a problem," Luca huffed with a lopsided grin.

"Leena and I will go into the barn through the window and take care of the demons there. There should be about ten of them. The sword will be at the top in a heavily guarded trunk."

"Heavily guarded by what?" I asked.

Corym didn't answer. He only rubbed a finger against his bottom lip. "Amara, your job is the most dangerous. We need you to create a distraction."

"A distraction? I don't think that's a good idea," I said.

Corym raised a brow. "Why not?"

"I don't think we should split up."

"It's what needs to be done." Leena stepped forward and put her hand on my shoulder. "I'll be fine."

"I'm going to the barn."

"No," both Leena and Corym said.

Corym stepped forward. "We need you where I have you planned. There are bound to be more demons than Dasyra could see, and our intel is about three days old. It wouldn't surprise me if their numbers have doubled. We need to weed them out into the open. Dasyra will assist you while we do the rest."

"You want to dangle her in front of them like a piece of meat," Vork said, agitation seeping into his tone.

I turned towards him. "I don't need your opinion on this."

"If you do your job," Corym said to me, ignoring Vork. "It'll keep the demons off of Leena and on you. In the grand scheme of things, it'll be you risking it all."

Vork took a step toward him. "A good leader wouldn't sacrifice one of their own just to complete a mission."

"I am not sacrificing her," Corym argued. "She is skilled and well-trained."

"She's only been a nephilim for a few weeks."

I leaned over to Leena with my arms crossed. "They must know I'm here, right?"

She shrugged. "I wouldn't hold your breath."

"Hey!" I yelled, interrupting their bickering. "It's not a sacrifice if I make it out alive." Shooting a pointed look at the lycan, I added, "Which I will, Vork. Corym isn't sacrificing anyone, because I am now volunteering for the task."

Vork whipped around, nostrils flared and defiance in his eyes. "Like hell you are."

I snapped and shoved the lycan as hard as my strength would allow, and yet that still didn't put enough distance between us. He simply stumbled back as if I was a slight inconvenience.

I had to have given it most if not all of my strength. Didn't I? How was he still so close?

With a dumbfounded look, he opened his mouth to say something else, but I cut him off.

"I'm not sure what more I need to say to get it through your thick skull that I belong to no one. You may soon be Chief, Vork, but I am a nephilim, so I outrank you. So shut the hell up and stay out of my way."

I turned from the rest of the group without bothering to see their reactions and stalked towards the farm's entrance. "Let's get this over with," I said.

Corym signaled Dasyra who silently shot her arrows at the demons patrolling the perimeter. With deadly precision, she aimed for their throats, which suppressed their screams and caused them to fall quickly.

The rest of the team took their positions.

Luca lurked in the shadows next to the house while Corym and Leena climbed up the side of the house and into the barn.

Dasyra nodded to me as I entered the threshold of the farm's property and glared the two demons standing out front.

"Only two?" I asked, pulling out my short swords. Grunts came from behind them in the barn, and I took my opportunity. I charged for the bigger demon on the right and slashed him across the neck. The other put up a little more of a fight, but nothing impressive. To my disappointment, he too quickly went down with a simple jab to the chest.

"Well, this is becoming uneventful."

There was a thud behind me and a nudge at my feet. A demon lay on the ground, dead with an arrow in its chest.

I looked up at Dasyra. She returned it with an exaggerated bow.

"Come on!" I yelled, quite uncomfortable putting myself in the spotlight, but I had to shake it off. "There has to be more of you out there! Are you really that scared of me? I'm guessing you probably saw how easily I killed your friends here. Not much of a threat, I'd say."

Just as I had hoped, demons began to file out from the shadows, armed with swords and blunt weapons of all sizes. I counted ten.

If Dasyra weren't here to help, I would be more worried, but I couldn't deny the fact I was nervous. It didn't take long for the adrenaline to kick in and mask the emotions buzzing in my body.

All at once, they ran, and my heart beat faster.

Two quickly fell at the hands of arrows, but eight still charged.

I side-stepped the group and slashed my swords across a demon's stomach as I tucked and rolled out of the way. The group halted and stared.

The arrows had also stopped, but why? I couldn't risk checking. If I did, they would have an opening. There was no doubting my skill, but it would mean my death if I were too confident.

I stood from my position, grip tightening on my swords. "Who's next?"

The demon in the middle took a single step forward, but before he could take another, a sword was pushed through the back of his head, exiting his mouth. His body shuddered, jerking when the blade was pulled out.

Vork stood behind him with a smile. "Tell me again how you don't need me."

My lip turned up in a snarl. "Still don't."

The demons turned their attention to Vork and attacked. He easily cut them down even after he was disarmed.

He ended the fight with blood splattered across his face and dripping down to stain his tunic. A half-dead demon crawled away from him.

He smirked, his eyes moving to mine. "Have I impressed you?"

"Not in the slightest."

He furrowed his brow and jerked his head back slightly, genuinely insulted. He picked up his sword, pushed the demon onto his back, and put pressure on his neck with his foot.

"Now I think we both know that's a lie."

"Why are you always so cocky?"

The demon struggled under the pressure but didn't take Vork's gaze away from mine.

"I just know when you're lying."

"Is that so?"

He waved the tip of the sword in small circles towards me. "You take a breath before you tell a lie. It's not noticeable to most. It's almost like you brace yourself because you're hoping it'll prepare you for what will happen after you spit those lies. Or maybe you hold your breath, hoping it stops you from doing so, giving yourself that extra second to make your final decision."

"I hate you," I sneered, still not paying any mind to the demon below him. "Truth or lie?"

The demon struggled with its last breath and went limp.

"Truth, it seems. I'll remedy that soon."

"How about you hold *your* breath?" I challenged.

There was a cry and a thud a few yards away from us. Dasyra stood on the watchtower and huffed a breath. She threw a demon over the edge.

"You two done flirting?" she yelled.

"I'm not flirting!" I shouted back.

"Lie," Vork muttered.

Oh, how I wish he would hold his breath.

Dasyra nocked an arrow. "Got more coming."

A new group of demons was coming from the forest, fully armed.

"Think you can keep up?" I asked him.

"Remember I saved you just a few moments ago?"

I waved my sword at him. "Details."

Vork didn't have a chance to respond as we were thrown into the fight again. I bobbed and weaved through the weapons coming my way. Here and there, they landed a hit, but I ignored the pain as best I could, knowing they would heal quickly.

While fighting off a demon, I caught sight of another one out of the corner of my eye. He was a behemoth and carried an axe almost the size of me.

Finishing my current opponent off with a deadly blow to the stomach, I ran towards the giant. He was so huge that he waddled with his legs fairly far apart. That's when I saw the opening. I slid in between his legs, cutting them in the process, and he fell to a knee. Taking the free moment, I rose and turned around to shove my swords into either side of his neck. Dislodging them, I braced for impact as another one charged.

With a crazed look in her eye, the demon didn't hold back and got a few good shallow hits on me with her machete. We both ended up holding our weapons to the other's neck and blocking the blows, our faces inches away from each other.

"You're dead," the demon sneered.

"You first."

Dasyra landed a shot on her shoulder. She howled in pain and dropped her weapon. Another arrow hit her chest, and she fell.

Though he didn't look to be struggling, Vork had three demons on him. I moved to help, but a jumble of sounds came from the barn.

Yells, grunts, thuds, and shatters.

The thing that worried me the most was a scream. My blood ran cold. I knew that scream.

Leena.

I ran to the barn without a second thought, peered inside, but it was deathly silent.

I slowly made my way in and followed a flight of stairs leading to the top. As I took those steps, a figure appeared at the top of the stairs. It was too dark, and despite the torches lining every other stud of the barn, I couldn't tell what it was, only that it had piercing red eyes.

"Get the hell out of here," Corym shouted. "Run!"

The creature slowly descended the stairs, never leaving my gaze.

"I'm not leaving," I said.

I'm *not* leaving her.

As I backed into the light, I saw the creature for what it was. A dog covered in black fur and even darker shadows that distorted its whole body. At one point, the shadows showed the dog with its fur; at other times, they shimmered to show only the skeleton. It stood over me with fangs as long as my hand and claws equally so.

"Are you okay?" I called, not daring to divert my gaze from the beast.

They didn't answer.

I took a breath, and the beast lunged. I jumped out of the way and landed on my side, scurrying to get back to my feet, but it swiped with its paw and sent me flying against the wall, disarming me. I pushed back and rolled to my feet, running up the stairs before it could land another blow.

Leena was lying in Corym's arms, her abdomen badly slashed, but the damned sword was in her right hand.

I rushed to their side and looked down at Leena. "Hey, you're going to be okay."

"Yeah, that hellhound is a hell of a bodyguard." She smiled weakly and held the sword out to me. "Take it to Vocova."

"You aren't dying," I said sternly. "Corym, get her out of here and take the sword."

"Amara." He shook his head.

"We aren't all going to make it out." My tone left no room for argument. "Take her. Now."

A familiar growl erupted behind them.

"Corym," I said, slowly backing away from them. "It's going to make a jump for you, but I have a plan. When you get a chance, you take it and get the hell out of here. Do you understand?"

"We can't."

"You can."

He said nothing as we stared at each other.

I wish it had lasted longer than it did.

The hellhound jumped, and I leaped towards it, pushing us both off the top floor. We collided with a stud holding part of the ceiling, and it brought down multiple torches. Fire began to spread around the barn, consuming the hay that lay on the floor and against the walls.

I picked up a stud piece and swung it at the beast's head.

Corym and Leena scurried past, the sword with them.

The fire continued to grow until it engulfed the whole barn.

With my arms at my sides, my fingers reached towards the flames, spreading out to touch their warmth. I let them engulf me completely.

"You're not the only one immune to fire," I said to the monster.

It snarled, but the barn doors flew open before it could gear up for a charge. Vork stood amongst the flames, immediately coughing, his skin starting to burn.

The hound turned to him.

"Vork, you idiot, get out of here!"

His only answer was another cough, eyes locking with the beast's. He was ready to take it on, but he wouldn't make it even if he tried.

The smoke was becoming unbearable. It curled around our limbs, sucking out the air with its tight and scorching hold. However, the hound didn't seem to be affected by it.

I quickly moved in front of Vork, grabbing his wrist. His gasps of pain from the fire's flames ceased. I looked over and saw the fire no longer continued to burn his flesh. I was somehow lending him my immunity.

Before I could think more on it, the beasts snarls brought me back and I locked with its eyes again.

How had this gone so wrong?

The lack of information provided had almost gotten Leena killed and now us.

Gods, to be anywhere but here. I should've convinced Leena to leave with me a long time ago. I could've done it. I would have tempted her with tales of the western isles and its beautiful beaches, and it would've worked.

Gods, take me to that place. Let me feel the warm sun and smell the salty air. I want to lay against the sand, knowing myself and my best friend are safe, and just... be.

The hound charged at us, and in the heat of the attack, Vork and I fought for who stood in the beast's way. Vork's arm clung to my midsection as we braced for the impact.

The broken stud in my hands pierced through its shoulder as we collided

A tingle ran through my whole body, starting from my hands and spreading to my head, then down to my feet. The foreign and unexpected sensation caused me to stiffen.

As we all fell, there was a pulsing in my ears, but I was unsure if it was adrenaline or something else. I wasn't going to deny what I saw though. A tear cut through the air. The burning barn began to turn to nothing but ashes.

A gasp was forced out of me as I was shoved, my head hitting the ground which wasn't as hard as I expected it to be. My rigid body did me no favors as it didn't absorb the impact well and my muscles strained as I rolled on the gritty ground.

I strained to open my eyes, and when I did, I was met with darkness. The barn's fire was nowhere in sight.

Groaning, I pushed myself upright despite a searing pain in my shoulder. It seemed the hound had taken a nice bite of it. More pain radiated from a deep cut traveling from my jaw down the side of my neck. Another sensation rattled against my hand, and this one was much worse.

I held my right hand up, my mouth opening in a silent scream as tears streamed down my face. I couldn't fathom I now had two fewer fingers, and blood was profusely slipping down my arm. Clutching my wound to my chest, I looked up through tears that wouldn't stop.

I, no, *we* were on a beach, and it would've been impossible to see if it hadn't been for the moon. The warm breeze smacked me in the face as I took in our surroundings more.

How in the hell did we end up here?

A few paces away, Vork sat upright, one hand cradling the other, and attempted to rise quickly.

The hellhound, not far off, was also finding its footing. It shook its whole body, charging forward once again.

CHAPTER 13

The hound struggled as he ran. Blood was pouring out of the wound on its shoulder, and it was tripping over its feet as it came towards us. If we moved fast enough, maybe we could find shelter in the trees on the horizon.

Where are we?

It was bleeding faster than we were, so we might have had a chance. That was blown all to hell when Vork growled and popped his wrist back into place. A grunt followed another popping sound.

He was shifting.

"Vork, don't!" I screamed.

It was no surprise to me that he didn't listen and went for the beast.

I went to stand but immediately fell the wounds on my shoulder and neck stinging.

As far as I could tell, Vork was winning, but that could change at any moment, and then what? I wasn't healing like I normally did, and if I was left here half dead with no weapons, then the hellhound would finish the job.

My hand curled around a mound of sand as I tried to breathe through the throbbing. A howl of pain ripped through the night, stabbing into my chest and my body stiffened. I knew that sound. I heard it during the attack at the academy.

The hellhound had its teeth sunk into Vork's upper thigh, and if he weighed any less, I'm sure the beast would have tried to shake him around.

With wobbly legs, I stood, attempting to trudge over to them. It took two steps, and my face was covered with sand once again.

Vork was losing now. He couldn't stabilize himself enough to get another blow in and was seconds away from losing his leg.

"Vork, you have to get up!"

I inched forward, and my hands came into contact with something hard under the sand. I pulled up a large conch shell. I now had a weapon, but I was still too far from him to do anything to help.

He was saving me *again*.

He was willing to die for me *again*.

"Vork! Get. Up!"

It was my family's attack all over again.

He was able to get purchase through the sand and twist enough to swipe his paw over the hound's face, making it release him

With each drag across the sandy ground, I was more within range of the two.

Vork snapped at it, which gave me enough time to muster up all the remaining energy I had to throw sand at the hound's face and launch the tip of the shell into its eye. The bellow it let out was deafening but was cut short when Vork's teeth clamped down on its neck. There was an audible crack, and the body went limp.

Letting out a breath of relief, I dropped to my knees.

Vork shifted and lay on his back.

"Goddamnit, Vork."

I crawled over and leaned in to examine him. The bite on his leg was bad, and I didn't have the tools to heal it or my own wounds. His nakedness also didn't help the situation. He was severely wounded, and now he had no protection from the elements. A chill came in as the wind skated against us, and he shivered.

"I've never had a woman say my name so many times in one day." He chuckled through pained breaths. "You just made my record."

"I never thought I'd be with you enough to say your name this often."

I looked around and saw a forest about a quarter of a mile inland. "This will be hard, but I need you to stand and lean on my good shoulder. We need to find cover."

Slowly, we both got to our feet, and he leaned against my good side before we limped onward. I didn't truly understand the severity of his wounds and fatigue until his form molded to mine. He was spent, and I didn't blame him. It seemed like he'd never had to fight a hellhound before but he did what he could. Every few minutes his cheek would rest on the top of my head as I pulled us along, truly showing how exhausted he was.

I had been in a lot of questionable and dangerous situations, but I hadn't been this worried in a while. It wasn't because we were both badly wounded, or that we were defenseless and one of us completely naked, or the fact more beasts or any other type of enemy could be lurking. It was the memory of the way I felt when Vork howled in agony. I knew what that feeling was, and it would get me killed if I held onto it.

When we finally reached the forest, I tried to put him down as gently as I could against a tree before sitting next to him. I tied fabric I ripped from my trousers over the nubs that used to be my fingers.

"How's your shoulder?" Vork asked.

I tried not to move it in response. "I could be without an arm, so I think it's an improvement."

"And your hand?" There was a touch of remorse brewing on his face.

"Don't do that," I said, holding his gaze. "While I wish you weren't here, you did save my life... again. And I'm grateful."

Vork was silent.

"I bet you never had to work this hard to get naked for a woman, have you?" I tried to keep a smile from forming on my lips.

"You are definitely the most difficult, I won't deny that," he said wryly.

I stifled a chuckle and looked out towards the forest's darkness.

Vork's next words were quiet. "But I would do it all again."

That damned feeling in my chest returned.

"Hopefully," he added, "next time it will be because you undress me and not because I'm saving you again. What's this, the second time? You're racking a tab up quickly."

"Okay," I huffed and stood. "We should start a fire so your dick doesn't fall off."

"Yes, we wouldn't want that."

"No." My eyes roamed down his bloodied, dirty body and landed on the topic of conversation. "What a shame that would be."

When my gaze returned to his, his eyes were storming with a dark and dangerous expression I could see myself folding over.

But that's not why we were here; my first priority was survival.

After about an hour, I had a decent amount of wood, and as I was making it, I prayed to whatever Divine was out there it wouldn't attract predators. Going through the night without a fire wasn't an option with Vork's lack of clothing and both our wounds refusing to heal.

I made a bed of grass next to the fire for him, then sat on a stump and shaped a piece of flint I found in the dried-up riverbed. Besides the crackling of the fire, the only other sound was my flint being shaped, which wasn't a good sign.

"I'll take first watch," I said, not looking up at him.

Vork was lying on his side, propped up on his elbow. I could feel his stormy eyes glaring at me through the flames.

"You know we'll probably die out here."

I checked the edge of the rock and blew the excess debris off. "Aren't you one for pleasant conversation?"

"I love the way blood brings out the color in your eyes."

That made me look up at him.

"Better?" he asked.

I hid my smile.

"Hard to believe the lycan prince hasn't been taught proper etiquette for having a pleasant conversation."

"It made you smile."

I relaxed my face. He did make me smile.

"You need to rest," I said, testing the rock's edge on my finger. It easily sliced through the pad of my thumb, but I didn't flinch. The cut was warm and then healed a few moments later.

"So do you. These wounds from the hound won't heal on their own. We need a healer."

The sting of my shoulder never went away, but I had pushed it aside as best I could. "I'm guessing it's because the hound was a product of Hell."

Vork nodded.

Unfortunately, it made sense. Nephilim were angelic beings, even if we were only half, but having a creature born of Hell do damage to us stunted our ability to heal. I imagined the same went for Vork. He wasn't angelic, but he was a supernatural being.

I opted to change the subject since he refused to rest. "Where do you think we are?"

"Somewhere in Ekros. I've been here a few times with my father on diplomatic missions. The air has a certain taste you only get from the burnt Mahlar Isle, which means we're probably at the tail end of the Kuno River. If we travel north, we should run into a town that can help or at least point us somewhere to get help."

I hated to admit it, but his plan was a good one. I simply nodded, letting silence come between us.

It unfortunately didn't last long.

"Do you want to talk about how we got here?"

There was a big crackle in the fire, shooting embers up into the sky.

"I don't know," I said." One minute we're fighting the dog, and the next we're dumped onto a beach."

"Maybe your powers are developing?"

It was a possibility. I didn't know much about being a nephilim, so I guessed it wouldn't be unheard of for powers to change and mature. Similar to Luca's, but I was going into this blind. Clearly, that would work against me if I had somehow transported us from Arabrosa all the way to the east coast of the continent.

"Let's just worry about getting back to the academy," I dodged.

Vork let the subject go as he stretched his hands above his head and laced his fingers behind it before lying down. The rest of his body stretched, almost how a dog would when trying to get comfortable. But as his calves and quads flexed, I caught myself looking longer than I should have. They stopped at the huge gash on his upper thigh, but I would be lying if I said my eyes didn't wander farther.

"You can do more than look, you know." His eyes were still closed, but a smirk stretched across his face.

I snorted. "I wouldn't give you the pleasure."

"Even if I could give you the same back?"

"I doubt you could."

He opened his eyes and looked at me. "Why so hostile?"

"You're just arrogant as shit and that annoys me. You want to challenge me? I'll challenge you right back."

"Or," he said a little too playfully, "you love this. You love you've found a man who can take a beating both with words and in the flesh."

"Love is a word that rarely makes an appearance in my vocabulary." This man's ego was absolutely insane. I stood and walked around to his side, pointing the newly sharpened blade at him. "You're delusional if you think you're the man I want. I've had plenty of men in my bed who give me just the right amount of fight I like."

"And it's not enough. You want more."

"Don't presume to know me."

Vork shrugged, then took hold of himself, never breaking eye contact.

A lump formed in my throat.

He stroked himself from base to tip. "Then walk away and prove me wrong. Or, you can pull down those pants and ride my cock until I really can't move."

"Is that how you get women to sleep with you?" I scoffed. "This is weak even for you."

Out of my peripheral vision, I saw his hand squeeze the tip, and I almost moved my gaze down.

"Believe it or not, the women I sleep with are more than willing."

Ah, there it is.

"This whole time you've been telling me what I want, but I think you want the same thing. You want, no, you *need* someone to challenge you. Someone who will put up a real fight because all these beautiful women are so willing to throw themselves at you. I imagine it can become a real bore."

I sank to my knees to straddle and finally looked down at him. Fuck to the gods if my mouth didn't water when I did. His hand never stopped moving, and he was hard enough to the point where he could be begging me to end his suffering. I looked back up at him and placed a hand on his good thigh to lean forward. The air was hotter than it was moments ago.

"Is that what you want, Vork? Me. Do you want me?"

"Does my hard cock tell you something different?"

Damnit, I couldn't do this right now. We were both wounded, and the only weapon we had was a rock about the size of my hand, which I happened to be using to graze his abdomen.

"This is dangerous," I whispered. "Whatever game we're playing."

He released himself and sat up slowly, so we were at eye level. "Then make it worth it."

Those eyes danced with mischief, and gods, did I want to indulge.

And so, I did.

Wrapping my hand in his thick hair, I gently kissed his lips, then pulled back to meet his eyes. They burned so deeply into mine I almost needed to look away. They traveled down to my lips, where his tongue darted out to wet the bottom one.

"I might be wounded, but you won't break me." His hand squeezed my ass and roughly pulled me closer, almost causing me to fall on him. "Kiss me."

I latched my lips to his and kissed him so fiercely he landed on his back with a thud. Our lips moved in sync, and with equal urgency. His were so damn soft and though he was the one on the ground, I had the feeling he thought he was the one in control.

Soon, both his hands were on my hips, and he urged me to grind. I stopped, pulling back.

"I'll hurt you if I do."

"Then hurt me," he gritted out.

I hesitated. He'd already been hurt protecting me twice, and now he wanted me to hurt him again?

"You need to stop doing that."

He cocked his head to the side. "Doing what?"

"Allowing me to be the cause of your pain."

"Awe," he cooed. "Are you worried about me?"

The tip of the pointed rock rested at the top of his right peck, and I added slight pressure, enough to draw a small bead of blood.

"No, I'm not going to be in your debt," I explained. "I'm not asking you to stick your neck out for me, so you need to stop protecting me. I won't marry you, and if you continue to try and be my savior, one day I'll let you die in the process."

He refused to flinch as I moved the blade closer to his nipple. "I'm not doing it as a tradeoff."

"Then why?"

"Is it hard to believe I actually care?"

The cut began to heal as I picked up the stone. "Looks like someone is developing feelings for me."

Vork said nothing, but his gaze was enough. What I said was true. Whatever was brewing in his mind was starting to surface, and he wouldn't hide it.

"You can't have feelings for me, Vork."

I didn't think he loved me, that was too strong a word for hardly knowing one another, but anything related to the emotion was enough.

By this time, his hands had found their way to my thighs and rested there comfortably while he refused to look anywhere but my eyes. I wasn't going to back down either.

"Have you ever let someone in?" He asked.

"Yes, and they were taken from me when I loved them back. They all were. It's easier not to allow that emotion to surface. The pain of losing them is greater than anything I've known."

He sat up as he had before, with his face close and his eyes searching mine, and he saw the truth of my pain. My heart was still there, but it had decayed at this point.

"You may not feel pain, but going through this life without embracing the love another can give you will leave you hollow. By the time you have grown old, you may look back at your life and wonder how much better it could have been if you had let someone in." He pushed a strand of hair away from my face and threaded his fingers behind my head to gently secure me in place. "It doesn't have to be me.

Not yet anyway." His smirk rose as quickly as it fell. "But don't deny yourself the love I'm sure you deserve."

I traced his lips with mine and breathed in his musk. "Love is not what I'm looking for."

"What is?"

I snaked my hand in between us and grabbed hold of him. His eyes fluttered closed for a moment, then found mine again as I worked him slowly with my hand.

"You feel good," I confessed.

"Fuck, don't stop."

And I didn't. I kept my pace steady while I crushed my lips to his and took his bottom lip between my teeth. He hissed when I bit down, and we both tasted blood, but he didn't stop. He kissed me back with the blood between our lips. Something... primal came over me, and the urgency grew. My whole body turned so hot it almost hurt.

Vork moved past my face and latched onto the base of my neck with his teeth and bit *hard*. A moan escaped me. I was supposed to be in control. Me, not him.

"Well, well, look at wa we got here."

We both froze.

"It a bit dangerous to be fuckin in da middle of da woods, yah?"

I was the first to look past the fire. A man and a woman stood with their hands full of weapons and disgusting looks on their faces.

"Some privacy would be nice," I sneered.

"Ah, darlin, but yous be in our territory." The man took a step forward into the light.

He was tall and stocky with a multi-pointed mace in his left hand, his other resting on the buckle of his pants.

The woman stood a bit shorter but was easily just as stocky. They were both dressed in dirty linen clothes patched up with different-colored cloth with various trinkets dangling from the side of their belts.

Scavengers weren't unheard of, especially in abandoned places. The woods made it easy for them to escape from the guards who pushed them out of respectable cities. They were typically convicted criminals who had served their sentence and were set free into the world, but their lives were over by that point. They weren't able to find work, and when there's no work, there's no food, safety, or security. But times had changed, and they created communities now. So, where there were a few, there were many, which meant more were not far behind.

"No need to be embarrassed," the woman said to Vork with a satisfied grin.

"Oh, I'm not. I'm honestly just waiting for someone to do something about it."

I looked down at him. "Are you serious? This is not the time."

He shrugged. "She pointed it out."

"I, ahh, could finish what she not, yah?" the woman offered.

"Well, I would've finished if you two had left us alone," I gritted. "What do you want?"

The man swung his mace up and tapped its neck in his free hand. "Like I done said, yous in our land. Was in our land is ours and dat," his eyes roamed around us, "means yous and yous lover there."

"We have nothing of value to give you. We're just passing through. If you tell us the nearest town, we'll be out of your hair by sunrise. It's only a few hours away."

"I don tink you hear good, yah?" the woman said sternly, taking a step forward. "Yous now our property."

If we fought, this wasn't going to end well for either party. Vork can't stand, and I have an almost useless arm with two fewer fingers, but I have a horrible suspicion there's not another way out of this.

I cast a glance at the man and then look back down at Vork. "What size are you?"

He looked over at him. "I think it'll do."

"You owe me."

He furrowed his brows and snorted. "Look at the state of me. I think it's you who owes me."

I stalked to the other side of the fire, still keeping my distance from the scavengers. It was hard to act like my wounds weren't throbbing as the moments passed. No doubt they could see we weren't in the best condition.

"Last chance," I suggested.

The man barked a laugh, took a big step, and swung his mace around his head to gain momentum and launch it at me. I ducked as fast as I could, but the top of my forehead still got clipped, sending me to the dirt.

They laughed at my downfall, clearly thinking I wouldn't get back up. They thought we were human; I'd use that to our advantage. I stayed on the ground, my hand covering my now-healed gash, and waited.

"Whaaa, this was it?" The man sang as he walked towards my body. "Ahh, go get da otha one. We might be able to sell dis one fo parts."

Just a few more steps.

One. Two. Three. Four.

I sat up and stabbed my sharp rock into his foot, then rooted it up through his neck. His look of surprise only lasted so long before he gurgled up blood and spat it in my face.

Leaving the rock where it was, I kindly took his mace and turned to the woman.

She screamed, tears now flooding her eyes, but instead of taking revenge like I thought she would, she went after Vork, placing him in a hold and putting a dagger to his throat.

I stilled.

"You killed my Pa!"

"If you had left us alone, no one would be dead right now."

Even more enraged, she pushed the dagger against Vork's skin and drew blood.

"Wouldn't you rather do that to the person who killed your father?" I asked with a calm voice.

"Or I kill him and den you, yah?"

"Try it. I'll string you up by your intestines in these damn woods, and then *you'll* be used for parts."

She hissed in return but showed no intent to move.

"How about you use that helpful advantage you have?" Vork suggested.

He was mental.

"I don't know how to control it. It could kill you."

"Well, I'll definitely die if you leave me like this."

Like he could see me mentally weighing my options, he sighed, and in a flash, the woman hiccupped and fell to the forest floor. It all happened so fast, I didn't see that he quite literally ripped out her throat.

"So you aren't completely helpless then," I deadpanned.

He threw the chunk of meat into the fire. "I'm only helpless when I'm dead. Not much experience with lycans, I take it?"

He'd be my first.

I undressed the man, throwing Vork his clothes and shoes. "They might be a bit big, but it'll do till we get to the next town."

He began to dress and wiped the excess blood off his hands. "We can't stay here."

Unfortunately, he was right. More scavengers were bound to be close by, and even if they weren't, predators would smell the bodies, and we wouldn't be able to fight them off. The fact we were able to handle these two was a miracle.

We snuffed out the fire and gathered what we could carry. The scavengers had enough material on them to wrap our wounds, and we took their weapons as well, a mace and a knife. Once we'd gathered everything of use, we headed north as Vork had suggested before.

CHAPTER 14

Vork didn't talk as we trudged along the beaten path we found, which was surprising. We had walked all night, and by the gods, we survived. The endless chirping of the birds and insects was a good sign.

With Vork's silence came an endless swirl of questions.

Was I really about to sleep with him? Why was he starting to make me feel like I cared? What was it about him that made me have these emotions?

The sun was finally rising, and we were barely moving. Each step was about an inch, and Vork's weight was pressing into me more and more.

I propped him up a bit. "Hey, ease up."

"Sorry," he muttered breathlessly, but the weight didn't lighten. He took a misstep, then started to stumble. I tried to stop him as best I could with my injured shoulder, but he fell on his back.

"Vork." I tapped his face, but no response. "Vork!"

Turning my head to the side, I leaned over his mouth, and his breath hit my ear. I sighed, resting my forehead on his chest in defeat.

I don't know how far we are from the next town, but unless we were less than an hour on foot from it, then there was only a slight chance he would make it. I was reasonably strong, but I was injured. Even if I wasn't, he was big and I'd have issues dragging him down a dirt path.

I checked his leg and tightened the cloth on the wound to secure it. Before I could sit back down, I felt the ground vibrate from a horde of hooves running towards us.

Cursing, I shot up to grab his arm and drag him off the road before we were trampled. Over the hill, I counted at least twenty riders. I crouched down next to him and watched as they passed.

They were the Emperor's men, adorned with blue saddles and gold-plated hardware. Two banner men flanked the group in the front, holding the Emperor's emblem, the shrike. Its wings outstretched and a crown hovering above its head.

The men rode by, but one slowed and stopped before us.

He was dressed in a dull purple robe buttoned up to his neck and ending just above his knees. A sword sat at his hip, and his leather pants and boots seemed as weathered as his mud-stained robe.

I stood, locking eyes with him, and waited for his reaction. His sharp, dark gaze held a shine, indicating curiosity.

He leaned forward and looked behind me at Vork. "It looks like you require some assistance."

"Do you know how far the nearest town is?"

He looked forward and then back at me. "About an hour out on horseback."

I almost sighed in relief. It would be about three hours to the town, and Vork needed attention now.

I nodded and knelt to check if he was still breathing.

"Do you still need assistance?"

"Yes," I said as if it wasn't obvious.

"You could ask nicely."

"You're the one who stopped."

The man chuckled with a bright smile. Crow's feet crinkled next to his eyes, and the smile lines were deep on his chocolate, freckled skin.

"You do not look like the type that plays well with others."

"I don't tend to."

He chuckled again and stayed on his horse, eyes roaming over me—over my luxium leathers.

"Peculiar armor you have there."

"Thanks," I deadpanned.

"What happened?"

"A pack of hounds." A small lie with some truth in it. "My friend passed out."

He gave us both a once-over. "He will die before you get him to the town."

"I'm aware," I gritted.

"What is your name?"

"Luna."

"Well, Luna, I will make you a deal. I have a powder that will help your friend get on his feet, but I require something from you."

"Is that so?"

"You owe me a favor. I can call on you at any point for this favor, and you will come to my aid."

"I'm guessing you won't tell me the terms of this favor?"

"You come to my aid when I call."

My eyes narrowed. "You're insisting on helping a near-dead stranger on the side of the road, and that is what you want in return?"

The man pulled out a pouch from under his robe and juggled it in his hand. "Would you like the assistance or not?"

I didn't see what he could possibly get out of this. Just aid when he called? Would that mean a contract to kill? A life of servitude?

"Katar!" A soldier shouted from ahead. "Rejoin the group."

"Offer expires soon," *Katar* said.

"Fine."

He opened the pouch, whispered some words inside, then closed it and threw it over. There was black sand inside.

"What am I supposed to do with this?"

"Sprinkle it on his wound. It will take a while to close, and he will need rest before he can get on his feet. Remember our deal, Luna. I call and you answer."

He had to know there was an enormous chance we'd never see each other again.

"You now have the mark of the Farkath Coven. Until our deal is satisfied, you will continue to bear it."

On the palm of my hand, where the pouch had fallen, a symbol was etched into the skin.

My chest tightened as my thumb hovered over the circle, an intricate design woven through it. "You marked me?" I had to remember to breathe because if I didn't, I feared I'd let my teeth grind so hard nothing but stumps would be left. "Who the hell do you think you are?"

"The man who saved your life and High Priest of the Farkath Coven. You are welcome... *Luna.*"

He took off after the other soldiers, leaving us.

Opening the pouch fully, I saw there was only enough for one. *Tricky fucking witch.*

I wasted no time in sprinkling the sand over Vork's wound. He was hurt the most out of the two of us, and I couldn't continue to carry him in my state. I needed him moving.

At first, nothing happened, and my anxiety got the better of me. What if this kills him? I would not only responsible for his injuries, but also his death. An innocent's death.

No, no, no, no. Please work.

As if their Divine had answered my prayers, Vork bolted up with a pained cry, and the wound began to sizzle and bubble.

Cursing, I threw the pouch to the side. I pulled him more into the woods under cover and sat behind him, closing my legs around his midsection to keep his thrashing at bay.

After a few more pained cries and jolts, he began to relax and was unconscious again. I unwrapped my legs from his body, leaned back against the tree, and breathed deeply. Vork groaned and moved his head to the side, causing it to rest against my cheek.

He smelled like blood, dirt, and smoke from our fire. Beads of sweat on his temple brushed against my skin, and though I wanted to move, I didn't. He needed his rest, and to be honest, so did I.

The air was cool this morning, but his body against mine kept me warm, so I laced my arms over his shoulders and leaned in against him as we both rested. Soon, our breaths became synced, and it started to lull me to sleep until he stirred.

"Don't leave," he murmured, so softly I almost didn't hear him.

I stayed still until he fell back asleep.

"Pr— promise me. You won't go. You won't leave." His breathing became more erratic, and he began to struggle again.

"Hey—"

"Ple... Please... Don't, don't, father..."

He was hallucinating.

"He won't survive. He can't..."

Vork was stuttering and shaking so badly I placed my hand over his forehead and pulled him close.

"I'm not going anywhere," I whispered against his temple and let my free hand grab his. "I'm here."

"Why did you take him?"

I shushed him and squeezed gently.

His breath calmed again as he slumped back against me. He let his fingers lace through mine and squeezed for a moment, seeming to return to sanity. "I'm sorry."

"It's okay."

He smacked his lips. "What did I say?"

"You said you wish you had a pint of wine and a fae whore," I lied, adding a chuckle to sell it.

"Well," he sighed. "That doesn't sound too bad."

I couldn't hold back my smile. "Get some rest. We'll make it to the nearest village today."

"How do you know?"

"Just shut up and rest."

He didn't argue with me. I'm unsure if it was because he wanted to listen or if he was exhausted from his fit. At this point, I didn't really care, because I began to doze off as well. I didn't realize it until I woke up surprisingly warm.

Instead of sitting upright, I was lying on my side. I sat up quickly. Vork was sitting back against the tree, looking outward.

He looked at me with a small smile. "Good morning."

Rubbing the sleep from my eyes, I noted the coat in my lap. "What's this?"

"You were shivering."

"You didn't have to."

"Just say thank you."

My lip curled in resistance. "That was nice of you."

"Close enough, I suppose."

I tossed it back to him and looked through the canopy of the trees. "How long was I out?"

"It's about high noon."

He really let me sleep.

"How do you feel?" I asked.

He stretched his leg out, showing its mobility. "All healed. Though I am still a bit weak. We both could benefit from food and water. You said the town wasn't far?"

I nodded. "We can get there in a few hours."

"Ready to tell me how you know that?"

Before I could answer, the throbbing in my shoulder came back. This time it stung so badly it took the breath out of me. The pulsing ran up my head, and black spots danced in my vision.

I didn't realize I had almost hit the ground until Vork was catching me in his arms and wrapping the coat back around me.

He cursed and jostled my body up to hold me with one arm under my knees and the other wrapped behind my back.

"Amara, is the town the direction we were headed in?"

I nodded, and then the black dots swarmed my vision, making me fall into the darkness I knew so well.

CHAPTER 15

The chill of the winter air caressed my skin. I had always admired the cold. Leena, on the other hand, preferred the hot summers in Ekros. The only reason she was out here was for me. She complained for the first few minutes, but after a while, it subsided, and we sat in silence as we watched the snow fall around us in the forest outside the academy.

"Do you ever think of life outside of school?" she asked me.

All the time. I had planned my escape to the west and the lands rumored to be across the rocky sea. My time here on Masos had come to a close long ago when my family was murdered. Even after Diana found me, I never felt like I belonged. All I felt was hollowness and loss, as if my purpose had died along with all those closest to me.

"Yes," I said simply.

"I always wanted to go to northern Ekros and see the Cliffs of Dua. I heard the covens there are happy to bring in outsiders. I think I would be a good healer for them. It's rumored the waters off the cliffs are crystal clear and blessed by their gods. It's tradition that once a babe is born, they are to be baptized in the waters and granted unimaginable happiness for their entire life."

"That's some water."

Leena pulled her coat tighter around her. "I don't believe that, of course, but they believe it, and that's all that matters."

"Faith has people believing very stupid things."

"It's not stupid."

I kept silent.

"Faith gives people purpose. It makes them feel whole. It brings a calm to the chaos that is the world around them."

"All the strife and hard times are done unto us by the faith the Clergy has pushed down everyone's throats," I argued. "Everything done is in the Divine's name. All good and all bad. It's toxic."

"Yes, it is," Leena agreed. "That's an example of faith being used as a weapon. But these people use their faith peacefully. They apparently stay out of the Clergy's religion and follow their own gods. They live a peaceful life doing what is right and bring happiness to those around them."

"Seems simple."

She shifted to face me. "It is, and it's what I want. A simple life."

I could see where she was going with this. "But the chance for a simple life was taken from you when you found you were a nephilim."

Leena nodded, sadness swimming in her eyes.

I hurt for her.

"It's impossible to escape my fate," she said. "If I refuse or even flee, I have no doubt they would take it out on my family. They wouldn't be safe."

I wouldn't put it past the Clergy to insist to the Emperor that the nephilim must play the part the Divine has drawn out for them. From what I've heard, the Emperor was an honorable man, but having snakes coiled around his arms and leaning over his shoulders to whisper "logic" in his ears clouded his judgment.

"Do you know who you are betrothed to?" I asked.

"I heard Vocova talking about the son of a fae lord in the Emperor's court. We're too young now, but in the coming ages I have no doubt they'll call me to court to meet him."

"I'm sorry."

"It's not something I can change." She shrugged, then her eyes brightened a bit. "What about you? What are your plans after?"

"To go west."

Leena smiled, and my heart chipped a bit. "That sounds amazing!

I've heard stories of those lands. Sirens are rumored to swim there. Real sirens! What an adventure that would be."

"Come with me."

Her head snapped back to me. "I couldn't. Did you not hear—"

"That's if you tell them you're leaving. Don't say a word. I'll stage it so you won't have to worry about anything."

Her eyes looked everywhere but at my face, and she rolled her lips between her teeth. No doubt playing out every possible scenario.

"You deserve happiness," I pressed. "I'm trying to give it to you."

Leena couldn't fool me with her facade. She was just like me, broken, but in a different way. Most people dreamed of a life like hers, but the reality was, nephilim weren't free.

Though the collar around her neck was golden and beautiful, it was still a collar. An invisible symbol of the crown's and the Clergy's ownership of her.

Her gaze finally connected with mine. "Why... why would you do something like that for me?"

"I don't know."

"Not good enough."

"I don't trust anyone. I've been on my own before, and to some degree, I am right now, but I've found some people deserve all the good in this world, and you're one of them. I've learned how to spot the good and bad in people, though I've been trained to ignore that, and you, Leena, are the good this continent needs. But if they want to use your goodness for their own gain and manipulate that, then they don't deserve you. You're entitled to a chance to have the life you want. I can try to give that to you. No rules, no betrothals, and no duties. Just life as you want and a destiny you can make for yourself."

I feared I had made her thoughts run wild at this point. She didn't respond for a good while, and we sat in silence, listening to the wind. We continued to watch the snow fall until it finally stopped, and an undisturbed blanket of white surrounded us.

"I'll think about it," she finally said, softly. "Thank you, Amara. I've never had a friend who truly cared about me like that."

Friend.

What a strange word for me. I had only been at the academy for two ages and hadn't had one of those in some time.

"We'll watch each other's backs," I stated. "I won't let anything happen to you."

Leena raised a brow. "Should I be preparing for battle?"

She was too young to know anything about fighting, which was one of the reasons I think I was drawn to her. She was so innocent, and I was so corrupt. I had hoped having someone like her in my life would bring back a portion of the humanity I had lost.

"You never know." I shrugged. "But it would be nice to have a nephilim on my side."

The smile she gave warmed me from the inside out and brought me a semblance of peace that lasted for a few ages...until the academy was attacked and I—

When I awoke, the smell of incense immediately assaulted me. It was stale and smoky, almost bad enough to make me cough.

The air was warm from a fire in the middle of the room. Though it wasn't the warmth I first felt, it was the odd sensation that another being there with me.

Behind me, there was a rustling of what sounded like bones on strings, clanging about as quick breezes found their way in. I opened my eyes to find Vork sitting in a wooden chair, peeling off dried mud from his trousers.

He looked completely healed and full of energy.

I finally let the cough out, grabbing my throat. I had never wanted water as much as I did in that moment. Like he had read my mind, Vork approached me with a cup.

He helped me sit up and let me guzzle down the liquid. I set the cup next to me and noted there was no throbbing at my shoulder, and my hand was wrapped correctly. I looked down and the only clothes I had on were a wrap to bind my breasts and a similar wrap around my bottom that stopped just a few inches past my hip.

"Where's my armor?" I asked, checking my whole body. The wounds were closed, but the scars remained on my face, neck, and thighs. I traced them with my fingers.

"I'll get them," Vork assured me. "They needed to remove every-thing to tend to your wounds."

I took in the dark space. We were in a healer's tent, which made sense when I considered the burning incense. It seemed to be twilight as the only light was the fire and the candles around the tent's perimeter. Other odds and ends only a healer would understand were stacked on the dressers and tables.

"Where are we?"

"A small mining town south of Ekros capital. Glin."

I rolled my cheek, feeling the pull of sore muscles and the scar on my face. My hand went back up to the scar, and I internally sighed.

"You're beautiful."

My eyes snapped up to him, his words leaving me at a loss for my own. I wasn't a stranger to scars, but having one on my face was unsettling.

Vork handed me my undergarments and armor.

"If it makes you feel any better, I have a nasty scar on my leg from the hound. We both got banged up pretty good."

"That just makes me ooze with happiness," I said, more dryly than I wanted to, but he ignored it.

I ripped the cloth covering my body off and changed into clean clothes, but stared at the soft, almost leather-like luxium armor. It would look like any old leather armor to the common eye, but anyone in the Emperor's or Clergy's circle would know precisely what it was, and therefore who I was. While getting rescued might not be a bad thing, I didn't have the best feeling about the Clergy finding us.

Vork sighed. "What's got you worked up now?"

Always looking to push my buttons. "I've got trust issues."

"I never would've thought." There was a smirk growing on his face. The bastard knew he was getting to me and was getting a kick out of it.

"You enjoy being the thorn in my ass, don't you?"

"Huh," he breathed while stalking around the table and making his way in front of me. "That's not the only thing I'd enjoy being in."

My lips pursed as his hand snaked around my lower back, yanking me till I collided with his chest. Though his hand wasn't touching skin, it sure felt that way. It spanned my entire lower back, almost throbbing with heat.

My neck tipped back, and I met his gaze. This time my eyes were hooded so much it was almost difficult to see him through my lashes.

"That excites you, doesn't it?" His words were laced with delicious poison, paralyzing me. "Tell me what else you want."

I swallowed the lump in my throat, pulling back a bit in an attempt to regain my head. "I want to get back to the academy."

Not a total lie

"No, I want to know what you really want. At this moment. Tell me what desires I can stir up for you, angel."

A cool and sudden breeze blew against my back.

"Do I need to give you two a few more moments?" The healer stood in the doorway with an unamused look on her face.

"No," I said, setting myself away from Vork. "Thank you for tending to my wounds."

She ignored my thanks and threw a log in the fire before going to a corner and rustling through her things.

"Do you have two horses you could spare?" I asked the woman. "We have a long way to travel."

Vork's head snapped to me. "Horses will take us weeks to get back to the—"

"Not if we travel with haste," I cut him off.

"Calm yourself, child," the healer said softly. "Katar already told me who you are and where he suspects you're headed."

"Who's Katar?" Vork asked.

I ignored him.

"How does he know that?"

"He is a High Priest of the Farkath Coven, and you'd do well to make nice with."

Vork shifted next to me, his body now rigid and jaw clenched tight at the information.

"He knows who you are," she continued, "because he has the gift of sight—although your armor is a dead giveaway. He knows where you came from, how you ended up here, and sometimes the future." She whipped around, causing the trinkets woven in her long, curly brown hair to almost slap her in the face. She held out something I thought I would never see again: my swords. "These are from Katar."

How in the hell did he get these? The last time I had seen them was in the burning barn back in Arabrosa.

I went to take them, but she tightened her grip. "Don't be too quick to make enemies here."

"I'm not—"

The seriousness in her dark eyes made me pause, and her face contorted with a frown, showing her wrinkles. She looked up at me with determination, her lips pursed so hard her cheeks became even more hollow than they were before.

"You have such a darkness in you, child, and if you continue to feed it, it will consume you entirely."

"I am aware of the darkness." I almost rolled my eyes, but she was right. I didn't want to make too many enemies in a foreign land when I needed help. So, I held back. "I know how to control it."

"Your history with the guild is not what I'm referring to."

I froze. Did Katar tell her? No one, except Diana and Leena, knew anything about my past life, and I wanted to keep it that way. I took a closer step toward her.

"It would be appreciated," I began in a deadly, but soft, whisper, "if you kept your knowledge of my life to yourself. Not everyone is so keen on exposing themselves like you seem to be."

The healer's gaze never faltered, but she let go of the swords and gave me a slight nod before looking over to Vork. "Keep this one close. He will be your anchor."

It was eerily quiet, and I suddenly felt she might be right. This feeling had consumed me ever since we landed on the beach. As stupid and noble as his efforts were, something had come out of them.

Respect.

"About those horses," Vork said. "It will take us some time to get to where we are going. Can you spare them?"

"Yes, but you were right. It will take you months depending on which roads you take and if you were to run into any trouble. Katar and the Emperor's men were headed west to the capital of Ekros. If you ride quickly and catch up to him, he may be able to help you get where you need to be."

"How?" I wasn't going to travel to someone when I didn't know exactly how they could help me.

"He will be able to transport you there," the healer explained. "It is not a widely known magic. Only a few High Priests are able to do it, and even then, it can come at a price."

"You seem uncertain about that," Vork said.

"It is up to the gods if they require a sacrifice to perform the magic."

The gods.

This talk could get the healer killed if the Emperor's men caught wind of her speaking of divine beings other than *the* Divine. She knew that, though, and she wasn't afraid. I admired that strength. Despite the fact there was a force much greater than her, it didn't stop her from believing in her faith.

I fumbled with my swords, noticing extra leather straps had been added that seemed to crisscross in the front. Vork came up behind me, helped me strap them to my back, and secured the buckle in my front.

"You should go." The healer produced another sword, this time much longer and thicker, from behind her and gave it to Vork. "Once Katar makes it into the capital's gates, I can't say it will be easy to get to him."

"What do you want in return for your services?" I asked.

Her brows furrowed.

"You must want something," I insisted.

I had found out the hard way nothing in this life is free.

"I want you to do the right thing when the time comes. Not what is right for you, but what is right for us. Masos and its people."

I didn't see how I had anything to do with the continent, but I nodded and left the tent. Vork followed a short time later.

When he came out, he had a pack strapped over one shoulder and another in his hand that he threw to me. He led us to the stables, where two horses were ready. I stuffed my armor into my pack, and we mounted our horses.

The air was cool but far warmer than the chilly mountains of

Arabrosa. I took a deep breath and savored the split moment of contentment I had. Maybe I did like warmer weather after all.

"That healer put a great deal of responsibility on you," Vork said as he drove his horse out of the stall. "Any idea what she meant?"

"Not a clue."

"What about the guild? Care to tell me about that?"

"No."

He said no more as we pushed our horses into a sprint and made our way to Katar.

Truthfully, I didn't want any answers regarding what the healer said. Ignorance was bliss in these situations, but I had a feeling Katar was going to do more than just take us home. I was afraid all of this—becoming a nephilim and everything else that had happened—had put something into motion I didn't want to be a part of. But if I've learned anything in my ages on this continent, it's that fate is very hard to control.

CHAPTER 16

WE RODE all night as fast as our horses would go. I underestimated how unaccustomed my body was to riding at full speed for hours. The skin between my thighs, where it rubbed against the saddle, was turning raw. My grip on the reins loosened a bit when we finally slowed down.

A camp was just below where we looked out over the ridge. There were three fires and three large tents. It was hard to see how many were standing guard, but even if we knew, we would have to walk in without hurting them. I doubted they would help if we so rudely killed the Emperor's men.

"Should we wait till daybreak?" I asked Vork.

"No reason for us to sleep without cover when they could provide one. We can go there and hopefully talk to this Katar in the morning."

I nodded in agreement, and we moved our horses down the path towards the camp.

"So," Vork began. "How did you meet this Katar?"

"Jealous?"

"I'm not the jealous type. When I want a woman, she tends to want me back. Jealousy isn't required."

"Cocky."

"I like to call it confidence."

"You would like to call it that." I rolled my eyes. "He was a man who was on the road before we got to Glin. He gave me a powder that healed your leg."

"What did he want in return?"

"An 'I owe you,' which worries me."

Vork placed one hand on his thigh and sighed. "I understand why you did it and appreciate it. I bet it was nice saving me for a change."

"It was a change I graciously accepted." I teased.

He barked a laugh, then trotted forward and stopped in front of me, causing my horse to stop as well. His laugh faded, and he looked at me with a hint of admiration.

"Thank you, Amara."

"You're welcome." Suddenly, I felt out of breath, like I had run for miles. Before he could prolong the intimate moment, I asked, "Did you have a sibling?"

He didn't flinch. "I did. A brother. A long time ago."

I didn't want to push too much. I had a hunch that might have been who he was hallucinating about yesterday. Though the answer was fleeting, there was hurt in his eyes. I had wanted to change the subject so the attention wasn't on me, but I regretted it.

"I didn't mean to bring back unpleasant memories."

Vork moved his horse along, and I followed.

"They weren't all unpleasant. I have many happy memories of him and our family."

"Would you tell me about him someday?"

"Of course." He turned his head, the moonlight hitting his face and highlighting the curiosity brewing in his features. "Would you also share a bit of your life with me?"

I thought for a moment. "Perhaps."

"Well, it's not a 'no,'" he said.

"No," I answered. "It's not."

That made his smile return, and I found myself smiling in the dark as well, but I quickly wiped it away and kept moving forward.

"I saw that."

"Shut up."

I increased my pace, forcing him to do the same to keep up.

"My brother died when he was fifteen ages. There is a ritual lycan boys must perform when they come of age. My older brother was next in line for the title of Chief and had to do the task alone."

I said nothing, letting him continue.

"The ritual was simple: within the woods lived the fierce beasts from which we had descended, the wolves. We were to survive all night and kill a wolf, then skin it for its pelt. My brother, being heir, had a more difficult task than the others."

For a moment, I could have sworn his eyes had a glassy sheen to them as he glared forward. He blinked and his posture straightened, pushing down whatever feeling was trying to emerge. I pitied him.

"There was a lone, grey wolf who lived in the woods. It was much bigger than most, even though some would consider it a runt that looked nothing like the others. But this beast was far superior to them. Everything about it was enhanced, making it even more impossible for a boy of fifteen to bring it down. I pleaded with my father to not allow him to do it, but it was useless. The next day, when my brother didn't come back by midday, we went out looking for him, and all we found was a hand we knew in our hearts belonged to him."

"How old were you?"

"I was ten ages."

This world was not kind to children, especially. I could, unfortunately, share his pain about that. "I'm sorry you had to witness that. You never truly heal from losing family, no matter how many ages have passed."

He turned to me. "You speak as if you understand."

"I do." I nodded. "I lost my whole family to a fire when I was very young."

Vork shared the same expression I gave him during his story. It was an understanding and a sorrow only those who lived with loss would know. We gave each other a comforting look, but were cut short when our horses were stopped, and arrows landed just in front of their feet.

"Halt," a soldier a few yards ahead commanded. "You are trespassing. State your purpose."

Vork spoke first. "We are here to see the High Priest you travel with. Katar."

"And you are?"

"Vork Lacelle. Commander of the Arabrosa pack."

Two more soldiers on horseback came to flank the one speaking. "And the woman?"

"Luna," I said quickly.

The soldier's eyes traveled down my person and back up with a stern gaze as he ordered, "Follow."

We pushed our horses to do as commanded.

"Luna?" Vork whispered to me.

I shook my head. He'd have to wait for an explanation.

In silence, we were led into the camp, the light from the torches leading the way. As we approached their front lines, we received stares. Whispers began to sprout from soldier's lips as many of them probably recognized Vork. Their eyes followed us until we reached one of the bigger tents.

We dismounted and were escorted in. A captain stood behind a table, looking down at the troop placements, with a lieutenant on his left and Katar on his right.

"Captain," the soldier announced, and they all looked up. "Commander Vork Lacelle of the Arabrosa pack and... Luna."

The captain stared at us in an eerie silence. His pointed ears twitched, maybe in irritation or curiosity. To be honest, I wasn't too sure. For all he knew, I was human and the fae were not fans.

Katar's eyes gleamed.

"What can I do for you, Commander?" The captain asked in a low voice. He was a big fae, taking up a considerable part of the other side of the table, and had a medium-length silver beard which showed his age and contrasted with his olive skin.

His lieutenant, who I could tell by the silver band he wore on his left upper arm, was the exact opposite of him. He was young, couldn't be more than twenty ages old, had no facial hair, was lean, and of average height. He looked confident but also a bit timid.

"Captain..." Vork began.

"Eldos," he said firmly.

"Captain Eldos, we have come to seek shelter for the night. We traveled to the Duen coven to seek special ingredients and knowledge for our healer. We are making the trip back now and would appreciate the assistance."

"Why did you travel so far east? Could you not seek aid from the coven in your territory?"

"They're not the most hospitable of neighbors. We tend to keep to ourselves."

A frown formed on Eldos' face, and his eyes went back to me. "Why do you travel with a human?"

"She is my serf. Bound to me for some time. Her father owed a great debt he couldn't pay, and she became the price."

"Arabrosa is a long way. You plan to travel there by horseback?"

"Yes, sir."

"I could allow Katar to assist with your travel." Eldos leaned in on his knuckles. "We've been trying to move our troops past the mountains you currently sit on."

"You are aware that due to laws put in place—"

"*No entity outside of the Arabrosa pack will be allowed in the mountains to protect the ancestral lands of our people.* Yes, I know," Eldos sighed. "Though those witches seem able to walk on your land."

"That's different."

"How hard you protect those rocks makes one think you have something to hide."

"If we do," Vork said simply but sternly, "then neither the Clergy nor the Emperor's men will know about it. Unless you all decide to set foot on our soil uninvited, but then you'd be risking war."

The captain's back straightened.

"Looks like you'll need cover to rest for your long journey on horseback, Commander. My soldiers will pitch a tent for you and your human. In the meantime, you may help yourself to whatever food is by the fire. Now, if you'll excuse me."

Eldos began to make his way out of the tent with his lieutenant, leaving us with Katar. When the tent flap closed, Katar let out a short chuckle.

"Well, I have to say, I didn't think I'd be seeing you both so soon."

I raised a brow. "I can assure you I shared the same notion."

"I assume you'd like to take the Captain's offer of transport without owing him anything in return?"

"Yes," Vork said simply.

"And why would I do that?" Katar asked, looking at me. "You already owe me a favor. Do you want to tack on another?"

"Because you know exactly who I am," I stated. "You know what my armor is made of, and you retrieved my swords for me. Don't play us for fools."

A smile was playing on his lips, but he tried to hide it. "I would never do such a thing." He placed a hand over his chest. "Of course I will help you."

"Why? Simply because you know what she is?" Vork asked.

"That's exactly why."

"You want nothing in return?"

"No." Katar turned his gaze to me. "A time will come when you need to make a decision and making the right one will be payment enough."

The healer from the village had said something similar to me. I simply nodded in agreement.

"Unfortunately," Katar said, "I have spent most of my day defending the troops from sazari, so my magic is spent. I will come to your tent just before dawn and assist you then."

We nodded our thanks, then Katar escorted us to our tent where he wished us goodnight.

Inside the tent, we found a single pile of clothes and furs for us to share. There was no fire, so it was almost as cold as the outside air and fairly hard to see, but not impossible.

"I will sleep over there." Vork motioned to the other side of the tent and began to make his way.

"No," I clipped quickly. "It's cold. You have no reason to suffer, and we're both adults."

There was a slight hesitation, but he nodded, and we both got into the bed after disarming and taking off our shoes. The cold had started to affect me, all the muscles in my body tensed under the light fur.

"Come here."

Vork pulled me into his arms, and we both lay on our sides, my face squished against his chest. It took a moment, but warmth came over me like a wave. My muscles relaxed, while my mind raced. I had never really thought about his smell until it was right under my nose. Smoky with a hint of something sweet—lavender, maybe. It was calming.

I collected lavender as a child, and its scent would blend with the smoke of the fires that warmed our home, creating a cozy oasis.. I had always missed it, but now it felt like I was back—like I was home.

"Are you always this warm?" I asked.

He gave a low chuckle that vibrated against my cheek. "I am."

I pushed forward to get closer, if that was even possible. His grip on me tightened slightly, and I found myself grinding my hips against him. I was the most comfortable I had been in a long time, and my body was beginning to have a mind of its own.

"Amara," Vork drew out in warning. "If you start this, there's no going back. I *will* finish it."

I looked up at him, and we both knew as soon as our eyes locked. We didn't want this to stop. Though we were as close as we could possibly be, it was like I was being pulled towards him. The thick air between us was growing tenser by the second. We stared at each other, our gazes flickering to each other's mouths, waiting for one of us to make the first move.

Vork unwrapped one of his arms and placed his hand on the back of my neck, securing it in place. If he could feel the nervous sweat pooling at my hairline, he made no mention of it as he touched his lips softly to mine.

My body began to hum in glorious heat, and I felt weak. This man could do whatever he wanted and I might have let him. I only felt his soft lips feathering against mine. All too soon, he pulled away and my mouth parted in protest as I stared at his lips, hoping they would return.

This mouth moved to the newly healed scars on the side of my face, tracing them down my neck until I was arched back in his arms. He breathed me in when he rested his face on my neck.

"I..." He shuddered around me as he let out a shaky breath.

He never finished his sentence, but he didn't have to. I understood. Somehow, I understood how he was feeling and how he couldn't put it into words. So, I did what our words couldn't explain and kissed him back.

My hands, still pinned between us, gripped his shirt, and his hold tightened on the back of my neck. My hips ground into him again, and I draped one of my legs over his hips.

Vork pulled away. "This is your last chance to turn back."

"Don't stop me again," I commanded in a dangerously low tone I wasn't even sure came from me. The lust had fogged my mind and laid over me like a blanket I was trapped in. I never wanted to be freed.

Let me suffocate. It felt too good.

His eyes almost rolled to the back of his head, trying to keep a grip on whatever control he had left, but I wanted it. I wanted him to let it go and give me whatever chaos was brewing in that head of his.

I pushed him over on his back and straddled his hips, but before I could move, he sat upright and brought our faces close together.

"I need—"

His breath hitched when I kissed up his neck and nibbled on his ear.

"What do you need, Vork?"

The pads of his fingers pushed into my back with a tight grip. "I need to feel that wet cunt of yours. I need to be in you. You want that, angel?"

I nodded before I could even think about how to respond.

His warm hands untucked my shirt and pulled it over my head, then moved to the tight cropped undershirt. Without a second to spare, his head dipped down and he took a bud in his mouth, making my body heat back up. I grasped the back of his head, making sure he wouldn't stop the delicious torture of his tongue.

Gods, why did it feel like this? Why did it feel *so* damn good?

Though the foreplay was nice, I needed more. I fumbled with his shirt and when he broke away from me, I crushed my lips to his again, pushing him back. But position was short-lived as he rolled us over so I was under him, pressing hard against my core and eliciting a not-so-silent moan.

His free hand slid down my stomach and pulled my waistband up so his fingers could press against my core.

"You're already so wet," he purred as his fingers circled my clit.

"Fuck. The things I want to do to you. I should be locked away in that prison where we first met."

The scene from our first meeting came flooding back. Sex barely crossed my mind with him then. I had a job to do. But now, here we are, tangled in cheap bedding with the Emperor's men just outside, and I would rather have my eyes gouged out than let this moment stop.

Tension began to build in my core, and my toes tingled.

"By the gods, how are you so good at this?"

If Vork's ego wasn't inflated before, it sure was now.

He gave me a quick kiss on the lips. "I'm very observant."

His eyes bore holes into mine, and the lust brewing in his gaze made me tip right over the edge. He took my hand in his and laced our fingers together, his other hand never stopping.

My eyes fluttered closed, ready to feel euphoria.

"Eyes on me." Vork's rough yet clear voice rang through my ears, and I instantly obeyed.

We connected again, my body stiff, and a loud moan slipped from my lips. There was fire in his eyes in the first few seconds of my orgasm, but after that, I saw only stars and black. My body was in such a stiff lock it hurt, but the euphoric feeling he was giving me overshadowed it tenfold.

"Fuck, fuck, fuck." I chanted as the pulses of the orgasm kept coming. My grip on his hand must have been painful, but he said nothing. When I came to and could finally see, Vork looked down at me with a satisfied look on his face.

"You make the prettiest sounds when you come."

I finally relaxed my body and eased my grip on his hand. He pulled his other out of my pants, and it was glistening with me.

"My, my," he sang. "What a mess you've made."

Vork sat up to pull down my pants and undo his, then took himself in his hand. My mouth watered with anticipation, looking up at him.

"You want it bad, don't you?"

A wave of lust rolled over me, and I had to keep my eyes from fluttering closed. "Yes, I do."

Still working himself, he asked, "What exactly is it you want?"

A few months ago, I could never have imagined myself saying these words to him or to any person in my bed: "I want you."

"Oh, I think you can do better than that."

I thought I'd be embarrassed to say what I did next, but it came out so easily.

"I want you to give me everything, Vork. I want every dirty word, every bite of my skin, every moan you can make. I want to feel you shudder when you slip into me for the first time, and I want to see that beautiful face wring up in pleasure when I clamp down tight as you come."

He hovered over me and placed himself at my entrance, his hands on either side of my head. When he slowly pushed in, I was truly worried I would come again just from that.

Euphoria danced across my skin as a stupidly wide grin formed on my face. Gods this was *good*. So good my chest hurt, and I gripped his forearms hard to keep him in place. He couldn't back down now.

Just like I wanted, Vork shuddered slightly once he was fully seated and breathed heavily into my neck. He pulled out painfully slow, then thrusted forward just the same.

I brought my knees up closer to my head to deepen the angle, and he wrapped an arm around my lower back to prop me up more.

He groaned and took a nip at the skin that connected my neck and shoulder. That simple act sent me into a frenzy, and I flexed my hips up into his thrust, begging to go deeper.

"Gods, you feel good," I muttered into his hair, grasping at it like a lifeline. "I need more."

He picked up the pace steadily and met my lips with a heavy kiss, causing my head to spin. "You're going to be the end of me."

I wished I could say I felt guilty for how deep my nails dug into his back or the grip my legs had on his waist, but I didn't care. The moment was pure bliss.

His thrusts became more abrupt, and I pulled his ear to my mouth. "Are you going to come for me, Vork?"

An aggressive growl erupted from him, making my toes curl. It was primal and gods I needed it.

He pulled me up so I was sitting on his lap and jerked up into me. I went to put my feet on the ground for more leverage, but he wouldn't allow it, pulling my legs back around his waist, then placing his hands on my back to hold me still. He was using me for his own release—just like I wanted. Vork had all the control here, and it was freeing .

His movements became shallower and more rhythmic. He was so close, but before he could find his release, my own came out of nowhere. I shuddered against him and moaned into his hair, clawing into his shoulders to hold on.

"Ah, I'm going to—"

He didn't get the chance to finish as a guttural groan was muffled into my neck, and his thrusts halted, finally giving me what I wanted.

Our breaths were erratic as we held each other for a moment. No words were spoken and none was needed as we stayed there, our foreheads touching.

This connection—it terrified me.

How could something so effortless be given to me with no consequences, no strings, and no stipulations?

For most of my life, I had been taught to believe anything good came with a price, and I always thought mine was whatever shard of my heart I had left.

He might not have known, but the lycan in my arms now held it.

CHAPTER 17

Vork woke before I did.

It must have been the scuffle coming from outside the tent that pulled him from sleep. I rubbed the dirt from my eyes and wrapped the fur around my chest. His arm lay in front of me. Maybe last night had made him forget I needed no shield.

Last night was... unexpected. The sex itself was something to remember, but that's not what stuck in my mind. It was his tenderness and the same I showed toward him, which I hadn't even known I was capable of.

After we had untangled our bodies and cleaned up, we lay down and faced one another, talking.

He told me about his life in the pack, how his mother was the kindest soul he had ever known, and how his father was equally so in certain predicaments. The pack was stationed in the Arabrosa mountain range, so it was constantly covered in snow except in the summer when the base of the mountain was covered in lush green. Apparently, the sweetest honey came from the bees who housed their hives in the pack's territory, and he wanted to show me.

I nodded and smiled in return. I didn't think I would ever make it there, but I didn't want to sour the moment.

The stories I told were not as sweet. The only good memories I could tell him were the ones with Leena when we were drinking in the middle of a blizzard under the grand oak of the academy's courtyard.

I shared the small amount of happy memories I had from when my family was still alive.

"Tell me about them," he said, but it sounded like a question.

I swallowed the lump in my throat, keeping my eyes locked on our entwined fingers.

"When I was young, I was part of a group called the Hollow's Guild high in the mountains of Arabrosa, past the pack's territory. My memory is hazy because I was so young, but when I became an orphan, I was given to my aunt, who was already struggling to provide for her own family, so she sold me off to the guild for ten silvers. I was young but old enough to develop a relationship with the leader. He taught me how to be an effective killer and thief."

Vork never said a word, but I could feel his eyes on me.

"My family. They were an interesting lot. A group of degenerates of all ages and races who were brought into the fold of the guild. Our leader, Nev, was killed in the fire that consumed our home." I took my hand out of his and inspected it. "Curious that the thing I am now immune to couldn't help me when I needed it. When I needed to save those I loved most."

He took my hand in his and kissed every knuckle until he got to my palm. "You can't do that to yourself."

"It's normal," I said with a sigh. "To wonder what could have been. But it was a long time ago, and doesn't hurt as much as it did when I was younger. It's hardened me. Made me into the person I am today. While I'm grateful for the lessons I've learned, I wish it hadn't happened at their expense."

We fell into a silence, which turned into a peaceful sleep until he stirred next to me, and someone came to our tent.

Katar pushed the flap open just enough to show his side profile. "Get dressed."

Then he was gone.

We put our clothes on, and Vork helped to strap my swords in place behind my back. When we were both clothed, I went to walk out of the tent, but his hand came around my front, catching the leather that crisscrossed there. He spun me around and pulled me to him, keeping his grip on the strap.

We locked eyes, and he flashed a teasing smile. My lips began quivering up to a returning one before he tugged again and kissed me.

It was brief but purposeful.

As he pulled away, I shoved him off playfully, still biting back that smile. We made our way to Katar, but he wasn't alone. There was another man with him, leaning against a post and fiddling with a coin between his slender fingers.

He stood tall, a hood covering the top part of his face, but I make out a scruffy grey beard. The long brown coat shielding him from the cold swayed in the wind, showing a scimitar strapped to his waist.

The visitor raised his head and pulled back the hood. His face was haggard, not from the ages that had passed but from the world's hardships. He is—or was—a warrior. For some, the ages of battle and killing took a toll on their souls. Most didn't make it to an old enough age to worry about such things, but this man—I could tell—had many internal scars.

But his eyes remained young. They were a bright, light blue, which reminded me of the clear pool waters that ran down the mountains of Arabrosa. Those eyes held whatever fight was left in him.

Katar held a hand out to the man. "May I introduce Silas, Commander of the Defiants."

I raised an eyebrow at him. "Consorting with rebels, Katar? Interesting to hear from someone so close to the Emperor."

"I have the same intentions as the Emperor," Katar said. "We serve Masos and its people. We simply have different ways of going about it."

"What is it you want?" I asked the commander.

Silas flipped the coin in the air and caught it, placing it in the small pocket of his shirt. "I'd like to request your aid."

"And why would I help you?"

"Because you're the only one who can, or we'll all die."

A slight pang of guilt hit me. Like when I did nothing to save my family. But back then, I couldn't. This time I might be able to.

But these people weren't my family.

They were strangers who had woken me at an ungodly hour.

I walked over to the campfire, which was now just smoldering embers, and grabbed the sack of water sitting next to it, taking a gulp.

"That doesn't tell me why I'd help you. You just told me you needed me. But I don't need you. Why would I put myself at risk when I don't even know or care about who you are?"

"Amara," Katar interjected before Silas could respond.

My palm began to warm, and I looked to see the mark he had given me starting to illuminate like a brand.

He wouldn't dare.

"Katar," I warned.

"I only wish for you to hear him speak."

"If you ask this and I accept, then you take this mark off. You will not get any free favors from me."

He nodded complacently. Too easily.

Silas followed me. "My people, your people, all those living on this continent, will either be enslaved or dead if you don't help us."

"Yes, I heard you the first time. Help you to do what exactly?"

"The simple answer? Win this war." He prompted me to walk towards the woods.

I could feel Vork and Katar behind us.

It was still dark out, the camp quiet, and no one had seen us. The timing was probably a part of Katar's plan. I imagined the favor he planted on my palm was always meant to be used at this moment. He had planned for me to meet Silas all along and knew I wouldn't listen unless I genuinely had to.

"What war are you referring to?" I asked Silas. "There's unrest on the continent like there always is, but I've seen no signs of a civil war."

I noticed his hand resting on the handle of his blade. He would be foolish to draw it, and I didn't believe he would. It was a habit of observation.

He seemed disappointed.

"That's because you aren't a part of it. This war has been going on for a long time, even before we were here. The Defiants, as the Clergy call us, are a free people who want the same for all. Shortly after the Clergy came together, a group of souls wanted a different life, a better one, where they were not ruled with cruelty. A witch, a human, a fae, and an angel all came together to fight for this, and they called themselves the Vanguard."

I almost snickered at the name.

"At the academy, we were taught the Defiants were in league with the demons and Lucifer. Is he the angel you speak of?"

Silas nodded. "He was indeed. It's an odd tale that Lucifer was cast out of Heaven. No, he left of his own free will, and contrary to popular belief, he was not the original snake in the garden who tempted the first humans of Masos."

"Can you get to the point where this somehow affects me?"

Silas stopped walking and turned to me.

"I believe the whole story will give you a better ability to understand our situation and stand with us. Now, as I was saying—" He continued to walk. "Lucifer was not the villain the Clergy had set him out to be, but they used him to solidify their claim of the righteous side of this war.

"After centuries, strange things began to happen on Masos. Demons had always been in existence. They were a part of life that balanced the scales, and we understood this, but during that strange time, the demons started to become more... bold. They were taking souls by force, and those who couldn't handle the transformation to a demon were turned into sazari.

"It went on until the Cleansing about fifteen ages ago. The Clergy claimed we were working with the demons, but we were fighting them off our land. The holy men saw an opportunity to hit us while we were weak and joined after our victory against the demon horde. We lost against the Clergy's forces and retreated further into the Isle." He sighed and looked down at his boots in defeat. "But now, the same problem has resurfaced. So, not only are we fighting the Clergy for our freedom, but we are fighting against a force that is seeking to take every soul they possibly can, but for what we don't know."

"I still don't know what you ask of me."

He stopped again and kept his eyes trained forward into the forest's darkness. "The Defiants have been fighting a silent war with the Clergy since their conception. We have learned how to keep them at bay and weaken them, but never truly defeat them. Unfortunately, I believe we need to pause those efforts and turn to a more dangerous threat. His name is Abaddon, the product of Lucifer and the mother of all chaos, Lilith."

Abaddon. Why did that name bring such a sense of familiarity?

Abaddon. Abaddon. Abaddon.

Abe— the bastard in my room all those nights ago. But why? What could the son of Lilith and Lucifer want with me?

Another finding clicked. He was a nephilim and a corrupted one at that. Part demon *and* angel. What a wild ride. No wonder they were so afraid of him. Who knew what devastation he could bring on. His existence was... wrong.

After all this talk about what Silas wants me to do, I still haven't received an answer. All I've gotten is a history lesson about his people.

"There is a prophecy," Katar joined, strolling to Silas' side. "It's quite simple. The daughter of that which is scorched and the son of pure vile will fight upon the golden fields of the birth of creation, and a fissure of clouded abyss will show itself to decide judgement of the world."

"Wow," I said. "That's some prophecy."

I had become bored with this conversation immediately after it started. The fate of Masos was not my concern. My own fate was the only thing I needed to worry about. It's all I've ever had to worry about. Especially now since I had a hunch this Abaddon character had tried to kidnap me from my bed.

Was he the one behind the first demon attack? But what for?

"I've heard what he had to say, and I'm not interested." I leveled a look at Katar, then turned to Silas. "Best of luck to you and your people, Silas."

I turned to begin my walk back to the camp, but he stomped up behind me.

"You," Silas shouted, "can stop all of this, but you would send my people, all of Masos' people, to die because you're too selfish to care about anyone but yourself?"

He was so close to my back now that my fingers were itching for a fight.

Before I could even think of whether or not that would be a good idea, Vork took a massive step in front of me, looming over my shoulder at Silas and pinning him with a glare.

"I see you have a lycan at your beck and call."

An unimpressed snicker came from me as I turned around to face him. His eyes were still locked with Vork's.

"You will not goad me into helping you with this war," I said. "A word to the wise: when you try to ask an assassin for help, make sure there is something in it for them. Otherwise, your cause is useless."

That made Silas' attention come back to me, his eyes softening to a plea. "I am not asking an assassin for assistance; I am asking a daughter of Michael, the Unburnt Nephilim, to help me save millions of lives. We will all soon be nothing if you do not stand with us. I implore you, Amara, please help us."

"Do you believe in destiny?" Katar asked from the background in a soft, calm voice.

I hadn't given it much thought.

"Every move you have made was to stay alive," he continued. "When you were a child, up until now, every decision has been based on your most basic instinct as a human and as an assassin to survive. But what if destiny needed you alive to fulfill what you were meant to do? Your whole life has been in the shadows alone. Now you have those who are not trying to bring you out of those shadows but walk beside you in them." He shook his head and held his hands out in exaggeration. "Destiny is one of the most powerful things in this world, Amara! If one runs from it, then destruction soon follows. One might think there is only *the* right decision to make, but that is not true. It's *your* decision. It is what you want *your* legacy to be. And whether you can live with Abaddon ruining this world or if you are willing to fight to save it, for yourself and for others."

"You're asking me to go against everything I've learned," I said in disbelief, "everything I am, to sacrifice for everyone else. That is a lofty price."

Katar nodded excessively and stepped forward to take my hands in his. "Yes, yes, it is. But if I have seen this prophecy, what makes you think Abaddon doesn't have a witch in his army that can see what I see? Whether you like it or not, he is coming for you. You may be skilled, but you cannot run from him, and even if you could, your friends cannot. Vork, the headmistress, the other nephilims, will all be at the mercy of a tyrant, and you could put a stop to it before any of them were hurt." He squeezed my hands slightly. "You are the daughter of light. Your destiny is intertwined. Take control of yours and put an end to Abaddon."

Many people had attempted to coax me into free services.

Please, don't kill me.

I implore you, save my brother from the soldiers.

Have mercy on us.

Do the right thing.

None of those pleas ever mattered to me. This one shouldn't matter either, but it did, and I hated it with every fiber of my being.

I pulled out from Katar's grasp and stomped away. Pushing the heels of my palms into my eyes, I listened to the sound of my breath.

A sigh of aggravation came from Silas. "We don't—"

"Shut up," Vork snapped.

The words from the healer played in my mind as I tried to fight the person I had become over the ages.

"I want you to do the right thing when the time comes. Not what is right for you, but what is right for us. Masos and its people."

Why did I have to do what was right for Masos? I hated myself for suddenly caring about all this. Even though I had been trained to kill and steal, I didn't think I had it in me to let thousands of people die because of my neglect. Not when I could have done something about it.

I felt his warmth before I heard him. Vork stood silently at my side, waiting for me to break it.

"I'm not sure what to do." I pulled my hands from my eyes and steadied myself from the stars in my vision. "A few hours ago, I was just trying to make it back to the academy, and now I'm told I'm a part of a prophecy and meant to save the continent. I didn't ask for this."

"You don't have to do anything you don't want to," Vork said sternly. "Prophecy be damned. You are not just this Unburnt Nephilim. You're Amara. You're your own person and you get to make your own destiny and live your life the way you choose. Don't allow a leader of misfits and a high priest to tell you who you are. You've lived by a code you've chosen to accept. If this prophecy is fulfilled, you will do it because you want to. Not because some old men told you it must be followed."

"Do your people believe in prophecies?"

He nodded.

"It's deeply rooted in our beliefs. Though they aren't as aggressive as the one they just sprung on you." Vork turned to me and placed a hand on the back of my neck, not pulling me to him, but to show he was there with me. "If you're afraid, don't be. You have support."

"We shared one night, and now you're willing to jump into battle with me?"

"Angel, the first time I met you in that damp, dark prison, I knew I would follow you wherever you needed me to go."

It hurt—the feeling brewing inside of me. My heart was pounding so loudly against my chest that if he weren't as close, I wouldn't even be able to hear his words.

He gently placed his forehead against mine, and guilt flooded my senses. It would consume me if I didn't do what I could. I could tell. It was already beginning.

I pulled back from Vork and looked at the witch and the rebel.

"What exactly do you need from me?"

CHAPTER 18

Silas left as dawn was about to break, but not before giving me the coin he was fiddling with. It was an invitation to his home on the Mahlar Isle, where the rebellion lived. If I was smart, I would sell that information to the Clergy and use the money to ferry off this continent, but recently my conscience had been getting in the way.

Silas explained when I was ready to come to the Cliffs of Dua on the easternmost side of Ekros and his people would bring me to him if I presented the coin. There, he would bring me into the fold of his plan, and preparations would begin.

I was so tired. All I wanted was to sleep in a bed I knew well and see my friend, so I could ensure her safety.

Did they get her to a healer in time? Please, gods, still be alive.

I held my palm out to Katar shortly after Silas left.

"Remove it. Now."

He gently moved his fingers over my palm, and the mark evaporated. I balled it into a fist.

"Don't ever pull me into anything like that again. Despite my newfound lineage, I'm a trained killer first, and I don't like being backed into a corner."

"It is almost dawn." He ignored my threat, or more so, promise. Cheeky witch. "I should transport you back home, yes?"

"Yes." Finally, the only thing I truly came here for, yet I somehow came out on the other side fighting with the Defiants.

"Have you ever tried portaling yourself?"

"I—no, I haven't. What do you know of that power?"

"I'm sure you were told I had the gift of sight." Indeed, the woman from Glin had mentioned it. "I saw you would portal yourself to the Ekros coast. Seeing how surprised you are by my knowledge of your power, it's safe to assume you didn't intend to transport yourselves there. Why didn't you try to portal home?"

"Because I don't know how."

"But you have not tried, so how would you know?"

My eyes were trained on Vork. I could see he wanted to scold me for not even trying to get us out of our current situation, but I didn't know where to begin. Perhaps he didn't say anything because he understood that.

"It is quite simple. Envision the place you wish to be portaled and it will appear. However, you must give it all your attention. If you muddle your mind too much, then it will not work."

"Is it that simple?"

"Dear girl, you are Michael's daughter. You have immense power; all you need to do is believe in that power. You can do great things if you do not fight who you are."

"Try it," Vork said. "The worst that can happen is that it doesn't work."

"But how did I get us to the coast? I'd never been there before."

"I never said you had to." Katar laced his hands together behind his back. "I said to envision where you wanted to go. If you had a location explained to you in detail, you could travel there."

I learned about Ekros only from Leena. She had told me about her family's holidays there and what she had read about the territory.

Odd that was enough at the time, but it had sounded like a beautiful land that I wanted to visit someday. Maybe that's why I thought of it at the time of the attack. Being there sounded better than a burning barn.

I reluctantly held up my hands, looking at Katar. He nodded in encouragement, and I focused. The first thing that popped into my mind was the oak tree in the academy's courtyard. By this time, there probably wouldn't be many leaves on its branches in the dead of winter. Though it still would be a sight. The grand look of it from behind the aged iron gates just outside, looking in towards it.

There was a slight pull on my fingers, willing the magic within me to produce as I instructed. The space in front of my fingertips beamed and rippled into a rainbow of colors about the size of my fist. The pull traveled up my arms till they tingled, and the portal expanded to about my height.

On the other side, the oak tree of the academy stood tall, just behind the gates. I lowered my hands, my mouth parting in awe.

This entire time, I could have portaled us to safety. Before, I wouldn't have felt any regret about it. I had wanted to stay far away from my other half and the powers it came with. But now, shame bubbled in my gut at the thought of the pain I could've prevented for Vork and myself.

Katar's lips curved in a satisfied smile.

"To close the portal, take the power you hold in your hand and will it to do so."

"Why does something so powerful come so easily to witches like you?" I asked.

"I know I do not look it, but I am one hundred and thirty-five ages old. Learning how to properly portal has taken me about three-fourths of my life. It is not easy to do for those who don't have the power naturally, but when you have the amount of raw power you do... well, you won't need most of your life to learn it."

Katar bid us farewell and returned to the camp. I stared into the portal.

"Vork—"

"You have made no promises to me," he said quickly.

He came up behind and traced his fingers down my arm, causing bumps to appear in their wake. "The night we shared was beyond words, but as painful as it is to admit, you did not fully give yourself to me. You are not bound by any contract."

It hurt a little.

He was right. The night we had shared could not be labeled by anything in the common tongue. I wanted more of it, but not if it meant giving up my freedom or taking on the duties that would be expected of me if I did. It made me glad he understood that. He understood me.

Maybe that's why I hadn't even attempted to open a portal. If I had, then it would mean to some degree, I had accepted the part of who I was that I didn't want to know at all. Now, I was being pulled into a war after these new emotions flooded me, and if I gave myself fully to Vork, then the part of myself I knew so well would begin to disappear, and I needed to hold onto her.

Vork's hand strayed down to mine.

"Ready when you are."

I took a breath and pulled him into the portal with me. Snow crunched under our boots as we crossed the line, and within seconds, we were swarmed by the witches and warriors tasked with protecting the grounds.

"State your name and business," one of the warriors asked, a hand ready on the hilt of his sword.

I turned to extend my hand and slowly closed it, which in turn closed the portal behind us.

"Amara Cohen. I'm a student of the school."

The warrior seemed fairly unimpressed.

"Students aren't supposed to be outside the gates at this hour, especially after the attack. You'll be sent straight to the headmistress."

I felt bodies coming at my back, and I turned my head.

"We will need to take the swords," he demanded.

"Put a finger on them, and I'll make sure they're the first thing I take off."

They stopped in their tracks and retreating back to their original positions.

We followed two warriors into the grounds with a witch trailing our rear. They were most definitely new. Though I could tell the academy had trained them well, I could see they were hesitant about bringing us in. If we were, in fact, who we said we were and they treated us in any way that was not respectful, then Diana would certainly have something to say.

We took turns down familiar hallways until we were at Diana's office. The warrior unlocked the door and held it open as we strolled in.

"Please wait here while we get the headmistress."

Vork sighed as he sank into one of the leather chairs. I paced around her office, too antsy to sit. My eyes trailed over the desk, all the paperwork stacked on one side and the rest neat as could be.

"I remember," Vork said, "you trying to stab me with a letter opener."

"Yes, I did, didn't I?" I held my pointer finger and thumb close together. "I was this close, too. What a shame that would've been. Wouldn't want to go and mess up that pretty face."

His eyes darkened, and he rubbed his bottom lip with his middle finger, a haunting smirk starting to emerge. Slouching further into the chair, his deep, husky voice vibrated against my ears. "Come here."

I took slow calculated steps forward, our gazes never diverting. A rush of excitement surged through my body and all the blood rushed down to my abdomen, burning like a furnace.

When I made it to him, I put my knee between his legs and leaned in, making him sit back in his chair. I took his jaw in my hand and skated my lips around the edge of his. His hand came up on my hip, his middle finger tracing circles.

"You," Vork breathed out, "are going to be a lot of trouble, aren't you?"

I forced his head to turn, trailed up to his ear, giving light kisses along the way, and nibbled the lobe.

"Fuck, you're going to be so much trouble."

Before we could sink into the feeling of each other, he cleared his throat. "We have company."

I pulled away and leaned back against Diana's desk just in time for her to open the door and exclaim, "Where the hell have you been? Are you alright?"

I snickered.

"Nice to see you too, Diana." She strutted over to me with impressive speed and hugged me tightly. I struggled to get out my next words. "Yes, we're fine. We just got a little sidetracked."

She gave me a once-over and raised a brow at my scars and lack of fingers. "By the Divine, Amara, what happened?"

"Apparently, I can portal, and I accidentally transported us to the Ekros coast," I stated, ignoring her gesture to my hand. "Everything is fine. We didn't run into any demons, and I was able to get us back."

"How? You can control your power already?"

"I had some help from a High Priest of the Farkath Coven."

"I need you to tell me—"

"Is Leena alive?"

Her face softened a bit. "She's fine. She's resting in her room."

I made for the door, but when I crossed by her, she took hold of my upper arm, causing me to pause.

"I need to know what happened."

"And I need to see Leena. I just told you what happened. Nothing more and nothing less."

Skepticism oozed out of her pores.

"Let me go, Diana."

She did instantly, and I rushed out of the room towards the Hold.

Walking through the intricate hallways, I began thinking about Silas, his request, and this Abaddon character. What did I have that he wanted? The puzzle pieces were there, but I couldn't put anything together.

On top of that, I was battling the feelings I had for the lycan I left in Diana's care. By the gods, what else could possibly be added to my life right now?

I shook away the thoughts as I came to Leena's door and knocked, pushing it open after a faint, "Come in." Leena was lying on her back with a rag over her eyes, which she moved once I stepped inside.

My heart dropped to the lowest pit of my stomach. She didn't look to be too banged up, but she was in pain.

"Amara!" Leena smiled at me and got out of bed as fast as her injuries would allow, pulling me into a tight hug. "You smell awful."

"Like a dog?"

Leena scrunched up her nose. "Among other things. Care to explain?"

I did. I told her everything that had happened, including the encounter with Silas and Katar. And I didn't leave out the bit about Vork. She's the only person I could trust with the truth.

Leena sat upright in her chair, sipping the tea I had made for her while I told her about my adventure.

"I had a feeling this enemy's front you were parading around wouldn't last long," she jested, looking at me from the cup's rim. "I could tell."

"Tell what?"

"That you were meant for each other."

I barked a laugh as I stretched out in her bedside chair and folded my hands on my stomach. "I think that's a bit of a stretch. I find him attractive, and he knows his way around a woman's body. I'm not going to pass up an opportunity like that, and we have an understanding."

"So, he's not pushing marriage?"

"Quite the opposite."

"Hmm," she hummed, not convinced. "I don't think he's given up."

"Leena, stop."

Of course she didn't.

"He wants you to want him the same way he wants you. He's waiting for you to believe it's a good match in its own right, not just for the sake of fulfilling the Clergy's wishes."

"Did you not hear the other part of my story? There's too much going on to even think about marriage. Besides, it's not what I want."

There was a moment of silence, and Leena gave me a look of such emotion, I broke eye contact.

In a fragile voice, she said, "I just want you to be happy. You've been through so much—too much—and I've seen what this world has done to you."

"I'm not sure I can do that to you."

"I don't know what you mean."

"Finn." I dared to speak his name, and it pained my heart to bring up something hurtful. But I was proving a point. "You lost him under horrible circumstances, and I couldn't stand to showcase a relationship in front of you knowing the pain you still carry after all these years."

"As much as I loved—" Leena took a huge gulp of air "—Finn, that doesn't affect you. Honestly, you holding back to gain happiness, on the chance to have what Finn and I did, angers me to no end. I'd be pissed if you stopped yourself from this because you want to spare my feelings. Don't you ever do that."

I held my hands up in defense and smiled. "No promises."

She rolled her eyes. "So, you can portal. Show me."

"I'm not sure I can. I feel very weak after doing it to get us back here, and I'm tired. I can show you another time."

"I can draw up a bath," she offered. "You're starting to smell up my room, but I don't want you to leave. We still have much to talk about."

I ended up drawing a bath for myself. Her flinching every other step she took was unnecessary; she needed rest.

When the bath was full, I sank into it and sighed as the water melted my whole body. Leena scooted the chair to my side and propped her feet on the tub.

"So, Silas," she sighed as she got comfortable. "Do you believe him?"

"I can't imagine why he'd weave a lie so intricate, especially with a high priest on his side. It's too messy. Too many moving pieces."

"He could just want you to be on his side for the war. This could be him trying to convince you his plan is legit. In all my ages and tutors, I've never heard of a person named Abaddon."

"I would be lying if I said I was completely confident in his story and myself, but—" *But for the first time in my life, I feel like I have this purpose to do good, to be good. I'm being pulled to do the right thing, and I want to.* "—It wouldn't be the worst thing to keep an eye on the action while I sit on the sidelines. At least until I know which side I'm on."

"Wow, you picking sides? Who would've guessed?"

I splashed her.

"I never said there were only two. I have my side as well."

She smirked, wiping the water off. "And your plans to leave?"

"I'm almost there. About two more well-paying jobs, then I can secure a boat out with some left over to get me started."

"What will you do there?"

I hadn't thought of that. I had been a thief and assassin all my life. I didn't know how to do anything else.

"I would have a garden," Leena went on, dreaming aloud. "My father had one when I was younger, and I used to help him tend to it every day. At first, I hated it. The dirt, the constant heat of the sun bearing down on us, and, by the divine, the bees that would buzz around his flowers would try to sting me every chance they got, I swear."

We chuckled.

I could imagine little Leena running for her life from some bees.

"But over time, I began to enjoy my time with him. My skin began to brown as much as it could, and once those bees learned I wasn't there for their flowers but for the vegetables growing next to them, they left me alone. I later found myself planting my own little square of flowers my father let me take care of all on my own." At this point, she was staring off into space, really trying to relive the life she had before. "If I could garden, I'd have flowers of all colors. Pinks, yellows, oranges, reds —oh, blues especially. The Divine, I love blue Delphiniums. I think I'd have a whole horde of them."

I scrubbed the dirt from under my fingernails and grabbed the sponge at the bottom of the tub. "Why don't you do it now? You have classes and training, but I'm sure there's enough time for you to have a small garden up here."

"Perhaps." The smile she gave me was less than convincing. "Later. But right now, there's too much to be done."

"Done?" I furrowed my brows. "Is there an extra class you're taking I don't know about? Or... a boy perhaps?"

"No," she sang out. "No boy and no extra class. It's just busy right now."

I didn't press anymore.

"Back to this Silas guy," Leena said. "What's the next step?"

"I haven't thought that far ahead."

"Are you going to meet him?"

I sighed. "I said I don't know, Leena."

"Sorry, sorry, it's just far."

"I never said where the meeting point was."

"Oh. Well, I assumed since you were over in Ekros, that's where he wanted to meet."

I continued to scrub away the days of filth, and we made small talk about the time we had missed. I explained my loss of fingers, she told me of her extensive healing process, and we laughed in between with jokes.

It felt good to be home, not the academy or the Hold, but with her. Home was wherever your happiness was, and Leena was mine.

CHAPTER 19

Later that night, I sat down with the others for dinner. I didn't tell them everything I had told Leena, and they didn't pry for more information. I was especially appreciative of Dasyra, who took the attention off me once she started talking about the raid.

Though I noted she was a bit paler than usual. Dark circles hovered under her eyes, and her lips slightly chapped. Her cup of wine hadn't been touched, and she hardly spoke until now.

We all sat in a dining room, minus Diana and Vork, finishing our food and lazily sipping our leftover wine.

"We did find something interesting about the sword the hellhound was protecting," Corym said as he slouched back in his chair at the head of the table, looking at me. "It wasn't Lucifer's blade. Though, we think we figured out how they're replicating luxium."

Adding to my list of interesting events early, I see.

"My contact was able to deconstruct the sword back to its raw form," Dasyra continued. "When they did, they saw it was composed of two main substances. Iron ore and a liquid."

I frowned. Liquid in a sword?

"The liquid was white, almost like a bright light. They thought the material was angel's grace."

"Has anyone ever seen angel's grace before?" I asked.

"Not that I'm aware of," Dasyra said.

"Then what proof does this contact have that it is what they say it is?"

She clenched her jaw. "I can guarantee you the contact is reliable."

"Then wouldn't it be easier to have the contact come here to explain this to us?"

Fire brewed behind her eyes, her hand tightening into a fist. "I hope you aren't insinuating my trust in my contact is misplaced, because if so, you're disrespecting the hell out of me."

"Easy, D," Leena jumped in with a gentle smile. "This just seems like a big accusation, and I don't think Amara wants anything to come back to bite us in the ass because we have no proof."

"I'm telling you," Dasyra pressed and blinked slowly. "The contact is sound, and the finding is legit."

"Fine, it's angel's grace," I agreed. "I believe you, but what good will this information do if we can't prove it? Diana will need some evidence, or all she'll see is melted iron and whatever the grace is made of."

"We aren't going to tell Vocova," Corym said, standing and looking at the bookcase behind him. "She doesn't know about the raids, so she can't know about this."

I rolled my eyes. "What do you plan to do then?"

His eyes jumped between me and Leena, and she shook her head. "Corym, she just got back."

"We don't have time to do this gently, Leena."

"What's the difference between today and holding out a little longer?" Luca asked, actual worry on his face.

Corym's stern face turned to his brother, a crease forming between his brows. "Hundreds dead. Thousands, if you want me to be completely honest. We don't. Have. Time."

"What's going on?" I said before they could start another conversation without me in it.

They all looked conflicted, except for Corym, that is. So, it wasn't just Leena holding onto a secret. And I had a feeling they were all holding onto the same thing.

"Am I or am I not a part of this team?" I asked.

"Of course you are!" Leena leaned over and placed her hand on mine. "You are, and we all know that. It's just…"

I pulled my hand away from her. "Seriously, Leena? Keeping secrets from *me*?"

There was a knock at the door, and a maid walked in. She curtsied and spoke quietly. "The Headmistress requests your presence in her office *immediately*. All of you."

"What's the hurry?" Dasyra asked.

"Clergyman Marcellus is here."

Not once in all my ages had the Clergyman made the trek through the mountains to get to the academy. From my understanding, he was in constant contact with Diana, but he never showed his face.

I couldn't care less about the Clergy. They had done nothing good for me, and what was brewing across the continent was evidence they weren't doing anything for its people either.

So, when we all filed into Diana's office and Clergyman Marcellus was sitting in her chair, it took all my willpower not to snarl in disgust.

Diana was standing to his right, and Vork to his left. Vork's jaw was slightly clenched, his right foot tapping occasionally.

Everyone gave a slight bow with a hand over their chest before taking their seats. I took mine as far away as possible, but it didn't go unnoticed. The clergyman raised a brow at my defiance, and Diana's expression was less than pleased. So, I stood, gave a small bow, then sat back down.

Marcellus wore the customary travel attire for a clergyman. His black robe lay just above his feet, deep red around its edges and a red tree knitted on his breast pocket. A thick red sash hung around his waist, tied in a fancy knot to the side. Countless silver buttons ran down the front of his robe, but the silver did not outshine the luxium bar he paraded around his neck.

How he got that I'll never know.

"Hello, children." His voice was smooth yet utterly irritating. The audacity to call us children. "I have come to bring news from the Emperor. But first, I want to address a rather serious matter."

His eyes scanned the room, and a wave of uneasiness came over me.

"I am aware of your late-night adventures, which will cease immediately." He looked at Corym. "You are their leader, are you not? I expected better. If I hear another rumor of your little group's antics, you all will be under constant supervision of a warrior until you are released from this academy and under the protection of the Holy City. Is that understood?"

The air around us grew cold at the Clergyman's promise. He said *released* as if we were prisoners being kept in a cell until they needed us.

Corym bowed his head in submission.

"Good. Now." Marcellus clapped his hands together. "The Emperor has decided it would be fitting for the nephilim to join us in the Holy City in two days' time for the Winter Solstice Gala. Amidst everything happening, we believe it would do the people some good to see their gifts from the Divine in good standing. And it will be the perfect time to publicly announce the engagement of the future Chief of the Arabrosa pack and Michael's heir."

Anger swept through me at being referred to as *Michael's heir*. I had a name, and I was sure he knew it.

Unfortunately, I had found everyone did.

"Are you aware the academy was attacked not too long ago?" I asked. "And that demons are threatening the school's borders as well as the Arabrosa pack's, yes? So why is the Emperor insistent on having us dress up for a dance?"

To my surprise, I didn't get the reaction I had hoped for from him. Marcellus was calm and collected. He steepled his fingers as his gaze bored into me.

"What will or will not be done with your gifts lies with the Clergy on the Emperor's orders, Ms. Cohen, and you will do well to remember who you are speaking to. I do not need to give details on military plans or discuss the continent's state with you. You are to do as you're told. Am I understood?"

Now, that response didn't surprise me. They were always clinging to power. Even when problems were brought to them directly, they still pushed them away.

True politicians.

"My word is final," Marcellus clipped. "Our warriors will take care of the academy's protection following the unfortunate events. Now, you will all pack your essentials for the trip to the Holy City, and the rest will be provided for you." He stood, and everyone else followed suit. Leaning over to Diana, I heard him say, "Make sure she is in line before she meets the Emperor."

She bowed her head slightly and watched as he walked out. His warrior, who had been standing guard, closed the door behind him.

Diana looked at Corym.

"Honestly, could not have been more discreet?" The venom spewing from her lips made me flinch.

"I thought we were being discreet," he said matter-of-factly. "You didn't know, so how did he?"

"Of course I knew," she scoffed and sat in her chair. "You think, as long as I have been headmistress of this institution, I do not know everything that goes on? I knew of your nightly outings, and I said nothing because you all needed it and were good at it. The continent also needed it. Having fewer demons on this land is a blessing, and the Clergy cannot control all the hordes them by themselves. Your talents will be wasted in the Holy City as trinkets for the crown."

At least that we could agree upon.

"I'll ask again," Corym pushed. "How did he know about the raids?"

Diana rubbed the pads of her fingers together as if to collect the pang of anger I could see coming up from his defiance. The deep, sinister voice she spoke with made me tense.

"Watch your tone, child," she said. "I have done everything to make sure you were not taken to that city earlier than they intended. I let you train as true warriors, which was not what the Clergy wanted, and I tried to cover your tracks when they began to believe you were involved with the raids. So, when you speak to me, it will be with nothing but the respect I am owed."

Corym took note as he nodded in apology.

"He knew because I was cornered with questions regarding Leena's state when you all returned. I have covered many secrets without outwardly lying to the Clergy, but when asked a direct question, I cannot lie. Marcellus was informed of that night *raid*, as you call it, but he does not know of any others. Keep this to yourselves." No one responded, and Diana nodded, satisfied. "Now, please pack your things for the trip. We will leave tomorrow morning."

Everyone began filing out of her office one by one, but before I could follow, she asked me to stay.

I leaned up against the wall, crossing my arms and trying not to look at Vork, who still stood next to Diana.

"I did not know of the clergyman's intentions to announce your engagement. I would have fought against it had I known, though I am not sure it would have done much good. But I would have been able to at least prepare you for it."

"There's no need," I said. "I'm not accepting."

There was a twitch between her brows. "Amara, I do hate to be the one to state the obvious, but this is not a choice. Your marriage to Vork is an order from the crown."

"Now, do you mean the actual crown or the ones wiping the crown's ass with their precious robes?"

No wonder they're black. It's to cover up the shit stains.

That caused Vork to snicker, which gained him a sharp eye from Diana.

"I do not think you understand the situation you are in," she said. "You either go into this marriage willingly—"

"Or I am forced?"

"No," Vork said sternly, then looked at Diana. "She will not be forced."

Diana pinched the bridge of her nose. "By the Divine's power, you both will be the literal end of me. We are out of options. Since you will not marry willingly and plan to refuse the union unless it's entered into willingly, then one, if not both of you, will be imprisoned. And while you, Amara, may be able to sneak out and vanish to another land, Vork does not have that luxury. He has an entire people who depend on him as their leader. And once they hear of his imprisonment, you are foolish to think another war will not come of this. Do you plan to make them suffer because you refuse to marry a man who you do seem to have feelings towards?"

"I—"

"Hush," she bit back, fairly hard. "Ever since I took you in, I have done everything in my power to protect you, to give you the life you deserve, and I had hoped one day you would find your way and no longer wander. Now... now you have a chance for a future, and you would dismiss it for what? Out of sheer defiance just for the sake of it?"

How had this suddenly become all about me? Vork was here, too, but I was the only one refusing the union. He had already accepted.

My hands curled into fists. "I don't understand how a marriage I didn't ask for is considered such an amazing future and deemed to be the only one I can have. What am I to do? Be a dutiful wife and agree to every whim my husband orders?"

Diana stood abruptly, pushing her chair back and almost hitting the wall.

"You would be a leader, you insolent child! You defy the Clergy already by being who you are, but that is not the problem. The issue is your public defiance of them. If you truly want to defy them with a purpose, then wait until you have the power to do so. You are a small nephilim with nothing but the roof of the academy over your head and powers you have yet to fully understand. Play this right, Amara. Be the leader you can be and then use your power to induce change." She stalked toward the exit, then turned around with one last word. "Or at least fake it until you have a real plan, because I can only shield you for so long."

Diana slammed the door behind her.

Vork gave a long whistle.

"Well, that was the most emotion I've seen from her in ages. You really know how to piss people off, don't you?"

I closed my eyes and sighed. "She's right. For all the irritation she brought me in that rant of hers, she's right."

"Hey." He came to me and planted his hand at the base of my neck. "Look at me."

I slowly opened my eyes.

"Don't agree to this union out of guilt."

"I didn't even think of how this would affect you." And part of me was pissed because of it. I grew up thinking the only way to stay alive was to be selfish. There's no need for that now. "The least I could do is show I support this to ensure you and your people don't suffer."

Vork shook his head. "We will be just fine."

"Speaking of, how have you been here all these moons when you're supposed to be ruling your people? Or commanding your army for that matter?"

The tips of his fingers began to slowly massage my scalp, almost making me sink into him.

"My father is still the Chief, and I have a second in command who acts on my behalf while I'm away," he explained. "I was instructed by my father securing your hand was of the utmost importance."

"I wonder why that is."

A dazzling smile appeared as he searched my gaze. "Probably because he wants grandchildren."

His lips relaxed a bit, his eyes still swimming in mine.

"Slow it down there, commander. I said I'd agree to the facade. I said nothing about actually going through with it."

"Still." He pulled me closer. "A man can dream, can't he?"

"Do you know what I dream of?"

"Hmm, tell me."

I dipped in close, brushing my lips against his. "Sleep."

"Oh, angel. You won't be doing much of that."

CHAPTER 20

Vork wasn't kidding about not sleeping. The first half of my night had us tangled in each other until sweat coated our bodies, and we couldn't physically move. I was consumed by the intoxicating smell, taste, and feel of lycan. But that wasn't the only reason I didn't get any rest.

A few hours later, I woke to Vork lying beside me with one arm and one leg hanging off the side of the bed, the other arm covering his eyes. The rest of the night was spent trying to figure out why the Clergy, not the Emperor, wanted us in the Holy City so badly. It was easy to see the crown itself didn't care if we were present at a ball.

That poor family had about as much power as I did, which was hardly any. They were puppets, and everyone knew it. Their control over the continent was slipping away with each passing age as the Clergy made more and more orders on behalf of the Emperor.

That was hardly my problem. At least, that's what I kept telling myself each time I thought about it. My old self, pre-nephilim, would have agreed and moved on, but now I've evolved, and with it has come all these damned emotions. Now, a part of me cared. I cared for Vork, and Diana was right: What would become of him if I didn't play my role?

My plans to get off this continent were starting to feel like a fantasy.

With a huff, I threw off the covers, pulled on my trousers and shirt, and walked across the cold stone floor to the dying fire in the corner. Nothing was left but softly glowing embers. I sat, leaning back against my heels and picked up the smoldering shards of wood.

I grabbed a handful and sighed in relief when they didn't burn. The wood was brittle as I closed my fist around it, but the warmth stayed in my hands.

A small gust of air tickled the back of my neck, and I turned. A man stood just a few feet behind me.

I wasn't afraid and he didn't have to introduce himself, because I already knew him. Something inside me just knew who my father was, even though I had never seen or talked to him.

"Michael."

I turned back to the fire.

"Amara." His voice was deep and soul-crushing. "Are you well?"

I didn't answer.

"Do not worry. Your companion cannot hear us."

"Why are you here?"

His boots thumped against the floor as he walked over to the wall next to the fireplace and sat. My eyes flickered to his, and I got a good look at him.

I could see why he was named the Divine's General. He looked like a man who held an abundance of power. The sureness of his bright blue eyes, the strong yet gentle brow that hovered over them, and the small amount of stubble from a shaven beard lingered lightly, blending in with his ear-length dark blond hair. He smiled at me.

I could also see why he might enamor others. He was a breath of calm and safety in this fucked up world.

"You," he said with a catch in his breath, "are even more beautiful in person." That soft smile never left his face. "Seeing your likeness from the Heavens does not do you justice."

I shifted so I sat fully on the ground and propped my leg up to rest my forearm on my knee. "Thanks. What do you want?"

"I have been following you since your birth. I know of your struggles and victories as the years have passed. I'm now seeing the chaos you're being pulled into, and I only wish to help."

"The only way you could help me is by killing the Clergy so I don't have to participate in this ridiculous party they have planned."

"Yes," he laughed and breathed out all in one. "They are a bit extravagant, aren't they?"

"Unless you can do that, you can be of no help."

"We cannot meddle in your society's affairs."

I ran my tongue over my teeth.

"Do you not see the world right now? Sazari and demons are ravaging the land while a corrupt leadership oversees everything, and you do nothing to stop it. What is your purpose if you can't make an exception when the world is burning?"

"I have seen countless worlds burn." Michael shrugged slightly. "This world is not yet there, but I am here now to help you stop that from happening."

The balls on this man.

"What makes you think I'm going to help you? If anything, I want this world to burn, so I don't have to deal with the shit happening in it."

"If that were true," he said, eyes boring into mine, "then you wouldn't have accepted the Defiants' token."

He really had been watching everything I was doing. I looked away, gritting my teeth. I didn't know what to say to that.

"So, how do you plan to help me, then?" I finally asked.

"You have questions for me."

"You know I do," I deadpanned.

"Then ask."

"Is my mother anyone of importance?"

He hesitated, then said, "Yes."

"And who is she?"

More hesitation. Silence stretched between us. I wanted to see if he could find his words and tell me the truth. Silence had a way of gnawing away at a person if it stayed too long. Eventually, they would spill their secrets.

"Your mother is a dangerous cre—woman. I would not seek her out."

Hardly an answer.

"Is she a part of this war between humans and demons?"

Michael sighed heavily. The way he sat against the wall with his arms propped on his knees made him look like an ordinary man. He had on distressed trousers, a shirt with the top few buttons undone, and boots that looked like they had traveled a few hundred miles.

But I wouldn't be in my current situation if my father were a regular man.

"Truthfully, I haven't seen your mother for quite some time, and I see no evidence of her involvement. However, she must be. The way Abaddon gained so much power so quickly..." He shook his head. "It is not possible he did it on his own."

"You think she's working with Abaddon?"

"I do."

"Fantastic. My mother is working against her child and helping the being who wants to take over Masos."

With those words, suspicion hit me.

Nephilims were the offspring of angels and humans, a taboo, temporary union. If my mother were human, how could she be useful in helping Abaddon to obtain power? It was a dangerous puzzle I was piecing together. Maybe even a longshot.

My mother had to be someone who mattered. A woman whose power was enough to decimate the continent, lead armies, or bring hell's fire through the world like a tsunami. That was the extent of my imagination at the time, but who knew how far her strength could go.

I decided to go out on a limb. Best case scenario, I was wrong. Worst case, I was right.

"Michael," I said with more calm than my wild mind was feeling. "Is Lilith my mother?"

He seemed surprised by my question, as if he hadn't expected me to ask the right one to get a direct answer from him.

He nodded his head slightly, and fear rolled through me.

"Amara, do not—"

"Shut up."

I was frozen.

My father was the angel Michael, and my mother was the Mother of Demons. Was that why I was the way I was? Why most of my life I didn't give a shit about anyone? There were two sides of me, fighting for dominance in one body.

Darkness was brewing beneath my skin while I tried to compensate for it by helping the Defiants. Was this why I never felt like I belonged? I never understood the struggle I had within myself, but now I saw why. I was trying to be good, but the bad could creep up so easily when I allowed it to.

I collected myself and threw daggers at him. "What possessed you to fuck your sworn enemy?"

I didn't know angels could have emotion, but that question looked like it hurt.

Good.

"It was ages ago when Abaddon first attempted to take over the Heavens," he explained. "Our forces easily defeated his, as he did not have many demons on his side at that time. But he did bring his mother. I fought her, and when we did...there was no clear winner. We were in a fit of passion. What happened was such a...a mortal experience. I could not fully understand it in the moment. Lilith was strong and beautiful. So beautiful it somehow only took her a few moments to break me." His gaze moved away from me as shame consumed him. "The only other person who knew what I did that day was Gabriel. He was the one who discovered Lilith was with child. Once she gave birth to you, I took you from Hell and left you in Diana's care."

"I was born in Hell?"

He nodded.

"Why didn't Diana take care of me from birth?"

"She did not know how to be a mother and did what she thought was best. She set you up with a family she believed would be best. I cannot believe she knew what would happen with your *aunt* when she gave you to the guild, but from what I could see, they were more of a family to you."

"Her finding me as a child later on wasn't an accident, was it?"

He shook his head. "I had informed her of your family's tragedy and that's when she placed herself in your path and took you to Clamore."

"I should hate you," I interrupted. "But I don't. What's done is done. We have bigger problems now than my origin. Abaddon may be using angels' grace to create his own luxium-like blades."

Michael clenched his hand into a fist. "Damn it."

"Damn it?"

"Angels with orders that venture outside the Heavens sometimes do not return, and we never knew why until now. They are making luxium blades with angel grace, you said?"

I nodded.

"Luxium like, yes. Or at least that's what one of our nephilims believes. But now, I must worry about the continent and the war between men. Not angels and demons."

"Man is flawed," he sighed, shaking his head.

"Everyone is flawed," I shot back. "Humans are weak, witches have a limit to their magic, nephilim are cursed to be Masos' golden children, and angels... well, they sleep with demons and create halflings. No one is perfect, Michael. Don't think you are above others simply because the Divine is your creator."

He did not respond.

I dropped the burned wood I had held in my hand for the entirety of our conversation. "Abaddon, Lilith's son, his father is Lucifer, right? Where is he in all of this?"

Another heavy sigh left Michael's lips. "I have not been able to find my brother since the beginning of this war."

"The ruler of hell is missing?"

"Ever since Abaddon began spiraling out of control, we've seen less and less of Lucifer. After a while, we were blocked from entering Hell when we attempted to see him."

"You think Abaddon killed his father?"

Michael raised a brow, a hint of a smirk on his lips. "It is impossible to kill my brother."

"From what I've learned, you are not indestructible."

"You misunderstand. Lucifer is the engineer of Hell. He is the foundation of that realm and cannot be killed. Even if there were a way to kill my brother, the whole system would crumble if he died. Besides the Divine, he is the only thing in this world that cannot be killed."

Who thought the angel everyone thought was cast out from the Heavens would be the most powerful of them all?

"What do you think happened to him then?"

"I don't know. That's what worries me."

I leaned back on my palms. "You're worried?"

"As you said, we are not perfect. My brother is... flawed, but he is still my brother, and I care for him. He broke away from us because he had different views on the Divine's world. However, there cannot be good without evil or light without darkness. Believe it or not, Lucifer brings balance to your world, and with Abaddon taking his seat of power, it shows how much we truly need my brother back on his throne."

Something clicked then. "Are you asking me something, Michael?"

He did nothing but look into my eyes.

"You want me to find out what happened to your brother? I didn't realize I was an errand girl."

"You are not."

"Then don't ask me for favors. I just told you I'm being pulled into a war between the humans. I hardly know what I'm doing now. Don't ask me to help you in your war."

His lips pressed into a thin line as he stood and glanced at Vork, still sleeping as if I were in the bed next to him.

"So," Michael said looking over at Vork. "You have a betrothed. The pup of the Arabrosa pack. Vork, yes?"

"I guess word travels fast, even up to the Heavens."

"He's a handsome candidate," Michael observed

"His physical features are not the problem. The Clergy paired us and now expect us to wed just because they say we are a perfect match."

His nose scrunched up in annoyance. "I have heard of these customs."

"Shouldn't you be out finding Lucifer?"

With another tight-lipped smile, he took a step back and developed his wings. "I will talk to you soon, daughter. Please know that if you should ever need me, I am always here."

I internally flinched at the word *daughter.*

There was a gust of wind, and Michael was gone. A moment later, Vork sat up and rubbed his eyes.

"What are you doing down there? You must be freezing."

"I don't seem to get cold."

"Be that as it may." He pulled down the covers and patted the mattress. "Come back to bed, because I do."

I got up and shed my clothing before joining him. "I thought lycans had fairly high temperatures."

Once I was settled, he pulled me close so my back was pressed to his *warm* chest. I relaxed and let his hold grow firm as he kissed the back of my head.

"You're right. I lied. Now, go back to sleep."

I smiled and let sleep take over.

CHAPTER 21

The carriages provided for our journey to the Holy City, courtesy of the Emperor, were of impeccable quality. They were spacious enough to comfortably house over six people, though not tall enough to stand. The cushions were made of the finest dark red velvet, and the same material framed the two windows on either side of the carriage, partially blocking the morning sun.

Marcellus, who was in the front carriage along with Corym, Luca, and Diana, had brought ten armed warriors with him to Clamore. They followed behind his carriage on horseback. Vork was among them.

I envied him. I didn't want to be in this stuffy, lavish box. I knew how to ride a horse, but Marcellus had refused my request, saying, *"It is not proper for someone of your stature to ride while there are warriors present who are completely capable of ensuring your safety."*

I kept my mouth shut and said no more on the subject. I knew others could be affected by my actions. The Clergy held a dangerous power, and I had to play by their rules—for now.

Unfortunately, those rules included sitting in a carriage with Dasyra, Leena, and two maids while we were dressed up like we were going straight to the gala.

We had all been forced into heavy, velvet-like dresses and corsets so tight they seemed to rearrange our organs. The dress itself had to have added at least ten pounds to our weight, and if we were caught in a fight, it would have definitely gotten in the way, and we couldn't have that. So, we made minor adjustments, swapping out our low heels for boots and pulling on a pair of trousers under our skirts.

The maids helping us to pack and dress had grimaced at this.

For the first half of the day, the maids tried their hardest to converse with us, but all they seemed to want to talk about was the eligible warriors who walked about the Holy City looking for a bride. Neither of us had any interest in this talk, but it was amusing to watch it unfold.

"Honestly, Kaben is the best choice," the brunette went on. "His family is so wealthy they own land *inside* the Holy City."

The second maid gasped.

"How could they own land inside? It belongs to the Clergy! Oh, what power they must hold. Do you think the Emperor had any say in it?"

"I bet he did. The Clergy have power, but the Emperor is just that, the Emperor. I couldn't imagine them doing anything without his permission."

"I can't wait to see him." The second maid fanned herself. "We must make sure we all look proper for this gala."

"Of course! Oh, so I had an idea for my hair. If I just—"

"Will you two shut the hell up?" Dasyra leaned forward over her knees, pushing her hands through her hair.

The two maids' mouths clamped shut, their eyes wide.

"For the entire day, all you two have been talking about are men. No, not men— boys. Boys who probably don't deserve to touch any woman on Masos. You've been chattering incessantly about what families will wear, who will be our matches, what gossip you've heard in the Clergy's halls, and now, I am this close to throwing you both out of this carriage so you can walk with the horses!"

I suppressed a chuckle, and Leena tried to hush Dasyra's outburst.

"D, how else are they going to pass the time?" she asked softly.

"Maybe sleeping?" She shouted as she sat back in her seat. "Servants can't get much sleep, so why not use this time to do that? If I hear one more peep out of either of you about this damn gala, I'm going to shove my foot so far down—"

"All right," Leena cut her off. "I think they understand."

With a huff, Dasyra crossed her hands over her chest and looked out the window.

I did the same and caught a glimpse of Vork on his horse. One hand was placed on the horn, the other on his thigh. He was conversing with another warrior who rode beside him, laughing at whatever he said.

A tickle rummaged through my stomach at the sound.

Vork shifted on his saddle, and his leg muscles flexed in response. God, he even looked powerful from behind, and I was stuck in this carriage in a ridiculous dress when all I wanted was to be the horse under him.

A lump in my throat formed.

I tore my gaze from his backside and looked past him through the trees. It was a sunny, cool day. Not a cloud in the sky, but one couldn't tell that from the forest we were currently riding through.

Despite the thick dress and the warmth of the carriage, a chill came over my skin, causing bumps to form.

Something was wrong.

"Stop the carriage," I yelled, but no one responded. I opened the door and stuck my body out. "Stop the carriage!"

The warriors in the front obeyed and came to a halt, causing everyone else to do the same.

Marcellus poked his head out the door. "What is the meaning of this?"

"A moment."

Marcellus gripped the door in annoyance. He was being handled by a nephilim around his own warriors. It made him seem incapable of keeping those below him in check. If he wanted to live, he'd have to get used to it.

"What is it? We have a half day's ride left."

I jumped out of the carriage and stared into the woods.

Vork motioned his horse and halted in front of me. "What do you see?"

"Nothing," I said. "I can't see anything, but I have a feeling."

"A feeling?"

"Something is following us."

"You have a feeling something is following us." He deadpanned, leaning on the horn of the saddle.

"That's what I said," I gritted out.

"And how do you know if you can't see anything?"

"I told you, a feeling."

"A feeling."

"A feeling," I repeated, more irritated.

Vork sighed and pinched the skin between his eyes. "You stopped this whole caravan because you felt something was following us."

"Look," I shot at him while glaring. "Maybe if you were better at being a warrior and not fooling about, then you would have noticed this miles ago."

"There is nothing there, Amara."

"Don't be condescending. I'm telling you something is out there."

Another warrior galloped up beside Vork.

"What's the problem?"

"She believes we are being followed."

Hunted would be more appropriate.

The warrior looked out, then back at us.

"Well, they haven't attacked, and we still have much ground to cover. We will deal with the threat, if there is one, when necessary." He looked down at me. "Unlike you, we have been trained to protect, so I suggest you get back in the carriage before you ruffle your skirts."

The warrior turned his horse around before I could get another word in.

"Please get back in the carriage," Vork pleaded.

I huffed through my nostrils and took a step in. "I hate this."

"I know. But it's only for a few days and then we'll be back at Clamore."

That didn't make me feel any better.

"Lieutenant," Marcellus addressed the man I had just spoken with. "As you were."

He bowed his head slightly and motioned his horse forward. "Let's move out!"

The Clergyman's carriage rolled forward, crunching the rocks as it went, until a warrior at the back of the caravan screamed, and everything stopped again.

He had fallen off his horse and was absent his arms. He wriggled in the dirt, and within his screams, he shouted a word that stole my breath.

"Sazari!"

The remaining soldiers drew their weapons. There was no other noise but the man's screams. The air grew stale and cold, just as before.

I'd barely made it into the carriage when the terror stopped me. There I was in a dress with no weapons, and sazari were tracking us. Only a fool wouldn't fear those damned things.

"We need to move," Vork ordered the lieutenant. "*Now!*"

It was already too late. A pack of sazari attacked from each side, pushing in. One of them locked their sights on me, leaping forward.

I grabbed the door's knob and slammed it shut as I flung myself into the carriage. The sazari pushed it onto two wheels, causing us to teeter back and forth.

The two maids held onto each other, crying.

"We're going to die," one of them sobbed.

Dasyra rolled her eyes, dug into her seat, and pulled out a rolled-up piece of leather. She unraveled it, revealing three long daggers.

"You sneak!" Leena exclaimed as she took one and handed another to me.

Gods bless her. Our luxium was packed with the rest of the luggage, but leave it to Dasyra to be prepared.

I wasted no time in cutting the skirt of my dress up to my hips, revealing the boots and trousers underneath.

Dasyra followed suit, but Leena stayed still.

"I'm going to stay here," she said. "I'm still pretty weak and will only be a liability." Her head tilted towards the maids. "I'll protect them."

Dasyra and I nodded in agreement, went out on separate sides, and joined the fight.

The remaining warriors flanked the Clergyman's carriage, all besides Vork, who stood closely by ours.

His sword slashed through every sazari that came his way, but I couldn't let him have all the fun.

A creature came up behind him as he was fighting off another, and I threw the dagger at the back of its skull. I picked up a fallen warrior's sword with my right hand and retrieved the dagger with my other.

"Don't say it," Vork growled as he pushed the monster off his sword.

"You—"

"Don't."

A sazari came up to my right, and I slashed the sword down. "Should have—"

"Amara," he groaned, dodging his own opponent.

"Listened to me."

We were back-to-back now.

"Are you done?"

I smirked and pushed off him.

There were two humans who had turned sazari standing in front of me. Drool fell from their uneven mouth, and blood dripped from their claws. The woman screamed and ran as she slashed her claws left and right, barely missing my skin. I went to bring the sword up, but she knocked it out of my grasp, bringing her claws down on my stomach.

She flung me back against the carriage, and the world started to spin. Lights danced in my vision as I checked where she hit me. The luxurious velvet of my dress was shredded, leaving the corset exposed but without damage.

"Guess it's not completely useless." I ripped off the rest of the dress, and the sazari lunged again. I side-swiped her and plunged the dagger into her neck.

Another stepped to start an attack but was met with an arrow between its eyes.

The lieutenant stood yards away, a bow in hand. He quickly nodded before jumping into the driver's seat of the ccergyman's carriage and taking off.

I hadn't seen Corym or Luca in the fight, so I assumed they were still in the carriage. Marcellus' orders, no doubt.

Vork followed the lieutenant's lead and jumped onto the second carriage's driver's seat. "Get in!"

"Dasyra?"

"She's inside. Now let's move!"

The sazari shrieked and growled behind us. There were hundreds of them, maybe even thousands. I couldn't tell. I could only see what the forest allowed me to see.

The noises from the sazari frightened the horses, and the carriage took off without me. I pushed my legs as fast as they would go, trying to catch up.

I got to the back end of the carriage and hopped onto the bottom ledge. On the way, I had swiped up a bow and a group of arrows from a dead soldier. A moment later there was a growl too close to my ears, and that's when I saw a hellhound just below.

"Good boy?"

It snapped as it lunged, barely missing my heels.

Fucking hell.

Wrapping the bow around my back, I threw the arrows on the carriage's top and breathed. I peered over my shoulder, waiting for the exact moment I needed.

The hound leaped again and I struck. I hoisted a leg up and kicked at the dog, giving me the power I needed to throw the leg over and swing onto the top. With bow and arrow in hand, I drew quickly and released, hitting the hound between the eyes.

My heart was hammering against my chest, almost bursting from the adrenaline.

"Are you with me?" Vork yelled from up front.

"Yes! Try and keep it steady."

I shot the arrows at the sazari that were getting too close, but I would run out soon, and I didn't have a plan after that. What else was there to do? The horses could only go so fast while pulling a carriage full of people, and there was an army of sazari behind us.

I frantically looked around for a way out of this mess, but I was only met with a more terrifying sight.

Abe— or Abaddon rather.

He was flying towards us, a cloud of smoke coming from his pale wings. His eyes were glowing with rage. He bared his teeth as he got closer, and I unloaded my last few arrows on him.

He dodged every single one as he charged, throwing me back against the roof once he got close. My head landed with an aggressive thud.

"Dear sister," Abaddon hissed in my face. "Did you think I wouldn't find you? That you were untouchable?"

I struggled under his weight, and a hearty laugh rumbled from his chest.

"This is your only chance to join me willingly."

I grabbed hold of his wrists, trying to pull his hands from my throat.

The fire, the power I knew was always within me, began to rise back to the surface. I had been so afraid of it before, afraid of who I might hurt in its wake, but that's what I was counting on now. My palms began to heat, emitting a small glow.

He laughed again. "Fire cannot hurt me."

"I'm not trying to hurt you."

There was a split second of confusion, then Vork sent a fist to his face, and Abaddon flew off the back, tumbling into the horde of beasts and disappearing.

"Who the hell is that?"

Ignoring his question, I took a deep breath, knowing what I had to do. I hadn't tried this since the sazari's attack at the academy, but there was no other choice.

I leaned on my knees, summoning the power again. Slowly, embers poured from my hands, and fire soon followed. It was as easy as hitting a target with my blade.

The fire was part of me.

It was me.

With a big huff, I unleashed the power onto the army of sazari, and they burned.

They *melted,* and I smiled as the heat hit my face.

That warmth, that power was... intoxicating.

The growls turned into pained whines as the army slowed and began to retreat into the forest. When I lowered my hands, the fire had already spread, and we had made it past the clearing, out of the forest. The flames flooding the tree line shimmered angry shades of red and orange as a body stepped out of the chaos.

I pushed the hair out of my face and saw the picture clearer. Abaddon was standing on the forest's edge, his wings gone. We were too far to make out his face, but I knew he was enraged at their defeat.

His hands were clenched at his sides, and he threw his head back, letting out a roar that would have shaken the mountains if we were close enough.

"That," I said to Vork, "was my brother."

CHAPTER 22

Vork hated the Holy City. The aura around him changed drastically when we saw the city on the horizon.

The sounds of city's hustle became clear as we got closer, making me envision what it looked like inside. I bet plenty of merchants were at their stalls selling fine jewelry, food, and otherworldly possessions available nowhere else. Children might even be playing among the adults trying to conduct business. It would be a nice reprieve from the war we've faced these past few weeks. To see genuine happiness on faces might even convince me our sacrifices, my sacrifices, were worth it.

As we approached, I got a better look at the wall protecting the Holy City's borders on the east side. It stood hundreds of feet above one's head, and there was only one way in and one way out, the solid iron gate in the front.

The city was inhabited only by those of high status. The Clergy did not allow slums to form, and those who didn't hold a high status tended to find work as merchants across the continent. Any humans found in the market streets were typically handmaidens to the fae who held office.

When the carriages pushed through the gates, there were small crowds gathered to welcome us. Marcellus opened his window and waved to his people.

I sat next to Vork in the driver's seat, my hands tightly wrapped around the cloak he had gifted me earlier.

He had not asked me to elaborate on the news I had shared. When I had moved to sit next to him for the duration of the ride, he kept silent. There was a chance the flood of sazari and Abaddon's attack had shaken me up, or maybe it was I didn't know how to explain fully.

I didn't know where to begin, because I didn't even have the whole story. I assumed he didn't press for answers, so I wouldn't pull away. On some level, I had begun to open up, and I could see where he could believe he would jeopardize that if he asked questions I didn't want to answer.

My mind wandered to Abaddon for a moment during our ride. He had a demon mother and an angelic father just like I did. Then I recalled his wings.

They were terrifying. The tips had claws that were angled to a point. The membrane almost looked cracked and tattered from battles, no doubt.

Would I gain wings too? Would they look like his? Did I already have them, and I just didn't know how to use them?

I couldn't speculate anymore because our carriage stopped at the inner circle of the city. This gate was the most heavily guarded, as it was the entrance to the Clergy's dwelling, the Emperor's palace, and the Divine's temple.

The heavy iron gate clanked. Three thick bars slid to the side as it unlocked, and the guards let us pass. On the other side was a long, white aisle leading to the building we were headed to.

While we were still far, I had to strain my neck to take it all in. It was dreadfully beautiful.

The structure was not as crisp as the white gracing every other building in the city, but that was due to its age. The limestone color took no awe from the building, because it stood greater than anything else.

The estate sat on two hundred acres of land with gardens and a small forest in the backyard. The main building, the palace, known as Elmira, had multiple columns with spires at the top that were staggered throughout the structure. Pointed arches connected each sizable part through an outdoor walkway

To the east was an enormous tower standing above them all, which housed the temple for the Divine. There was a picture within the stained glass of the tower, clear as day for all to see. A tree engrossed in a vibrant orange fire glistened in the sun.

"Impressed?"

I glanced at Vork's stoic expression. "You aren't?"

He shrugged. "I've been here more times than I care to remember."

"I'm not thrilled to be here either, but you must admit it's a sight to see."

Vork shifted his gaze to me, eyes soft. "I've seen better."

I turned my head to look at the tower, but it was simply to hide a small smile and possible blush from him. He made me blush. Who was I becoming?

We approached the front doors of the Elmira, and Vork pulled the reins to stop the carriage.

"Tell you what," he sighed, resting his forearms on his knees. "You tell me who Abaddon is to you, and I'll tell you my history with this place. A little give and take. Think of it like a game."

He hopped off the seat and walked to the other side of the carriage, opening the door before holding his hand out.

I took it and stepped down. "Games are for children."

He smirked, and his eyes gleamed. "Not all."

Before I could respond, a female servant stood before us, a smile plastered on her face.

"Hello, welcome to the Holy City. My name is Eira, and I will be your lady in waiting during your stay here."

Eira was dressed in a grey linen dress that ended just above her ankles and had long sleeves that extended past her wrists. Black hair was hidden underneath a white head wrap. She fidgeted with the apron tied to her front, her smile never faltering.

"Hi, Eira, I'm—"

"Oh! I know who you are. I was so excited when Clergyman Marcellus told me of my position. Please follow me, and I will show you to your room where you can freshen up before dinner with the rest of the Clergymen and the royal family. All your belongings will be brought to you."

I looked at Vork, and he nodded with a small smile. "Go on. I'll find you before dinner."

I returned the expression, then turned to follow Eira, but I quickly began losing her, partly because I was still taking in the structures around me and all their glory. My eyes roamed over to the others as they made their way into Elmira and landed on Diana, who was talking to Marcellus. The expressions on their faces sent a subtle ping of worry through me, but before I could analyze it further, Eira came back to hurry me along.

Pulling my eyes away, I jogged to keep up.

"So, Eira, how long have you worked for the Clergy?"

"A few months," she said as she rounded a corner, still with a smile on her face. "They are very generous and have made me feel right at home."

"How did you come into their employment?"

"I lost my family in a fire a year ago and was on the road looking for work. The Clergy saw potential in me and took me in. I can't complain. The bed is comfortable, there's always a new adventure to be found, and I've made friends quickly."

We came to a door and she ushered me in.

The room was beautiful and far more attractive than mine at the Hold. The walls were painted a dark blue, and intricate tapestries hung over them. A large bed sat in the far left with a gold canopy hanging from the ceiling and flowing down either side.

A fire roared on the other side of the room, and candles had been lit all around.

Two large doors led to a balcony, which I inched towards but was stopped when Eira walked briskly in front of the wardrobe.

Some minutes passed as servants came in with my things and unloaded all the unnecessary dresses our maids packed.

"This," she said, pulling out a dark green gown, "is your dinner dress. I can help you get into it."

I threw my cloak on the bed. "When is dinner?"

Eira froze, staring at my lack of clothing and boots.

"Um, in an hour."

I kicked off my shoes. "The dress I was wearing wasn't battle appropriate."

"You *fought*?"

I internally rolled my eyes. This again.

"I did. Can you help me out of this corset?"

I caught a glimpse of her in the mirror as she assisted me, still wearing a smile.

"You don't have to smile constantly around me, Eira. You're free to relax."

"No need to worry. I am relaxed, and I love smiling. I'm hoping it will rub off on others."

In return, I gave her a weak one and let out a breath when the corset came fully off. As Eira walked around to the other side of the dress, her feet got caught in the fabric, and she fell.

Reaching my arms around her waist, I held her firm but quickly let go when she yelped in pain.

When she fell, her smile finally faltered.

"Shit, sorry!" I kneeled next to her. "Are you okay?"

Eira clutched her waist and exhaled. "Yes. I'm sorry I tripped."

"You have nothing to apologize for."

She looked up, and her smile was back. "Thank you for your concern. Now, let's get you in that dress?"

I didn't move from the floor. "Has someone hurt you?"

"No!" She kept her eyes away from mine. "I am perfectly fine."

"Look at me."

She refused.

"Eira," I commanded. "I said, look at me."

Reluctantly, she did.

"Who were you attending before me?"

She fumbled with the cloth in her hand, her smile falling again. "Clergyman Marcellus."

I understood.

There was something about men abusing women that set a fire under me to deal some vengeance. But I knew I couldn't do that here, so instead I listened. I would listen, collect, and wait.

"Please, Amara, he's a good man. He didn't hurt me. I don't want to lose my job."

I stayed silent.

Her eyes searched mine, glassing over with tears.

"Please—"

"Stop," I said. "I'm not forcing you to tell me anything you don't want to. But, Eira." I stood, maintaining a healthy distance to keep her as comfortable as possible. "I can be an ally if you need it."

At that moment, the door opened to reveal Vork, who moved his gaze from me, naked from the waist up, and then back to Eira.

"I'm sorry," Eira began. "I—"

Vork held up his hand. "It's fine. You can take your leave."

Eira laid the dress down and did a slight curtsey before rushing out and closing the door behind her.

"Well." He leaned against the closed door. "I did not expect to find you like this. Though I have to say I'm not disappointed."

I ignored his comment and moved to the dress. "Are you going to help, or did you just say that to get rid of her?"

He pushed off the door, coming to me. "I can help." His hands settled along my waist, drawing lazy, small circles with his thumb. His touch left a burning sensation in its wake as he moved to the underside of my breast, and those thumbs brushed over the nipples. "After I fuck you."

"I was hoping you would say that." I took one of his hands in mine and hit a pressure point, causing him to bend a knee. I smirked down at him.

I *needed* this.

I lightly took his jaw in my hand.

Right where I wanted him, under my control. I rubbed my thumb over his bottom lip, and his sharp teeth caught its pad. I didn't flinch as a bead of blood oozed out. He gently kissed it away, and my stomach fluttered.

I leaned in to press my lips against his, but before they made contact, he broke my grip and shot up, grabbing me in his arms and laying me beneath him.

He swiftly pulled my trousers off before coming back up to cage me in his arms that lay on either side of my head.

I tried to kiss him, but he pulled away.

My brows drew together. "Kiss me."

"Oh no, angel. You've got to work harder than that. What do I look like, a cheap whore?"

I grabbed a handful of his hair and yanked as hard as I could until he eased up on the cage he had me in. Wrapping my foot around his calf, I bucked my hips up and flipped us. Once he was seated below me, I pulled his shirt open.

There he was, hair tossed and completely out of place, shirt opened, buttons lying on the floor, some rolling away from us still.

I admired my work.

"Now you look like a cheap whore." I smirked. "Care to do your job?"

Both hands grabbed my ass, hauling me to his chest. "You're going to make us late for dinner."

"I don't care."

Without another word, I lifted myself to undo his pants and push them down far enough to where I could grab him. Lining him up with my entrance, I slowly sat. We groaned in sync, warmth surrounding us.

Every damn time felt like pure bliss. I couldn't explain it.

And gods, I didn't want an explanation.

I just didn't want it to stop.

At first, my movements were slow and purposeful, but I needed more. My hips jerked, grinding against him with such a powerful need we moved a few inches.

Somewhere in the heat of it all, he picked me up and stood, but I didn't stop. I wrapped my legs around his waist and held on for dear life while trying to create as much friction as I could.

When he took us to the bed, I finally got my lips on his and kissed him fiercely. I tightly gripped his ass, pulling him farther into me, if that were even possible, and lost my breath when he angled my bottom up to ram into me deeper.

"The Divine, you take me so well. I need you to squeeze me, angel."

I complied, tightening around him. His loud moan set me off, and my toes curled, ready to give him everything.

"How close are you?"

"So close," I gasped, my eyes shut so tight I was starting to see stars. "Ah, I'm right there."

He placed one hand on the headboard next to my head, and the other hand cupped my throat while his thrusts became more aggressive.

"You're such a dirty little thing, aren't you?" Vork grunted. "Who's the whore now?"

If this was what the Heavens the Clergy spoke of looked like, then I was all for it. I felt so free in that moment, like a piece of clay ready to be molded however he wanted. I lay there, feeling him against my body, and all the things around us didn't matter. It was just us, and I *loved* it.

Too soon, he pulled away to flip me so I was on all fours and hoisted me back by my hair, his mouth hot against my neck.

I reached behind and rubbed my hand against his muscled thigh. "Please."

He gave my neck a deep kiss before his thrusts became powerful once more. I arched up into him, trying to deepen his touch as my skin lit like a fire. My nails dug into his thigh, a silent plea for more.

More. More. More.

The thrusts were slow but purposeful, and it didn't take me long to clench and unravel around him.

"Oh gods, Vork!"

He let go of my hair and I crashed to the bed, entirely spent. His searing touch gripped my hips tightly until he found his release with my name on his lips.

———◆———

WE STAYED in each other's arms for a moment longer, silent but content, until we cleaned off and began to dress for dinner. Vork had to call a servant to bring him another shirt since his buttons were all over the floor and impossible to find.

I pulled on the dress and moved my hair to the side, so Vork could do the buttons on the back. It was made of dark green lace that came up to just below my collarbone and sleeves that belled towards the end of my elbow. Gold trim circled my waist and ran through each sleeve, while a thicker strip climbed from my waist to my neckline. The bodice was fitted enough that no corset was needed, and the skirt flared out below.

"I think Marcellus is abusing Eira," I said. "Though it seems she would never turn on her master."

"Don't be so sure. People in this city might have a smile or a look of content on their face, but I've found very quickly it's only a mask."

Vork's hands were warm and rough on my skin as he linked the last few buttons.

"Vork," I said, spinning around and gazing at him. "I can trust you."

It wasn't a question but a statement. One I was hoping he'd confirm was true.

"Yes." He stroked my cheek with the back of his hand. "You have me."

"If you're lying..."

He grabbed the back of my head, lacing his fingers through my hair. "You'll kill me."

His other hand pulled my waist to his, and our lips crushed together. I wanted something simple, soft, and quick, but that's not what he had in mind.

He wanted me again, and I was so close to giving it to him. The kiss was almost enough to make me dizzy. But I placed my hands on his chest and pulled away, though not enough to break his embrace.

"I need to tell you something."

"I guess it's something that can't wait till later?"

I moved out of his arms and went to the vanity so I could wrap my hair while I told him everything about Michael's visit.

Vork took it better than I thought he would. My family tree made things a bit more complicated, but he showed no signs of worry or stress. After I told him, I finished getting ready and slipped on my heels at the end of the bed.

"I'm trusting you, Vork. Please don't make me feel it was in vain."

"My, my, angel," he cooed as he stalked over and wrapped me in his arms again. "Does this mean you like me?"

I couldn't contain the smile.

"I might hate you a little less than I did a few days ago."

His breath was hot against the shell of my ear, making my skin as warm as the fire in the corner. "That wouldn't have to do with how many times you came with my name on those pretty lips, would it?"

Before I could answer with a witty response, Eira knocked and let herself in. She curtsied. "Dinner is waiting. Everyone has gathered in the hall."

Vork dismissed her with a nod and wrapped my arm around his.

"Thank you," I murmured. "For letting me tell you on my own time."

It was like a weight had been lifted off my shoulders when I realized I could confide in him. It was hard, something had been clawing at my brain since the night of Michael's visit, but talking to him had been a lot easier than I thought it would be.

He kissed the top of my head and escorted me out.

As we walked down the hall, all that could be heard was the clicking of our shoes, which showed how empty this place could be. It was holy ground, but I was starting to feel more and more uneasy.

We took a few more turns, then stood in front of two double doors. My feet suddenly weighed heavier than I could ever remember. I never backed down from a fight or a challenge, but I was almost prepared to throw that mindset out the window if it meant I didn't have to have dinner with the Clergy and the royal family.

There were many things I disliked about the Clergy. Their posh way of living while others suffered, their inability to truly stop the war that had been raging on for the past ages, or maybe it was just their faces. Granted, I had never met a clergyman beside Marcellus, but I had known at first glance there was a malice under his skin that ran deep into the marrow of his bones. Tonight, I would have the unfortunate pleasure of meeting the other two.

Vork placed his other hand over mine and glided his thumb over my three fingers, which rested on his arm.

"I'm here."

And I felt it.

Physically, I knew he had me because I eased up on my grip, but he was *really* there. He was someone I could depend on. Vork was there, and I felt it. At that moment, he was mine, and I was his.

Undeniably.

CHAPTER 23

A LONG WOODEN TABLE, already set, stood in the middle of the room lit by multiple candlesticks running down its length.

Did they eat this way for every meal? It was incredibly depressing.

The Emperor sat at the head, with a gold crown on his head and his pointed ears sticking out from the sides. His face was laced with concern as he spoke to Clergyman Marcellus.

His crown was made of intricately woven spirals forming a point just above the center of his forehead. It took all my strength to move my eyes from the emerald that sat at the top to look at the Empress on his left, who was in a conversation with the clergyman sitting next to Marcellus. Next to him was another clergyman, a vacant seat, Corym, and then Luca.

Next to the empress was a young girl who couldn't have been more than eighteen ages old. She had a scowl on her face that would no doubt leave lines, given how deeply they were embedded in her skin. It was a shame. She was beautiful, with forest green eyes and freckles covering her nose and under her eyes, but they couldn't clearly be seen because of her horrible frown.

There was a vacant seat next to her, and then Diana, Leena, and Dasyra were at the end.

A servant came to my side and motioned me to the empty seat next to who I assumed was the princess. With hesitation, I let go of Vork's arm, and we went to stand behind our chairs.

"Welcome!" the clergyman sitting next to Marcellus boasted with a wide grin. "Amara, let me please begin this meal by saying it is so wonderful to meet you in the flesh finally. Your travels are already very well known."

I gave a soft smile and dipped my head. "Thank you, Clergyman…"

"Salvadore," he finished. "I apologize for not properly introducing myself. I am Salvadore Tauya. Please allow me to introduce you to the Emperor of Masos, Protector of the continent, and the Divine's rightfully chosen, Emperor Neiven Pelleas Aien Virra VIII."

I did a very poor and unpracticed curtsey while Vork bowed.

"Welcome," the Emperor said in a silky tone. "This is my wife, Empress Sana, and my daughter, Keunwysa."

The Empress gave us both a gentle smile while the Princess stayed in her scowling state.

"Please sit. I'm sure you are both hungry from the long journey," Empress Sana offered.

"I bet that's not why they're hungry," Luca whispered loud enough for everyone to hear.

Corym flicked his brother on the ear, quick enough for no one to pay any mind, but to my horror, I blushed at the surge of truth.

"Amara," Marcellus interjected with his hand out to the other clergyman. "This is Clergyman Landis."

Landis took his cup in his perkily manicured dark hand and raised it in greeting. I did the same.

The dinner began with the first course of soup, and light chatter filled the room. I kept quiet for the most part unless someone directly asked me a question. While everyone was busy talking amongst themselves and indulging in light-hearted jokes, I simply watched.

The rumors appeared to be true. The Emperor held no power and was simply a figurehead for the Clergy. Vork had once told me before, the Clergy believed it was easier to have a single ruler presented to the people while they took to the shadows to do what needed to be done.

If they were making decisions in front of the people, then they would hardly get away with their usual crimes. Those crimes included the smuggling of goods and people, stealing from the poor to pay for their lavish lifestyles, and who knew what else.

The Emperor engaged in conversation with the clergymen while the Empress and Princess remained silent, only speaking when spoken to.

Marcellus held all the power in the room, but Salvadore was the extrovert among them. He engaged in conversation with everyone and could hold on for as long as he wanted to. I had to admit, Marcellus needed someone like him in the Clergy. He was a man who held his decorum perfectly, said the right things when needed, and could be the face of them if things were to ever spiral out of control.

Landis was a quiet man. Every so often, he would respond to Salvadore's statements and say a few words to Diana, but other than that, he was soft-spoken. I would normally keep a watchful eye on someone like Landis, but Salvadore was the trickster of the group. His mannerisms gave him away.

On the surface, he was a people pleaser. He smiled when necessary, laughed at dry jokes, and showed false interest in his conversations, but I could see past that. It was in his eyes.

The others continued to engage in conversation, and Vork was pulled in as well. It was like he belonged at the table. What an odd thing to see.

I swirled the cup in my hand, looking down at the wine as the next course was brought out. My eyes darted to Salvadore and saw his mouth was about to spit something I'd have to listen to, so I turned to the princess.

"So, Keunwysa," I began, "how old are you?"

"Just, Keun."

"Okay. How old are you, Keun?"

She cut into her food and popped a piece of meat into her mouth. "I hardly see why it matters. I am the princess, and that's all you need to know."

I looked away, taking a sip of wine. "Just trying to make conversation."

"Well, don't. I don't need to make conversation with common folk."

Oh, this one needs a beating.

"I bet you're not popular within your city, are you, Princess?" There was such venom in my voice. I hoped she heard it.

"I hardly care."

"You'll care when they storm Elmira and hang you from your toes."

The princess clutched her silver fork and knife in her hands and snapped, "Ignorant peasant."

"Ungrateful brat."

Keun's eyes widened, and she turned her angered gaze to me. "You can't speak to me like that."

"I beg you to do something about it." Putting the cup down, I went to cut my food and began eating.

"I could have any one of these guards take you out to our courtyard and have you whipped."

"Careful there, Princess. Don't be a tease."

"You're disgusting," she sneered.

I smirked. "You have no idea."

"You want a conversation? Fine." Keun put down her silverware and spoke a bit *too* loudly. "What happened to your hand?"

The whole room went silent.

I sighed internally. Here we go.

"A demon bit my fingers off."

Not the whole truth, but we didn't need any more restrictions on our movements, seeing as how Marcellus already knew of the raids.

"I couldn't imagine."

"No, you couldn't."

The air grew thick around us, but Salvadore cut through it like butter.

"Amara, you must tell us of your tale. Of course, we've heard it from others, but to hear it from the source would be extraordinary."

With gritted teeth, I put on a smile and told them of my travels with Vork, omitting the fact raiding a demon den was what got us there, and our road to the Holy City. It wasn't a tale I wanted to romanticize, but others at the table couldn't help but do so. I also left out the bit about Katar, lest they ask any questions I couldn't answer. A few more lies were woven into the story to make it sound more interesting than it was.

The food had finally stopped coming, and the servants began to clear the table. At that point, everyone except Vork and Landis seemed warmed up by the wine they had been drinking all evening. I might be able to get away from these people sooner than I had thought. Then, Salvadore shot me with another request.

"May we see?"

I placed my cup on the table. "Your eminence?"

"Your power, child, your power!"

"I don't know if that—"

"I," Keun said, "would love to see it. Maybe she'll burn herself from the inside out."

"Keun," the Empress chastised.

I reluctantly grabbed a candlestick and held the flame under my left hand. It swallowed the stick as it rose to my fingers.

I had practiced just a bit during my training, enough to where I had a handle on small flames. What I had done to Abaddon hours before was something I'd like to put in the luck category, especially how I had produced my own flames. I hadn't been sure I could even do that, but at the moment it had just felt natural.

The room was quiet, the only sound the flames crackling in the fireplace. Salvadore stood from his place and walked to me with interest.

"Magnificent! You truly are a wonder!"

Though I had a strong desire to turn and bolt, I refused to move because I worried if I did, I might just throw the fire into the man's face.

Disgust rolled through me at being made to put on a show like an animal.

This was the one time I didn't consider the princess a thorn in my side, because she began to talk about something that locked everyone's attention on her. My shoulders loosened until I noticed Salvadore still gawking.

I extinguished the flames, pushed out of my chair and went to the large fireplace, searching for a reprieve from the stares. Despite its warmth, the fire was like a cool breeze compared to the dinner table. Unfortunately, my time alone didn't last.

Salvadore moved behind me and dared to place a hand on my shoulder. "You are exquisite. Can you produce more?"

"Yes, but I don't think now is the time."

I held my breath but refused to show any discomfort. Though I knew Vork could see right through me. I didn't have to look to know his eyes had been on us ever since the Clergyman came over to me.

Salvadore glided his hands over my back, letting them creep down lower to rest at the base. He moved in close, his mouth hanging over my ear.

"You are an amazing creature, little nephilim. What a shame you have a betrothed."

Clergymen were not celibate. They refused to marry due to their higher calling to the Divine, but of course, they could indulge in their fantasies as long as they did not give in fully to one woman who would come over their duties to Masos.

"He is a good man," I said, throwing a heated gaze to him.

"Mhm," Salvadore hummed as he sipped his wine. "And is your union with him strictly monogamous?"

"Yes," I gritted out, stepping to the side so his hands dropped.

I could still feel them on me as if his touch had been embedded into my dress and skin.

"I wonder if that could be adjusted."

I turned to look at him.

"Clergyman Salvadore, you seem like a very well-educated man. Do you think it is wise to gamble with the commander's betrothed?"

"Ah, but he is a commander, not a chief."

"This is true." A servant came by to place a drink in my hand. "But it's not him you have to worry about."

His eyebrows rose. "Threats?"

"I wouldn't dare." I took a sip of wine. "Though threats can be effective, I believe promises have better results."

He chuckled. "You are not as I expected."

"Why is that?'

"I had heard of a nephilim named Amara, who was the daughter of Michael. She was said to be fiery, and her passion showed through her stature as a true leader. Yet tonight, you hardly spoke a word unless directly addressed."

"I've begun to learn new things daily, Clergyman."

Salvadore placed a hand on the mantle and took a step closer. "And what have you learned today, child?"

"Looks can be very deceiving."

"Oh." He cocked an eyebrow. "Am I to see this passionate and fiery nephilim sometime soon?"

"You sound hopeful."

"That I am."

Trying to contain the bile forcing its way up my throat, I took another sip of wine. "Be careful with your hopes, your eminence, the fire you so much desire might not be what you're looking for."

"Is it wrong for a man to want warmth? Especially when it comes from something so mesmerizing?"

"Oh, not at all," I said matter-of-factly. "It's just that the fire I have and the fire you want so badly are not the same."

Salvadore held my gaze, smirking. "You doubt my ability to control it?"

I gulped the rest of my drink and took his hand to place my empty cup in it before I leaned over and whispered, "I doubt it very much."

CHAPTER 24

I HATED the person staring back at me in the tall mirror of my boudoir. I hated the dress I was wearing, and I hated I was being shown off *again*. Only this time, it was my body being put on display. My dress for the gala was far more revealing than the long-sleeved green one I'd worn to dinner the previous night, making me miss it.

My current dress was made of a thick satin material that only extended to mid-thigh, apparently some version of a skirt. My breasts were covered and the collar went up to my neck, but there was a slit in the middle from the collarbone down to the middle of my chest. The sleeves were made of an airy material that frilled at the shoulders, lay flat against the elbow, and then flared out again at the wrists. The sheer material acted as a coat to the satin slip, held together by buttons in the front that then opened up at the knees, separating as I walked.

Damned if I didn't feel like a slave who was going up for auction. I hoped neither Leena nor Dasyra would be dressed this way. It was embarrassing and surprising such holy men would want our bodies shown off at all.

Maybe not, seeing how Clergyman Salvadore had spoken to me last night.

I would play by their rules because, though I didn't know how yet, I planned to find out just how involved the Clergy were in this war.

Eira stood behind me as she hoisted my long, dark locks into a twist on top of my head.

"I want to apologize," I said as I watched her. "Your business is your own."

She continued pinning and smiled. "It's alright. Thank you for your concern, but there is nothing to be worried about. I am fine."

"Of course."

I let her pin the last hair into place and turned around, wrapping my hands in hers.

I was starting to pity the girl. Next to the negligence of children, men beating women was the one thing I could not abide by, especially those who are unable to help themselves. Though I wanted to continue to extend a helping hand, I stopped myself from saying anything and dropped my grip on hers. It would only lead to unnecessary attachments, which I didn't have time for.

"You look lovely," Eira said.

I gently smiled at her work and stood to continue getting ready.

With a sigh, Eira cursed and her painted smile melted.

"Amara, what I'm about to tell you is dangerous, but I do need your help."

I internally cursed. And here the attachment began, but I couldn't turn her away now. I motioned for her to sit.

Eira ran a shaky hand over her head, removing the head wrap. Her dark curls flowing over her shoulders.

"I'm honestly unsure if you can, but I loathe the Clergy. Landis and Salvadorc have never done anything to hurt me, but they've never stopped Marcellus from his..." She took a breath. "I've been here for about two ages. I didn't lie to you when I said my home was destroyed in a fire, but not everyone died. My brother, Iziah, was out in the fields planting seeds for the new season when the fire broke out, and I was down by the river washing our linen. I don't know how the fire started; I only know the Clergy's guard was there waiting for my brother and me when we returned.

"By the time I got there, they already had him on a horse with his hands tied, and when they saw me running back home, they took me as well."

Eira placed her hands on her knees and looked up to keep herself from crying.

"I, um… don't know why they kept me alive, but I know why they kept my brother. Marcellus has him locked up somewhere in this damned place, and I need your help to free him. He could learn something from you. I might be his sister, but you are the person he needs."

"Why would he need me?"

"He's one of you. He's a nephilim."

I shook my head. "You mean to tell me the Clergy has a nephilim locked away like a prisoner here in Elmira? For what purpose?"

"He keeps them alive."

The Clergy were said to be over a century old. No one knew exactly how they had kept their youth for so long. Their explanation to Masos was, *it is by the Divine's power.*

But a boy? For how long? Surely not a century.

By the gods, this was mental.

"Care to elaborate?"

"Iziah is the son of the angel Raphael. Raphael is a natural healer, and this gift was passed down to my brother." Eira looked as if she were about to vomit. "I think the clergymen are feeding off his grace and somehow using his powers to keep them alive."

"You said you have been here for two ages. What were they doing to keep themselves alive before your brother? It's not like nephilims are easy to come by."

She might have thought I didn't see it, but she hesitated for a split second before she said, "I have no idea, but all I know is they could feed off his grace for who knows how long. If I don't get him out of here, then he'll be a prisoner for as long as he lives."

I rolled my lips between my teeth. "Do you have a plan for afterward? I'm assuming once they find out it was you who orchestrated all this, they'll kill you and take your brother back to his holding place."

"That's not for you to worry about."

I sat back on my hands. I wasn't doing anything if I didn't know the whole plan.

Eira stood, pacing around the room as she tugged on her head wrap in nervousness. "Amara, please, I have a plan. I just need you to trust me. Get my brother out, and meet me at the entrance of Elmira when the moon is at its highest."

I didn't speak.

When Eira took notice my silence, she got on her knees and took my hands.

"Please," she begged. "You're the first person who has offered me any friendship. I know your time here has been brief, but I feel I can trust you. Is my feeling right?"

Her eyes were trained on me, pleading for the answer.

"You can trust me, and I will help you, but I don't need to tell you how dangerous this is, not for me but for you both. Your brother is Raphael's son, one of the most powerful angels. If anyone finds out who he is, then you will be hunted. They will kill you and take your brother."

Eira squeezed harder. "I promise. We'll be fine."

I sighed and closed my eyes. "All right. Where is your brother?"

"At the northwest wing in Marcellus' chambers, there is a trap door under his bed. I don't know for certain if that is where Iziah is, but I can't imagine the Clergy's life source being kept elsewhere. When Marcellus called me to... tend to him, he would often order me to sleep on the floor, and all those nights I would stare at the trap door wondering if my brother could be down there."

I nodded, the wheels in my mind already beginning to turn. "You said you wanted me to meet you at the entrance of Elmira. How do I get him there without being seen?"

Eira stood.

"With the gala happening, no one will notice. The personal guard for the Clergy will be attending the party, and that will be their main concern." She reached into the pocket of her apron and handed me a paper. "This is the layout of the servant's hallways we use while serving those in Elmira. Take those marked on the paper, and you'll be led right out the front door."

"You know," I mused, lifting a brow. "I could be killed if I get caught."

Eira snorted. "They wouldn't dare."

I knew she was right, but I was worried about the aftermath if I were caught.

"Get ready for your departure, and I will get it done."

Another nephilim. And he's being used by the Clergy. These vile, degenerate men would meet their comeuppance.

I hoped I was the one to give it to them.

CHAPTER 25

The food was amazing, the music never ended, and the entertainment was impressive. It was a night everyone would remember.

I definitely would. It was annoyingly perfect.

Musicians played various songs to keep the crowd engaged, and cups were never left any less than half empty, with one servant for every two guests.

Scattered around the room were small round tables about the size of my arm span where a man or woman with exceptionally flexible limbs performed. They showcased their talents; if the dancing did not keep the guests engaged, that did. Or it may have been the man who could breathe fire in the far corner or the cat-like beast in a cage on the other end of the ballroom.

Though I hardly wanted to be here, I appreciated there were other things to gawk at besides the "Girl of Fire." The new pet name had sprung from Salvadore's lips, and word had traveled fast. Too fast.

I took a sip of the sweet wine before a servant came to fill it back to the brim. Across the way, Vork was chatting with a man. Though everyone was dressed to impress, this man was adorned with a necklace dripping in jewels that took up most of his chest. He held a cane in his left hand and the hand of an older woman in his right. Clearly he was someone of importance.

My eyes moved back to Vork.

He wore a dark blue velvet jacket clipped up to his neck and adorned with golden embellishments around the shoulders. Blue and yellow stripes were stitched into his right breast pocket, and gold buttons traveled down to his trousers. They were of the same material as his jacket and clung to him in the best possible ways.

"Handsome, isn't he?" A high-pitched but elegant voice crept up next to me.

"He is indeed."

The woman was a bit shorter than I and was dressed in a soft gold and pink dress that puffed out a few inches from her waist with elaborate lace at her train. Her equally deep golden hair was pinned in a bun, loose strands framing her face.

"I heard he is to be married."

"Yes, I had heard the same. I wonder who she is." I made a show of searching around before looking back at her.

"Well, whoever she is, I pity her."

"Why is that?"

Her eyes swung back to Vork. "Being betrothed won't stop the attempts on him. He's too valuable for that."

Interesting.

"Valuable because he's the next in line to lead the Arabrosa pack?"

"Yes," she said blissfully as if daydreaming it was her with him right now. "The amount of power that woman would have…" She trailed off and cleared her throat in a very polite manner. "Anyways, I believe I may try myself tonight."

I raised a brow at her. To say I didn't feel a bit of jealousy would be a lie, but irritation was what took over me the most at that very moment. Irritation that she was stomping all over what wasn't hers. Territorial didn't begin to cover how I felt.

"Are you an old flame?" I guessed.

She smiled now, looking at me with sparkling blue eyes. "Yes, you could say that. It doesn't necessarily mean it has burnt out. There could always be something still there burning no matter how small."

"And you believe you're going to reignite this old flame?"

"Oh, I do hope so. He won't remember his betrothed when I'm done with him."

I had to stop myself from busting out in laughter. The number of times I had that lycan wrapped around my finger would impress their Divine. "What do you plan to do?"

She looked at me in shock. "What, so you can steal my ideas? No," she said, drawing the word out, "I can't have that."

That cracked a smile on my face. "I promise you I will not steal anything."

I don't need them.

"Hello."

His warm voice laced around me as he joined us.

"Vork," the woman said in awe. She gave him a slight curtsey, and he bowed.

His thick hair was pulled behind his ears, keeping his locks out of his face and showing off that dazzling smile.

"My new friend here," I said with a smile, "was telling me something about an old flame—how you two knew each other." I turned to her. "Wasn't that right?"

"Ah, yes, I was telling her that an old flame can still have heat brewing despite the time that has passed." The woman bit her bottom lip as she looked up at Vork. "And it may still be able to burn just as brightly as the day it was first lit."

"Or it might be just as cold and dead as it was the day it was snuffed out," I suggested.

That caught her off guard. Her eyes shot to me in irritation for butting into her chance.

Vork, on the other hand, seemed content to watch the scene unfold.

"I beg your pardon?" She exclaimed in a very demure way. Expected from a woman of high status.

"Seeing as how you incessantly keep talking about your plans to get into the Commander's pants, I know very well you heard and understood the words that came out of my mouth."

A strained smile played on her lips as her eyes darted between me and Vork. "Would you be so kind as to excuse the Commander and I?"

I snorted. "No."

"Beg your pardon?"

"If you beg anymore, you might as well be on your knees."

That finally got her to shut up.

"May I introduce my betrothed?" Vork said with his arm out. "Amara, daughter of Michael."

And *that* caused her to drop her jaw.

"I would say pleased to meet you," I bit out, "but since you yammered away about how you plan to undermine my union, I'm going to say you can go fuck yourself."

The woman straightened her back and scurried off, the party swallowing her.

"You look beautiful." Vork's voice was deliciously warm in my ear.

"I feel ridiculous. Is this considered fashion in the Holy City?"

"Apparently," he sighed, looking at himself. "I feel like one of those soldier dolls playing dress up."

"Do you want to be played with?" I took another sip of my drink and smirked.

"Careful, angel."

"Or what?"

He leaned in next to my ear, leaving his hands laced behind his back. "Or I'll ruin that dress of yours in front of all these people."

"You expect me to believe you'll take me with an audience?"

"Would you like that?"

"No," I shot back. "I don't share."

"Well," he hummed. "Neither do I, but I don't plan to lay a single hand on you here tonight."

"Then—"

"I wouldn't sit down," he interrupted. "Unless you want to stain the back of that pretty little dress with your wetness. I imagine it will be quite noticeable with that color."

My grip tightened on the cup. "You play a dangerous game, Commander."

Vork pecked the side of my head and stood up straight, looking into the crowd. "The whole room has been buzzing about you nephilim tonight. It first started when a fae girl and Corym walked in. I think they're trying to upstage us and be the Holy City's favorite. What do you say we change their mind with a dance?"

I glanced up and then around us with hesitation. "I'm a fighter, not a dancer."

"You," he said in a low tone, putting his hand on my lower back and guiding us towards the dance floor, "are a nephilim of many talents. I have no doubt this can be added to the list."

I reluctantly handed my cup to a servant as we reached the middle of the floor. His left hand fell on my hip, his other engulfed mine, and we moved so gracefully it was like I was doing nothing at all as he led.

Despite other couples being there, including the rest of the group with their partners, I could feel the eyes on us. My hands began to sweat, and my heartbeat sped up almost as fast as the beat of the music.

"Look at me," Vork said as he pulled me closer. "Just me."

I locked my eyes with his and followed his lead.

He swung me gently around, never missing a beat. He was experienced in this, and I was grateful.

"I wonder," I began, "how many other women you must have paraded on a dance floor to become this good. That old flame, perhaps?"

"Jealous?" He smirked. "In all honesty, I don't even remember her name. She may have been someone I met in my younger ages. When I turned sixteen, my father was hellbent on finding me a wife. I was put on show similar to how you were last night." He squeezed my hand slightly. "I'm sorry you were put through that."

"We do what we must to survive."

We separated for a moment, circling each other, before coming back together, his chest against mine once more.

I brought my hand to the base of his neck and lightly grabbed his hair. "About these other women. I'm dying to know why none of them stuck. Did they realize how much work you would be and ran?"

"I'm insulted."

I snorted to keep a laugh from escaping and moved my hand back to his shoulder.

"It was the other way around. Most women I met, though they were lovely, were a bit too high maintenance for me, and they weren't you."

My eyes shot to his as my cheeks warmed. I didn't even realize the song had ended. His hand squeezed mine and thankfully the next song began, our feet moving on beat.

"You had no idea I even existed when you met them," I argued.

"Not true. I always knew you were out there. I just had to find you. Or I guess in our case, you found me, didn't you?"

The night I had tried to evade him in the prison felt like a lifetime ago. I wasn't a nephilim; I was just an assassin fulfilling a contract. I had no attraction to anyone or anything besides the coin I received.

Now, I'm dancing in the most expensive dress I'll ever care to wear at the most heavily guarded and known place on the continent.

"I guess I did find you." I hesitated momentarily before speaking my next words, because I couldn't go back once I said them. "Vork, I need you to do something for me."

"This already sounds like trouble."

I pulled back.

"I haven't even said anything."

"You, angel, are always trouble."

I rolled my eyes, but he had a point. "Keep your composure. I found out another nephilim is here, named Iziah."

He kept his eyes forward and did as I said. "Where?"

"In Marcellus' bed chamber."

"Why would he keep a nephilim there?"

He twirled me around and brought me back to his chest.

"He is the son of Raphael. The Clergy are using his powers to keep them alive. I don't have time to explain more, but I need you to meet me in the northwest wing at Marcellus' chambers a quarter before peak. Can you do that?"

The song ended, and we stood still as everyone clapped, but he acted as if we were alone. The clapping faded in the background, his look keeping me focused on him.

He held my chin between his thumb and pointer finger.

"For you, always." Vork brought his lips down on mine, and they touched with beautiful warmth. I couldn't stop until someone cleared their throat.

It was a fae girl.

"Mind if I cut in?"

Knowing eyes were on us at all times, I gave her a tight-lipped smile and took a step back.

"Of course."

"I'll come find you," Vork pressed.

I nodded and walked away as he swept her across the dance floor.

I reached the side of the room with a drink in hand and spotted Diana a few steps away. I raised my cup to her.

She glided across the floor to me. "Hiding so you don't have to retell the story of your travels?"

"How did you know?"

She smiled and shrugged. "A hunch."

"The party is nice." I looked up at the shining decorations and the elaborate food table at the head of the room. "A little extra, but I expected nothing less from the Clergy."

"Yes, extravagance is their forte."

A fae couple came up to us with smiles, shaking hands, and expressing excitement about meeting the Girl of Fire.

Internally, I screamed.

Of course, they inquired about our recent travels and asked if I could pick up a candlestick and let the flames dance across my hand. Luckily, Diana was quick to tell them how inappropriate that would be, and they easily changed the subject before taking their leave.

Despite the guests' laughing, dancing, and gluttonous actions, I couldn't shake the feeling something was off. Perhaps it was because of what I was about to do. The nerves covered me like a thick blanket of snow, chilling me to the bone. Making me almost immobile, but I had to act.

"There is something I need to tell you," I said to Diana as I motioned her away from the crowd. "There is another nephilim here."

She moved in closer.

"I don't have the details." I chose my next words carefully. "But I know he's being kept in the cellars in the south corridor. I mean to free him. Can you help me? Meet me there at a quarter before the peak."

She nodded. "Of course, but why do you think the Clergy has a nephilim imprisoned? That's a bold accusation."

"I don't know, but I plan to find out."

When we parted ways, I realized why I truly hated those of high status. They were normally all the same: dressed in beautiful clothing, perfume so strong one could vomit from the smell, and the same belief that everyone who wasn't at the ball was beneath them.

I chatted with multiple people in that category, and it took everything in me not to set fire to their pretty dresses and suits.

The next time I looked up through the floor-to-ceiling windows, the moon told me it was time. I set down my drink and excused myself from a conversation I was having with a fae ambassador.

Bobbing through the crowd, I finally reached the edge of the room and found the servants' corridors. I took a breath once inside.

Eira was right, the corridors were almost empty of the Clergy's guards. After studying the map she'd given me, I made my way down the halls until I rounded the corner to Marcellus' room.

Two guards stood on either side of the door. I halted and fixed my back on the corner in the shadows.

From the quick picture I got, both of the guards had swords on their right hips. It was simple, shouldn't be too difficult.

I pushed off the wall and slapped on a wide smile.

"Hi there." I beamed at them. "What are you doing out here? There's a party going on. Don't you ever take a break?"

"This is our post for tonight, ma'am," the guard to the right said, his voice monotone.

"So, you'll be here all night?"

He nodded.

"How boring! If you won't leave your post, will you at least have a drink with me?"

He shook his head and looked forward. "Not while on duty, ma'am."

I sighed internally and looked to the young guard. "How about you? Don't let me have all the fun."

His eyes bounced from me to the wall in front of him, then back to me. He was nervous and conflicted, wanting to say yes but knowing he had to say no. So, instead, he didn't say anything at all.

I put my hand on his chest. "Come on. One drink?"

The other guard grabbed my upper arm and tugged. "I said no. We are on duty, and you need to go back the way you came."

"Ow."

"You need to leave."

With lightning speed, I brought my other hand down on his inner elbow to break his hold and used my newly freed arm to bring that elbow to his face. He fell with a loud thud.

I looked back to the young guard who drew his sword.

He looked steady as a veteran warrior, but his eyes told me differently.

"I'm not going to kill you," I told him. "But it will hurt."

He charged me with his sword in the air, ready to strike. I dipped, pushed my hand up through the opening of his arms, grabbed his jaw, picked him up, and slammed him on the ground. He'd have a nasty headache, but other than that, he would be fine.

After opening the doors to the room, I dragged the bodies into the suite and closed the door behind me.

Thick golden curtains hung over the bed and window, and an enormous fur rug had been placed just at the end of the bed. The smell of cigars lingered in the room, and wood burned in the fireplace.

Before I got off task, I went to the bed and pushed it to the side a few times until I saw what Eira had described—a trap door. It was locked, but I didn't come this far to let a lock stop me.

Grabbing the iron lock, I began to pull, the metal creaking from the tension. When my muscles couldn't take it anymore, I stopped and let out a sigh, noting the lock was distorted from my efforts. I grabbed it again, this time heating the metal with my hand. Once it melted enough, I yanked again, and the lock snapped off.

I threw the hatch open. The hole was shallow but deep enough that someone standing couldn't just jump out.

"Iziah? Are you down there?"

No answer.

I retrieved a lit candlestick from the bedside table and returned, peering in. There was a body curled up on the dank floor.

"Your sister Eira sent me," I said. "I'm here to get you out."

The man lifted his head and looked up with squinted eyes. "Eira?"

"Yes, now I'm going to reach out, and I need you to grab hold of me, okay?"

"Well, this is unsettling," said a voice from behind.

I pulled out of the hole and looked at the door, unsurprised to find them there.

Diana stood with her hands on her hips and a blank expression.

"You're here," I breathed.

"I am. You told me to meet you here."

"I told you to meet me in the cellars."

She took a step forward. "I saw where you were going and assumed it was where you wanted me to meet you, so I followed."

She thought she had me.

"We are at the north end of Elmira," I said. "I told you to meet me in the cellars to the south. You never thought maybe I was coming here for my own purposes and you should go to the southern cellars like we agreed?"

She smiled, faintly strained. "Well, I'm here now. And I want to help Iziah. So, let's do that."

Diana moved towards the trap door, but I stepped to the side, blocking her.

"I never told you his name."

Her smile fell slowly, and she rolled her eyes.

A mass came hurtling toward my face, but I dodged just in time. I took the small opening provided and kicked her backward to create distance between us.

Diana flew back, but before she could hit the floor, she developed huge wings that slowed her down enough for her to land on her feet.

My jaw dropped. "You're an angel?"

Diana straightened and waved a hand over her face, removing her fae facade. "No, darling, I'm far more powerful. A Dominion."

A damned Dominion.

Powerful beings, even above angels until they refused to participate in the battle against Lucifer. After that, the angels rallied together to take over their power and have resided over the Dominions ever since.

They were given the job of protecting nephilim when our population was abundant before the war, but now they were hard to come by because only a handful of us remained.

I assumed she had been meant to guide the nephilim at Clamore, but it hadn't worked out in her favor.

"You knew Iziah was here and being used by the Clergy," I accused, then I let all my other accusations come to light, whether there was fact to them or not. "I bet it doesn't stop there. You knew who I was before my powers came in, and you let the demons into the school. How else could they get into a place like Clamore?" Flashes of bright fire flooded my vision, and the memory of that demon's hands on me brought bile up my throat, making my next words difficult. "The only person who wanted to kidnap me was Abaddon. He tried not too long ago, and I put together that the first time, it was him as well. You let down the defenses so Abaddon could come into my room. You're working with him, aren't you?"

She clapped.

"Well done, Amara. I see all those years in classes were good for something. I'm not going to lie. I was worried about you for a little bit."

"You lied to me. You were the one person I could count on!" My voice had grown louder with every word I spat, tears threatening to spill over. "How long has this been going on?"

"I'm not going to lie," Vocova mused as she glided around the room and thumbed through the books on the shelves. "I grew attached to you for a little while. As a Dominion, I can't have children of my own. When I found you again all those ages ago, I almost took your arm for trying to steal from me, but then I figured it would be so much better for you to see me as a mother. What better way to keep my eye on you than to raise you?"

"So, what, you were going just to deliver me to Abaddon?"

Vocova turned sharply and held out her finger. "No, I was supposed to keep my cover going for as long as possible. You seemed to figure it out, though. How?"

"You can thank my training," I spat through gritted teeth. "My gut is often never wrong."

"Clever little thing."

Vocova continued looking over Marcellus' belongings, then stopped at his desk, pulled out a stack of papers, and sifted through them.

"I'm guessing," she mused as her eyes kept searching. "You were also planning to look for proof of the Clergy's deceit when you came here. Some sort of connection to Abaddon?"

"They're kidnapping angels, aren't they?" I tried.

She barked a laugh. "Oh no, child. They are not."

"Abaddon is doing it for them?"

She shrugged. "No."

A fucking lie.

I narrowed my eyes and balled my fists.

"What do you want?"

"Abaddon needs you alive. That much is clear. He needs you to get to the tree, but what he truly desires is what's in the tree."

"The tree?" I asked as I watched her still sifting through the papers on the clergyman's desk.

"Come now, child. I can't tell you all my secrets."

"You clearly think highly of yourself. There's a chance I will beat you, take Iziah, and get out of here unscathed."

The Dominion let out a boisterous laugh and set the paper on the desk before stalking slowly towards me.

"I am as old as your father. You think a nephilim who has only just come into their power will be able to subdue me? That's cute."

"Before I started training with the nephilim, I was also trained by you. Did you forget you taught me all your tricks?"

"Well," Vocova said, fluttering her did midnight blue wings and manifesting a gleaming silver great sword. "Let's see how much you remember."

As she struck, I dove out of the way towards the unconscious soldiers to grab one of their swords, but with the help of her wings, Vocova glided across the room and kicked me away. I slammed against the bookshelf.

The shelves splintered and jabbed into my back, leaving a radiating pain that shook through my whole body. Books fell between us, hitting me in the face as they went.

"I will give you one chance," she breathed out, resting her sword on her shoulder. "To come with me willingly, or I can beat you down then drag you out."

I moved the fallen paintings and books off myself and stood. Sweat dripped down my brow, and blood seeped from a cut on my jaw that closed seconds later.

"If you truly knew me, then you would know I'm not going down without a fight."

Vocova smiled with malice. "Excellent."

She came for me again, and I rolled. When she swung, I caught her arm and disarmed her with a quick yank down, then threw my elbow against her face.

Vocova recovered and wasted no time making her next assault. She grabbed me hard by the throat before soaring across the room and slamming me against another bookcase.

"I'm so bored with always hearing your name." She pulled me off the wall and slammed me back into it, making my head wobble. "*Amara is the key. Amara is the one. Amara is the power we need to succeed.*"

Vocova flung me against the wall a third time, taking some of the stone out, before picking me up by the throat again. "If I didn't know any better, I'd say Abaddon might actually be obsessed with you."

I smiled, showing my blood-stained teeth. "Jealous?"

She frowned and grabbed the back of my head, forcing me to look in a mirror.

"Look at you," Vocova commanded. "You're as pathetic as your father. You have weaknesses and look at where your heart has led you. Here, with me about to rearrange your entire face because you can't help but be a hero. One last piece of advice from a mentor: you need to let that heart turn black and cold, or it will get you killed."

"Your words are worth nothing to me. Just like you are worth nothing to Abaddon."

Vocova shoved my head into the mirror. The shards cut into my face, my skin going slick with blood. Though they would heal, it might take longer than usual because I was so weak.

She smashed my head in again, and blood dripped into my eyes, but I could see her admiring the handy work that was my face.

I gargled.

"What was that?" she asked.

I tried to form the words, but I choked on the blood and spit pooling in my mouth.

She leaned closer. "Come again?"

"Sometimes," I spat up the blood. "Having a heart tends to work out."

"And why's that?"

I spat again before taking a breath and giving her a beaming smile. "Allies."

"You're all alone. You clearly don't trust them enough since they aren't here to help. Your friends are utterly useless."

The bell tower outside Elmira struck, and I sighed in relief.

"I'm not alone."

The door slammed open, hitting the wall and almost breaking it. Vork stood at the entryway with Corym and Dasyra at his side. None were armed, but that didn't stop them from entering the fight, and for that, I was grateful.

"Unless," Vork said slowly with conviction, "you want me to rip those wings off your back, I suggest you take your hands off of her."

Vocova jerked me in front of her as she faced them, holding onto my hair. "You think you can challenge me?"

"Now, Vocova!" Vork tsked. "If I have to say it again, you won't be alive much longer after that."

She let go of me, and I slumped to the ground, trying to keep my head from hitting the floor as I went.

Her wings fluttered, shaking off whatever debris was left from our fight.

Flashes of shock, disgust, fear, and anger brewed on all of my friends' faces as they took in Vocova's true form.

"What the hell is wrong with you?" Corym yelled. "Diana, you trained us... you mentored us!"

"Sorry to break your heart," she snipped, with narrowed eyes, "but it's not always about you. There are bigger things at play here besides your feelings."

"I'm going to enjoy killing you," Dasyra hissed, taking a step forward, but Vork held out an arm to stop her. "What are you doing?" she snapped at him.

"You're foolish if you think you can take her," Vork said, ensuring his eyes never left Vocova. "She's centuries old and has about as much power as Michael."

"So, what? Are we supposed just to let her walk away?" Dasyra asked in disbelief.

Vork shook his head. "I didn't say that. I said you're foolish if you think *you* can take her."

Vocova took slow steps backward. "Now, children, no need to get defensive. Would it help if a girl had done this all for love?"

No one answered as they continued to glare at her.

"No?" She sighed. "Well, I guess that's my cue."

She held her sword up high, and the pommel glowed so brightly it rendered us blind for a split second—that's all she needed. The window broke, and Vocova flew out, leaving us behind.

My breath escaped me when I felt the cool night's breeze. A layer of worry and dread peeling off of me as she escaped.

"Get the nephilim," Vork ordered Corym and Dasyra, who quickly went to the trap door.

His attention went directly to me, rushing to my side and pulling me up to sit against the wall. His hand barely lay on my cheek.

"Hey."

"You came."

His brows drew together. "Of course, I came. I'm sorry I didn't get here sooner."

I took a deep breath and lifted my head from his hand. "It worked out the way it was supposed to."

"You meant to get yourself hurt?"

I nodded.

I could feel the healing beginning as my strength slowly returned. My eyes could fully open now without much effort. A rib cracked back into place, causing me to flinch.

"If you had come too soon," I explained. "I wouldn't have been able to confirm she was the mole. I only suspected."

"When did you figure out there was a mole?"

I flinched again as another bone cracked into place.

"It was a gut feeling. There were so many notes from the Clergy on her desk back at the academy. Her attitude towards me and our union also changed. It was slight, but I noticed. Also, the demons and Abaddon were able to get onto the grounds too easily. She had a spell from a powerful witch placed on the grounds ages ago to keep their kind out. She's the only person with the power to allow things like that into her home."

Vork huffed a laugh and smeared away blood from my cheek with his thumb. "You are a devilish little nephilim."

I smiled back and pulled on him to help me stand while Dasyra and Corym hoisted Iziah from the hole.

He looked worse than I felt.

The fragile boy had nothing but rags on. His dark locks were matted down to his shoulder, and his face was so sunken he must not have eaten in weeks.

"Iziah," I breathed out in relief. "Your sister sent me to get you. We have to meet her out front quickly."

His bony hand grasped his shirt sleeve to pull it back up. "What debt is she in for this service?"

"None. It's a favor that doesn't need to be returned with anything."

"Everything has a price."

Though blood was still on my face, my wounds had healed, and I was able to stand up straight.

"Iziah, your sister owes me nothing. Now we need to move."

Vork threw a heavy cloak, courtesy of Clergyman Marcellus' wardrobe, over Iziah's shoulders and ushered him out of the room.

"Thank you both." I spoke before the others could leave. "For coming."

It was a foreign feeling, trusting again.

Dasyra put her arm over my shoulder. "You're not alone. Ever. You call on us, and we're there."

"Yes," Corym agreed. "Though the Clergy will not take Vocova's deceit very well."

I shook my head.

"The Clergy must be in league with the demons on some level. I'm hoping this will prove it." I pulled out the papers I was able to snag during the fight. "But first, let's ensure Iziah makes it to his sister in one piece."

They nodded, and we made our way towards the door. A loud crash and screams followed. We bolted out of the room and down the halls to the front of Elmira.

What if everyone saw him, and the scream was a reaction to something so homely looking being in a place of such elegance? Iziah would be thrown back into the hole and probably tortured to reveal who helped him. Then, the rescue truly would have been for nothing.

The thought made my legs pump faster, and we made it to the front of the building in time to see Iziah safely run into Eira's arms, but Vork's eyes were trained towards the ballroom doors.

Screams echoed behind the doors. When they opened, people flooded out with horror on their faces. I was hauled back by an arm away from the crowd and under the arches of the hallway.

"What's going on?" Dasyra asked over the screams.

"It's the Defiants," Eira answered, hugging Iziah closer.

"They're here to kill the Clergymen?"

Eira shook her head. "No, it would do us no good to kill them in their own home."

Us.

I trained my eyes on her. "Their plan?"

"A kidnapping."

"The Clergymen?"

Eira took a few steps back with Iziah, gazing at me.

"I hope you can forgive me."

I shouldn't have trusted her. I had willingly offered her help expecting nothing in return. I should have known trusting anyone I didn't already know would be a mistake.

"This was a setup," I breathed, balling my fists.

"I did need your help," Eira argued. "You were the only one who could—would help me once I told you my story."

"I had a deal with Silas."

"This isn't about your deal. I took the best opportunity to get my brother out. You were perfect."

It was people like Eira who kept me from trusting others. I had extended a helping hand without expecting anything in return, and like before, it backfired. The relationships I had with Vork and the others had softened me.

I had let my emotions get the better of me, and now, the others and I were paying for it with a betrayal.

Heat began to pour from my hands as I locked eyes with Eira.

"Amara," Vork warned me, grabbing my forearm.

Armed Defiants surrounded us. There was no way out.

Hotheaded as I was, I couldn't bring myself to kill everyone.

"You better have a damn good reason for doing this," I threatened Eira. "Because if you don't, I'll bring hell to your front door."

The corner of Eira's lips curled up. "I know."

CHAPTER 26

Within moments of being captured, our hands were bound and we were all blindfolded.

A gust skated past us. I was pushed forward, and the air turned hotter. The winds continued to swirl around us, and the smell of salt was in the air.

A gull called to my right and continued as it flew overhead. Clamoring followed just ahead as boots fell on wooden planks, the creak of rope being hauled, and bags thrown every which way.

We were near docks.

I was pushed forward again, and this time, my feet landed on the wood I had heard a few moments ago. I was moving at an incline, onto a ship.

We were all placed next to each other, sitting against the side of the ship, still blindfolded. As we cast off, the ship started rocking aggressively against the waves. The shipmates were barking orders to one another, sails were being let down, and crates were moved. So much movement was going on it was hard to pinpoint who to listen to gain any information.

But then I heard that voice.

"Bas, trim that sail, boy! You were taught better than that."

"Right. Sorry, Captain!"

Footfalls scurried away amongst the other sailors, and I turned my head towards the captain as if I could see her.

"Captain," another crew member said. "Your brother is not doing well. I can't break his fever."

She cursed. "We'll be home soon. Do what you can until then."

"Yes, ma'am."

I propped my knees up, putting my bound hands on top.

"So," I sang. "Captain is a big step up from servant."

There was no response.

"I know it's you, Eira."

The clicking of boots came my way in a slow stride.

"We'll be home soon, and then we can talk."

I tipped my head back as if looking directly into her eyes. "Or we can talk now. I've got nothing to do."

"Well, I have a ship to direct, so you'll have to wait."

"Why take us?" I clipped. "We had an agreement that I would come to him when I was ready. I don't think he would jeopardize my willingness to help by kidnapping me."

"Things have... escalated—"

"What the fuck does that mean?"

"—and like I said," she continued, "I needed my brother out of there. Now if you'll excuse me, I have work to do." Eira stomped off and began barking more orders, her voice getting fainter as she moved away.

"Well, this turned out to be a fun night," Vork sighed.

I turned my head to him. "Was that a joke I just heard you tell?"

"Tried to tell," Corym chimed in.

"We could use a mood lightener," the lycan defended.

Corym snorted. "Not from you."

"Anyone but you," Luca agreed.

I sucked in both of my lips to keep a laugh from coming out.

"Alright," Vork said. "Fine."

"I thought it was very funny, Vork," I snickered.

"Shut it."

I tightened my lips and kept the rest of the laughs to myself.

A few moments passed, and I could feel the hover of Vork's shoulder mere centimeters away from mine. I swallowed the lump in my throat and leaned into his arm.

Surprised by the sudden physical touch, he went rigid for a moment but relaxed when I nestled more into his side and rested my head against his shoulder.

"I never got the chance to ask how you are," he said.

I creased my brows, not that he would have seen it. "What do you mean? My wounds are healed. I'm okay."

"You know that's not what I meant."

Oh. He was asking about Vocova's betrayal.

"I'm fine."

I wasn't, though. I was angry, disappointed, and broken-hearted. The only person who I thought was in my corner, aside from Leena, ended up being the enemy's right hand. For all intents and purposes, she had been like a mother. She was always there to counsel me as I grew, and now it all felt like it was for nothing.

I had put so much trust into Vocova I didn't even consider the person closest to me was the one who betrayed me.

I knew now it would be impossible for anyone to simply be given my trust. They would have to earn it, and it would not be as easy as it had been for Eira.

They would need to bleed for me to trust them.

I had given Vocova all those ages of trust, and it wasn't enough. So, what about the people who sat next to me on the boat, tied and blind-folded? I had only known four out of five of them for a few months.

What had they done to gain my trust? Been my friends and mentors while I tried to learn how to be a nephilim? It all could have been an act. Came to my rescue when I found out Vocova's secret? Vork could have very well been in on it and coaxed them to follow.

Vork.

Was he worthy of trust? He had been around when I was most vulnerable, physically and mentally. He could be my downfall.

"Amara."

I came back. "Yes?"

"Are you really fine?"

No, it wasn't him. I knew he didn't want any harm to come to me.

Physically or emotionally. He didn't need to put it into words. It was all in action. His touch was always laced with such care, whether firm or gentle—his ability to truly listen and be supportive, but not being afraid to speak up either.

I wasn't going to overanalyze this.

I could trust him.

He was home.

"Yes," I said with certainty as I leaned into him more. He rested his cheek on the top of my head, and I breathed in his scent. "I will be."

———◆———

I DIDN'T EVEN REALIZE I had fallen asleep until I woke up with the smell of soot raiding my nostrils. My brain was awake, but I hadn't yet opened my eyes. I twitched my nose to keep from sneezing.

We must be at the Mahlar Isle. No other place on Masos was as depressing as this. It was a desolate plain well known in the history books. The site of the Cleansing all those ages ago. On the island's west side, there was nothing but sand and bone left over from the original war.

It finally clicked.

The Defiants were still hiding out on the island. It was the perfect cover.

By order of the Emperor, no one was permitted to set foot on the Isle. Even ships that travelled up and down the coast had to keep a certain distance from it lest they be dragged to the depths of Hell, or so warned the Clergy.

Once we docked, the crew members hoisted us off the ship and into rowboats they used to take ashore.

I sat at the bow of the boat with Leena leaning against me.

"Got any feelings?" I asked.

"They're calm," Leena whispered. "I smell smoke and fire. One would think a different emotion would show itself, but they're not worried."

"Because it's our home," one man said from the stern. "Everyone else is so scared of this island they never venture near it, but we pay no mind to the rumors."

"And you aren't worried about demons circling your base?"

The man snorted. "Demons?"

"The Clergy warns the gates of Hell are at your front door."

"There are no demons here. The last time any set foot on the island was during the war."

"And how have you managed that?"

"Magic, of course," he said matter-of-factly.

Of course.

I rolled my eyes under the blindfold. A simple spell would not hold back beings like Abaddon or Vocova.

The longboat jerked as the bow hit land, and men climbed out to pull it to shore. One of them picked me up by the shoulders and placed me on the sand.

"Can you ease up on the restraints?" Dasyra called with an irritated tone.

"Not until we get to camp." It was the same man I had been talking to earlier.

"I'm getting tired of walking. Carry me?"

The mystery man scoffed. "Absolutely not.'

"Come on, I don't weigh much. I'll walk if you just take the restraints off."

We all snickered at her complaints.

"I said no."

"Touchy, touchy," Dasyra tsked. "Fine, if you insist."

There was no way she was giving up so easily, and we all knew that.

"So, what's your name, big guy? You sound like a big guy. I'm Dasyra."

He groaned and placed a hand on my shoulders, pushing me to move forward faster.

"Easy," Vork warned with a snarl.

The man must have been handling the others the same way.

Dasyra yelped, and I heard her stumble. "Come on, give me your name!"

"Oh, will you shut your mouth?" one man complained.

"Just tell her your damn name," another shouted.

The whole group stopped, and the scuff of his shoes told me our mystery man had spun around.

"Ramon!" he yelled. "Now, will you please grace us with peace? You haven't stopped talking since we got you on the damn boat!"

"Ramon," Dasyra chuckled in victory. "Well, it's nice to meet you. Think we can shake hands?"

I promptly burned off the ropes binding me and lifted the blindfold to see everyone was now free. Ramon's deeply tanned skin wrinkled with surprise.

"How did you—"

"If you wanted us to come to your home," I said, rubbing my raw skin, "all you had to do was ask."

"I'm just following orders."

Dasyra stepped forward. "And why did your Captain want us bound and blindfolded?"

"The Captain, though her intentions were and are pure, knew you wouldn't come willingly since she had deceived you."

I furrowed my brows. "Not true."

Silas and I had understood each other. None of this made sense.

"And," Ramon continued, "it was easier to take you amidst the chaos instead of explaining our reasoning while a fight was going on."

"So why are we here?" Vork asked.

"I can't tell you."

I looked to the sky in annoyance, then back to Ramon. "You tell us what's going on, or we aren't moving, and if you want to fight us, then I welcome you to try."

"I am not in Silas' inner circle. All I heard him tell the Captain is your brother's plans are accelerating."

If air consumed by thick smoke could get any denser, it did at that moment.

"How did you—"

"What's he talking about?" Corym asked.

I didn't answer. Fuck this could not have happened at a worse time.

"Lead the way," I said to Ramon.

The sailors, Vork, and I began to walk, but the other nephilim refused to move.

Corym's anger got the best of him, and he screamed, "Amara!"

His tone stopped me.

"Abaddon," I said calmly, without turning, "is my half-brother."

"Is he another of Michael's heirs?"

There was a tightness in my chest at having to unceremoniously reveal my dirty little secret.

"No, we share the same mother."

"What the hell is going on?" Corym pressed.

"Our mother is Lilith. Abaddon's father is Lucifer."

"Amara, how long have you known?" Luca asked.

I looked at him and found some comfort in his kind eyes. "I found out a few days ago."

Venom laced Corym's next words. "With everything going on, you didn't think we should have been told ?"

I slid my hand down the side of my face. No, I didn't.

Corym snorted. "And now you act like you would rather be anywhere else than here with us."

"Because I do!" I screamed at him. I almost pulled the hair from my head. "I want to be anywhere but here. I don't want to be a nephilim. I don't want to be a part of this little ragtag team of broken half-angels. I don't want to be the 'Girl of Fire.' All I want, all I've wanted for as long as I could remember, is to collect enough money and get off this damned rock. But then you all screwed it up. I don't want any of this! I don't want any of *you*."

I didn't entirely mean the last bit, but I had already said it, so the damage was done.

The pain on Leena's face— the fact I was the one who brought it upon her almost made me reach towards her, but I knew it would do more harm than good. I had to look away, but the next face almost shattered me.

Vork's look of disappointment tightened my chest, and my hands began to sweat. Suddenly I regretted what I said. I was...embarrassed. I had never felt this way before.

I didn't like it.

A strong wind skated by us as the silence built. Tensions rose, and my body heated with the anger that had fueled my words.

Corym stalked over to me and bent down enough to be at eye level, staring into my stern gaze.

"If you don't want us," he said in a low tone. "Fine. If you don't want to be with us, fine. Leave. Take one of the boats and sail to wherever you want. But when Abaddon comes for you—hell, if your mother comes for you—don't you dare try to find refuge with any of us. We would lay down our swords for each other, including you, but since you've made your intentions clear, you are on your own."

"I've been on my own for years. Abandonment is nothing new for me."

"You don't see it, do you?"

"See what?" I spat.

"The common denominator is you. Have you ever considered you were the problem?"

My nails dug into the palms of my hands.

"Enough," Ramon shouted from the front.

More armed Defiants came up from behind, too many for even the nephilims to fight off.

"You've talked enough," one said. "Now move, or we make you move."

With a quick breath, Corym moved past me, shoving into my shoulder as he went.

The others followed. Leena's eyes held mine briefly before she stormed past.

What I said had nothing to do with Leena, never her. Though with her kind heart, there was no way she would accept my apology, at least not now. The others were her family, and I had hurt them.

"Well done," Vork whispered while waiting for me to move.

As we walked, the sandy dunes and harsh sun turned into lush greenery and illuminating light. We soon came to a pathway between the mountains.

The air turned from dry to humid as birds chirped on the long limbs of the trees that covered them. There were so many colors of flowers. I wish it brought me some happiness, but past events had soured my mood.

"How is this possible?" Luca asked.

"The war was long ago," Ramon shouted from the front. "It also didn't scorch everything like people believe. Our home lies just beyond this path."

A small blue bird swooped down on a branch next to Luca and chirped in his face.

He smiled, and the bird cocked its head to the side. "I've never seen this species before."

"It's called a Jenu, and they have acid-like saliva," one of the Defiants said. "I wouldn't put your hands near its beak."

Luca quickly jumped back.

Dasyra let out a snicker and pushed him forward.

Our group went through a small dark tunnel and were met with the same greenery we had seen on the other side. It was a paradise.

Children were playing, giggling as they chased after each other. Merchants were trading at their stalls, selling different goods such as food and pelts. The market was the first thing we saw, and beyond that was a town center with a square platform.

Ramon took a hard right and led us down the base of the mountainside. Above us were dwellings built into the side of the mountain. Elaborate columns held the roofs up, and the linens lining the windows flowed in the breeze.

This was more than I thought possible.

"We've had plenty of time to build," Ramon said.

I gazed up at the rows of houses going as far up as the peak.

"Impressive."

"Come," Ramon said. "The Commander is this way."

We climbed a few floors and walked into the mountain where we were left in a room with an enormous round table. We took our seats as if this were second nature to all of us.

I took the last seat at the end of the table and unease skittered over me as their eyes bore into mine.

I could avoid them earlier because I was at the back of the group during our trudge up to the camp, but now I was face-to-face with their anger.

The trained assassin in me truly didn't care, and she needed to be brought back. They could be mad, but my survival came first.

The nephilim in me, though, had a pain in her chest that wouldn't stop. For the first time in a very long time, she felt regret—regret that she may have ruined the one chance she had at a connection with others.

The double wooden doors opened, and Silas entered with Eira and Iziah at his side.

Iziah looked much better than the last time I had seen him. His washed hair was a light brown, and the color in his tanned skin was returning despite having been held in a hole as long as he was.

Eira was in trousers with a scimitar strapped to her side. She looked nothing like the helpless servant I had met at Elmira. No, she looked like a leader, a captain, and a deceiver. But I really couldn't judge her for the last one too much because I was one as well.

"Good morning," Silas said with a soft smile as he sat in one of the three seats left. "It's good to see you all again."

"Again?" Vork spoke next to me.

I sat back in the chair and scraped my nails against the wooden armrests. "I guess I wasn't the only one holding secrets, huh?" I shot a look at Corym, who refused to meet my eye.

"We—"

"Owe Amara an apology," I finished for him.

He scoffed.

"You," I began slowly, venom spewing from my lips, "judged me for withholding information I had learned only days ago, exiled me from the group, and had the nerve to keep it to yourselves you all are working with the Defiants? At least I only just learned about my family tree. You all have been keeping this from me for months. And you sit here all mighty, thinking what you did was justified? You can kiss my ass. Matter of fact. Get on your fucking knees and apologize."

"Amara—" Leena started.

"How dare you?" I cut her off. "How dare you keep something like this from me. We've known each other for ages, so how long have you kept this secret? Months? Since we first became friends?"

She flinched at my words, and for the very first time, I didn't care. She deserved them. Leena was working with the rebels—hell, was even a full-fledged part of their group for all I knew.

I had kept a secret from her, yes, but I had intended to tell her shortly after the gala. I had intended to tell them all, but never got the chance. Months have passed since I had become a part of their group. They had ample opportunity to tell me about this, and they hadn't.

Was this why they were going on the raids? Hoping to find out information for the Defiants?

"I'm sorry."

My head whirled back to Corym as he spoke.

"There was a reason for keeping you in the dark this long, but I am sorry it came to a head like this."

Was he sorry he got caught lying, or was he sorry he ever lied in the first place? I ignored his apology and turned to Silas.

"Looks like you couldn't wait for me to come to you," I sneered. "What's so urgent you had to have your little workers stage a kidnapping to get me here."

Silas gave Eira a disappointed look before answering. "I apologize on how Eira handled things. That was not the intended plan. Her brother was not to be retrieved until after your arrival. But you are here now. So," he tapped his finger on the chair's armrest, "where to begin..."

"Iziah," I said. "Where does he stand in your ranks?"

"He is one of my lieutenants. His area of expertise lies in infiltration."

It clicked in my head.

"You were there to find answers, weren't you, Iziah?" I asked the boy. "Is there any truth to your sister's story?"

He lifted his head high. "Does it matter? I got what was needed."

I suppose it didn't matter now. It was over.

"And what was needed?"

"Abaddon's plan," Silas finished.

There was an odd and unnecessary pause.

"Then educate us," Vork insisted.

"I first need to decipher what side you are on," Eira said, her gaze bouncing between Vork and myself.

Dasyra placed her boot on the table's edge. "You truly think they're spies?"

"I have thousands of lives I am responsible for," Eira said. "If I am going to unleash a Lycan Commander and his mate in our home, then I will make damn sure they are not here to harm my people."

"You brought us here, remember?" I pointed out. "You stole us, actually." I tilted my head in mock consideration. "Wait, no, you came to me first. And now you wonder if I'm trustworthy?"

"Yes, and now I will see if that was a mistake."

Taking off her thick leather gloves, Eira moved around the table towards me. Before she could get too close, Vork stood, blocking her way.

"Down, boy," she sneered at him.

I sighed as I stood.

"It's fine. Let her do what needs to be done so we can move on."

He took a small step to the side, and Eira placed herself before me.

"Now, hold still and don't fight it. It's much easier that way."

I braced myself as Eira put her hands on either side of my face and kissed me. I froze as she pulled me in by the waist, deepening the kiss. That's when I saw everything I could remember about my life.

I was five, pickpocketing for food and thieving where I could. Then, I was taken in by a man whom I regarded as my father. The man who taught me everything.

It flashed to my first kill, and what a kill it was. A slender baker beating on his wife and half-age-old child. That one had stuck with me, but it passed quickly.

The picture around me spiraled and moved to show the first time I had met Leena. Then, it phased into the bonfire at Clamore, when the sazari attacked.

For a moment, I was warm. It was something I hadn't felt till I was in Vork's arms, and thought I wouldn't feel anywhere else, but I did.

I was next to Leena, who was talking to me, but she was muted, and I couldn't hear what she was saying.

The others were right where I remembered them to be one night when we all drank and let the conversation flow. Luca's jokes had everyone crying by the end of the night, and Dasyra's drinks—boy, were they strong. They were all so happy.

We were so happy.

I hadn't seen any of us smile like that since.

Corym looked up and gave me a warm smile that almost caused me to smile back, but I was pulled away and pushed into another scene where Vork was bleeding in my arms after the sazari attack.

We moved again to the moment at the farm when I had fought alongside the others and sacrificed myself to the hellhound to save them. There was pride in seeing how I'd had them at my back, but it began to crack as I remembered how I had treated them.

The scenes kept moving, from Vork's bed to Vocova's betrayal and then to the present moment.

Eira gently pulled away from me and stared into my now watery eyes. "You hold in so much pain."

I didn't speak as I tried to blink away the tears before they fell.

"They are true, Silas." Eira lowered her hands and moved back to his side.

"What are you?" I finally asked.

"I am a witch of the Bemle Coven from the Northern mountains of Eatren."

Eatren was a land north of Masos. Like the far north, it was well known for its bitterly cold climate. Hardly anyone lived there aside from witches due to the inhabitable conditions.

Is that how we had portaled to the Isles? Eira seemed too young to be able to portal, but at this point, nothing surprised me.

"Witches shouldn't be able do that." Dasyra spoke with skepticism. "What are you really?"

"And you know about the abilities of witches how?" Eira's head tilted in question.

Dasyra's jaw clenched ever so slightly, her eyes narrowing. "I've done my research."

"I'm not lying," Eira said. "I am a witch, but I am from a small faction within the coven. The word is too complicated for the common tongue, but I believe a Gazer is what your people call it."

"A Gazer?" Corym questioned.

"A person who can see your past by touch," Dasyra explained, her curious stare roaming over Eira. "They can do much more if they have training, though. They can alter your memories, make you forget some, and maybe even create lies. They aren't held in high regard once their power is discovered."

The seat scraped across the floor as I pulled it out and sat. "So, you looked at my memories to see if we were who we said we were. How did that work for you?"

"When I look into your memories, I don't just see, I feel. I felt your love and devotion towards these people. I also felt your drive to protect them. No matter how broken your heart may be in this moment, it is true. It's true for them. I don't need to see any more to know you and the Commander are who you say you are."

Before anyone could speak on what Eira had revealed, I leaned back in the seat, and said, "Since that's out of the way." I locked eyes with Silas. "Care to begin?"

CHAPTER 27

SILAS WAS A GENTLE SOUL, or at least that's what I had thought when I first met him. A man who didn't have an aggressive bone in his body, and though I couldn't tell if that was true, I did know he was cautious.

Cautious enough to want us tested to know our true intentions and to keep his people safe. I admired people like that. Masos needed leaders who acted as he did.

"How much do you know of your brother?" Silas asked.

"Not much," I confessed. "I didn't know about him until a few days ago." Up until then, I didn't even know myself. "I know he is the first to be born of Lilith, but I'm not sure what to make of him. Is he a demon or a nephilim?"

Whatever he was, I suppose we're the same, both with angelic fathers and a demonic mother.

"There is no known word for what you are. We weren't aware something like you existed," Silas answered.

Great, even more out of place than I was before.

"You are Amara." Leena leaned in, her eyes gleaming with determination. "Our friend."

I didn't know how to respond. A few moments ago we were at each other's throats. I was still fuming from it.

"So," Vork pressed to turn the conversation. "You were going to tell us of this plan?"

Before Silas could continue, a man came to place a glass of wine in front of him and then quickly took his leave.

Silas took a sip of the liquid and sighed. "We've found that Abaddon needs Amara to get into the Garden. She is the only non-angel to create a gateway and allow others in. The first question you should be asking is *why*."

"Can trained witches not just create a portal?" Vork asked.

"No." Silas shook his head. "This is different. Though she is not fully angel, she has a right to the Garden and its entrance no mortal has. That and no one has ever seen the Garden, so portaling there would be difficult."

"My first thought," I began, "would be he wanted to gain access to the Garden so he could mine luxium and create weapons capable of killing angels. Though, I can't imagine him gathering hordes of demons and sazari just to gain access to it."

Silas rolled the stem of his glass between his fingers. "From the information gathered by Iziah, we now know Abaddon plans to use you all to unleash the four Druxa of Old."

My brows drew together. "Druxa of Old?"

The double doors opened again and in strutted Katar. His high priest robes fluttered behind him as he made his way to the back of Silas' chair, placing his hands on the top. His eyes floated past everyone and then landed on me with a knowing smile—a smile that knew I was as irritated as I looked, remembering the bind he had put me in not too long ago.

His long fingers wrapped around the top of the chair's spikes, and he leaned in a bit.

"Nice to see you again, Amara."

"So, you're how they portaled us to the boats," I accused.

His dazzling smile grew as he shrugged.

Before I could kill him with any venomous words, Silas began talking again and Katar moved to the back of the room, out of sight.

"The Druxa of Old are four beings who were brought into creation when life on this world came to be."

Eira extended her arms and produced a vision of a fire in the darkness above the stone table.

"It is believed this world came into being by fire. There was a single flame that lit the Divine's night. By their will, the world was born from this flame, and so was all the life in it."

The vision moved to show the daily lives of the people in Masos. Farmers were in their fields, fishermen hoisted nets into their boats, and fae ruled in their political seats.

"But, with life came the greed of all."

Scenes of war filled the space above the table. There were screams, deafening to the ears, and enough blood to blind a person. Emperor Bardhyl, the first ruler of Masos and Emperor Neiven's ancestor, sat on a marble throne, wearing a golden crown filled with starlight.

"Through years of constant wars between noble families across the continent came about the Druxa of Old," Silas continued.

Four dark shadow beings stood in front of us. I couldn't see their faces or tell what race they were. These beings were just eerie, and even though they weren't real, they drained all light from the room. It wasn't a feeling of sadness, or anger, or despair, but rather nothing. It was absolutely nothing. I felt absent from all feelings for a moment.

The picture rippled but stayed focused on the Druxa.

"The four Druxa represent the four sins of Masos. The Druxa of War feeds off of strife and aggression. Where there are wars, battles, and petty fights, this Druxa will harness those emotions and create chaos tenfold.

"The Druxa of Famine follows closely behind, wiping out all who survive War's carnage, and after comes the Druxa of Death, taking everyone who withstood Famine.

"The last of the Druxa is the most powerful, the Pale Druxa. From it, the other Druxa's were born. It is all of these beings combined into one, and it feeds off of any ill in the world and amplifies it." Eira moved her hand over the vision, and it changed to a battle in the Heavens. "The Divine and their angels fought off the Druxa and banished them to a place no one but angels could reach... Until now, that is."

I white-knuckled the armrests of my chair. "The Garden."

Silas nodded, and the picture changed to a silhouette of a tree with thousands of branches, its leaves blowing in the wind.

"The Tree of Life, to be more specific," Silas continued. "Abaddon needs the children of Michael, Gabriel, and Raphael to open the seal at the tree's base."

"And what happens when the seal is opened?" Leena asked.

"The end."

"Cryptic," Luca deadpanned.

"The tree," Eira began, "holds all the life on Masos. When a leaf falls, it signifies someone's passing. When new buds are formed, a new soul is being made. Under the tree, directly in the middle of its trunk, is the seal. The seal is what keeps the souls of the Druxa at bay. It's their prison."

"Who put them there?"

"Michael, Gabriel, and Raphael, many years ago, before the nephilim existed," Silas explained. "When the Druxa came into existence, the angels, including Lucifer, knew they would be the end of all life and impossible to control. It took the brothers over a decade to finally capture them and put them in their cage. And now Abaddon wants to free them."

Dasyra scratched her head. "But if the King of Hell himself couldn't control the Druxa, what makes Abaddon so different?"

"We don't know. Whether he can control them or not makes no difference. He can't set them free."

"That still doesn't explain why he needs the angels' children," Vork argued.

"The souls," Silas said simply, as his eyes scanning our faces, "need a body."

"Convenient," Luca said, crossing his arms and sitting back in his chair, "that Gabriel would have two children so Abaddon's plan could work."

Silas took a sip of his drink and peered at Luca over the rim. "Convenience or fate?"

That uneasiness that had entered the room before made an appearance again when Silas spoke those words, though this time it was much stronger. We were sacrifices, vessels.

"For the first three Druxa to be let out of their confinement, the Pale Druxa must kill an innocent. In theory, if the Pale Druxa is released but able to suppress the need to kill, the end will not come." Silas danced his fingertips on his upper lip in thought. "The Pale Druxa will be whoever's blood touches the seal first. I assume Abaddon will choose out of you all."

"He's got to choose Amara," Luca said, his cheek resting on his hand. "Who else would he pick?"

"Why not you, Corym or, Iziah?" Dasyra asked.

He raised his eyebrow and pushed her leg off the table. "Really? Do you think Abaddon would choose either of us over his sister? Clearly, he's a sick sociopath, and the Pale Druxa has to kill the first innocent. Why would he let anyone else suffer like that when he could make it happen to Michael's kid?"

"What will your next move be?" Vork asked Silas, ending the argument. "You're telling us a problem, but we haven't heard a solution."

"We have to keep you all moving."

Before all of this came to be, all I ever wanted was to get off of Masos. This was my chance. But I wouldn't really be living; I'd be running away constantly.

"We can't run," Corym shot back. "Are we supposed to run from Abaddon for the rest of our lives? No, that's no way to live. That's no way for *us* to live."

Silas raised a brow. "I need you alive while I formulate a better plan. We need to buy time."

"That's insane," Luca clipped. "We need to fight."

"Would you have me put a sword in every woman and child's hand to fight against the horde of demons? Would you have me throw people who are against the Clergy at their gates and have their army rip them to shreds? Or what about the sazari? You look into a child's eyes and tell them they must be as quick as a nephilim to stay alive against one of those beasts. Or tell them if they're lucky, the sazari will bite off their heads and they'll feel no pain."

Corym shook his head. "The only people who would take up arms are those who would want to. We would never force anyone to fight against their will, but if they want to learn, we can teach them. You have soldiers here. You're telling me with one hundred percent certainty they don't want to end this?"

Silas held the bridge of his nose. "There are soldiers here to protect the compound, not to be used in a war."

Dasyra fiddled with the wood splintering on her chair. "Have you asked them?"

"Asked them what?" Silas gritted out, clearly trying to keep his composure.

Impressive, I'll give him that.

"If they are happy with their lives. If they want to continue to live this way. Have you asked your people if they are content hiding behind the mountainside, or if they want to fight for their land?"

"We're going around in circles here, young nephilim." Silas looked at us all. "Fight who? The Clergy, the demons or your brother?"

He had a point. The compound had a maximum of a thousand soldiers who were already trained. From the looks of it, there were another five hundred men who looked healthy enough to be armed, and that didn't include the women who wanted to participate.

It still wouldn't be enough.

They would be slaughtered before the fight formally began if they had to fight three different armies. They couldn't fight them all. There was no way the sazari could be talked to, and while Abaddon's horde of demons was the main problem, the Clergy posed their own threat.

From our time in the Holy City, I made the conclusion that all three were linked. Abaddon had demons and sazari fighting on his side and with Vocova's betrayal, it only made sense they were working together. Masos was being attacked by three separate groups.

I looked around the room, but the sound from everyone's mouths was dulled. Corym and Silas were still arguing. Vork had joined in on it while Dasyra, Luca, and Leena engaged in their own dispute.

There was a ringing in my ear that wouldn't stop. It was the reality of the situation in front of us. This had to be dealt with, or the whole world would become nothing.

I sighed internally. My conscience was starting to make an appearance again.

Fuck.

"Okay," I said.

They kept arguing. Of course, they didn't hear me. I could hardly bring myself to say it again because it would mean I was truly about to play a part in this.

"Enough!" I yelled loud enough that the room finally fell silent, and all eyes turned to me.

"What?" Corym clipped.

The words fell out of my mouth slowly. "I said, that is enough. We don't know for certain if Abaddon plans to use me as the Pale Druxa. He could use any of us; none of us is truly safe. Our best option is to separate for now. At least until we have an actual plan of action. "

Leena pulled herself to the edge of her seat. "Split up?"

"Yes." It pained me to say.

"You can't be serious," she scoffed. "We're stronger together."

"But we aren't," I argued. "Think about it. Abaddon needs four of us: me, Corym, Luca, and Iziah. If we all stay together, it would be easy for Abaddon to pick us up and take us straight to the tree."

"You mean you," Corym shot out. "This is all avoidable so long as you don't open the portal for him."

"That is true."

"So just don't open the portal. Done."

My fingers twitched, almost curling into a fist. I let out a quick, short breath. "In the case I am forced, then we're all fucked."

"Vork, you should take Amara to your pack," Dasyra suggested. "Iziah can stay here with Eira. Corym and Leena will go with the Farkath Coven, and I can take Luca to—my coven." She hesitated. "In the south."

"Your coven?" Corym pressed. "Good to know Amara isn't the only one keeping secrets."

Dasyra whirled, her hot gaze meeting his. "Oh, piss off, you pretentious goodie-goodie. Some of us have a past we don't care to speak of."

"So, what?" Luca asked. "We all hide out and stay separated for how long?"

Silas lightly slapped his hands on the armrests. "As long as it takes to formulate a real plan."

"We plan to build our forces and fight," I said. "Train your people, and recruit who you can on the mainland."

Silas considered, then shook his head. "That won't be enough."

I sighed. "I'll handle the rest. I believe I can get the angels to join our fight."

"I'm sorry," Luca coughed. "Did you say angels? Like our parents?"

"Yes. Michael wants me to find Lucifer; once I do, I'll have them join us to repay the favor. Then, hopefully, along with any reinforcements Silas can find, we'll have a chance."

"You've talked to your dad?" Luca asked.

"Once."

That was enough for me.

Silas stood and buttoned his jacket. "I will muster up any more citizens who will fight. With any luck, I may find some witches along the way. You can stay here briefly to get your affairs in order, but come the next moon phase, you will all need to be elsewhere."

Silas took his leave, and Iziah and Eira followed suit.

When they left the room, they took something with them. It was like whatever small string held this group together began to loosen as soon as the door shut. Whatever friendship we had with one another was more fragile than ever. We had been pulled into a plan without being adequately prepared, and now we were being tested and separated.

I had heard some friendships can manifest into another life, and I had begun to think about that more deeply with them—with my friends. But now I worried we were being torn apart and our ability to trust was being stripped away. I only hoped we could survive this. If not, maybe we could find each other again in the next life.

CHAPTER 28

THAT NIGHT, the moon was at its fullest and there was no one in sight near the port. The people of the compound had turned in for the night, minus the guards who patrolled the area.

It was quiet to some degree, but we didn't welcome the silence. The only sounds were the fire crackling in front of us and the waves lapping against the shore.

Dasyra, Leena, and I stood looking into the flames without a word. It was Leena's idea to come together and fix whatever had broken between us not too long ago.

"Well," Dasyra said, breaking the silence first, "this is tense."

Leena rolled her lips between her teeth. "Even though we're standing right in front of each other, it seems we are more separated now than ever." She pulled over a bucket that had been and took a seat. "If we're going to survive or even hope to stop this, we need to trust each other."

I crossed my arms.

"I find it very irritating you all need to know my past to trust me. Conveniently leaving out the fact you all kept this—" I gestured to the compound "—from me. You were working with the Defiants long before I came into the picture."

"It wasn't out of spite, Amara," Luca said from across the way with such a soft voice a human probably wouldn't have been able to pick it up. He and Corym took their places in front of the fire with the rest of us. "This... revolt is not just about us. You saw how many people and families are here, and if we went around telling anyone about our involvement, we would endanger them."

"Trust goes both ways, Luca. If you want to know about my past, then you should have told me about yours."

Leena rubbed her hands through her hair and kept her head down. Maybe she was starting to see this was pointless and might have done more harm than good.

We were about to go to war and being allies at odds with each other wasn't an option. That would mean not only the death of the Defiants but ours, too. If I was to be this leader everyone claimed I was, then... fuck, I better start acting like it.

For our survival. For theirs.

I stood, reaching the pit and placing my hand within the flames. For a moment, I was at peace. The noise of our problems faded, and only warmth was left.

"Before any of you knew me," I began, "I was part of a guild of thieves and assassins. It's where I learned to be who I was. What I am now."

"Was that a good place for you?" Luca asked. "Did you like it?"

I lifted my hand from the flames and watched the excess fire dance around my skin. "It was all I ever knew."

I blew on it to extinguish the fire.

"Yes, but was it *home*?" Luca pushed.

"I suppose, in a way. There were a select few who meant something to me, but the guild itself? No, it wasn't. They took me in, and fed and clothed me, but they also made me into a killer. The training was physically and mentally abusive. When you're a child, it's easy to be groomed into what others want you to be, and I was coming along very quickly." There was silence for a moment. Though all eyes were trained on me, I never moved my gaze from the flames. "I miss Nev because he was the only father figure I could remember having, but I don't miss that place... Just him."

"How did you get to Clamore?" Luca asked.

"I tried to pickpocket Vocova."

That earned me a few chuckles.

"Or so I thought," I said with a small sigh. "Turns out she was looking for me. Michael gave me to her after I was taken from my mother. Diana placed me with a family, and when those parents died, my *aunt* sold me to the Guild—they became my family. After the fire destroyed my home and everyone in it, I took to the streets and had to become a thief to survive. One day I tried to steal from Vocova. But now I know she purposefully introduced herself back into my life. I haven't figured out why yet."

"Wow," Dasyra laughed. "Even when you were a kid, you had balls. I knew I liked you for a reason."

"And you?" I pressed. "Witch?"

Dasyra rubbed her eyes with the inside of her palms before looking up, resting her forearms on her knees.

"I won't go into detail, but I come from a land called Nekeri, far south of Masos. There, I was a part of the Onena Coven. A war broke out between covens, and when I found my family was dead, I fled here. That's when my powers of clairvoyance came in. It took me straight to Clamore."

Leena leaned back in her chair, resting on the back. "Do you not have magic?"

There was a look on Dasyra's face I couldn't place, but it was gone as quickly as it had shown. "I don't really know how to answer that."

Silence rolled over us once again.

"Anyone else have any depressing stories to share?" Dasyra asked. "I have to say, after being betrayed by Vocova, learning of Abaddon's plan, and swapping sad stories, I'm ready for a good night's sleep."

"Hush." Leena hit the side of her arm. "This was good. If we're going to trust each other, and I mean *really* trust each other, then we can't lie. There's only us. We're the only nephilim in this world. There is strength in numbers."

Dasyra groaned and threw her head back. "The Divine, I'm going to throw up. You know where there's strength? In sleep."

"We should get some rest," Corym agreed. "We have some decisions to make in the next few days."

Everyone began making their way back to the main building, but I stayed. Leena turned to me before she left.

"You okay?"

"Yeah, just need a few moments."

She put a hand on my shoulder. "You know you're allowed to feel. Give yourself a break."

I gave her a weak smile.

"Don't stay out too long."

"Yes, *mother*."

She huffed a laugh and kissed me lightly on the head before following after the others.

It only took a moment after they all left for the tears I'd been holding back to come running down my face.

The pressure I was under was beginning to break me, and I was supposed to be unbreakable.

The assassin, the thief, the warrior, the nephilim. I was powerful. I was resilient. I was what our enemies feared. Or at least I was supposed to be. But right now, I felt so small sitting beneath the Heavens that could go on for ages. Would I be enough for them?

Could I be strong enough to win this war and be by their side in battle? Could I convince the angels to fight alongside us? Did I have the power to end it? Because of this, I have to kill my brother. We had no sibling bond to speak of, but we were still blood, could I go through with it? And then, of course, there was the biggest question of all.

How do you kill an immortal ruler of Hell?

CHAPTER 29

The following night, Vork stood before me, armored up and ready to travel. He had just finished strapping on his leathers and securing his sword to his back.

A knock came at the door, and I went to open it.

A witch was going to help Vork travel to his father. Though I was able to portal us once before, I still didn't know how to properly do it, and if he ended up somewhere he wasn't supposed to be, then he would have no help.

The witch on the other side of the door was one I knew, unfortunately.

"Katar," I breathed with a slight bit of irritation. "I would say it's fancy seeing you here, but it doesn't surprise me you're the only witch who can portal."

"Charming as ever." He chuckled. "May I?"

I stepped to the side, allowing him to enter.

"Vork," the witch said.

"Katar." He nodded back.

"It's good to see you well."

Vork only nodded again.

"What are you going to tell your father?" Katar asked.

Vork looked down at me as I fixed the buckle on his chest, making sure the sword was secure...again.

"The truth. Masos is in danger, and so are we. If he wants the pack to survive in the long run, he'll support us."

"And if that does not work?"

"We go with plan B."

"Which is..." Katar pressed.

I pulled on the strap to test its sturdiness. "We marry."

The High Priest raised a brow and shrugged. "That is a good plan. Old people love solidifying their family line."

Vork looked back down at me. "Don't burn the place down while I'm gone."

I gave him a small smile and lightly hit his chest. "Just get back in one piece."

"I'll do my best. It depends on whether he says yes and how hard he'll fight me on it."

"I'd be surprised. I've been refusing you this whole time, and now I'm saying I'll marry. You'd think he would jump at the opportunity."

"I'll be fine and come back with good news." He pressed his forehead to mine and breathed in deeply.

"Travel safely," I said with my eyes closed. The following words flew out of my mouth without a second thought, "Come back to me."

Vork smirked.

"Don't worry, angel, you can't keep me away for too long."

That made me smile, though I didn't move from his embrace. I didn't want to lose the warmth of him against me.

"I'll return with an army, and we'll win this war." Vork touched my head, threading his fingers through the loose strands.

I pulled back and placed my hand on the back of his head, mimicking his motions.

We gave each other a knowing look. A look where we both understood what was at stake but still hated we were parting ways.

Katar stood a few feet from us and held his hands out to his sides. I took that as my cue to step back and allow him to begin.

He moved his hands as he began a chant that neither Vork nor I understood. That sparked his magic, and a portal rippled open at our side. Katar held it open.

Vork gave me a quick wink before stepping toward the one thing that could help us win. When he faded into the portal, Katar closed it behind him, the room fell silent, and a wind skated back at us.

At all once, it was like the wind had pushed away all my good feelings.

I was used to not being with him throughout the day, but him not being in the compound at all made me wary. It was how I felt when I worried about Leena— the fear of not knowing if I could be there to protect her. But I couldn't worry about Vork that way. I shouldn't.

He was a Lycan Commander after all. He had plenty of training and had proved he was skilled against sazari and demons.

In the wake of his absence, I was forced to come to terms with the fact Vork now held a part of me I had unknowingly given, and when he left, he took it with him.

———◆———

I was exhausted.

When I came to, my eyes were so heavy and dry it was almost painful to open them, so I didn't. I lay there with my head— against nothing... I forced open my eyes, and the blinding light created a throbbing pain in my head. I squinted hard and when the pain finally subsided, I slowly opened them.

I wasn't laying down; I was standing in the middle of a field with the sun's rays bearing down on me.

The wind was blowing so hard my nightdress, which I hadn't remembered going to bed in, almost felt like it would come off. My hair whipped around me all the same, and when I went to push it out of view, I noticed my hand. All five fingers were still intact.

Looking down, I focused on my unmarked hand, and nerves began to kick in. I touched the side of my face but there was nothing except for smooth skin. There were no scars from the hellhound or the other fights I'd been in over the past few months. Everything was healed.

There was a yell of laughter across the field. A man grabbed a woman around the waist, lifted her off her feet, and spun her around.

The wind died down into a calm breeze, which coupled with the beautiful weather, set the perfect scene. They looked happy in their own paradise.

It created a sort of sadness in me.

"Beautiful, aren't they?"

To my right stood a man looking off at the couple with an unreadable expression. There was a decent distance between us, but I still had to tilt my head up to look at him. His rich, dark hair was tied back at the nape of his neck, and the wind seemed not to affect him at all.

"They are," I said simply. "I'm envious."

"Do you not have this with the lycan?"

"Our feelings aren't the problem. It's the world around us. It isn't as perfect as theirs is."

"This," the stranger sighed, never taking his eyes off them, "did not last long."

"Am I dreaming?"

The side of his lips quirked up. "Do you think you are dead?"

"Am I?'

"No," he chuckled. "This is not the place you would go if you were dead."

"And where would I go?"

"Hoping to alter your fate?"

I shrugged, pushing my hair back again. "What if I am?"

"It does not work like that. Your fate is written in your blood and the soul that resides in you." He looked down at me, his green eyes almost glowing, and smirked again. "Or so they say."

I wasn't looking to alter my fate. If anything, I didn't believe in it in the first place, but I had to be dreaming. There was no other way all my wounds would be healed.

"You must be my uncle, Raphael?"

The man wrinkled his nose. "No, I am not my brother. He is much scrawnier than I."

"Gabriel then."

He rolled his eyes. "I can see where you might think that. We bear a strong resemblance to each other."

"I know all angels are related in some aspect because they came from the Divine, but I have no other guesses."

"That is expected." He cocked his head to the side, a bit of annoyance in his tone. "I am not talked about much or well-liked."

"You're Lucifer."

He nodded and looked out into the endlessness of the field.

"My father is looking for you."

"I have heard."

Irritation boiled as I turned to face him. "And you didn't think it would be more productive to use whatever resources you're using right now to contact him and not your niece?"

"He cannot help me where I am, nor can you. Not yet, anyway."

Less than helpful.

"Is this real?"

Lucifer shrugged. "It was."

"This dream isn't my memory."

He said nothing, only continued to stare.

"Is that you?"

There was a pause before he let out a small, almost unnoticeable, sigh. "It is—it was, but this was long ago."

"What is the significance of this place?"

Lucifer began to step forward, and I followed. His hand danced over the tops of the grass as we got closer.

"It's not so much the place as who is here."

"The woman?" I followed his line of sight to the couple still chasing each other in the field, and that's when I noticed a little head bobbing up and down in the tall grass. More laughter filled the air, but it wasn't the woman's or the man's; it was a child's. A small girl no taller than their hips chased after them.

"Is that—"

"My daughter, yes. I believe you have already met."

"When?"

He stopped and looked down at me.

I had seen those eyes before. They held an anger in them that, at first, I didn't understand, but now I saw where the anger came from. I understood.

"Keunwysa."

"Yes," he said simply.

"And who is the mother?"

"I believe you know her as well."

He motioned for us to continue walking, and when we reached the family, who was oblivious to us, I saw the face of the woman. She looked different in this memory than when I had met her.

"Empress Sana was your wife?"

"We never married," Lucifer whispered, his head down. He let the grass dance under his fingertips.

To see an angel, *the* Angel of Hell, affected so much by love was very strange. Very...human.

"But in our hearts, that did not matter," he continued. "We loved one another, and that was enough."

I took in the rest of our surroundings, including a small cottage to the left with a smoking chimney and a pen with chickens, a pig, and a horse in the stable to its side. They did look happy. They looked as if they had a simple yet beautiful life.

"What happened?" I finally willed myself to ask.

"My son." Lucifer's voice lowered at the statement, and his hands balled into fists. "Michael had come to me about Abaddon, and after a while, we realized my simple talks with him were not sufficient. I was forced to return to my kingdom and take care of him personally, with force.

"I promised Sana I would be back, but I should not have made that promise...." His voice was small, something I never would have expected from Lucifer. "When I went to handle my son, I found he and his mother had joined forces. Together they put me into the prison I am now in."

"And that's when the war broke out?"

He shook his head. "The war between humans and demons had raged for ages even before my union with Sana. Abaddon had just made it worse when I was not there to control my demons."

"So, you had the power to stop their attacks in the first place?" My voice grew louder. "You could have stopped all of this from happening."

"There will always be conflict," he said with eerie calmness. "It is inevitable. There will always be good and bad. Take away one, and everything will fall apart. My demons created enough conflict to maintain the balance. Every strike had a purpose, but with Abaddon, it was different. He wanted it all, and he wanted it out of violence. His mother helped him create my prison, and I have not been able to escape ever since."

"So, are you here to tell me how to free you?"

"No, I am here to tell you how to defeat my son."

"Can he even be killed? He's the child of the King of Hell and the Mother of Demons. Does that not warrant immortality?"

"He can be killed. I promise you this."

"All right, *Uncle*," I pressed with venom, "then spill it."

"It is her. She is the key."

"You expect me to believe the negative and brutally rude princess of Masos is supposed to kill her brother and the most dangerous demon on the continent? I know you've been locked up for a while, but I promise you, if she doesn't crack from knowing her lineage first, then she'll die before she can even get close to him."

Laughter from ahead took me out of the conversation. If we hadn't been so engrossed in the task at hand, then I might have been able to enjoy the small amount of happiness Lucifer had been able to have.

"She knows who she is," Lucifer said. "Michael assisted with that. Always the better angel." He shook his head and laughed. "Once he heard of my disappearance, he flew to Sana and helped relocate her and Keunwysa to the Holy City, protecting them. After that, I heard about her union with the Emperor and how my daughter was now the Princess of Masos.

"Within that time, Michael had educated Keunwysa on her lineage and her powers that came on at a young age. She was only ten when she learned of her true power, though it is something she must keep from the public. If anyone were to hear she was the daughter of the fallen angel, then they would surely burn her at the stake. The Clergy made sure to douse my reputation with plenty of the foul deeds done in my name, though I had not committed them personally."

A pain twisted in my chest for the bastard. He was the fallen angel we had been taught to fear, but as far as I could tell—at least in the memory before us and in the person I saw standing next to me—he was a man in love who understood the importance of family.

Another pain flared at the fact Michael could go to his brother's child and have a relationship with her, but not with his own. That pain turned to a piping hot brand of anger that burned up my throat.

"How is Keun supposed to help kill Abaddon?"

Lucifer raised a brow at her nickname but didn't acknowledge it further.

"She can summon the pit of Ibith. It is a hole deeper than even my Hell, and the fires there burn bright and hot, and are endless. It is said that it is where all life originated, and unless willed by the Divine, anything that comes into contact with its fire will burn. It is the only thing powerful enough to stop him."

"And she'll just willingly help us? It seems easy when you say it, but we first need to get Abaddon in the flesh and then get Keun to open the pit and somehow get him in it."

Lucifer shrugged. "That is for you to piece together. I have given you the tools needed to finish it."

Arrogant.

"And what of your freedom? Will you tell me where you are so we can send help?"

"No," he said curtly. "My cage is tied to Abaddon's life. There is no way to free me unless he is dead, and as soon as he is, I will be able to free myself. If I told you or any of my brothers or sisters my whereabouts, then they would die for no reason."

I raised a brow.

"I may be known as the Devil, but I love my family and will protect them at all costs, which is why I am helping you. It is taking everything in my being to enlist help from the few demons who are still loyal to me to get this message to you. Please do not let it be in vain, as I cannot do this again. This is up to you to stop, Amara. It should not be your responsibility, but I am asking you to save my family. I fear if you and Keunwysa cannot, then everything will be destroyed, because I was not strong enough to kill my son when I should have."

CHAPTER 30

FROM A YOUNG AGE, my life was never easy. I was an orphan not once but twice. I was turned into a thief and a killer, and I was good at it. There were no age day celebrations or special hugs when I felt sad. No one tucked me in at night and told me of their love for me. Though, I'm now beginning to see the blessings I'd had.

I had no mother or father, but I'd had the guild. Affection was not shown like in a typical family, but the care we had for one another was undeniable, which is probably why it hurt so badly when I lost them.

Looking at who I had now, I could see how lucky I was.

These past few months had been more emotionally and physically stressful than any other time in my life, and yet I was grateful. I was thankful for the family I now had in the nephilim—in Vork. We would die for one another. It was a feeling I never thought I would have.

I had a new sense of purpose as I listened to the wind brush through the trees giving me shade. The chaos of the leaves rustling brought a sort of calm.

I no longer felt the need to run. I needed to fight. I needed to protect those I cared about, and to do that, I needed to play my part in this war.

Not too long ago, I was crying on the beach with an over-whelming desire to run away, not ready to lead anyone. On all accounts, I should still feel that way. I should have been scared and worried, but as I sat with my legs crossed in the camp's garden surrounded by lush greenery and colorful flowers, I felt nothing but content.

For once, my mind and body were at ease. I cared for nothing but how the little light through the trees warmed my skin, and how the grass rubbed against my legs through the skirt I had been given. I was at peace.

I dipped my head back and sighed. Soft footfalls came my way.

"I don't think I've ever seen you so relaxed."

I smirked and looked up at Leena.

"Me either."

Her smile brought warmth all around us, and the sun exaggerated the golden highlights weaving through her natural red hair. She gathered the fabric of her dress in one hand and sat next to me.

"Vork has been gone for almost a week with no word. Are you worried?"

"No."

I would feel it. There was something in me that would begin to tug at my stomach and gnaw at my chest if he were in danger. I would know.

"And if he comes back with news you must marry?"

"Then we shall marry." I lay back, placing my hands behind my head, and looked at the trees above.

"Do you love him?"

"Yes," I said without hesitation. She was too quiet for too long, so I looked over to her. "What?"

There was a bright grin on her face. "You've changed, and I'm glad to see it. You seem happy."

I looked back up at the trees.

Happiness.

That's what I was feeling? I never wanted it to stop.

"Who else do you plan to tell about Keun?" Leena asked.

"No one outside our circle. I'll tell Vork when he returns."

She left it at that and lay beside me, looking at the same place I was. Birds chirped above us, and gulls bellowed just off the shore.

"Do you remember when I was so sure there was a siren in the lake back on the school grounds?"

I snorted. "How could I forget? You wouldn't stop talking about it until I finally went there with you."

"And then you pushed me in to make me go see if she was down there. It took me hours to get the moss out of my hair. Thank you very much." We both chuckled at the memory. The bright green had stood out all too well in her hair. "And we never even saw it."

"I'm pretty sure the lore says they're saltwater animals... so there wouldn't have been one in the lake."

"Shut up. I was young and believed almost anything." Leena rolled her eyes and gave my side a shove. "Anyways, you felt so bad you cared for me for three days after that. I wasn't hurt or upset about my hair, and I was fine overall. Yet, you still looked after me." She turned her head to me. "That's what you do. You're a protector. You've been protecting me for as long as I've known you and sometimes even seemed to care more about me than yourself. But remember, others can do the same for you. Especially Vork."

I looked at her.

"You," she continued, "deserve all the happiness he can give you. It's your turn to be protected and loved deeply. When this is all over, I can't wait to see the life you two will have."

I raised my eyebrow a bit, my stomach feeling a bit uneasy. "That's if we survive this. Thinking too far into the future is pointless. Especially with a war going on. Anything can happen."

Leena pulled my hand from under my head and locked her fingers with mine. Her eyes piercing.

"You two will live a full and happy life. I know it."

The depth of her words showed in her gaze. They never faltered, even after she said them. I wasn't sure if she believed them to be prophecies or dreams. Either way, I squeezed her hand in comfort and went back to staring at the treetops.

Vork returned two weeks later with news his father would assist if we married. His rationale was he couldn't go to war for someone who was not of his pack. I understood it, and even if I didn't, it wouldn't matter because we needed an army, and the pack could provide one.

Shortly after Vork arrived, we all gathered at Silas's round table to discuss what I had learned about Princess Keun. It was a glimmer of hope in the dark haze the multiple battles had cast over us. Finally, we weren't going to be fighting with our eyes covered. But of course, with it came significant risk.

We couldn't entrust something like the retrieval of the continent's princess to any foot soldiers or allow Iziah or Eira to return to the castle. This had to be someone who was stealthy and could come and go without being seen. Luckily, the best person for the job was very well-trained.

I, accompanied by Dasyra, would infiltrate Elmira and bring the princess back without leaving so much as a footprint on the sands to indicate we were there.

We debated for a long while about who would take on the mission and how going myself was too dangerous.

"It's war," I said to them. "No part of this is supposed to be easy. Lives are being lost daily, but we could be one step closer to ending it. This is the answer to your better plan, Silas. It's not me who will end the war— it's her."

They eventually saw reason and agreed. It was decided the wedding would take place in two days, and then two days after that, we would move forward with the plan. The longer we held off, the more time we would leave for error and could possibly miss our opportunity.

Two days after the meeting, I sat in my boudoir, watching as Dasyra dipped her brush into the soot-filled canister one last time before applying a thin line of black to my top lid.

"There," she breathed in victory. "All done."

I barely recognized myself under the makeup, and my hair had never been so intricately braided. I had to admit, I looked damn good.

Leena worked to adjust the last strands of hair as the braid fell down my back, and we locked eyes in the mirror.

"You're beautiful."

I returned the smile in kind and stood from the vanity to retrieve the dress from the bed. It was a gift from Nareus, my soon-to-be father-in-law.

It was typical attire for a bride in their culture. The dark red dress was long, hanging to the top of my feet with a small train flowing behind. Each of the sleeves were structured and firm, while the rest of the dress was made of a soft, flowy material. Thick straps crisscrossed over my chest, leaving bits of skin exposed down to the top of my navel. The back, by contrast, was completely covered.

Dasyra stood near the window as Leena helped me get dressed.

"It looks like it's going to storm," Dasyra said, gazing at the sky. "Do you think they'll cancel the wedding?"

Leena fastened the zipper at the back of the dress.

"No," I said. "They'll see it as a sign the Divine is weeping tears of joy. If anything, they'll be more excited by the fact."

"But all our work will go to waste because of the rain," Dasyra pouted.

Leena rolled her eyes and tried to suppress her smirk as she pulled me to the full-length mirror. She held my shoulders from behind and peered at our reflections.

"There is still time to back out."

Staring at myself, I ran my hands down the front of the dress.

"If I do, then we won't have the support of the Arabrosa pack. We need them and the angels if we're going to survive. Also," I hesitated, embarrassed to say the next words aloud, "I wouldn't mind marrying him."

Dasyra draped her arm over the mirror's top and leaned in with her other hand on her hip. "You're happy?"

I nodded.

"And you love him?"

A smile played on my lips as I looked at myself in the mirror, and butterflies fluttered in my stomach.

"Well, color me speechless," Dasyra said in a shocked tone. "Amara is in love, Leena."

Before I could respond, there was a knock at the door, and Vork filled the frame.

His black jacket fell to his knees, still unbuttoned to show the clean shirt underneath. He wore a similar shade of trousers, and his hair was a bit unruly. He didn't look proper for a wedding, but I didn't care, I saw him, not the fancy clothing. I saw the man, and he saw me, too.

Leena moved out of the way, and when our eyes locked, a look of shock painted his face. But it quickly morphed into an expression that heated me to my core. After gawking some more, he finally willed his feet to bring him to stand before me, but he remained silent.

His eyes searched mine, and the level of intimacy he was showing almost made me turn away, but I couldn't. This man was about to be my husband, so I needed to accept the love he showed me. I looked back at him, the same emotion shining in my own eyes.

He was perfect.

"What, no compliments?" Dasyra chastised. "We worked hard to prepare your bride."

As if she had said nothing to him, his eyes stayed locked on mine, and he placed a finger under my chin. "She's perfect."

The side of my lip twitched. "Ready to be tied down, Lycan?"

He took my hand and began pulling us to the door.

Dasyra and Leena followed as we walked hand in hand down to the beach where everyone waited. We walked in silence, understanding words no longer needed to be exchanged to show how one feels when there was a connection not even their Divine could destroy.

As we came out of the stone hallway of the compound to the beach, we were met with groups of people divided by an aisle down the middle. A High Priestess from the Arabrosa pack stood at the end. Everyone's eyes were on us.

People from the Arabrosa pack stood to the right and the Defiants stood to the left, but neither of us took our eyes off the High Priestess in her simple grey robe.

When we reached the end, our hands still entangled, the heavens roared loudly and began to weep.

The High Priestess then spoke.

"It is a glorious day that the Divine should grant us this storm upon the bonding of these two. The first union between a Lycan and a Nephilim."

The High Priestess picked up a small bowl and dagger from the altar behind her, then continued in a language I didn't understand.

Vork turned, so we were facing one another.

"She's blessing the blade," he whispered to me.

The High Priestess returned to us, and Vork extended his right hand. She brought the sharp blade down on the pad of his thumb and let the blood drip into the bowl.

I did the same when the High Priestess turned her gaze to me. Our blood mixed, and she closed her eyes, saying another string of words in the unknown language.

The rain began to fall harder, and by this time, we were soaked.

My gaze moved from my now-healed finger to Vork's eyes, and the way he gazed at me stopped everything around us. Nothing else but this moment mattered to me. Only him.

With his free and wounded hand, Vork brought his thumb to my forehead and created a line down the middle to the crossroad of my brows.

He motioned for me to do the same.

"My finger," I said. "It healed."

I gave my hand back to the High Priestess, and she created the wound again. I followed the same action he had with me, but before I could put my hand down, he caught it in his grasp and lightly held the wound to his lips.

I did the same to him.

It should have caught me off guard, but the tangy taste of his blood did everything but that. Knowing what we were doing was real and how the feelings were truly there for both of us made me feel even more alive.

All too soon, he took his finger away from my mouth and wrapped his hand around my forearm.

He and the High Priestess said more unknown words to me, his eyes never leaving mine. They seemed like a promise or a declaration; whatever it was, it would change me, and there was no going back.

Not that I would ever want to.

I wanted this.

I wanted him.

"Repeat after me," he said, and I did.

The intricate language rolled off my tongue, but it wasn't nearly as elegant as when he had said the words.

When I was done, the High Priestess poured the mixed blood and rainwater over our linked arms.

"It is done."

The crowd was still silent, and thunder roared again loudly, the shore waves threatening to move inland.

"In this moment," Vork said over the noise with water cascading down his face, "and until my last, I am bound to you."

He was translating the oath.

"I am yours. I am your lover, your servant, your protection, and your sword. To the hellfire and the heavens above, there is no place my soul will not find you again in our next existence. Because my very being is and has always been made for you."

I no longer knew if my face was thoroughly wet from the rain or if it was tears. This man had broken me down into thousands of pieces like the sand we stood on, yet he had all the power to put me back together, and he did. He took away everything and yet gave back so much more.

"For you," I vowed.

The biggest smile played on his lips as he pulled me in for a kiss. Our lips moved in effortless sync, and our bodies molded to one another. The guests around us began to cheer. We pulled away with smiles on our faces, then turned to the guests, and their cheers grew louder.

I saw my friends all celebrating and giving me big smiles and nods of congratulations. I scanned the crowd to see Vork's side, where his father and other high-ranking pack members stood, also in good cheer.

The rain had eased up a bit, allowing me to see through the stone archway we had entered through. I squinted and saw a man leaning on his side under the stone. It wasn't clear enough to make out his face, but he was tall and had broad shoulders.

People came flocking to us, offering congratulations, which tore my eyes away from the man. There was a kiss on my cheek and a tight hug around my neck before I could look back to the shadows, and when I did, he was no longer there. His back was to us and wings developed behind him, so massive they stretched past the archway on each side.

The wings shot him up into the sky, and when my eyes swung to the top of the hallway where I expected to see him flying, he wasn't there.

It was as if he had vanished during his ascent to the Heavens. But he had been here, and he'd left behind proof of his existence leaning against the bottom of the wall.

With my hand wrapped around his arm, Vork guided us down the aisle to the archway where the object was. He pulled me to him, lightly brushing the back of his hand against my cheek.

"How inappropriate would it be for me to steal you away without even going to the celebration?"

"Very," I snorted. "Seeing how many high-ranking members of your pack came. They wouldn't be thrilled."

He smiled in response, and I turned to see what the angel had left.

It was a huge sword that came up to my elbow made of gleaming steel that would no doubt reflect the sun if it were out.

"A sword?" Vork questioned.

It was simple. No writing, indents, or jewels. I picked it up with two hands, as it was too heavy for just one, and when I did, it began to glow an angry orange. It was the color of molten lava and threatened to burn anyone who met its end, minus two individuals.

"From my father." I held it up as high as my arms would allow. "A flaming sword."

I held it between us, and the heat must have warmed Vork's face, because he grimaced. I moved the sword to my left hand and let the tip rest on the stone walkway.

"Why would he give you his sword?"

This was no longer his sword. The handle molded to my grasp, and a tingle ran up my arm.

"He's preparing me."

Out of my peripheral vision, I saw a movement, and before us stood the crowd with their hands over their shoulders and their heads bowed. It was a sign of respect for a warrior who had won many battles, a leader with enormous power, and it was directed toward us.

A gesture to show they had found their earthly-bound general who would lead them into battle. With us was the sword of flames, that would aid in our victory.

CHAPTER 31

I sat in an ornate wooden chair at the head of multiple rows of people who were drinking, cheering, and when I looked close enough, fucking.

What a party our wedding had turned out to be. Get enough drink into even the most respectable aristocrat, and they'll begin to spill all their secrets.

It's how I found out demons and sazari were threatening the pack's northeastern borders and pushing into their land. There were whispers of my new father-in-law losing his grip on power, and despite this marriage helping to solidify his claim, he was being challenged by packs all over the continent.

I was alone in my chair, sipping red wine, that was making my head a bit fuzzy, and looking at Vork conversing with his pack members. Some were older, no doubt his father's acquaintances, and others were around his age. Possibly childhood friends. My own friends sat to my right.

Corym was cozying up to a beautiful girl. Leena was being Leena, making everyone around her laugh or smile in pure joy, but it was Luca and Dasyra who piqued my interest most.

They both sat straddling the bench beneath them, pulled close in a conversation. Her foot sat right behind his backside, making them even closer. His hand stroked hers, which was wrapped around a large stein, and her eyes pierced into his with determination.

Oh, he was in trouble.

I brought the wine to my lips and looked back at my husband.

Husband.

I didn't think I'd ever get used to that, but I had to admit I liked it. He still carried on talking to those around him about who knows what, and I emptied my cup.

A cupbearer came quickly to refill, and I regretted not stopping him. It's hard to get a nephilim drunk, but not impossible. I swapped my wine for the nearby water and chugged as much as I could.

"Hi."

Hanging onto the back of my throne was a man with an exceedingly bright smile painted on his face. His teeth gleamed against his dark skin, and it was all I could look at until I met his eyes. They were warm brown and stood out beautifully against his complexion, but I found my gaze returning to his smile and how the apples of his cheeks lifted with the expression.

His right arm was draped over the back of the chair, while his other hand held a cup, his index finger threaded through the thin handle.

"Hi," I parroted back. "To what do I owe the pleasure?"

"I assure you." He moved to sit on the table and took my hand before kissing the top. "The pleasure is surely mine."

I and raised a brow. "I guess it is."

He sat upright and pushed back his coarse hair; the braided locks traveled down his back. "I am Mathias of the Arabrosa pack."

I made an 'o' with my mouth and took another sip of water. "To what do I owe the pleasure, Mathias?"

"I felt it rude I had not met the sparkling bride that has been so highly talked about."

"I wouldn't use the term 'sparkling' to describe me."

"How would you describe yourself?"

"Menacing, puissant, maybe even bewitching."

He momentarily contemplated, then pointed a finger at me, wagging it around. "I think I agree with all those."

It wasn't until I looked closer at those warm eyes I noticed a slight glaze.

"You're drunk," I said aloud.

"I'd add observant to that list. But yes, just a tad. A lycan doesn't tend to stay that way for long, so I try to ride the high as long as possible."

I could understand. I wasn't sure how soon my sobriety would come, but I wished my tipsy state would stay a bit longer. It was a nice reprieve.

I chugged the rest of my water, leaving the chalice on the table, and sat back.

"I'm sure you could be using your inebriated state to woo someone else in this room besides the newlywed."

He waved his hand over my cup, and after a faint glow, it was full again, this time with wine.

"I promise you, my lady, if I intended to seduce you, you'd know." Mathias handed me my cup and clinked it before taking another sip of his own drink.

I had never seen a lycan do magic before. I looked down skeptically at the liquid.

"I have a witch in my ancestry," he answered my puzzled look. "I got lucky to be able to do very basic magic."

"Well, if this is all you have to offer, then I understand why you're up here with me instead of any eligible women in the room. Your game is horrible."

I smirked and took a sip of the wine. It was sweeter this time.

He scoffed.

"I'll have you know I am very well desired by women. In fact, I have my eyes on a beautiful redhead currently." He looked across the room, locked eyes with her, and waved. "Anyways, I'd dare not anger the Blood Commander, so my duties have me attending to other needs."

Blood Commander?

"And those would be?"

"Well," Mathias said, his cheeky smile still plastered on. "I am what one might call a 'right-hand man' to Vork. We've been close since we could walk and have always referred to each other as brothers. Since I am his only known brother, there is a custom."

"And that would be?" I asked again.

"There must be a duel between the newlywed and a warrior of the Chief's choice. He's chosen me to be his representative."

I nearly choked on my own spit in laughter. "You want me to fight you? Right now? While you're hammered?"

"I am not hammered. I'm actually starting to sober up, unfortunately. So, what'll it be, oh bewitching goddess? Will you fight me?"

This was absurd. It's supposed to be a celebration. "To what end?"

"Till one of us submits or passes out."

He stood and downed his drink before putting his hand out for me to take. He was serious. Was this actually a custom? I'm in a dress for fuck's sake.

Without thinking, I looked around the room and instantly met Vork's eyes. There was mischief in his gaze and a hint of a challenge. He didn't think I would do it. He thought I'd back down. No, he knew I wouldn't.

Without breaking eye contact, I took Mathias' hand, and he escorted me to the middle of the room, where he began to clear a space for us. A rhythm of hoots sounding almost like a chant echoed as we walked. When we got there, Mathias approached Vork where stood in front of the group.

"I'll go easy on her," Mathias said to him with a smile.

"Honestly," Vork chuckled, "It's not her I'm worried about."

His friend's smile faltered but was replaced quickly with a snort. "We'll see."

Mathias turned to face me, undoing the top button of his dress shirt and rolling up his sleeves.

"Till yield or unconsciousness!" Vork yelled above the chanting till it abruptly stopped, and all one could hear was the roaring fires in the room. "You may begin."

Mathias held his hands up in preparation and began circling me. I mirrored his steps, letting my heels be the only sound I focused on for the moment.

"I won't yield," I stated.

"Then this'll be fun."

He lunged. My damned shoes threw me off balance when I dodged, and I fell to the ground. He didn't waste any time in charging for me again and bringing his right foot down hard where my body just was. I had rolled away just in time.

Mathias moved quickly, constantly keeping me moving and expecting me to be on the defensive the entire time. Normally, I'd do that so he would tire out, and I could strike. That's what the assassin would do, not the nephilim.

The next punch came with a lot of force to the abdomen, but I took the blow, toppling over to find my breath. With my grip on his fist, I pulled him forward enough to bring my knee up to his stomach, throwing an uppercut to his jaw and a kick hard enough to push him back.

He lay on the floor gasping for air and digging at his chest where my foot landed. "You almost impaled me!"

"It wasn't that hard."

"*I could've died!*"

"Stop whining," I said, pulling my heels off and throwing them to the side. "I knew what I was doing."

He eventually got up but still had hands on his knees for support. "This isn't to the death."

"I'm aware." I shrugged and placed my hand on the edge of the lit brazier. "But keep in mind, if I wanted you dead, it wouldn't be with a heel to the heart." I tugged at it so the hot coals formed a line across our space.

Mathias' eyes moved tentatively from me to the fire and back again.

"What's wrong? Afraid to singe your fur?"

He tentatively took a small step forward to then abruptly stop before he got too close.

"That's okay. I'll come to you." I walked through the flames, the light clinging to my fingertips and my body warming. When I was a good foot or two in front of him, I lifted my hand below my chin and blew.

Embers sparked from the flames on my fingertips and scattered across his face, causing him to flinch and giving me the opening I needed.

I went for his legs, but Mathias recovered quicker than anticipated. He blocked my initial attack and the fists I threw his way.

We ended up with our hands on each other's necks, our other hands raised in defense, and our heads leaned back against the holds.

"You fight dirty, don't you?" He mused between clenched teeth.

I let go of his chin to break his hold on me, only to have him push me back into one of the wooden tables where guests were currently sitting. They all scurried away when they realized the chaos that had literally been thrown at them.

The crowd's cheering was still running rampant in the background. The room turned hotter, and I searched for Vork in the crowd.

There was too much going on. The crowd, the fire crackling around me, the intense throbbing I had in my head from getting knocked around, and the blood I just seemed to notice oozing out of my nose.

I came back to reality right as a fist was hurtling towards my face. There was an audible crunch, and those close enough to hear sighed in pain. I fell back on the table and gasped, unable to breathe through my nostrils.

Mathias didn't attack again, so I could sit up and cradle my face. "You broke my nose."

He shrugged back at me. "I play dirty."

Fair enough.

I grabbed my nose and popped it back into place, already feeling it beginning to heal.

"Well, come on then," I sighed and lifted both hands, palms up, curling my fingers toward myself in challenge.

Unfortunately, Mathias was happy to oblige and lunged for me. I scrounged for anything that lay behind me and came back with a wooden plate I swung at him. There was a crack, and at first, I thought it was his cheek or maybe I had paid him back for my nose, but I looked down, and the wood was broken in half.

"I'm much more durable than you think," he boasted.

I raised a brow and made my way to the empty throne beside mine. They were both made of a deep wood, carved to perfection, with intricate details on the arms and the backrest. It would be a shame to ruin it, but when inspiration struck, it was wrong to ignore it.

On either side of the back rest was a column of wood with a heavy ball at the top. I gripped the ball and used my other hand to break through the base. I did the same with the other side, then faced Mathias.

His expression was indifferent, but he didn't know that for months, day in and day out, I had trained with weapons like these.

Stalking towards him, I twirled the wood in my hands, gauging how highly off balance they were.

"Oh, you're fucked now, pretty boy!" Dasyra hollered out with a hearty chuckle.

We were at it again, but now I was truly in my element. I dodged most of his hits, and the ones he did land, I returned with a more brutal force. It got to the point where his crimson blood started to accumulate so much his face was completely covered, and it dripped down to his shirt.

If I did any more of this, then he wouldn't heal quickly enough, and I'd really hurt him.

I threw the wood to the ground and bent down till we were at eye level as he wiped away the blood from his nose. "Do you yield?"

"Not a chance, pyro."

I won't lie; I expected him to. Mathias had a lot of resolve. I was glad someone like him stood behind Vork, but this needed to end.

Taking a clump of his locks in my hand, I pulled him to his feet to walk towards the line of fire left from the brazier. I pushed him to his knees and then forward till I rested my knee on his back, keeping him immobile and his face inches from the fire.

He tried to move away, but I held firm.

I bent down till my mouth was at his ear. "I like you, Mathias. You're a worthy opponent, and I can tell an even better brother to Vork. I'm sorry we met under such... violent circumstances, but I'd like to wrap up this evening, so if you wouldn't mind—" I lowered my voice to a command, "Yield."

I could see the wheels turning in his head to fabricate some sort of escape, but he had nowhere to go. When he put his hand up in defeat, the room erupted in cheers, and their chants began again.

I sighed and released my hold to turn him over and extend my arm. I could see the irritation on his face at his defeat, but it was slowly overshadowed by a smile as he took my arm and let me hoist him up.

"Congratulations on the nuptials." Mathias bowed, then moved to the side.

Vork scooped me up and wrapped his arms around my upper thighs, hoisting me in the air for all to see.

I chanted with them. The high of the win and adrenaline coursed through my veins as he walked me around the edge of the ring. When we made our way around again, I wiggled so he would let me down. I grabbed the back of his head and crushed his lips to mine, tasting him and the blood that mixed between our lips.

I broke the kiss first. "Any more unknown trials you want to tell me about?"

"No, angel," he chuckled.

"Good. Take me to bed."

His eyebrows shot up, but I crushed our lips together again before he could get a word out. He hoisted me up again, wrapped my legs around his waist, and began to move.

I paid no attention to where he was going or to those around us. All I knew was I needed him, and I had worked so hard to have him.

After a few more seconds of walking, he opened a door and walked us into a room. Without breaking our kiss, he slammed me against the door he had just closed and locked. I groaned at the sharp pain that radiated up my spine from the impact, but I refused to let it get in the way.

I took a bite out of his bottom lip while ripping the front of his shirt, giving me access to his neck and chest.

He hissed at the sudden pain and dug his fingers into the flesh of my ass while grinding into me. It almost sent me over the edge. My whole body was tingling, and I didn't want it to stop.

My lips traveled down his jaw to his neck, where I took another bite, being careful not to break skin but still putting force behind it.

He was mine.

"Fuck." He strung out the word as he moved again, and I was sat on a large oak table situated in the middle of our room, the intricate design of the edge digging into my legs.

Vork flattened his hand on my chest to push me back. I arched into his touch as his hand traveled down my body to the place that hurt the most. He moved the fabric there aside and scissored his fingers just on the edge of me.

I was soaked, and I wasn't ashamed.

"What a good girl."

"Yes." It came out so breathlessly, like I needed him to breathe, and I did. If I didn't have him, I would drop dead. I yearned for him in this moment and every other.

"Tell me how bad you want it. I want to see what pretty little declarations I can get out of that foul mouth of yours."

I trembled when his fingers came together to circle around my clit in lazy circles. My hips jerked forward of their own volition, begging for more friction.

He stopped moving and placed his free hand on my chest.

"You're not in control here," he commanded, moving that hand to my throat and placing a firm grip on it. "You may be a powerful nephilim to the world, but you're mine here. Mine to toy with, mine to tease, mine to fuck. Don't get it twisted, angel. I'll be happy to give you a proper recollection of what that means."

I grabbed the hand at my neck.

"Do you want me?"

His eyes softened ever so slightly. "More than the air I breathe."

"Kiss me."

He happily obliged, crushing his lips back to mine, our tongues connecting and creating total bliss.

I pulled him on top of me as much as the angle would allow. I needed to feel his body on mine, his skin connected to mine, but before that could happen, I flung him off me, and he landed with a thud on the hard ground, then looked at me in disbelief.

I hopped off the table and undid the fabric at my neck, allowing the dress to fall to the ground.

"I fought for you," I said as his haunting gaze rolled over my body. "I believe now you need to earn the prize that bled for you. Catch me if you can, pup."

I took off in a sprint, making my way to the bed, but he was faster than I thought. He blocked me in seconds, making this less of a game than I had intended. I shuffled back as he stalked forward, undoing the remaining buttons of his shirt.

My bottom hit the dressing screen positioned close to the window. I yanked down the silk robe hanging from the edge and put it on.

It looked like I would have to expand my range. I sauntered over to him, but just before he grabbed hold, I spun out and finally made my way to the door.

When I got it open, the hallway light bled into the room. Vork's eyes darkened, and his hand twitched ever so slightly, wanting to grasp something so far out of his reach.

His shoulders moved slowly but forcefully up and down.

A wide, mischievous smile formed on my face as I drank him in.

Oh, I was in trouble.

"Amara," he warned, but it wasn't a warning for me. It was a delicious promise.

Finally.

I puckered my lips to blow a quick kiss then ran down the hall.

The blood pumping in my ears muted all else, and my eyes were locked on only what was in front of me. My adrenaline kept me from focusing on anything but moving my feet.

I was fleeing from a predator, but I knew at the end of it all, there would be nothing but pure bliss. I was too excited to think about anything but my husband fucking me hard against any surface he could find.

"Run, run all you want, little rabbit."

How was he so close already?

"I know your scent, and when I get you—" He let out a guttural laugh that sent shivers down my entire body. "Oh, when I get you..."

I took turns wherever I could to keep moving forward. I had no idea where I was. I had explored the fort, but no more than I really had to, and I'd never been in this part of this building before.

It was more refined than other parts. Old, red carpet ran down the center of the halls with gold trim on either side. Small fire sconces lit it up well against the rough brick walls. Besides that, there wasn't much to the decor outside the rooms.

I was stopped abruptly, cool iron jutting against my stomach, and my front end teetering over the edge of a balcony to an empty lounge below. A fire was roaring in the huge stone fireplace, casting a glow around the room. A large chaise lounge sat in the middle, but before I could make out anymore my head was yanked back.

"Gotcha."

Thick fingers wound in my strands with a vise grip making me lose my breath. Vork's own was hot on my neck just below the ear. He gave me a tiny kiss on that sensitive skin before using his other hand to pull the robe aside and expose more skin, his lips leaving a sear of lust in their wake.

I moaned a chuckle. "That's because I wanted you to catch me. Don't tell me you actually thought you could on your own?"

He took a hard nip at my lobe and I yelped in protest. His free hand traveled from the collar of the robe down to the underside of my breast, where he lingered for a moment over the satin material, teasing my already scorching skin.

I pulled against the grip on my hair and angled myself to look at him. My heart was racing as if I was still running, my body temperature had to be dangerously high, and I felt drunk, though the effects of the alcohol had worn off.

Vork's fingers found their way into the robe's opening, and he ran the tips of his fingers up and down, in between my breasts, making me shudder.

I said his name so breathlessly it took everything I had to make it loud enough for him to hear. "Don't tease me."

"Oh?" He pulled back slowly, now tracing circles. "You tease me running around these halls in this pathetic excuse for a robe." His fingers traveled farther down until they lightly grazed the curls that covered me. "I think you've earned this punishment. You—" He slid two fingers between my folds, making my breath hitch, and used the wetness to circle me slowly a few times before bringing them back up. "Deserve this."

I went to protest, but he put those wet fingers in my mouth.

"Suck," he demanded.

Too eagerly, I complied, running my tongue against the rough pads of his fingers.

Vork ripped his fingers from my mouth and turned me before hoisting me up and linking my legs around his waist. His lips met mine in a demanding kiss, muting the noise of my heartbeat in my ears. I could feel, see, and hear nothing but him.

He took us down the small staircase to the lounge faster than I realized because we were already sitting when I pulled away from him.

I rested my arms over his shoulders and ran my hands through his loose hair. My eyes locked with his, and in that moment, I saw more than the lycan or the Blood Commander— I saw my husband.

"What are you thinking about?" he asked.

"All those months ago when I didn't want anything to do with you."

A smile played on his lips.

"At the time, I hated your presence. Every time you spoke was like a knife to my ears..." I paused, and his smile faltered. "But... how much I yearned for you at the same time was... not like me. There was a part of me that was missing, and the rest was broken. Leena glued together those broken pieces, but that missing half was with you. I was too stubborn to admit it." I clasped my hands on his cheeks and rested my head on his. "Everything I am from now till the end is for you."

He beamed, holding me at the nape of my neck. The grey storms of his eyes brewing as they darkened with hooded lids. "You are my soul. Don't you ever part from me."

The kiss was gentle and loving—or longing, like this was the first and last time we'd ever hold each other. His hands, tender, slid down my side and hoisted me closer before the kiss became demanding.

Ah, there he was.

"On your knees."

Part of me wanted to play this game he had started, but I was too wound up. I *needed* the relief now. So, I ignored him. Despite the grip he had, I pulled hard enough to crush my lips to his again, but he was rigid against me, his lips unmoving.

He grunted in what I hoped was frustration, but I knew that wasn't true. His other hand wrapped around my throat, and he forced me back.

"I know those ears on that pretty little head work. Don't act like you didn't hear me."

"I heard you fine. It's just not what I want."

"I—" His touch became softer, his thumb tracing my bottom lip. "—will always put you first. I will always genuinely care about your wants and needs." His hand went to its original position and squeezed, blocking my airway a bit. "But not tonight."

Everything happened so fast, the only thing I could see or feel was the dull pain of my knees hitting the carpet and my eyes level with Vork's crotch.

The corners of his mouth turned up in a sexy smirk, and he said nothing while looking down at the strings of his trousers. I glanced up and couldn't hold back a smirk of my own.

Sliding my hands slowly from his knees up to his thighs, I bent forward to take one of the strings in my mouth and pulled slowly. Butterflies flew in my stomach at his slightly parted mouth and almost hazy eyes.

Once untied, I looped my tongue under the crossing of the string and pulled it loose.

"You've done this before," he guessed.

I shrugged with a smirk. "Once or twice."

After pulling his trousers fully off, I took hold of him and dragged my tongue from the base till my lips wrapped around the tip.

I looked up, and the sight alone was enough to make me whimper against him. He leaned his back up with his eyes closed, and his arms wide, resting on the back of the ornate furniture, shirt open to show his abs flexing with every suck I gave him.

The air grew hot. I was scorching and *desperate* to see him unravel. My mouth traveled down his length until he hit the back of my throat, and I swallowed, constricting my hold even more.

Vork hissed as he tangled his fingers in my hair and closed his fist.

I came up and wrapped my hand around his length, twisting as I began bobbing again. I massaged his balls in my other hand and they tightened.

"Amara, stop."

Oh no. No, I won't.

I kept going and switched hands, so I cupped him with more wetness.

"Stop."

No.

He now had a death grip on my head, and he ripped me away.

"Enough."

His voice was so powerful and twisted I couldn't help but submit for a second. That second was all he needed to push me to the floor, to my front, and pin me there.

The fire was hot on my face as his full weight pressed into me.

"You dirty girl. You were going to make me come, weren't you?"

"That's the whole reason I'm here."

"But you wanted to force it out of me." He propped up to place a pillow underneath my hips. "Like I said, you're not the one in control."

Without warning, he pushed into me smooth and slow. The sensation made my eyes roll to the back of my head, and I finally submitted fully. It was pure euphoria.

Never mind the feeling of him inside me, it was his weight on my back, keeping me safe, and his ragged breath against my hair, letting me know he felt it too.

One of his hands held my hip in place as he ground against me, while the other pinned my hands above my head, our fingers lacing together. I swirled into the pillow, adding a delicious friction.

If their Divine could grant me one favor, I would ask for this moment to stretch on for as long as possible.

Vork thrusted deep enough to push me forward and rub me against the pillow.

"Yes," I moaned for him.

He pushed up, releasing my hand to grip the back of my neck as he rhythmically rolled his hips, eliciting a whimper—*a fucking whimper*—from me.

"This is what you want?"

"Gods, yes. *Yes.*"

The thrusts became short and quick, making my toes curl and sparks lighting under my skin.

"Come on, angel, give me what's mine."

All too quickly, my body seized up, and I clenched around him, screaming his name, my nails scratching the rug below us.

As I caught my breath, Vork soon followed and pushed all his weight on me as he came with the sexiest moan, warming me all over again.

I wasn't sure how long we lay there, but enough time passed I remembered closing my eyes to his warmth on my back and opening them to find our hands intertwined in our bed.

I lifted his hand to my lips before falling asleep again with happiness.

CHAPTER 32

I woke up to warmth and a steady heartbeat the next morning. The sun had barely risen above the horizon, and the birds chirped from their nests. A cool sea breeze pushed through the curtains and skimmed over our intertwined bodies.

Vork slept with one hand behind his head and the other tucked behind my knee, which was draped over his body. My head lay comfortably on his chest, and my fingers lightly stroked the hairs there.

He looked so peaceful. It was different from other times I had woken up beside him. Last night's ceremony had changed something in us.

"That tickles."

I halted my movements. "I didn't mean to wake you."

He briefly let go of my leg to stretch, making it sound like every bone in his body was cracking. He turned on his side, wrapping his arms around me after tucking my head beneath his chin.

He breathed in. "Hmm, good morning, wife."

"That should sound strange to me." I smiled against his chest and pulled back to look at him. "But it doesn't."

"Good." Vork raked his hands up and down my back. "I'd hate for you to regret this."

I caught his lips in mine with a tender kiss. "Never."

This was the calm I had been searching for my whole life—the home I always wanted. For so long, I had been trying to flee this continent, freeing myself from the earthly cage that was Masos, but for once, I was glad I hadn't gone through with it. My reasoning lay right next me, holding me in his arms and making me feel safe. Whole.

"Mathias referred to you last night as the Blood Commander. What is that?"

Vork's body went rigid for a split second. "It's a name I try not to live up to, but sometimes he is needed."

It didn't seem he wanted to elaborate, so I changed the subject. "So, what's next?"

"What? Last night wasn't sufficient?"

"No, last night was too good. I'm afraid I'm addicted to you now." He hugged me tighter. "But what I'm referring to is your father and his pack. What will they do?"

He let me go so I could lie on his arm. "My father will return home with the elders. There have been some complications with other packs trying to move into our territory and breaking the treaty."

"They're doing this while there's a war— *wars*," I corrected, "going on?"

"Just because we're fighting against the Clergy and your brother doesn't mean anyone else knows. As far as the citizens are concerned, the Clergy is doing exactly what they're meant to— counseling the Emperor and showing them the path to the Divine. As for your brother, we are the only ones aware of what's happening with him. For now, we're on our own."

"That makes me wonder, how are we going to convince everyone threats are coming from each side?"

Vork's brows creased for a moment as he stroked my hair. His touch was almost soothing enough to draw me into a sleep. "One thing at a time, angel. Let's get the princess first, and then we'll plan our next steps."

I sighed loudly. There were so many moving pieces, and everything was so unpredictable, but I suppose that was war.

"Hey." Vork gently fisted my hair. "Come back to me."

I melted into his embrace and kissed him softly.

"Let me fuck you at least one more time before we start preparing for war again," he said.

He caged me under him, and what he did next was far from fucking. It was more intimate than that. His gaze never left mine as he entered me, and I almost came undone right then.

My legs wrapped around his waist to try and pull him closer with each thrust pushing me closer and closer to the edge. He grabbed my ass and angled me up, going in deeper and breathing heavily against my neck.

Vork didn't utter dirty words or commands like last night. In this moment, it was just us. We were connected in ways neither of us understood, but it felt right, like we owned a piece of one another.

The friction of him against me had me feeling high. I wanted to be present in this moment and never let it go. It was intoxicating, and as I tried to hold on, he pulled back so he was looking at me again, his movements slow and purposeful.

Looking into that gaze, my heart swelled and tears threatened to blur my eyes. I wished I could describe the feeling, but the emotions this lycan was brewing in me were making me experience something I'd never thought was possible.

This connection was real, powerful... dangerous—to us and to those who might oppose us.

His breath hitched, and the rhythm picked up to where I couldn't hold it anymore. My heart skipped a beat, and I held onto his back as my vision went black at the bliss of being with him. I pulled him closer as if he would be ripped from me.

I couldn't let go.

I wouldn't.

Vork followed me over the edge and collapsed on top of me. Our heartbeats pounded against our chests as if they were about to jump out and join each other.

I wrapped my arms more securely around him. All too soon, he tried to move but my hold held firm.

"I don't want to crush you."

"You move, and I'll kill you."

His chuckle spread warmth all over my body, and he snuggled more into my hold.

"I fear," he said, still a bit winded, "you have me wrapped about your finger, angel."

I laughed and kissed his head again. "All a part of my plan."

The moment of silence we had in each other's arms was short-lived. A banging sound came from our door.

"Amara, open up!"

Bang. Bang. Bang. Bang.

I groaned and rolled us over so I was on top. "Go away!"

The banging never let up.

"Alright, alright." I reluctantly pulled away from Vork, wincing a bit as he withdrew from me, and threw on the robe at the end of the bed.

The banging kept coming until I threw open the door to see Leena standing there, fully clothed and ready for a fight.

"We need to move. *Now*. The Clergy are overthrowing the Emperor. We could lose Keun."

I looked at Vork, who was already hopping into his trousers, then ran through the halls to Silas's round table.

"Your gear has been brought to the room, and you can get ready while we discuss our plan," Leena said.

We took a sharp turn and scurried down the hall further.

Breathless, I asked, "How did you know about this?"

"We learned it from Dasyra. She's with the others at the round table, waiting for you. She has a contact within the Holy City, and they notified her just recently."

I didn't have time to ask for specifics, and I didn't care. Dasyra had her own secrets, and those secrets had just given us the edge to retrieve the princess.

By the time we arrived at the round table, everyone was there, like Leena had said. A look of guilt passed over their faces as I scrambled in. It was just a few hours after my wedding night. And though that night had been unforgettable, and I wished it had lasted longer, I was here now— there was work to be done, or everything we had planned would go to shit.

Leena picked up my armor from the nearby chair and rushed to the privacy screen set up in the corner. Quickly, I dropped the robe and began dressing into the layers she had given me before she helped me with the armor.

"If Dasyra's sources are correct," Silas began, looking at a layout of Elmira on the table in front of him, "then the mutiny began just before first light, and we've already missed our advantage. We need to do this quickly. There's a small dock off the coast, about a mile north of the eastern water gate. We can enter there and begin the search."

Once the last of my leather armor was placed and my boots pulled up to my knees, I joined the group. "Do we know where Keun is?"

"There's a room on the dungeon level. A place where the royal family was planned to be taken if any attacks were to find their way to their doorstep."

"Bet they didn't expect the threat to come from within," Luca murmured.

"No, they didn't." Dasyra crossed her arms. "Which makes me think they aren't there. The Clergy controlled everything for the Emperor. Who's to say this panic room wasn't their idea? If I were them, it would be the last place I would go. It's compromised."

"How do we even know the princess in the palace anymore? They all could have fled," I said.

Dasyra nodded. "That's a possibility, but I know how to locate her. I just need something of hers."

"A locator spell?"

"In a sense. I'm gifted with clairvoyance already, so instead of a spell to locate her, it's more of a spell to enhance what I already have."

"I thought you couldn't do magic?" I asked.

She was able to ignore my question when Luca asked one of his own.

He leaned into her side and said in a low voice, "are you sure?"

She replied in a similar hushed tone, "I have to try."

I ignored the exchange and what it might mean for the time being and held out my hand. We didn't have time for backstories. "Can you use my blood? Since we are related."

"That would be perfect." Dasyra sliced my palm with one of her daggers, held my hands in hers, and began to speak foreign words.

The table below us trembled, and her grip tightened. A small amount of blood began to trickle from her nostril, but she never let up.

"D," Luca said, grabbing hold of her shoulder.

Her eyes opened, glowing a soft lavender, and her brows pulled upright in stress. But she never let up on her words. They elegantly rolled off her tongue as blood began to seep from both nostrils.

"For the love of the Divine," Luca pleaded, his grasp clutching onto her now. "D, stop."

It ended as quickly as it had started, and Dasyra released my hand.

"There." She wiped the blood from her face and pointed to a small room on the northeast side of the castle. "She's being hidden in a servant's quarters."

Dasyra's eyes glazed over a bit, looking like she might lose consciousness.

"Then we move now," Silas ordered. "Dasyra and Amara, prepare yourselves. You'll leave within the hour."

Luca pulled Dasyra over to the side and steadied her against the wall. Before I could address them, Leena came to my side.

"Are you hopeful about this?"

I kept my eyes on Dasyra. "About the plan in general or getting the princess?"

"I was talking about the princess, but sure, let's talk about the whole process."

"I think," I said, turning my gaze to her and leaning on the table, "Dasyra and I won't have a problem retrieving her. As for what to do afterwards... well, that seems like a problem for when we return."

"It's not smart to go into war without a plan."

She was right. It was messy and unpredictable. She was using my words against me.

"Most people don't need to fight an army of sazari and the son of the Devil— who wants to bring about the end of days—all while getting stuck in the middle of a revolution with rebels and a mutiny within the government itself." I shrugged. "We work with what we got."

Leena nodded in agreement.

"What's going on with Dasyra? Do I need to be worried about her?" I asked.

We trained our eyes on her and Luca, who were still in the corner.

"I don't know what's going on," Leena said. "But she's a solid warrior. She'll have your back no matter what's going on personally."

I left it at that and went back to my room. On the way there, I ran into Vork who was walking in the opposite direction. A hint of a smile crept onto my face.

We met in the middle of the hall.

"Where did you scurry off to?" I asked. "I thought you would've been close behind when I left."

He was also dressed in battle attire: simple breeches and a brown leather chest guard held together by straps on his shoulder. His longsword, bigger than the sword Michael had left me, was strapped to his hip.

"Mathias came in, not long after you left, with word the bordering pack started moving into our land. My father is preparing for an attack."

I pinched the bridge of my nose and sighed heavily. Fucking hell, *another* war.

"Hey," he said, grabbing my shoulders and squeezing. "I'll be here to see you off and I'll make sure to be here shortly after you return. It should be a simple in and out retrieval."

Should be.

"You and Mathias?" I was a bit hurt I wasn't involved in those plans.

"I want you there, but you have a duty here. This petty attempt to take our lands won't last long." He assured me again. "I'll go to organize the troops and then return."

This would be our reality, but hopefully only for a short time. So much chaos was brewing on all sides of us, of course he'd need to deal with pack business, too. Vork had an obligation and responsibility to his people. I wouldn't stand in the way of that, but he could still see the worry on my face, so he pulled me in and rested his head against mine.

"It'll be okay, angel."

"This is one hell of a honeymoon."

He threaded his hand in my low braid and angled my face up.

"It'll be okay," he repeated before giving me a gentle kiss that I returned in kind.

I grabbed hold of the bottom of his leathers and pulled him closer.

Unfortunately, he eventually pulled us apart, breathless. "How long till you leave?"

"An hour."

A wicked grin developed on his face, and he groaned, "Perfect."

He hoisted me over his shoulder and carried me towards our room.

"I just put my armor on!"

"Like that'll stop me," Vork snorted.

My laughs echoed through the hall as I let my husband carry me with a stupid grin on my face.

CHAPTER 33

I WAS MORE nervous than I should have been. In all my ages of life, I had only felt anxious at the beginning of my life as a thief and an assassin.

For my first sting, I had to pickpocket a wealthy merchant. I was young and still new to the trade, but it wasn't the act of illegal activity that made me nervous, no, it was getting caught. Even at a young age, I excelled in combat, getting away unhurt wasn't my worry. It was the boy I was with whom I was afraid for. He wasn't a favorite among the others at the guild due to his lack of promise, but it didn't stop us from working together.

I'd seen the reprimands that followed whenever he made a mistake, and the scars were not forming well. However, with this job, if he was caught, the merchant would kill him before the guild could get their hands on him.

Perhaps that was why I was so nervous now. I had people I cared about going into harm's way, just like back then. I also had something to live for— someone to return home to. This could all be taken away from me in an instant, and I had waited my whole life to feel this sense of security.

I was drawn out of my worry when Vork and I reached the court-yard. Everyone was there to see us off.

"Elmira is protected by wards that only a select few of their witches can work through," Dasyra instructed. "We'll have to portal within their gardens. I can navigate us from there."

"I can't portal somewhere I haven't seen. Can you describe it to me?"

"It's too big for me to remember the whole thing, but I can recall the details of the entrance to Elmira. An ornate, wooden double door lies before a vast terrace. Around it is three entrances to the gardens from the north, east, and west, lined with waist-high pristine shrubs. Different flowers are on each end as the rows extend into the garden.

"At the east are the orange tiger lilies, surrounding a marble foundation of a shrike. Blood red roses are planted in three large circles to the north, and past them is another path leading into the woods. West of there is a stone table, big enough to hold the royal family and the Clergy. The stone is weathered and smooth to the touch in some places." Dasyra took a breath. "Is that enough to go on?"

"I'd say it's sufficient."

Leena approached and pulled me into a tight hug, then leaned her head against mine. "I don't need to tell you to be careful."

"No, you don't, but it's still nice to hear."

When we separated, I nodded to Luca, Corym, Silas, Eira, and Iziah.

Vork took me in a hug and kissed the top of my head. "Give 'em hell, yeah?"

I looked up and smiled in a way only he could bring out in me. "What else is the daughter of Lilith to do?"

I took a few steps back and stretched out my arms. The familiar tingle ran from my chest down to my fingertip as a portal to the palace opened. "See you soon."

———◆———

As Dasyra led the way through the garden and into Elmira, it was quieter than I had anticipated. Those big doors she told me about were locked up tight, but luckily, her clairvoyance came in handy.

It was the first time I had ever seen it in action, though there was barely anything to actually see. There was a ripple in the air, like the fumes from a fire when it distorts the view and makes things blurry, but that was it. After she figured out which way to go, we found ourselves in a back alley full of mud and gunk, but also finally in front of an unlocked door.

Inside, the gothic halls were messy, broken statues scattered all over the floor. Discarded scraps of linen, food, and the occasional blood splatter were also present.

It didn't look like a power grab but a war zone. Those who remained loyal to the Emperor must have resisted.

Dasyra and I unsheathed our weapons as we crept down the hall, still weary of the silence we were met with.

If I remembered the plans correctly, we were to follow this hall all the way down, make a left and another left, and then go downstairs to find the hall with the room where the princess was being held.

We made it halfway down the hall when a group of soldiers jogged past at the end. We flattened ourselves against the opposite wall with slow and steady steps and waited for them to pass. Letting my breath release, I nodded, and we began our walk again.

After a few steps forward, a straggler of the group passed, pausing midway and fixing his helmet. His eyes locked on us, and he froze.

"I—I— Intruder!" He fumbled, pulling out his sword, barely holding it up. "Stay where you are!"

"We don't have time for this." Dasyra pulled out one of her knives, preparing to throw it, but I put my hand on her shoulder.

"He's scared. Looks like just a kid. Let's not kill the young."

She took a harder look, twirled the blade in her hand, and put it back in its place. "Hard to see anything with that goofy helmet taking over most of his head."

The emblem on his chest's armor, the Emperor's coat of arms, had a strike, but it had been scratched off. He was with the Clergy.

"Well," Dasyra said with her arms outstretched. "Come on then."

The boy let out a battle cry and charged right for her. She didn't even bother with taking out another weapon. When he was close enough to strike, he left a huge opening allowing her disarm him and twirl him away from her.

She held the sword up and juggled it in each hand. "Such a weighty weapon. This the only one they could give you?"

The soldier discarded his helmet with heavy puffs. "Don't make me hurt a woman."

She snorted. "As honorable as that is— I'd *love* to see you try."

And try, he did.

He came at her again, this time low to grab her by the waist, but she caught him by the throat and pushed him on his back. Her foot was replaced by her hand, and she kept enough pressure to cause him a bit of alarm.

"Kill me already," he gritted out.

"Kill you? I'm not in the business of killing kids. Beating their ass, well that's another thing entirely." She kicked him out cold and threw the sword on the ground. "Now where—"

She was interrupted by a slew of soldiers running toward us, no doubt hearing the boy's previous alarm.

Dasyra drew out her luxium katana, the black blade glistening against the gold hilt with an intricate design embedded in it. The handle was wrapped in a dark blue material that matched the woven design in the holder, outlined in gold.

As the soldiers approached, one of them turned to another and ordered him to inform the Clergymen of our presence. We couldn't let him get away.

Dasyra knew this and was quick to act. I had never seen her move with such swiftness as she bobbed and weaved through the guards. She came up directly behind her target and blindsided him by twirling to his front. That gave her katana the opportunity to find the sliver of skin at his neck between his armor.

The fight was over quickly. It was only four soldiers with less than ideal training.

We pushed on, but before I could get more than a few steps forward, a high-pitched ringing drilled into my left side. I forced my weight on the wall beside me, clutching my head.

Dasyra's hand lay on my shoulder. "What is it? What's wrong?"

"I— don't— know," I gritted out. "It's like a pickaxe is scraping away at my eardrum."

In the background, the sound of faint footfalls reached me.

"I don't mean to add to this surprise headache of yours, but we need to move."

The ringing slammed against my head again. Almost like a plea.

Dragging my feet, I made my way to a corridor leading down to what felt like the source of the sound.

"There," I said simply.

Dasyra sighed heavily and put my arm over her shoulders. "Let's go."

The spiral stone staircase was lit by torches every few feet and got colder the further down we went. At the base of the stairs was a wooden door with a lock bolted into it.

I moved towards it and outstretched my hand to her. "Lend me a dagger."

Dasyra flipped the handle my way, and I used the fine point to pick the lock. It wasn't the best, but I had done more with less. I kept maneuvering it until I finally heard the old bolt click.

When we opened the door, I was mortified by what I saw.

A woman, *an angel,* was hung, hands and feet stretched out by a thick chain wrapped around each of them. Her golden-brown wings were also spread, a hook in each one. Blood leaked from the wounds, creating a heaping pool at her feet.

A thick band of metal laced around her neck, chafing into the skin and leaving it incredibly raw. Her auburn hair stuck to her face, and sweat beaded at her hairline.

Dasyra quickly closed the door behind us. "What did you just bring us to?"

I stood just below, looking up at her dangling head. Her eyes were closed. I realized the ringing had finally stopped. Though I was too far away to touch her, I raised my hand as if to cup her face. That's when she woke.

She breathed in a shallow breath, and her eyes slowly opened, showing dark blue irises.

"It worked. You found me."

I lowered my hand and took a step back. "I did."

"I do not expect you to free me."

It was an unfortunate truth. We didn't come here for her, and even if we did find a way to get her down, we couldn't carry her deadweight. Not to mention, people might notice a half-dead angel being dragged around the palace halls.

"What is this?" Dasyra asked again.

"They're draining her grace," I explained. "I didn't think the Clergy would be so bold as to do it in their own home."

"I need you to extract the last of my grace and give it to my daughter," the angel wheezed.

My eyes locked with Dasyra's.

"Don't look at me," she said. "I don't know who this is."

"There's a vial on the table at the edge of the room." The angel's voice was barely a whisper. "Please give it to Leena. Let my essence guide her when I cannot."

My mouth opened but nothing came out. All I could do was look at the angel's state and calculate how I could get Leena's mother home. How would I tell her what happened here? Helplessness crashed into me.

"I—I don't know how," I finally managed to say.

Dasyra reached for the vial tentatively. "I can."

How did she all of a sudden know this?

She dragged over a small ladder to reach the angel's neck, then pushed her hair away to reveal the nape.

The angel's hooded eyes trailed over to me. "Tamiel." She forced out the word with the last of the energy she had within her. "My name is Tamiel."

Strange words flowed from Dasyra's lips, and a white glowing mist traveled from the center of the angel's chest, upward and out of the incision already there. Dasyra placed it in the vial and sealed it with the cork before shoving it in her pocket.

The angel had no life left in her. My heart skipped a beat and sweat beaded at my hairline. We had found a heavenly being who was strung up like cattle and tortured. If the Clergy was doing this, what else were they capable of?

"You were the contact," I said, "who knew the luxium blade was made from grace."

Her gaze was firm as she nodded.

What else did she know?

"Amara, we need to move. We can't afford any more detours."

I let the topic be as we raced back up the stairs. The princess was the objective.

The ringing in my ears and the pain it brought ceased once the angel had taken her last breath—a heavenly being...gone. The halls were quiet as we pushed on.

Dasyra took a sharp turn, landing us in front of a modest wooden door. She slowly opened it, and we were met with two servants huddled close to one another, sobs escaping them when they saw our weapons.

Putting her blade away, Dasyra held her hands up. "Hey, we're not here to hurt you. We—"

A dark flash came out of the corner of my eye and headed straight for Dasyra. I intercepted and disarmed the attacker while flipping them over, sending them tumbling across the floor. The mace they had held skittered to a stop next to my feet. They quickly gained their footing, and we were looking at the tip of an arrow held by the princess.

"Woah, woah, Princess Keun, we're here to save you!" Dasyra said quickly.

"Your father sent us," I said calmly.

The princess pulled back on the bowstring. "The Clergy took my father."

"Not that one," I corrected.

The tension slowly started to dissipate as realization set in. Keun lowered her bow. "Do you know where he is?"

"No." I stepped forward tentatively. "He told me you would know who you are and agree to come with us. You are the one person who can help end the war."

Keun barked a laugh. "How can I do anything? I'm the bastard princess of a probably already dead emperor. I will not be able to stop the Clergy from doing anything."

"Other wars are happening." I picked up her discarded mace and held it out to her. "I know it's hard to see right now, but the continent is falling apart. We can tell you more back at the compound, but we have to move."

There was hesitation on her end. Her eyes darted back and forth between Dasyra and me before she taking her mace back.

"Alright, *cousin*," Keun spat. "Anyway, out of here?"

Dasyra pulled the curtains from the window, fanning the layer of dust into the air and letting in the morning light. She had a very proud look on her face. "I've got an idea."

"Why can't we just use the stairs?" Keun asked.

"Because there are guards, it's quicker to go out the window. Amara can't portal within the walls of this place."

The princess looked puzzled.

I shrugged and helped Dasyra braid the fabric together in long strands, anchoring them so we could rappel down the outer wall. It was quick work, and once on the ground, I was ready to return to the garden, but footsteps sounded behind us, and I sighed heavily.

A small group of soldiers flooded in, more close behind after they raised an alarm alerting the whole area. They started closing in on us, their weapons drawn.

There's no way, I thought. But I had to try.

I held out my arms and envisioned the courtyard of the hold, the magic tingling across my fingertips as it shimmered open.

"How?" Dasyra yelled. "The wards don't extend this far?"

"I guess not, now let's move!" I shot back.

We only had moments until we'd be captured. Keun went first, then Dasyra.

I took steps to follow, but something clamped hard on my ankle and a growing pain vibrated up my leg. An arrow had been shot clean through. The arrowhead expanded to a star and was connected to a long, thick chain. The guard used it as leverage and yanked hard, throwing me off balance and making me land face-first into the muck.

I clawed my way forward, my nails digging into the mud as I looked for purchase. On the other side of the portal, Leena and Vork began to make their way to me.

"No!" Anxiety brewed deep within me as I pushed a gust of fire at them and they stopped.

The guards were closing in on all sides. Everyone would be in danger if I didn't close the portal soon. The Clergy couldn't have me *and* the princess.

Before I could close it, another arrow pierced through my hand, and I was flipped over, flopping onto my back. A ringing sounded in my ears as my head collided with the ground, and the air escaped my lungs. There was a weight on my chest like my lungs had just been pulverized into the earth. My head spun as I tried to sit up and close the door.

My vision was blurry, but I could see Vork take another step. Corym firmly grasped his arm.

At first, I couldn't make out what they were saying, but I assumed Corym was trying to reason with him to not take an unnecessary risk. The ringing in my ears lessened, and their words started to become clearer.

"Don't." Corym wasn't speaking loudly; I was just that close.

I was so, *so* close to escape, yet not close enough to save myself. But I was to save the others.

"Don't?" Vork said in disbelief. My hearing came back bit by bit. "... wife... shit and mud.... Save..."

Corym pulled him closer and tightened his hold, arguing again.

Another arrow pierced my shoulder when I sat up, and I couldn't keep in the shriek that left me. I had been battered and stabbed three times now, and my strength was waning. Vork broke his gaze with Corym to look at me. Guilt ran through me when our gazes met.

We were married only last night, and we were already about to lose each other. I could see the fight behind his eyes just before rage engulfed him, and he pushed through Corym and everyone else who tried to hold him back.

"Amara!" His voice changed. Deeper, more feral and dangerous. If they didn't let him go soon, then they would be the ones who'd truly be in danger.

Everything around me bled away as I watched him struggling. I wasn't going to make it. I needed to close the portal, or they would all die, and all this would have been for nothing.

"Vork!" He couldn't hear me. Not over the rage he was clawing through to get to me. "Vork, look at me!"

His movements calmed, but his breathing was still ragged.

"It'll be okay," I whispered, only for him to hear. "You'll find me, and it'll be okay."

"Amara." His voice cracked, tears threatening his eyes. "Don't you part from me."

The burning from the arrows couldn't compare to the pain in my heart. He had spoken those words last night, while we held each other close, and I was already breaking the unspoken promise I'd made to him.

"I'm so sorry."

"Don't do it." Vork looked to the others who held him. "Get off!"

"I'll see you soon."

It took all my strength to bring both hands together and close the portal, but I did it.

Only a second after Leena jumped through and landed in front of me.

She stood and threw the daggers strapped to her belt at the closest guards. There was a ringing in my ears and a tightness in my chest from what I had done.

Leena slid down next to me and took my face in her hands. "Are you all right?"

"You idiot. Why did you do that?" I shuddered out a shaky breath, and my head started to go limp, all my energy depleted.

Leena held my head close to her chest, tears filling her eyes as she looked towards the running guards. "It's going to be okay."

I knew all too well it wouldn't be.

CHAPTER 34

I WAS BROUGHT in as the Emperor's golden child on my first visit to the Holy City. Loved by those who didn't know me and treated with the utmost respect. I had almost forgotten how that felt as I was pushed towards the shouts of a crowd and led to the front gates of Elmira.

I was alone.

The guards had separated me from Leena as soon as they closed in on us. Though I feared for her, I also feared for myself.

This morning, I had been happy. Now, I was a prisoner, a thick collar around my neck.

Only when I was pushed into the sun's light could I truly see the crowd gathered—the guards were holding me by a stick connected to my collar, and my hands were bound behind me. I was pushed to my knees and bent over to look at the marble floor.

The Clergyman was spitting his venomous, persuasive words to the crowd. How unfortunate I was that all of his sheep had come to flock on this day. It was the perfect place for him to continue their plan. A plan which was becoming clearer by the second.

"These nephilims," Salvadore continued, "were once thought to be the Divine's prized children. Beings on this earth who were sent to us, so we could bask in the Divine's true glory and who would protect us if needed. But as you can see." He gestured to me. "We were wrong about this lot. Especially the famed Girl of Fire."

The crowd began to yell shouts of agreement.

He took short strides over to me and brought my head up, grabbing my hair and yanking. "But do not fear! This collar she wears was made especially for her. It prevents her from using her powers, so you are safe." His voice grew low, so only I could hear. "Never doubt me again."

I winced at the reference to our chat at that long ago dinner, but I moved my gaze up to his as Salvadore smiled at the crowd in reassurance.

"I don't need my powers to peel the skin off your bones, holy man," I spat.

His perfectly practiced smile almost faltered, but he regained his composure quick enough that no one noticed. He released my head and stooped down to my ear. "It seems you have no regard for your own life, but I know whose life you do care for, and oh, do we have a treat for you."

There was a rattling of chains, a struggling breath, and when I looked up, it was as if my whole world became contained in that moment. Leena was there, an identical collar around her neck, and her hands were bound behind her in chains. She was pushed forward next to me.

"Are you alright?" Leena asked.

"I'm fine. Did they hurt you?"

"No."

"Not yet," Vocova said as she walked past me to the other side of Leena. "But we will."

I wasn't sure how long she had been there, but it was of no surprise to me.

Salvadore held his hands up to silence the crowd's shouting and clamoring, then Vocova took a step forward, raising her voice so the crowd could hear every word.

"With a broken heart, I say what your clergyman tells you is true. These nephilims were found to be in league with demons!"

The people let out loud gasps and talked amongst themselves. Of course, they would believe whatever the Clergy said. For all they knew, the Clergy had kept the demons at bay, not us.

They don't know the truth of their fate, and how could they? It was an outlandish idea.

"Furthermore," Vocova continued, "we caught them kidnapping Princess Keunwysa, and the Divine knows what they would have done with her. We can only fear the worst."

Ridiculous. Even though the Princess was taken—saved, and came willingly, they still pretend she is safe in her room. They were grasping at any and all power they could, even if it meant demonizing us.

"That is a lie!" Leena spat as she shook in her bonds. "The Princess needs protection from you! You are working with the demons. *You* are who the people need to fear!"

Vocova laughed, and Salvadore followed suit.

"You nephilims will do anything to bolster your stories and keep yourselves from burning at the stake."

A wagon was rolled to the side of the steps. Wood was piled onto a platform, and a log stood vertically in the center.

"Though, unfortunately, this will not help." Vocova crooked her fingers, and the soldiers holding Leena pushed her over.

From that moment on, everything was chaos. The crowd's jeering turned into an uproar. Leena's cries of resistance blended in with the sounds of my own screams as they pushed her towards the pyre.

"No!" Leena struggled against their hold, planting her feet firmly into the ground to halt them.

"Let her go!" I yelled. "Take me! I was the one who planned the whole ruse. Let her live, Vocova, damn you. Let her go!"

She ignored my pleas, keeping her eyes on Leena.

"Diana, please," Leena tried. "I have been with you for most of my life. You have taught me since I was a girl. Please, you can stop this."

Vocova put her hand up to stop the guards from hoisting Leena up onto the platform and placed a hand on her tear-stained cheek.

"You nephilims think you're *so* smart, " she whispered so only we could hear. "But you forgot your proper place amongst beings like me. This was destined, and I can promise you your little family will soon meet the same fate. Though I admit we have something a little more interesting in store for Amara." She gently patted Leena's cheek and stepped back as the guards continued. "Burn well."

They secured her completely to the post with iron chains around her torso and waited for the command to light the fire.

No, no, no, no. NO! Not again, not again.

Why is it always for me?

I kicked and tugged to get to Leena, and the guards took every chance they could to stab the tip of their blades into my back, but it didn't stop me. They jabbed so much my bare feet began to slip in the pool of blood now on the marble floors.

"Not for me!" I shrieked. "Vocova, stop this!"

"Let this be a message." She spoke over my continued screams and struggles. "Anyone associated with the nephilims or the Defiants will meet the same fate you see here today. Any assistance to the enemy, including the nephilim, will be considered an act of treason against your Emperor and a threat to life as you know it. This cannot and will not be tolerated."

With those last words, Vocova nodded to the soldier with the fire, and he dropped it at Leena's feet. Genuine fear I never thought I'd experience again hit me all at once.

With the one soldier gripping the stick and holding my collar in place, another had gotten close enough to pull my head back, making me watch. The soldier's grip grew so tight and pulled my neck so taut I began to lose feeling. My strength and power may have been taken away, but they couldn't take away my training.

I pulled my left arm so hard it popped out of the socket, but I was too focused to worry about the pain. I kicked my left leg out to dispose of soldier holding my collar, and then to the one gripping my hair. The remaining soldier didn't have enough time to react before I head butted him and made a run for the pyre.

The fire had almost risen to Leena's feet when I jumped onto the platform and tried to find a way to undo her bonds.

"Amara," she breathed with more tears running down her face. "Get off."

"Shut up."

I tried pushing at the vertical log to loosen it, and that's when I noticed the fire at our feet was starting to burn us.

It burned me.

I hadn't known the feeling of a burn until that moment, and I screamed out in pain but didn't stop pushing my good shoulder against the post. I didn't care what happened to me. The fire could melt the flesh from my bones, and I still wouldn't stop.

"You'll die if you stay." Leena coughed and brought her knee between us.

"So will you!"

"Amara," she said as softly as she could through the pain. "It's my time, but it's not yet yours. You have time to make this right." Her eyes were glassy. "Make this right."

"Leena—"

With that knee between us, she extended her leg and pushed me off the pyre as the flames grew to her torso.

I cried out when I landed on my dislocated shoulder, but Leena's screams masked mine.

I sat up, looking upon the burning pyre of my best friend through blurry vision. Dying because of me. Burning. All because my powers were taken from me. I was *again* useless.

The flames grew so large they now covered her entire body. The screams were deafening, but they were more than screams to me. Everything in me began to break. Those screams were tears in my soul. They grew bigger and more pain spilled out as the seconds went by.

It was when Leena's screams stopped that mine began. I hunched over and let out a wail so frightening the crowd, even the soldiers, ceased their shouting and cheering.

Other than my screams, the only sound was the crackling of the fire. When I had used the last of my breath, all the energy drained out of me, and I looked up at her remains.

The chaos swimming in my head took over, and then just as quickly as everything moved, it was quiet. With a tear-stained face, I looked over to Vocova, who bore an expression I couldn't and didn't care to place.

"I want you to remember this moment!" I screamed out at her through my cries and trembling lips. "I want you to remember the pain you inflicted today, the chaos you brought, the war that will become your end. Because when I get out of these chains, I want you to remember what started this as I plunge my hand into your chest, rip out your heart, and burn it in front of your cold, dead eyes. I will bring the fires of Hell and the rains from the Heavens down on you and the whole fucking Clergy. This I promise you."

It was small, but there was a tentative step back from her before she opened her mouth to speak. Soldiers had grabbed me again before she could reply.

They jerked me back so fast my shoulder popped incorrectly in the socket and tied a rope higher up my arms to my elbows so I was more restricted.

"Take her to the cells," Salvadore stepped in.

The soldiers did as they were told and took me down to my new holding.

I still had no idea how long they planned to keep me there, or if they had the means to kill me. Usually, in these instances, I would already be planning ways to escape and mapping out my revenge.

Though that wasn't possible now, my heart wasn't broken into a thousand pieces; it had been destroyed.

The sad truth was I loved her, and I had waited too long to tell her.

CHAPTER 35

"By the Divine, you are beautiful."

"You're only saying that because I was in an awful mood moments ago."

Vork placed his cheek on the top of my head. "Not true."

"Liar."

He gave me a wolfish grin and placed his hand on my stomach. "I promise you this isn't a lie. You have filled a hole in me I didn't know needed to be filled. You, Milar." He gestured to the little boy playing with the dog at his ankles, then rubbed my stomach in circles. "And little Leena. You're all I'll ever need."

A knife nicked at my heart, spilling the tears I had been holding back for so long.

"I miss her."

He kissed my head and pulled me close in silence. Silence he knew I needed. No words would be able to fill the void I had in me.

I looked over his arm at Milar playing in the grass, and the tears continued, but a smile played on my lips. The boy was perfect and the spitting image of his father. His chestnut hair flowed down over his ears, and his eyes were even more enchanting than Vork's, which made it difficult for me to deny him anything. One look with those eyes and the boy could have anything he wanted.

Though I knew the child I was carrying would look nothing like me, I hoped I'd see a little bit of Leena in her soul—the friend who was killed by the demons.

Those fucking demons.

The day it happened was still fuzzy, but what I did remember was Leena being burned alive, and I had been helpless to save her. If it weren't for the Clergy... for Vork, then I would be dead too.

The land Vork and I had been offered in the Arabrosa pack's territory was a beautiful lodge nestled in the mountains. We were grateful to have this home to raise our children and to live in peace after the war had ended with the angels' help.

"Do you know when we are to expect your father?" Vork asked as he continued to stroke my hair.

I blinked away the excess tears and watched Milar grasp blades of grass and throw it up in the air. For a moment, I could have sworn it was water falling to the ground and not the grass, but I blinked and it was as it was.

I pulled away, wiped my face, then leaned back on my hands. I dug my fingers into the soft grass behind me, feeling for the cushion, but for another moment, it almost felt slick and cold.

"Last we spoke, he said it would be Milar's birthday. He should come in three days."

Being blessed by all three of the high angels was an honor. One the product of a lycan and a nephilim was deserving of.

"What if we took Milar to him?" Vork asked.

Quirking my eyebrow, I took my gaze off the boy and moved it to him. "To Michael? We don't even know where he is. He could be in the Heavens for all we know."

"I don't suspect Michael would stray far from his grandchildren. He must be somewhere on Masos."

There was a movement that had me putting my hand on my stomach to soothe the baby.

"Perhaps, but I'm enjoying our time together. My father can wait."

Milar squealed in glee as he threw up more grass into the breeze. Like a scratch in my mind, I again saw a blur of water where the grass was. But as quickly as it came, it went away.

The baby kicked fiercely, causing me to double over a bit.

Vork was closer to me in a blink. With worry on his face.

"I'm fine," I said. "The baby has a hell of a kick, and my mind is playing tricks on me. I think I should go lie down."

Vork helped me to my feet and kissed my head again.

"Don't stay out too long. Dinner will be ready at sunset," I said, turning toward the house.

"Of course, love."

"Love?" I stopped and turned back, a confused smile on my face.

"What?" He smiled back. "I can't change it up? You prefer…"

I let the moment drag on before I realized he wouldn't finish. "Angel."

"Ah, of course. Maybe I need to lie down with you since my mind is starting to deceive me."

I returned to the house with a hand on my aching back for support. The warm breeze brought bumps on my cold skin. It was a tad damp and clammy. I didn't understand why. I had done nothing all day but lie in the grass.

When I returned to our room, I stood before the bureau and barely recognized myself in its mirror. It felt like only yesterday I was with the Clergy in the war against the demons.

How had I gotten to this point of happiness? With a family, no less. I never imagined to be as blessed as I was.

As if I were trying to wake up from a dream, I pushed at the nubs of my pinky and ring finger. The soreness was still there, though the injury happened long ago, and that's how I knew this was real.

I was really happy, and I could let those thoughts be.

"You still look tired," Vork said, appearing behind me.

"I have doubts."

"About?"

I didn't answer. I couldn't put doubts in his mind. He didn't deserve it.

He wrapped his arms around me and placed his chin on my head. "You can tell me."

"This feels too good to be true. I'm happy… very happy. So happy and at peace I'm afraid none of this is real."

"I understand." He laced his fingers with mine and squeezed. "But I hope you know, whether this is real or not, I am proud of how far you've come. As a person, as my wife, and as a mother."

My heart constricted as I locked eyes with him in the mirror.

"I do love you," he whispered against my hair.

It felt odd. We had said it once on our wedding night. We did love one another, there was no doubt about it, but that was not how we expressed it—not in those words.

"For you," I said with a hint of a smile.

His brows furrowed slightly. "What's for me?"

I didn't repeat it or give him a chance to right the wrong as I bucked him off and faced him. "Who are you?"

"Amara, what—"

"You're not Vork. Not the man I know."

He took a step toward me. "Come on, Am—"

I swung my fist with all my strength, sending him hurling into the wall. After a few seconds of groaning in pain, he slowly got up and moved his head back to meet my eyes. His face was broken. His left eye was missing, and the other one he had was pitch black, void of a pupil, making him haunting.

When he stood straight, his demeanor changed completely. With a scratchy, low voice, he asked, "What gave me away?"

I closed my eyes and shook my head, but I was no longer in paradise when I opened them. Instead of sun and a light breeze, I was confined in a dark, damp, hot room.

There was a throbbing and burning sensation in both my hands that I found were pinned above my head. Before my eyes could focus, that pain settled in first.

A whimper escaped my lips before I could contain it.

A sharp sting came to my cheek. "I asked you a question. What gave me away?"

The blistering pain was from my hands being hammered down by a thick, long iron nail that created a trail of blood down my arms and onto my head. The nail would begin moving through my hands if I slumped down too much.

I looked up at the man and saw the marks of a witch on his hands. A witch turned demon? "You—you said… 'I love you.'"

"Hmmm, and you do not say that to one another?"

I shook my head.

"Noted for next time."

My head rolled to the side, and whatever little food they had given me the day before came up.

"How long?" I spat.

The man didn't answer as he walked out of view.

"How long have you had me here?"

There was metal clanking from behind.

"About two weeks. We almost had you, though."

I spat out the remaining bile in my mouth. "Had me what?"

The witch, or demon rather, came back around, a hot poker in his hand. "Reveal the location of Michael. Now that you're awake, maybe I can ask you, and we can get an actual answer."

The poker was held up to my cheek, its warmth reaching for me. Though, I didn't welcome it. The collar still held back my powers.

"Where is Michael?"

At first, I didn't answer. The witch lightly touched my skin, but quickly removed the poker before it could do any severe damage.

"Where is Michael?"

For as long as they had me, this question had been asked, and my answer had always been the same.

"I don't know where he is."

"You wouldn't be lying to me now, would you?"

I would lie if I needed to, but my answer was honest. I had no idea where Michael was; if he was in the Heavens, I didn't know how to get there.

"No, I'm not lying."

"Hmmm." The witch hummed with annoyance as he ripped off the cloth covering my body. After a slow glance at my naked self, he took the tip of the poker and placed it at the middle of my chest, then slowly trailed it down to my navel.

I shook from my blinding pain that ripped through my body. My hands pulled from the iron pinning me down, but I didn't care. The heat was worse at that moment.

The room was then filled with the stench of burning flesh, bile, and blood. When he stopped at my navel, the witch held the poker there and gave it a gentle push. My screaming started to wane as I began to lose consciousness.

"Linx, that will be all," a smooth voice ordered.

The burning ceased, and breath re-entered my lungs. Linx put down the poker and left the cell, the door closing with a loud bang.

The clacking of heels rang in my ears, and I sensed a presence in front of me.

"You do not look well."

I looked up and saw Vocova, polished and pristine as ever. If she wasn't the traitor I knew her to be, then I would see her as a glowing light in this damp, depressing cell.

"I don't know why. I feel great," I snapped.

"Well, it's nice he hasn't broken your spirit yet. What a waste that would be."

I smiled through my blood-stained teeth. "It warms my heart knowing you care."

Vocova said nothing as she sat in a wooden chair she had placed in front of me. Crossing her legs, she began to pick at her nails.

"I'm surprised you aren't foaming at the mouth with anger for what I did to your friend." I almost allowed my fists to clench. "I was sure as soon as you saw my face, you'd be clawing through the filth of this cell to get to me. Why is that not so?"

Though my smile was innocent, my tone and eyes showed disgust. "Your time will come."

"To be honest with you, I think this is all a waste of time. I believe you're telling the truth, and you have no idea where Michael is. He is the general of angels for a reason. If he were to be so easily found, they would be a weak lot, wouldn't they?" She sighed and cast her eyes on me. "No, I'm looking for someone else. Someone you helped escape."

I blinked.

"We knew of the Defiants' stronghold on the Isle. See, I had my own spy on the inside, and when he did away with their little protection spell, I had soldiers storm it soon after. However, not many people were left—including the princess." Vocova uncrossed and recrossed her legs with a sigh at my continued silence. "You know she was worthless. I truly don't understand why you're upset. Her power over emotion was impressive, but it was unnecessary and constrained. Her combat skills were also subpar."

"Enough." I pulled on the restraints, more blood spilling.

Vocova held her hands up with a malicious grin. "I'm just stating facts. You can find nice girls anywhere, Amara. She wasn't special."

All sound but her voice muted. My vision tunneled in on just her face. I looked at her mouth and could see the venom spewing, but it was replaced with another voice. This one was intimate and silken. Speaking in a tongue I had not understood before that moment.

She doesn't deserve to live, the soothing, low voice whispered. *Every moment she spends walking this land, she prevents you from becoming what you are.*

I leaned into it.

She killed Leena. She will kill the rest— Vork. Too long you have been alone. You deserve what you have with the lycan. She will take it away just like she took Leena.

Vocova's words came back into focus.

"...I'm sure he would've found use for her. His appetite tends to be a bit more... damaging. But I do know Landis has a thing for redheads."

Kill her, it said.

With a hard yank, I was whirled around—out of my body—to look at the scene. Vocova sat gracefully in her chair, and I—well, I looked feral.

My eyes had turned from brown to a pitch black that bled down my cheeks, a single red pinpoint creating my pupil. My canines had elongated to a deadly point, and my skin glowed with a dark tint. As if a heated wind skated by, my hair brushed out of my face. I was thrust back into my body, and the words I spoke next were in that unfamiliar tongue.

"Be careful of the next words you speak, Dominion." The guttural voice boomed in the small space. Vocova's mask faltered. *"It will decide how I will kill you."*

"How do you know that language?" Her facade came back as quickly as it went. "I'd love to see your attempt."

A reedy shriek exploded from my mouth, and Vocova jumped from her seat, taking a step back. I pulled my hands and feet forward, pushing out of the nails.

Before I could make any real progress, Vocova dosed me with something in the neck that instantly calmed me.

"Well," she breathed in relief, throwing the syringe to the table. "That was interesting. I never thought your demon side would show its face. Now, where is the princess?"

Feeling the drug, I asked lazily, "And what do you want with her?"

"I have my own plans that need to be put in action, but that isn't the question you should be asking me, is it?"

I winced as I readjusted myself, and the nail dug into my hands. "What should I be asking you then?"

Vocova let go of my hair and gripped my chin, forcing me to look at her. *"If I tell you what you want to know, do you vow to spare my child?"*

My eyebrows immediately pulled together in confusion, and if it weren't for the poker that had almost worked its way through my abdomen, my whole body would have gone cold.

No, it was too soon.

"You're lying." I breathed, fighting through the mixed emotions.

Vocova smirked. "Am I?"

"You couldn't possibly know."

"Couldn't I?"

"For fuck's sake. Cut the shit, Vocova. I don't have time for your petty little games."

She rewarded the words with a hearty laugh as she sat back in the chair.

"My dear, all you have is time. Unless, of course, I let the torture continue, then you might be dead in two days. But no, I need you to tell me where the princess is. If not—" her voice moved down an octave "—I will peel that baby from your stomach and let you watch as I destroy it. Or..." She pondered for a moment. "Maybe I'll let it live and raise it as my own. How heartbreaking it would be for you to see your child mature without knowing their mother. To be mothered by your enemy."

I collected as much saliva as possible and spat it in her direction. It didn't go far, only to her feet.

"Killing you is going to be my greatest deed."

She laughed. "I cannot be killed."

"You are no god. Therefore, you can die."

"I have been around since the dawn of time. I have seen civilizations of this world rise and crumble to dust, and I come out just the same. In pure freedom of the Heavens."

"It'll be hard to fly when I rip your wings from your back and watch you choke on your feathers."

Her smile slowly fell, and she asked again, "Where is she?"

"The princess is with the others. You have no way of getting to her."

"*Where?*"

I stayed silent. If they weren't at the compound, it was yet another thing I didn't know.

It took one, two, three, four, five droplets of water to hit the stone floor till Vocova stood and knocked on the iron door.

"If you want to try my patience, Amara, fine." The door opened, but before she walked through, she turned halfway. "You think you'll somehow get out and find your way back to your dog and your mangled family, but I want to snuff that idea out of you right now. You will not leave these four walls. You're thinking you'll lose the baby, get out, and make another. You won't. The only remnant of your old life will be the child you're carrying. Remember that the next time you decide to hold your tongue."

She shut the door behind her, and I was forced back into darkness. Frigid stone beneath me began to feel like a blessing while my chest and stomach continued to burn from the poker. The incessant dripping of water never stopped, but after a while, I couldn't hear it over my sobs.

I began to believe Vocova was right. I was never going to get out of here. Even if the others did come for me, it would be some time before they could come up with a plan that would actually work. Coming now, while the city was on guard, was too risky. They would have to wait for things to calm down, which could take weeks or months.

I truly didn't know if I'd survive that long, because I knew nothing.

Knowledge was power, not my flames; and even in that, I was powerless.

I knew a new day had come when I heard the footsteps outside my cell door.

One, two, three, four, five, six, seven, eight steps the guard took from wherever they came to change with the night guard. The night guard then took ten steps the way the new guard had come, probably because they were shorter than the day guard. After that, there was more silence until a servant came in to shove some bread down my throat and give me water.

Once they left, I had no way to tell time. There was no window for fresh air or sunlight, and I was so deep in the city's belly no sound could get in or out unless it was right outside my door.

After some time, Linx came back in with new ways to try to cut, squeeze, burn, rip, or stab information out of me about Michael's whereabouts. My answer remained the same, and I think my torturer knew I was telling the truth. He just didn't care. He liked to see me in pain. A nephilim at his disposal for an infinite amount of time, and he could do anything but kill me.

Getting answers out of me wasn't his only goal. He would muddle my mind to make me see myself doing horrible things. Things the demon side of me would do.

I had rejected that part ever since I learned of my lineage, but Linx was making me question who I really was. There were times when I was alone in my cell, and I could feel her clawing at the shell of my being, prying her way to the surface. Whatever strength I had left in me was used to keep her from coming out, but I didn't know how long that would last. I didn't know how many more sessions my soul could take until it completely broke, and I lost who I was.

Though I had reached the point where I was about to pray to their Divine to make it all stop and end it—despite the supposed child I was carrying—I held myself back, even though I knew I would lose it anyway. It was only a matter of time. With the physical and mental stress I was under, my body would reject the baby. I could barely keep myself alive.

I knew the day was almost over when Linx left, and the servant came in to wash the floor of my bodily fluids. The servant went and then came back with bread and water again.

My eyes were closed when he came back in and put something to my lips. It wasn't bread but salty and silky. I opened my eyes and saw he held a piece of meat. I slowly but eagerly took it in my mouth, and my stomach turned instantly, but I did my best to keep it down.

When I finished the first piece, he gave me a second, a third, and then some water. After I took two huge gulps, I breathed in relief and locked eyes with him.

He was a middle-aged man with no hair and thick, dark eyebrows. His face was still too dark to make out despite the torch he had set to the side, but his eyes looked brown since I couldn't tell any other color. He was short and stocky, his head just hitting my shoulders.

The robes he wore were simple and grey with rope woven around his waist and then over his chest in an *X*. He was a eunuch. It wasn't unheard of for them to be within the city's walls. Most of them were servants or prisoners whose only way to survive was to repent, become a eunuch, and serve the Divine through the Emperor or the Clergy.

I smacked my lips together to work up enough saliva to form words. "How long?"

"A full moon's cycle. We are currently halfway through the next."

I closed my eyes and almost let myself cry. Six weeks I had been down here. Six weeks I had known nothing but pain and darkness, and I was no closer to leaving this place.

We spoke no more as he continued to feed me and then left. Shortly after, he returned with another man who came in with a leather bag in his hand.

Odd. This session was off schedule. I assumed he was here to resume Linx's work but was surprised when he started to unpack ointments and clean cloth.

A doctor was here to tend to my wounds.

I didn't question the assistance, but one look at the servant, who was looking intently as the doctor worked, told me it was him. I gave him the saddest excuse for a smile, and he nodded back.

The doctor applied the ointment to my wounds, and gave me some elixir that took away the throbbing temporarily.

That night, I was finally able to sleep without waking from the pain.

———◆———

THE PAIN WAS DULLED, but the memories of my failures and utter despair clouded my mind still.

The heartbreak on Vork's face right before I closed the portal tore whatever heart I had left into pieces. Every day, my life slipped away, and little by little, I felt our bond thinning.

I can only imagine the pain he must be feeling because I refused to let him and the others get captured. I was trying to be selfless, but in the end, it was selfish to leave him and the others like that. It was thoughtless of me not to keep the portal open so they could help. Maybe Leena would be alive if I had. Perhaps I would still be with him, and our baby would grow in a healthy, safe home. But that was another dream to add to the collection. Even if I weren't here, we'd be at war. The baby would never truly be safe.

I would never see Vork again.

His calloused hands on my skin would feel like the finest silk now compared to the rough stone rubbing against my feet. I could imagine the feeling of his breath on the back of my neck, warming me with the simplest of touches. I could even see the adventurous and love-filled life we'd have together, and though I know it would never come true, it's all that kept me sane during these dark days and nights.

It was also the only thing keeping me from spiraling into that darkness, but tonight I hit my ultimate low. I let the memory of Leena's screams and melting skin into my sight, and I couldn't control the tears and screams that followed. No one came in to check. They let me scream.

The purest soul I had ever met had the worst death imaginable, and what's worse is that I, the Unburnt Nephilim, couldn't save her. I was made to walk through the flames, and in all the moments of near-death experiences I'd had, I had never felt so vulnerable.

I remember the remnants of the pyre after it was over as if I were still there. The ash stained the white marble beneath us, and the wood's skeleton was so brittle a simple touch would cause it to crumble.

The only thing left of Leena was her charred body. She was slumped over, but her head was frozen, thrown back, her mouth still open from her screams. That's how she died. With fire burning through her. Forever left to scream to the Heavens for help, but it never came.

I cried until I had nothing left in me. The sadness didn't melt away, it hardened. I took a deep breath and closed my eyes letting the feeling wash over me. To mask the pain.

"Open your eyes, child."

The voice was seductive, calm, and oddly warm.

When I did, I saw a woman standing before me. She stood at least seven feet tall, her body long, slender, and tinted with pale skin that contrasted against her piercing molten gold eyes. She wore a sheer mesh material that hung gracefully over her curves and fell to the floor. Four horns protruded from her head, swooping slightly up and then down, fanning out like a crown. Under them, her thick black hair hung down her back and over her breasts to rest just above her navel.

Her gleaming eyes bored into mine.

A look of pity and disappointment passed over her face.

She took in the state I was in and then the room, along with the tools previously used on me, still fresh with my blood.

I knew exactly who she was, not because of her aura, which was dangerous, powerful, and intoxicating all at once. She was a force that would drive this world and others to the brink of extinction. But that wasn't the tell.

No, I knew because a child always knows.

I fought through the exhaustion to speak, but my words came out as little more than a wheeze.

"Hello, Mother."

CHAPTER 36

Vork

MATHIAS and I stepped through Katar's portal, and I quickly realized we were not in pack territory.

Yes, we were within the forest at the base of Arabrosa's mountains, but it wasn't home.

There wasn't a single sound, minus our tentative footsteps. There were no birds, no small critters running around the forest floor — only us.

"Why do I have a horrible feeling the witch did this intentionally?" Mathias sighed, his eyes darting all around him.

The *fucking* Divine.

I didn't want to believe that. Katar had helped Amara and I when we needed it and even recruited us to join the cause. Why would he try to dispose of us now? He would have nothing to gain from this. He wanted to help them—to help the Defiants and end the war.

Or he didn't.

My stomach turned as I calculated the possibilities. It could have been a mistake. It had to be. He had done much to help the Defiants, but he was a High Priest for the Emperor and, in turn, the Clergy. He had access to them. Was he working as a double agent for the Defiants, or was he truly in league with the Clergy, posing as an ally of the Defiants when—in reality—his loyalty lay with the holy men all along?

A High Priest of his stature and experience made it hard to believe he had made the mistake of not putting us into pack territory. My father had temporarily rectified the wards he had up so Katar could bring us home.

I always had my suspicions about him, but there was no proof of his deceit. The only information I had to go on was a conversation I overheard my father having with the elders about a High Priest who was motivated to obtaining power in any way they could. Katar was the only High Priest outside Arabrosa I met, but I couldn't damn him because of a sliver of information I overheard.

This predicament we were in now made me think differently. He was corrupt.

"I think you may be right," I finally confessed. Worry stabbed through my whole body like needles.

Now that I was out of the way and right where Katar wanted me, what was happening back at the compound?

The hair on my arms stood up, and my ears perked at a noise coming from the right. A very faint but distinct shriek came for us. I knew the sound all too well.

"Run," I commanded my friend, and we took off.

The sazari truly had made it close to the pack borders, and hopefully, my father would close that protection soon, whether we made it in time or not. He couldn't put his people at risk, not even for his heir.

Though we were running as fast as we could, I could feel the creatures getting close. The snarls and cracking of bones as their bodies hit the trees and made their way to us was evidence enough.

We knew these woods well and knew they would be on us before we reached the pack borders.

There was one thing that could save us, and only by the grace of the Divine would they provide.

I took a hard right, and Mathias followed.

"You're headed for their territory!"

That was the idea. The adrenaline pushed me to move faster without even thinking of exactly where I was going besides the direction of our possible saving grace. Mathias was close on my heels, trying to match the speed.

Our momentum rewarded us with slamming smack into a ward that flung us back. The world around us spun, I landed with a thud and a shriek came from under me.

There was a dull pain radiating through my whole body, and my head—like the world around me moments ago—spun out of control.

As I pushed up on my side, I grabbed my head.

"Easy on the family jewels, Vork!"

Before I could respond, Mathias pushed me off him and worked up to his feet as slowly as I did. He had his hand wrapped around his nose and a pop sounded.

Unfortunately, that was his second broken nose within forty-eight hours.

"Fucking hell, mate. You couldn't see that coming?"

I snorted. "How could I? It's *invisible*."

I made my way to the ward's edge and started banging on it.

Sazari were getting closer each second. We had only a minute or two until we would be completely overrun.

We couldn't let up. They had to know we were here. So, we continued banging, sending ripples through the ward. We weren't strong enough to break it. We just needed to make a little noise.

A moment later, a woman materialized in front of us, safe behind the ward. She stood tall and firm, her long black hair braided intricately out of her face and down her back. Those commanding eyes held us both in our place, unable to bang anymore.

Her face held no scar or blemish, just a straight jawline with high and defined cheekbones and warm, golden skin. Around her left nostril were two gold rings that complemented the gold hanging from her earlobes.

"You should know better, son of Nareus," she said.

"Sazari are close behind us. Please let us in," I pleaded.

She looked behind us to see they were indeed close. "And why would I do that?"

"Because you are currently occupying pack land solely because the Commander and his family are generous enough to let you live here,"

Mathias spat with another bang on the ward. "The least you could do is grant us temporary asylum."

She raised a brow. "My ancestors colonized these lands long before you dogs pissed on their mark."

"Please," I tried again. "What do you want?"

The snarls grew closer. They were a mile away, and that distance would be eaten up in seconds.

"I want our land to extend to the Red Stream in the east."

My teeth clenched. "That's over forty acres."

"You have less than forty seconds to live." She stepped forward and ran a finger over the ward, letting it ripple at her touch. "Forty seconds to lose your life or forty acres to save it. Your choice."

My heart was rattling against my chest and my mouth became increasingly dry before I finally shot out the word, "Fine."

"Wonderful," she deadpanned as she gripped our shirts and pulled us through the ward.

The creatures were coming over the horizon, but before I could get a good look, she said something in her native tongue and the world shifted abruptly.

When everything stilled again, an overwhelming urge to vomit flooded me. I doubled over with my hands on my knees and tried to steady my breathing.

Mathias, on the other hand, didn't even try to hold it back and everything he ate this morning made a reappearance.

The sour stench hit my nose instantly, and I looked away. "The Divine, Mathias, really?"

"Oh, piss off, you bloke. You did this to me. You're lucky this isn't on you."

I ignored him and took stock of our surroundings. We stood in a dimly lit tent with colorful small lanterns floating in the air linked with a thin glowing line that sparkled similar to stars in the night sky.

Other than us and the lanterns, and a thick wooden chair at the back, the space was empty.

The woman cocked a brow at our uneasy state as she strode towards the chair and sat gracefully.

"I don't believe we've met," I said, standing straight and finally catching my breath. "I remember the leader of the Highmore Coven being a bit older."

"That was my mother. She died many moons ago."

I bowed my head. "I am sorry for your loss."

"I am Soraya," she said curtly, ignoring my condolences. "Why were you beyond your pack borders in land where sazari roam?"

I explained our situation, how a High Priest had betrayed us, and how we needed passage back to the compound.

"I just granted you sanctuary, and now you ask another favor?"

"Hardly a favor," Mathias grumbled. "You were given a substantial part of the woods."

"You mean returned."

"Enough," I ordered my second. "I am not asking for a favor. I am requesting we make another deal."

He took a step towards me. "More land?"

I ignored his worry and kept my eyes locked on Soraya. "No. The High Priest who was responsible for the death of your grandmother and the capture of your people."

Her eyes narrowed, and she crossed her legs in curiosity. "What do you know of this?"

"I may know the person responsible."

"You knew," she spat, her face hardening and the lights above glowing brighter. "How long?"

"It's not my responsibility to speak on the internal conflict of the witches. You portal us back where we need to be, and I'll give you both, but you won't like it."

"I—"

"There's a catch," I stated simply.

Soraya pursed her lips.

"After you portal us back, help my pack against the sazari and the other packs threatening our borders."

I'd come here to help my people. I knew the threats they were facing, but I hadn't known about the ones at the compound. I had to go back, but I couldn't leave our home defenseless.

"You want me to put my people's lives at risk?"

"I'm not asking you to fight, I'm asking you to help protect. The protection around your coven seems durable. Something like that would do just fine."

She cocked her head to the side. "Deal."

After I told her of the location, she opened the portal. Before I stepped through after Mathias, Soraya called out to me.

"The information," she demanded.

I turned to her, and, with a twinge of sadness, I said, "I don't have solid proof of this, but it may be a place for you to start. I'd investigate the Farkath Coven."

———◆———

WHAT I SAW upon our return was utter chaos. Houses were on fire, blood filled the streets, and people were screaming and running to find safety—from what I couldn't tell. I was back in the courtyard where I had seen Amara off, and the portal was open again.

The princess and Dasyra had made it back, but I saw her, my wife, pinned down in filth through the window, grabbing for purchase to make it back.

I paid no mind to the carnage swirling around me as I charged toward her, but she threw a gust of fire, stopping me in my tracks.

An arrow pierced through her hand, pulling her back toward the group of soldiers.

My heart ceased beating at the picture in front of me.

I *needed* to help her. I *needed* to get to her.

The next cries she bellowed ripped my guts from the inside and I took a step toward her. Before I could get far, a hand gripped my arm, holding me back.

"Don't."

With nostrils flared, I slowly looked down at the hand holding me before looking to the young nephilim who the limb belonged to and who clearly had no regard for his life. Being this close to a lycan while it was on the verge of rage was dangerous, even more so if they were close to shifting.

"Don't? *My wife* is pinned down in shit and mud, and you expect me not to come to her aid? I'll shred that arm from your body if you don't let go."

"We have the princess." Corym moved in closer to try and intensify his lackluster gaze of intimidation. "Soldiers are pouring in on their side and ours. They won't kill her; they need her. We will find her, but we don't stand a chance if you go through there." I ignored him and moved forward again, but Corym tightened his hold. "Silas is dead! We don't have a leader. Seeing as how you're the highest-ranking warrior, that responsibility now falls to you. You have to be smart about this. You have to put the needs of the many before one singular person."

But this wasn't just any person. It was my whole world and soul wrapped in one, my whole reason for being, and she was literally being ripped away.

"I can't."

My eyes met hers as an arrow pierced her shoulder and she wailed. I couldn't physically feel the pain she was experiencing, and yet I could. Everything around me was breaking.

I twisted out of Corym's hold to bolt for her again. Finally, I was closer. I took one, two, three, four steps and could feel the slight gust of wind from the portal.

Almost there.

Just a few more steps and—

Hands grabbed me from all around, holding me back so I couldn't get to her. "Amara!"

My nails elongated, not able to keep the lycan at bay any longer. I didn't want to hurt her friends, but she mattered more. She was the only thing that mattered.

My clawed hand grabbed whoever held me with the most strength, which happened to be Luca. His cry of pain halted me for less than a second. He was just a kid doing what he thought was right.

I didn't want to hurt him... but I needed her. The pain he was feeling was fleeting, and he would heal, but I knew I wouldn't recover from losing her. So, I kept pushing.

"Vork!" Amara shouted. I didn't stop. "Vork, look at me!"

My furious eyes snapped to hers, stilling my movements. The other nephilims struggled against me still.

"It'll be okay. You'll find me, and it'll be okay."

"Amara, don't," I pleaded, voice breaking and tears clouding my vision. "Don't you part from me."

"I'm so sorry."

"Don't do it!" Through blurry vision, I looked at those holding me. *"Get off!"*

A soft smile spread across Amara's lips as tears filled her eyes. "I'll see you soon."

The portal closed, and my movements halted, but the tight grip of the others didn't let up. It was done. I couldn't get to her. I had failed as a protector, as a husband.

My ears felt like they were filled with water, eyes equally so. Tears fell. My still clawed hands began to shake, and my heart raced.

Bones began to subtly crack and pop as my shift began. A sharp pain shot into my gums as my canines slowly protruded.

The sensation was uncomfortable, trying to fight the shift like this. Not once in all my ages of living had my shift been out of control. It was always quick and with a purpose, but this time it was coming from a side I didn't know if I could control.

"Vork. Vork!" Corym pushed the others off, and then shook me. "Get a grip! She's fine. We need to move. Get a hold of yourself."

He started this. If he had never stopped me, the others would have never followed. It's him. *Him.*

Without thinking, I sent a clean uppercut to Corym's jaw and was going to hit him again, but Dasyra blocked my path, though she kept her hands off.

"Vork, he's an asshole. Don't listen to him. Listen to me. Hey!" She snapped her fingers, and my eyes locked with hers. "Amara is the strongest person I know. Corym is right, they won't kill her. She will weather what comes next, but we won't if we stay here."

With a ragged breath, I looked at Dasyra, but I didn't really see her. The shock rippled through me, planting my feet firmly in the dirt.

"Vork, please. She'd be pissed if she made this sacrifice for you to fuck it up by not acting. *Let's. Move.*"

For me. She had put herself at risk, and I would be stupid to not take this time she had given us. Like a hot poker to cattle, I blinked and everything began to move normally.

"The boats," I said to her. "Get as many people as you can to the boats."

"The boats." Dasyra nodded in agreement and sprang to action, telling the others, and everyone headed for the harbor.

Corym was still rubbing his jaw, blood pooling at the corner of his mouth.

"Sorry," I grumbled. "And tell Luca I'm sorry. I didn't mean to hurt him."

"He's an understanding kid. He won't take it personally." He spat out the blood and took off towards the harbor before turning around briefly to say, "That one's free."

The whole compound was either burning or had been destroyed with who knew what kind of weapons the Clergy had in their arsenal we were unaware of.

When I saw the boats in the distance, my heart sank at how few Defiants were left. Only three ships worth of people were visible and most were women and children. The men who could were fighting, so the others would escape.

As I looked toward the fighting, I saw soldiers with the Emperor's sigil of the strike on their armor, but it was scratched out.

The soldiers barreled through the Defiants in overwhelming numbers. These people weren't fighters. They wanted to be, but they weren't, and they were dying quickly because of it.

While making my way to the boats, I took out as many soldiers as I could with an axe left by a fallen Defiant. Many landed their blades on me, but I still stood. I had to. There was no other option. I wouldn't let her pain be for nothing.

I picked up a man whose ankle was twisted unnaturally and pushed through the fighting to reach the last ship at the dock.

"Take off!" I screamed as I ran up the ramp. "Now!"

I placed the man down and went to the stern, looking back at what we had left. The Clergy's archers knocked their arrows down, aimed, and let loose.

"Arrows! Take cover!"

At the edge of the boat was an elderly woman who was frozen in fear. I slid over to her, took the top of the nearest barrel, and covered us. The thunk of arrow tips hit the deck; unfortunately, some people. Their screams were followed closely by others.

"Row, goddamnit!"

The ship finally began to move quickly enough to be out of the archers' range. Standing at the helm, I saw many hadn't made it past the arrows.

"Where will we go?" Dasyra came up beside me.

"My home is the only safe place for us. We'll go north of the continent and through a pass that leads there."

She nodded in agreement.

The Divine, this hurt so bad. "I need her back."

Dasyra placed a hand on my shoulder. "I'll get her back once we make landfall. You have to help these people. I promise I'll get her back to you." There was a pause before she spoke again. "What will you do once you have them within your borders?"

I took in the cries coming from behind me, people mourning those who were lost in the fight and those whose bodies lay on the deck, so close to freedom. The waves slapped against the boat's hull, and I was able to use the sound to focus on the eerily calm surrounding me as I looked back at the burning compound.

Rage filled me, yes, but something else coated it. Contentment... because the Clergy was going to burn in the very flames they had set upon this place. If they did this here, then the pack land wouldn't be safe from them either.

This... silence. This blessed silence was the calm before the battle I was going to bring down on our enemies.

"Prepare for war."

www.ingramcontent.com/pod-product-compliance
Lightning Source LLC
Chambersburg PA
CBHW020311160726
47992CB00004B/1480